Soft Voices Whispering

ABOUT THE AUTHOR

Adrienne Dines was born in Dublin in 1959 and spent her childhood living in the south of Ireland. After graduating from University of Dublin, Trinity College in 1981, she moved to Weybridge in Surrey to teach. Marriage to a BP oilman saw her packed off to Aberdeen for ten years where she taught in a variety of secondary schools, wrote poetry and speeches and gave birth to three sons. On moving back to Weybridge in 1995, she continued writing speeches – for world champion canoeists, social functions and even ordinations. Many of her speeches are delivered in verse as it affords her the freedom to 'blame it on the rhyme.' She began writing her first novel as an exercise in following a character to see what would unfold. *Soft Voices Whispering* is the result of this journey.

Adrienne's novel, *Toppling Miss April* was published by Transita in 2005 and *The Jigsaw Maker* in 2006. Publication of *Soft Voices Whispering* also in 2006 fulfils an ambition to 'hit the ground running'!

Soft Voices Whispering

ADRIENNE DINES

transita

For Kieran
First story for a first son.

Published by Transita
Spring Hill House, Spring Hill Road
Oxford OX5 1RX. United Kingdom.
Tel: (01865) 375796. Fax: (01865) 379162.
email: info@transita.co.uk
http://www.transita.co.uk

British Library Cataloguing in Publication Data
A catalogue record for this book is available from the British Library

ISBN 10: 1-905175-29-9
ISBN 13: 978-1-905175-29-1

Cover design by Baseline Arts Ltd, Oxford
Produced for Transita by Deer Park Productions, Tavistock
Typeset by PDQ Typesetting, Newcastle-under-Lyme
Printed and bound by Bookmarque, Croydon

ACKNOWLEDGEMENTS

I am so grateful to the following people:

As ever, my husband, Tim and sons Kieran, Tom and Freddy; my parents Tom and Lall Phillips; parents-in-law, Edward and Marjorie Dines, my sister Margie Kennedy and brother Tom Phillips are always supportive.

A special thanks to my younger sister Caroline McNiff who read this story when it was much longer (and meandered) – and still loved it!

My friend Yvonne Fitzpatrick Grimes brought me along to the writing class in the first place. I'm glad I wasn't good looking enough to distract her admirer and had to resort to writing instead. Margaret Ireland listened to all the ideas and treated even the duff ones with respect. Stephen Smith, poet, ran the classes with skill and patience and made us all believe we had something to say.

My friend Meg Shreve (Gardiner), like Caroline, patiently read every word and urged me to join the American Women of Surrey Writers' Group and learn how to focus.

The other American Writers – Nancy Fraser in Switzerland, Mary Albanese, Suzanne Davidovac, Tammye Huf, Kelly Gerrard, Jennifer Spears and Heejung Westcoat, are wise in their advice and constant in their support. Sue Bohane – I am grateful to you for all the same reasons.

To my editor, Julia Williams, for agreeing that stories need to be told in their own time and for her astute editing.

To the nuns who peopled my schooldays and made such a strong impact on an impressionable child.

Finally, thanks to Nikki Read, Giles Lewis, Helen Moreno, Ros Loten, and all at Transita Publishing who are encouraging and approachable.

You're all great!

PROLOGUE

A S SHE NEARED THE DOOR the humming grew louder, like a warning inside her head. By the time her hand was on the latch, it was roaring in her ears. Deafened by the force of it she pushed the door open and stood on the threshold, staring at the sight. She wasn't sure what she had expected to see – her father maybe, but not this.

Matty Hurley was the first to hear the screams. He had just reached the lane when they started and he beckoned to the others to hurry.

The three of them raced up the lane as fast as they could with Matty, having neither age nor flesh to hinder him, in the lead. As he rounded the corner of the yard, Eleanor flew past him, arms outstretched. For a moment he thought she was being chased but there was no-one coming behind her, only the darkened empty house with its back door swinging open. He stood where he was, watching as she ran straight into the waiting arms of the two men behind.

'You'll be all right now, Elly,' he called and for a moment she paused and turned to look at him. The screaming stopped and she shook her head. Then she ran again, away from her invisible devils with nothing at all behind but the rain and the hounds of hell snapping at her heels.

KILDORAN 1980
CHAPTER 1

T HURSDAY WAS FREEZING. Though it was still mid-autumn, an unseasonably cold wind whistled into Kildoran and the sky was dreary. Mourners huddled in their cars, reluctant to leave the warmth till the last possible minute.

It came earlier than expected. Though the National School had been given the day off as a gesture of respect to their recently departed headmistress, the pupils were all under instruction to be at the church in plenty of time and, unwilling to risk the wrath of Sister Bernard, the school deputy, the clock had no sooner struck the half hour than hordes of children appeared in the church forecourt. The older girls, glad of an opportunity to show off their obedient goodness, took up position on the front steps; the rest shambled into place behind them.

Emer Fagan watched from the gate and sighed. As usual the biggest shambles was forming in that part of the queue occupied by her son, Gareth, and his friends. She hurried across the forecourt to settle them before Sister Bernard arrived. Other parents, themselves past pupils and well aware of the consequences of bad behaviour, had the same idea. Within seconds of the first jostle, car doors opened and the forecourt was full. Warning *Whist, will you!* and *Get in line* they ushered the queue into order and what seemed like the entire population of Kildoran filed quietly into the church in respectful silence.

Once inside, the congregation had reason to be thankful to the deceased, for her popularity packing the church with

3

mourners, whose numbers provided more in the way of physical warmth than the unpredictable central heating system ever would. The front two pews were still unoccupied, the next were filled with nuns of every shape and description and a few of the local dignitaries. Behind them, the pupils of Kildoran National School shuffled into their places – due in part to the solemnity of the occasion and in part to the fact that in most cases their parents were watching their every move. At the very back, nurses from the old folks' home wheeled in some of the home's more able residents: some sad at the passing of an old friend; some nervous at this reminder that it might be their turn next; and some simply glad of the opportunity of a day out and a fine tea at the end of it.

When the chief mourners arrived, all the shuffling and snuffling stopped and the congregation rose to watch as a sombre group of the convent sisters and relatives of the deceased made their way up the aisle. Some of the younger nuns were red eyed and the older ones too but all had an air of dignified serenity about them. The children watched them with interest. The nuns looked different from usual; every pleat was freshly pressed and even their beads looked polished. Sister Bernard nodded in acknowledgement at the pristine appearance of her class and the children smiled back. Good behaviour, however difficult to maintain, was usually worth it, and the prospect of a story from Sister Bernard's big storybook was always a better proposition than a half hour's Maths on a Friday afternoon.

At the back of the group a few strangers walked. One was obviously the Mother General and the crowd watched her with interest, still surprised that she had considered the occasion important enough to warrant coming all the way from England to attend. She was smaller than the onlookers had speculated, and not as old or forbidding-looking either. She was looking around the church wistfully, as if she wanted to drink in the sight of every corner of it. Every so often her eyes would rest on a face in the congregation and she'd nod slightly.

Beside her a tall nun walked, head down, looking neither right nor left. She moved up the aisle as if her feet were on runners and didn't raise her head till she reached the pews at the front where Mother General was taking her seat. It quickly became obvious that no amount of bottom shuffling was going to create room for her there so after a minute's muttering, she turned to find a space further back down the church. Her task made it impossible for her to keep her head bowed and she found herself looking into a sea of faces.

'Over here, Sister!' a voice called her and she turned to where a large ruddy-faced farmer's wife, wearing a coat at least two sizes too small, was beckoning her into a space. Glad to escape the eyes that followed her search, the tall nun squeezed in, and instantly regretted it. For all that she had her Sunday best on, the farmer's wife had brought more than a little of the farm with her. It hovered in the air and filled the nun's nostrils.

'Are you all right there, Sister, have you enough room?' Bridie Hennessy rested a rough red hand on her arm.

The nun raised her head and her expression was cold. She pulled her arm away. 'Perfectly fine, thank you.'

Bridie's hand was left hanging in space. 'Right so,' she said, and promptly turning her attention to the child who was tugging at her skirt, didn't appear to notice the rebuff.

Behind her, Emer Fagan did. She had been watching Gareth over on the other side of the aisle, hoping he'd resist the temptation to start pucking the fellows on either side of him before the service even started. Something about the nun's demeanour caught her eye. She looked to be in her late fifties, thin and pale-faced and her movements were stiff. For all that she had only come in and taken her place in a pew, there was an unmistakable air of hostility about her. Emer felt a chill suddenly.

At the very back of the church, one of the Home's residents was watching the scene, her face confused and anxious.

'Are you warm enough, Mrs Byrne?' the young nurse assigned to her asked as she attempted to pull the blanket further over on her lap.

Nell Byrne held the blanket firmly.

'I'm not cold,' she growled through gritted teeth.

'Well, you're shivering,' the nurse persisted.

'Not cold,' the old woman looked at her with a face blazing with anger. She began twisting the edge of her blanket. 'You don't know – you can't see—'

The nurse bent down and took her hand. 'What's the matter, Mrs Byrne? See what?'

Nell's voice sank to a whisper. 'You can't—' She straightened up but her voice sank even further so that the girl had difficulty hearing her.

Later, as the congregation buttoned up and prepared for the long walk to Kildoran Cemetery, Emer stopped to talk to the nurse.

'Mam looks bothered, Bridget. Is she having a bad day?'

Bridget shrugged. 'God help her, Emer,' she said, 'but she's very confused sometimes.'

'Why? Did something happen?'

'Well—' Bridget tucked the rug tightly around Nell's knees before she turned to Emer. 'She'd been nodding off just before the service started, when she leaned forward all of a sudden and stared up towards the front of the church. I swear to you she was as white as a sheet. *You can't be here,* she said, *you can't be. You're dead.* Honestly, what did she expect? Weren't we at a funeral?'

Sister Bernard was silent when the children came into school next day. Still full of energy from their day off, the fourth class trooped into their classroom in a raggedy bunch and took an age to get themselves and their bags organised. It wasn't until the last of the desk-lids was slammed that they noticed that she had been sitting there watching them and hadn't started giving out about the commotion yet. Instead she smiled and told them they were all very good and she was proud of them. She said that even Mother General and the visitors had commented on what well behaved children they had been. She said they had done her proud. Then she folded her hands in her lap and her voice grew soft and shaky. She looked at them and said she had a bit of news.

Just as she opened her mouth, there was a knock on the door. Gareth Fagan, on door duty this week, rose and opened it. There was a pause before anyone came in and when she did, the children were dismayed to see it was the nun from the funeral, the tall one who had sat beside Eilish Hennessy's mammy at mass with a face on her as if it was a terrible place to be and hadn't offered anyone her hand at the 'sign of peace' though several people had offered theirs to her.

Seas suas anois!

The children obeyed the order to stand and eyed the newcomer warily. Sister Bernard stood, looked sheepish.

'Say "hello" to Sister Pius, children.'

'*Dia dhuit*, Sister Pius,' thirty voices sang with more synchronisation than sincerity.

Sister Pius nodded towards them but said nothing.

'Now, children,' Sister Bernard continued, fiddling with the crucifix which hung from the rosary on her belt, 'this is the bit of news I was going to tell you about.' She paused as if the words were difficult and then lifted her head. 'I am going away for a little while.' There was a murmur of dismay as some of the brighter children, eyes on Pius' stern face, realised what the implications of this statement might be. 'It's only for a few months. In the meantime, you are very lucky to have Sister Pius here as your teacher.' She paused and waited for a reaction. None came, neither from the children nor the stern-faced woman at her side. 'These are very good children, Sister Pius. They all know how to behave themselves and they do lovely writing in their copybooks.' She smiled encouragement at the class, hoping for someone to say the right thing and break the silence, which hung heavy over her usually lively pupils.

Peter O'Rourke looked at her seriously. 'Are *you* going to die, Sister?'

Sister Bernard laughed. 'We're all going to die eventually, Peter, but not yet! No, I'm going to go across to England for a little while with Mother General and then I'll be back here to stay.'

'Will you be our teacher again then?' Peter didn't look at all consoled.

'God willing, Peter. Now enough of your chatter – get out your copybooks and let Sister Pius here see what good children you can be.'

There was a pause before the inevitable scraping and clattering started. Desk lids were raised and dropped and books were pulled out of bags. Bernard waited for the hubbub to subside before she went to the door. Gareth was still standing there. He held out a grubby hand to her.

'Goodbye for now, then, Sister Bernard. We'll be very good.'

Bernard smiled at him and ruffled his untidy hair. 'I know you will. Aren't you all grand boys and girls.' She shot a warning look at the ruffians in the back row. 'Of course, I'll be hearing all about it and if word reaches me that anyone is forgetting his homework, or his manners ... ' The threat hovered in the air between them but the children could hear the affection in her voice. *'Slan anois!'* She raised a hand and was out the door before anyone could say another word.

For a minute they all sat regarding the closed door and then turned their attention to the woman now standing behind the teacher's desk. She seemed to have forgotten they were there and was just staring at the desk. Very slowly, she was running her fingers around the edges of it and appeared to be whispering something to herself. The children looked from one to the other and wondered who should speak first. As he was standing anyway, Gareth supposed it should be him. Looking to Peter for encouragement, he approached the desk.

'It's a very old desk, you know. Sister Bernard said it was here from the time the school was opened.' As she didn't look up, he supposed it was okay to continue. 'It has a special way of opening, not a lock but a catch with a spring on it. You have to practise to be able to get it right. Sister Bernard showed us. Look, you just push – ow!'

As if she'd come unsprung herself, the tall nun suddenly came to life. Without looking at him, her hand shot out and caught his wrist and he was surprised at the strength of her.

'Leave it!' Her voice was very quiet but every child in the room heard it clearly.

Gareth squirmed in her grip. 'But I was only going to—'

'I said, leave it.' She looked at him and her face was as cold as her voice. Unlike Sister Bernard, Sister Pius had no colour in her face at all. Even her eyes were cold. They looked as if they had once been blue but now the colour had all been washed out. Gareth lowered his eyes.

'I thought I had just been told that you were able to behave yourselves? This is a fine example of disobedience with which to start the day, I must say. Who gave you permission to be out of your chair?'

'I don't need to get permission! I'm on door duty. I—'

'In my class, you need permission. In my class there will be no disobedience. Sit down.' She dropped Gareth's hand and watched his retreating back as he made his way to his desk. '*I was only trying to help,*' he whispered to the little boy who was waiting for him, sympathy written all over his face. When he reached his desk he sat down and turned to look at her again, obviously wrestling with emotions. Within a few seconds he had made his decision, his hand shot up.

'Sister?'

She looked at him.

'If you'd like to know how to open it, I could explain to you from here?'

Without taking her eyes from his face, Pius reached out her hand and jiggled the catch on the side of the desk. With a *click* of its well-used hinges, the lid lifted.

'I need no instruction, thank you,' she said, though she didn't sound grateful at all. 'Now if you have work to do, get on with it.'

The children were speechless. Sister Bernard had assured them that the hinge on the fourth class desk was a secret known only to good children yet this horrible woman knew how to work it without even being shown. And she hadn't even looked pleased when it came open the first time! Sister Bernard always looked pleased when it worked. Gareth and Peter sneaked a glance at one another and sighed. Things were certainly looking different round here and they weren't looking good. They would have to keep their heads down and stay as far out of her way as they could – and they would start from now. It seemed that the whole class had the same idea. Every head bowed and there was no sound in the room save the scratching of sharpened pencils and the sniffling of Eilish Hennessy's ever-runny nose.

Sister Pius watched them until the calm of concentration descended on the group. Then she reached into the desk and pulled out the large roll-book that took up most of the space in there. As she folded the cover over to reveal neat rows of ticks, she sighed quietly to herself. So this was it then. She had been sent to Kildoran out of the blue with barely a minute's warning to replace some country nun who was off to take a course in preparation for a new role – and she herself just back from Rome, ready to take on the task of transcription of the texts for which she had spent years preparing. As if all her quiet preparation counted for nothing she was packed off, left with strangers ...

'Ah, but you won't be among strangers,' Mother General's voice whispered from somewhere at the back of her memory.

'Yes, I will.'

Mother Mary smiled and shook her head slowly. 'Would it be so dreadful for you, Sister? Could you not go there for a short time even?'

Pius clasped her hands tightly till she could feel the blood tingle in protest at the top of her fingers. 'I have nothing to go there for, Mother. I have nothing to teach them.'

The fear that was growing stronger by the minute forced her to make one last stand.

Mother Mary straightened up and her voice was firm. 'You will go to Kildoran, Sister, not because of what you have to teach. You will go to Kildoran because of what you have to learn.'

Sister Pius stood up and walked stiffly to the door. As she left the room her was heart pounding and the sound of water was rushing in her ears. Already she could hear voices in her head, crooning their gentle threats. From the far end of the corridor the sisters were coming up for lunch and knowing that she wasn't ready to face them yet, she turned and rested her forehead against the cool wood of the study door. From inside she could hear snatches of Mother Mary's voice as she prayed aloud to the crucifix over her desk.

'Well, Lord,' it said, 'it's taken a while but we got there – if this is what you had in mind all along. . As usual, your will be done, Amen.'

And now Pius was sitting here, at the teacher's desk in the fourth class classroom in Kildoran National School. In front of her, thirty children kept their heads down and probably considered that was the best place to keep them. Pius looked at them. They needn't worry, she thought to herself. This won't be for long.

Strengthened by that resolve she let her eye slide down the list of names. Maura Aherne, Joseph Brady, Helen Burke, Patricia Doherty, Gareth Fagan – Fagan! Which one was he? As if he had heard his name, Gareth raised his head and looked at her. Pius stared back and this time she didn't look cold at all. Two bright spots of colour blazed in her cheeks.

'Are you Gareth Fagan?' she asked.

'I am, Sister,' he said. 'My daddy's John Fagan from the shop.'

'John Fagan? Your father's *John* Fagan?' Then she shook her head. 'Of course he is,' she said crossly. 'You are John Fagan's son from the shop.' She picked up her pen and started to put her ticks down the column of names.

Her hand was shaking.

CHAPTER 2

'CAN I GIVE YOU A HAND THERE, SISTER?' Emer Fagan's voice was manna from Heaven to Sister Agnes, the convent cook, as sweating, she struggled down the convent steps.

'The blessings of God on you, another minute there and I would have dropped the lot of them!'

Emer took the pile of cloths that were being let fall into her arms. 'Where are we off to then?'

'The Sacristy,' Agnes nodded towards the side door of the church. 'We'd started a clear out of the store rooms before Mother Rosalie—' Her voice trailed off and Emer looked at her sympathetically.

'You'll miss her.'

'Aye,' Agnes heaved her load and headed over to the Sacristy door, 'still, it was a grand funeral. I didn't know there were that many people in the county! You know, she probably taught every woman in this parish at one time or another.' She indicated an empty shelf. 'Here, put the smaller cloths on this shelf and we'll have the long ones there – it'll be easier for Father Martin to reach them.'

Within minutes the pile was stacked tidily and Agnes wiped a hand across her forehead. 'Thanks for that, Emer. I'm not feeling so good today. Hope I haven't picked up a chill from the other day.' She held open the door and the two of them stepped into the cold air. 'I saw your mother there. How is she?'

Emer shrugged. 'Up and down, Sister, mostly down these days. There's not much you can do for her really and she doesn't have any will to do anything for herself. She just sits there, glaring into space, making life as difficult as possible for the poor girls who have to look after her. Apparently she gets very agitated after our visits and gives them a hard time on account of it.'

'Does she know you've been? Does she know who you are?'

Emer turned and though her expression was calm enough her voice was angry. 'She knows very well who we are. She always addresses Gareth by name and seems to remember everything that he told her from the visit before.'

'And yourself?'

'No, she doesn't address me – if that's what you're asking. I get the occasional look but few words and then only instructions.'

Sister Agnes looked at the troubled face. 'Don't be cross with her, Emer. She doesn't mean any of it. Your mother wasn't designed to cope on her own.' She patted Emer gently on the shoulder. 'She's well looked after where she is and I'm sure she appreciates your visits even if she doesn't say so to you.'

'Maybe.' Emer sighed. 'Anyway, I'd better make a move. There's a delivery due in soon and I can't leave Cora on her own to take charge of it – you'd never know where she'd put things!'

'Cora Hennessey, is it? Bridie's eldest?'

'Yes. She still hasn't made up her mind about going back to school to have another bash at the Inter Cert so John said we should take her on for the time being, keep her out of harm's way.'

'That was kind of him.' Sister Agnes sounded surprised.

'It was – an unexpected display of charity.' Emer pulled her coat tighter around her. 'I'm off.'

Agnes locked the sacristy door. 'Mind yourself now, God bless!'

''Bye!'

Agnes watched Emer walking back up the path towards Fagan's Bar and Grocery. Unexpected acts of kindness my backside! That was likely all right. Poor Emer. She was such a timid thing, she seemed to carry the weight of the world on her shoulders – unlike her husband who carried only the weight of a prosperous stomach on his. Cross with herself for such uncharitable thoughts, she hurried back to the convent. *More's the pity you couldn't tidy away your bad mind as easily, Agnes Dowling.* She glanced towards the window and heard the rumble of the delivery truck crossing the bridge. She didn't like John Fagan, never had, and that was the size of it. He was only a few years younger than herself, had been in the same class as her brother at school but he wouldn't ever let on he remembered that. He wasn't a man to admit to his real age – or anything else that could be attributed to him either.

Agnes recalled the pale face of John Fagan's wife and shook her head. Through the window she could see the canopy at the front of the grocery side of Fagan's fluttering in the breeze and she knew that inside the shop, Emer would already be busy stacking and carrying while her lazy husband sat and smoked at the bar and didn't lift a finger to help her. He'd use the excuse of his weak heart.

If he had a heart at all.

The door was wide open and the shop full of boxes when Gareth arrived in from school. Bill Brady, the delivery man, was leaning on the counter with one elbow, gossiping.

'It's the weekend after next and we're going to be staying with them for the whole week before! Oh now, very la-di-da, I can tell you, Mrs Fagan.' His chest puffed out with pride. 'They have a house near the sea with a sitting room *and* a drawing room!'

'Isn't that lovely? Your mother must be very pleased.' Emer smiled at him.

'Pleased me arse,' Bridie Hennessy muttered, as if she was talking to herself but with a voice raised high enough that the whole place could hear. Today, she had forsaken the coat and was wrapped instead in layers of patterned skirts and faded woollen cardigans. Her face was sweaty as she bent down between two stacks of boxes and Gareth could see that if her backside moved only another little bit, her huge skirts would swing around and knock the whole lot. She always seemed to take up a lot of space and there was a smell about her that stayed in the shop even after she had gone out the door, a smell like smoke and soggy cornflakes and lots of people in a warm room close together. She was watching Bill Brady with the waves of a huge smile playing around her lips.

Bill did not look amused. He stood up very straight and held his chest high so that it looked bigger than the belly below. 'And what exactly do you mean by that, Mrs Hennessy?' he asked, his voice so posh you'd almost think he had a sitting room *and* a drawing room himself instead of just two rooms for the six of them and an outside toilet.

'I mean,' she said, 'that a family as grand as the one you're describing could surely afford the luxury of a decent engagement? That we'd at least have seen herself home for the weekend to visit her poor old mother and give us a chance to see the weight of jewels she's condemned to wear on her finger? That—'

'A pound of rashers, did you say, Mrs Hennessy?' Emer said quickly, as if she had not realised that Bridie was in the middle of explaining something to Bill Brady.

Bridie stopped and looked at Emer. Gareth liked the way she looked at his mother. No matter what she was saying or who she was giving out about, she always had a kind smile on her for Emer Fagan and when she spoke, she was always polite.

'It might have been, indeed, Emer, but now that I stop to think about it a bit, I think in fact tonight we might manage two pounds—' she turned to Bill and gave him a quick wink '—to celebrate the wedding, like.'

That seemed like a very friendly thing to Gareth but Bill didn't look friendly at all. His mouth was shut so tight that the lips had all been sucked inside and the red of his cheeks had turned to purple. If he had been looking at Gareth the way he was looking at Mrs Hennessy, Gareth was sure he'd have been about to get a belt of Bill's fist. But Bill would never hit a woman, even one as big as Bridie Hennessy; he just stared at her for a short while till his face went back to his usual colour.

'Aren't you the grand one to be talking about decent weddings now, Mrs Hennessy,' he said eventually. 'I've lived in this place all my life and so have you, and I don't remember yours.' He smiled as if he had said something very clever.

Bridie smiled back. 'Sure, how could you – I never had one. God, they're grand rashers!' And she reached out and took the parcel Emer was holding out to her.

The purple was back. 'All them children—?'

Bridie looked at him as if she had only just noticed him. 'What about them?'

'There must be half a dozen of them—' Bill sounded very upset.

'Eight in fact – so far.' Bridie patted her stomach and winked.

Bill waited a minute while the purple of his face faded to pink then he folded his arms and said very slowly, 'You know, a lot of people round here have noticed that only a couple of them look like your Sam.'

The big woman hoisted her breasts and slowly buttoned the front of her cardigan. 'That's right,' she said and started to walk towards the door, 'only a couple of mine look like my Sam but I'll tell you what,' and a great big smile evened out all the lines on her face, 'all of yours do!'

Only that she door slammed behind her that very minute, Gareth was sure Bill would have gone for her and hit her a clout. He banged his fist on the counter instead and said terrible words that had Emer going as red as he had been a few seconds before.

'Aul bitch!' he managed to say without opening his teeth at all.

'Hush there, Bill, don't mind her. She's only trying to get a rise out of you – you weren't too kind to her yourself!'

'Kind to her?' Bill was still breathing as if he'd run for miles. 'The kindest thing you could do for that one would be to put her down!'

'Bill Brady! One more word like that out of you and I'll ask you to go home and come back here another day when you're feeling more Christian!'

Bill shook his head and looked at her. 'Oh Jaysus, would you listen to me? I'm terrible sorry. That one has me turned into a rip as bad as herself.'

Emer smiled. 'There's no harm in Bridie Hennessy, Bill, and well you know it.'

'I do not.' Bill straightened up and fixed the front of his shirt where it had crumpled around his braces. 'Anyway, what was it I saying?'

'The wedding,' Gareth said.

'Gareth Fagan! How long have you been standing there?' Emer Fagan looked at him crossly.

'I wasn't standing, I was sitting – I didn't want Mrs Hennessy to see me.' He caught his mother's eye. 'Some boys made Eilish Hennessy cry in school today and it wasn't me. But she might give out to me anyway.'

Bill Brady chuckled. 'I'm right behind you, son. I'm nearly afraid of her meself.' He winked at Gareth.

Emer ruffled his hair. 'Go on and do your homework. Don't forget to say hello to your daddy first.'

Gareth shrugged. 'Okay.' He went across to the bar side but there was no sign of his father – only sulky Cora was there. 'Where's Daddy?'

She shrugged, and then when he didn't move, gestured towards the door that led to the storeroom. Without bothering to acknowledge her scant effort, Gareth pushed open the heavy door and jumped down the steep stone steps to the cellar. He could hear his father moving around below. 'Daddy, are you here?'

'What do you want?'

'I'm just in from school, Mammy said to come and say hello.'

'Did she now?' John Fagan pulled the cigarette out of the corner of his mouth and regarded his son with mild amusement. 'Are you sure she didn't send you down to spy on me?'

'No! What am I supposed to be spying about?'

John looked at the cigarette before dropping it onto the floor and grinding it with the sole of his shoe. 'Oh now, who knows what your mammy would be watching out for. She's a spoilsport.'

Gareth felt he should say something in his mother's defence but it was so unusual for his father to stop and have a chat with him that he didn't want to lose the moment. 'Is it that you're having a cigarette?'

'That's my business.' His father sounded bored already.

'In school they said smoking was bad for you.'

'Oh for God's sake – you're nearly as bad as your mother. Cora! Come in here a minute.'

'Yes, Mr Fagan?' As if she had been waiting outside, Cora appeared at the door and leaned lazily against the frame. 'Is there something I can do for you?'

His father smiled as if she had just said something really witty. 'Plenty, I'm sure,' he said and she giggled as if that was clever too. 'But for the moment, I could do with a sandwich. Don't bother Mrs Fagan – go on down to the kitchen yourself and make me one.'

'With mustard?'

His father was watching the girl very closely. 'Oh, as hot as you can make it. I like it like that.'

'Mr Fagan – you're awful!' Cora was acting as if liking plenty of mustard was some sort of crime but his father was smiling. Gareth looked from one to the other, confused. He didn't like Cora Hennessey. He didn't like the way she hung her coat behind the door in the kitchen, its perfumey smell

21

filling the doorway. She turned now and went into the kitchen and Gareth waited for his father to talk to him again but John Fagan seemed to have lost interest. He was bent over his books, humming to himself. Gareth left him there and went up to his room to start on the hordes of homework Sister Pius liked to set. Downstairs he could hear the sounds of his mother moving boxes in the shop and Cora fussing around the kitchen, opening cupboards as if she owned the place. After a few minutes she left the kitchen and he could hear her at the storeroom door.

"Bye, Mr Fagan. Thanks, Mr Fagan. See you all tomorrow!'

His father shouted up from the store but before Gareth could hear his mother's goodbye, Cora was out the door and away. Then it was just the three of them. Putting his pencil down, he strained to hear if Mammy and Daddy were chatting but they weren't – only the odd sound of boxes being moved and people going about their business, and the quiet, and everyone on their own.

Emer had just finished sorting out the broken bits from the biscuit box when Gareth came downstairs looking for food. His eyes lit up when he spotted the plate of broken Club Milks but darkened when he looked at her.

'What's wrong, Mammy, were you crying?'

'Crying? What would I have to cry about? It's only the onions. There's a special way of doing them. You have to peel them first and then run them under the cold tap for a minute. That way, when you slice them, there's no gas coming off them to make your eyes water. Here, drink your milk.' She forced a smile and kept it steady till the little shoulders relaxed and he started to drink. Sitting opposite him, she tried to think of what to talk about to distract him but the biscuits did the trick. Each one had to be examined closely. It couldn't be eaten straight off; it had to be stripped clean of chocolate first. It was a ritual.

Emer watched, lulled by the slow, pleasurable process. His precision and patience pleased her. It was so unlike his father. For years she watched John throw his ample weight around and when a heart attack brought him to his knees a year ago, he took it not as a warning about his excessive lifestyle, but as an excuse to bully her further. Emer felt the pricking behind her eyes.

'Mammy,' Gareth was watching her again. 'What makes people not like you?'

How could he know?

'I mean, if they'd never met you before?'

He didn't know. He was talking about someone else. He took a deep breath. 'Sister Pius hates me.'

Emer smiled. 'Of course she doesn't. She hasn't been here long enough to hate anyone.'

'Well, she hates me – everyone says so. I don't even have to be doing anything. Even when Joey's bold and I'm nowhere near him she looks at me as if I made him do it and she said that I am a bad influence and what could you expect anyway - and other times she can't even remember my name!' Warmed to the theme now, the words flowed freely. 'She gets her mean face on her and says, *I suppose Noel Fagan knows all about it but of course, he'll be the picture of innocence,* and Noel Lynch says *I don't,* and she says *I wasn't talking to you* and then she'll point at me and I'll say *I'm Gareth,* and then she'll get red and say *Don't you answer me back, boy.*'

'She calls you Noel Fagan?'

'She did, three times. She hates me so she won't even remember my proper name.' His eyes filled and his fists were clenched.

'I'm sure she doesn't hate you, pet. Maybe she's just a bit old and forgetful.'

'She does! Sometimes when she's correcting my copy and there's no mistake on it, she turns over the cover and looks at it and then at me and then she puts a tick on real fast as if it's all just stupid anyway,' he gulped.

'All right, all right, calm down. Maybe she's lonely for her friends in England and it's them she's thinking about when she looks up and not you at all. You stay being a good boy and if we get a chance we'll take Daddy's car into Kilkenny on Saturday and Peter can come too. Would you like that?'

Gareth's face brightened. 'Thanks, Mammy! Can I watch the telly upstairs for a while before the tea is ready?'

Emer nodded.

Grabbing his comic for company, he took the stairs two at a time and she smiled at how easily his good humour could be restored. She was biased of course, but she could still see that he was a good child. Of course the woman didn't hate him; how could she? Funny though – her calling him Noel. Emer shuddered. If her husband was a bully, his older brother was a hundred times worse. She hadn't seen him in years and for all any of them knew he might be dead. She threw sausages on the pan and shook it crossly. Well, she wouldn't mourn him. She hadn't thought about him for years and now that stupid nun had brought him into her mind again.

She touched her arm where she knew a nasty bruise would appear by the end of the day and she tried not to think of her husband either, focusing instead on the spitting fat in

24

the pan. By the time Gareth came down to the kitchen again she was humming in tune to the radio and she sent him out to fetch his father before the teatime shoppers came in for their last minute eggs and Calvita. The three of them sat, Gareth all chat again, John buried in the *Evening Press*, avoiding her eye. As she served the food, she realised with a sickening jolt why the boy was looking at her so closely. On his plate there were sausages, potatoes and some peas.

There were no onions.

CHAPTER 3

'Jaysus, Aggie! YOU'RE WARM IN YOUR LEATHERS gardening on a day like today!' Bridie's voice boomed ahead of her as she lumbered down Kildoran Main Street towards the convent gate.

Smiling, Agnes turned to greet her friend. She laid her trowel and fork on the side of the barrow and held out her hand to take the basket from her panting visitor. As she did so, she noticed the change in Bridie's face – the pallor pale, the dark, hungry shadows under her eyes – and the twinkle in them. Then she saw the belly that bulged even more than usual between the stretched sides of Bridie's coat.

'And how many of you would I be offering a cup of tea to, may I ask?'

'Ah, go on out a' that!' Bridie's chest rattled with laughter.

Inside it was warm and smelled of bread and nuns. Glad that the kitchen was empty but for the two of them Agnes lifted a tea towel from a tray of hot scones and started to butter them.

'You're very cheerful today, Bridie.' Agnes put a buttered scone on her plate. 'Thank God.'

'Ah, it isn't God I have to thank for my good humour,' Bridie chuckled. 'It's my Sam and the good Sister Pius.'

'Pius?' Agnes tried to hide her surprise. 'Well, I'm glad to hear that. We can't get her to relax with us here at all. She seems to prefer her own company.'

Bridie took a bite of her scone. 'I don't think anyone could enjoy that one's company, Agnes – even herself.'

'So what's she done to you?'

26

Bridie chuckled. 'She came to visit me, you know, a couple of days ago – after I'd ignored three letters summoning me to go see her. I was at the window in the kitchen when I spotted her, picking her way across the yard to the kitchen door. Oh, she's a prissy one – too prim to raise her skirts or part her knees far enough to get to the door quickly. There'll be shite soaked into the hem of her habit for two washings at least!'

Agnes was torn between the obligation of loyalty to a fellow sister and a very human desire to hear the rest of the story. The latter won. 'So what did she want? It wasn't a social visit?'

'Indeed it wasn't! No sooner was she through the door with her nostrils pinned to her forehead, than she informed me that my Eilish was having a rough time of it in school – being teased.

And what about, Sister Pius? said I.

'Well, she was swallowing as if she had just found the cure to a thirst and her eyes were darting around the room. Then she spotted the beds and you should have seen the look on her face! You know yourself, it's *"first up, best dressed"* in my house and if you don't make it on time, you might as well stay put. Two of little ones had and wasn't one of them after piddling?'

This room, says she, as if she was the queen herself come to visit, *reeks of disorder.*

And is my Eilish or my housekeeping you wanted to talk to me about? Well – she didn't know where to look.

Eilish – obviously, says she, scanning the room like a frightened rabbit. *She's being teased in school and she won't speak up for herself and –* by now I thought she was well on the way to her first heart attack – she was actually spitting. She looked at me as if I was a heathen and in the kitchen of my own house and she the visitor – not even invited. *They say that Eilish doesn't look like the rest of your children, that she has a different father.*

Bridie took another bite of her scone. 'Can you imagine? What could you say to that?'

Agnes shrugged. She couldn't imagine why Pius would take such an interest in any of the children. She always gave the impression that the less she had to do with them the better. And there she was, putting herself in line for the sharp tongue of Bridie Hennessey – and especially on the age-old question of the eclectic Hennessey clan. Maybe she considered it her duty to civilise the natives – she certainly hadn't any desire to become one of them. 'Goodness, Bridie, what did you say to that at all?'

A great wave of mirth washed over Bridie and Agnes had to wait till it subsided before she could make out the answer.

'Nothing – nothing at all,' Bridie spluttered. 'What's there to say?' and she burst out laughing again. 'I just hitched up my skirt and started to pull the wet clothes off the bed. I had them slung over the line to dry out before she opened her mouth again.

Well? Have you no answer to that?

'And did you?'

'Indeed I did,' Bridie heaved herself to her feet. 'I took off the old apron I had on and I stood right in the middle of the kitchen like this and look!' With her left hand she circled her stomach in slow and sensuous movements. *I have an answer for anyone who cares to hear it. I told her. Eilish has no 'different' father. No indeed.* She started to laugh again. *Sure she's had the same father since the night she was conceived!*

Despite herself, Agnes had to smile. 'Whist now,' she said eventually, 'and sit yourself down. I shouldn't be party to such disrespect. She was only trying to let you know what was going on.'

'Aye.' Bridie sat down again but she was obviously uncomfortable. She shifted her position on the chair in an effort to lessen the aches that were stretching and poking their way across her stomach. 'There's little going on that gets past me.'

Agnes watched pain fight the pleasure on her companion's ruddy face, 'Or me.' She pointed to Bridie's stomach. 'Are you well enough for all this? The doctor hasn't said it's too soon?'

'I'm grand,' Bridie pushed another crumbly scone into her mouth. 'Sure, isn't providing patients for the good doctor what I'm best at doing? That and shocking nuns!' And as she threw back her head to laugh, her watering eyes caught those of her friend and they laughed together.

The following morning, Agnes woke up with a terrible cold. Her eyes streamed and her head seemed stuffed with peppery slime. She sniffed and sneezed her way through matins and leaving early, stood waiting by the bell board for the others to emerge. It was obvious to her by now that she'd not be fit enough to make the weekly visit to St Thomas' Nursing Home and hoped to find a replacement quickly. Many of the elderly folk in residence there had neither relatives who could visit nor relatives who would and a friendly face from the convent was a welcome sight. She usually brought food with her too: fresh crusty rolls, sausages – and a drop of something creamy for the home's sole male resident.

'Well now, thank you, Sister', he'd beamed at her the first time she brought out the bottle, 'You have a rare understanding of the common man's needs – and you a creature of the cloth!'

'God forgive you, Matty Hurley – that's a desperate thing to say!' Agnes chided him but they both knew she didn't mind. They'd been friends since childhood when everyone, Matty included, expected that one day he'd marry the love of his life – Agnes' older sister, Connie. But Connie died of TB in her teens and Matty never replaced her. He worked hard, too hard, till it eventually took a toll on his health and left him an old man before his time. But his friendship with Agnes remained strong and sometimes in the twinkle of his rheumy eyes she'd catch a glimpse of the man he used to be.

'And crusty rolls with a slice of thick ham! Well, isn't that lovely!" Matty said without fail every Tuesday when she handed him his little parcel. 'I'll enjoy that. It'll be grand to have a bite to eat that doesn't feel as if Matron has chewed it herself first.'

Agnes secretly agreed with him. Sadie Flynn and her faithful staff took the chapter on 'Feeding the Elderly' very seriously indeed. Everything was mashed, pureed, liquidized or boiled soft – ardently rendered digestible – and at the same time bland or totally tasteless. Watching the listless food being wheeled in on the trolley, Agnes wondered if the last bit of goodness it ever possessed had fled for fear of being whipped, beaten or boiled alive. Little wonder then the home's bathroom windowsill was crowded with beakers containing rows of rarely used false teeth – all spotless and generally inserted only for Mass or visitors – never for mealtimes. Nevertheless, respect for Matron Flynn's integrity made her hold her tongue and quietly supplement Matty's needs with her own weekly offerings.

That was why she felt this visit was so important. If she was homebound because of her cold, it was imperative she found someone else to do the visit for her.

One by one the sisters filed past her out of chapel. One by one and with sincere regret in their eyes and voices, they recounted commitments already made that day. Only Pius was left inside, still kneeling at her small lectern praying. Agnes didn't like to bother her but today there didn't seem to be any other option. If she was unfit to go, then she would have to ask Sister Pius to do the visit for her.

Sister Pius was surprised to feel the tap on her shoulder and looked up to see the kindly face of Sister Agnes looking down at her.

'Pardon me, Sister,' the face grew red with embarrassment, 'I don't like to disturb you but I wondered if I might ask you a favour, a big favour.'

With a barely suppressed sigh, Pius replied, 'Of course.'

'Oh, bless you, Sister,' Agnes beamed, 'I'm sure you'll enjoy it!'

Pius doubted that. There was little she enjoyed – and two minutes later, when she heard what the request was, her doubts were more than confirmed.

'The gentleman's name is?' Pius stood stiffly watching Agnes carefully wrap the brown loaf in waxed paper.

'Matty – Mathew Hurley in full though he's always been Matty to me.'

'Matty Hurley.' Pius repeated and though there was a note of finality in her voice, her lips were parted as if she was about to say something else.

Agnes folded the paper neatly at the sides and tucking the parcel under her arm, shuffled over to the drawer for the scissors and a piece of string. 'He's been a friend of my family for years – more like a brother really.'

'Who are your family?'

If Agnes was surprised at this show of interest, she wasn't going to comment on it. 'Dowlings. My family were local. We farmed part of that hill beyond the village where they're doing all the building now. The whole hill is due to be "developed" as they say. You know, some people still refer to it as Dowlings' Hill though if the truth were known we had only a small part of it. The other side, most of it, belonged to the Hurleys.'

'Dowlings and Hurleys.' Pius' voice was very soft as if she was talking to herself.

Agnes pulled the string around her parcel twice and started to knot it. 'Further down, at the bottom of the Hill there was an old woman called the Widda Meaney, local midwife and wise woman. She was well known for miles around here.' She pulled the knot tight and snipped the string, 'And then, God help them, at the top of the hill, beyond the Hurleys, were the Morrisseys. There! That should hold tight!' With a smile she held the parcel out to Pius and was shocked to see the other woman had grown deathly pale. She was clutching the table as if for support and the bones in the back of her hands seemed to shine through translucent skin. 'Sister, are you all right?'

Pius seemed to be struggling for breath. 'I'm fine. Fine. Please continue.'

'Well, I—'Agnes was at a loss to remember what she had been talking about.

'You said there were other families on the hill.'

'Oh yes. The Widda, as I said, and the Morrisseys ...' She shook her head sadly at the memory. 'Who knows? It's not a nice story and most probably not entirely true either.'

'Tell me!' By now Pius was leaning across the table and the two bright spots of colour were blazing in her cheeks.

Confused, Agnes pushed the parcel across the table towards her. 'Well, I'm not sure, Sister. I was just a child at the time but local legend has it that there was a terrible incident that wiped the family out. After that nobody went near the place for years and now word is that the developers have finally managed to buy up all the land—'

Pius snatched the parcel off the table. 'So they're all dead then.' It sounded like an announcement.

'Nobody really knows. There haven't been Morrisseys in these—'

But Pius had already turned and was walking out of the kitchen. Agnes stood and watched her as the door closed and then she pulled her shawl more tightly around her shoulders. Suddenly she felt cold and clammy. Her neck and shoulders were aching and her head was beginning to throb. Somewhere the conversation had left her behind and she wasn't quite sure why.

As she walked down the long polished corridor outside the kitchen, Pius clutched the parcel closely to her chest. Her breath was coming in small gasps and there were beads of sweat on her forehead. She wanted to drop the parcel into the bin and run for her life but there was nowhere to run to now.

It was too late.

There was the usual flurry of excitement when the doorbell rang at St Thomas' Nursing Home. As Matron led Emer into the dining room a circle of old ladies turned to watch her. Recognising a familiar face, a few smiled and others reached out to catch her hand and her attention. Within minutes she was privy to a wealth of gossip: whose cat was dead; which nurse was suspected of having a new boyfriend; whose teeth had gone missing – even who was suspected to have taken them. Careful to acknowledge every attention, Emer kept an eye on the sun lounge at the far end of the dining room where her mother and Matty Hurley always sat. Both were in their usual seats – her mother at one end tucked as far as possible out of sight; Matty at the other, by the door. Though he joked that he was truly 'Blessed amongst women,' Emer suspected that he was actually quite lonely and the chair by his side was an invitation to anyone who was prepared neither to mother nor smother him, to sit a while and keep him company. He waved when he saw her and she was glad of the opportunity to break free of the soft hands and head for the sun lounge.

At the door, one of the young nurses stopped her. 'Emer, hello!'

'Hello Bridget – how are you?'

'Fine, fine. You might find your mother a bit on the quiet side today. She's been a bit "off" recently.'

'What sort of "off"?'

'Well, moody-like.' Bridget caught Emer's eye and the two of them smiled. *That'll be a change*, Emer thought and the look on Bridget's face was evidence enough she wasn't the only one thinking it. 'Anyway, I'm sure the visit will cheer her up. Someone for you, Nell!' The young nurse went into the sun lounge, a damp tea towel still in her hands. 'C'mere and I'll straighten that cushion for you.' She laid the towel on the window-sill and, bending over the old woman, caught hold of the cushion and attempted to straighten it.

Nell made no move to assist her. She sat still and heavy as an old rock, for all the world as if she was unaware that there was anyone there.

Emer and Matty watched her. While the young nurse heaved and panted, the old woman remained motionless – even when the girl managed to haul the large limp cushion out from its crumpled position and smooth it carefully against the back of the chair.

'There!' She said. 'Comfortable now, are you?' Then she turned, red-faced with exertion, beads of sweat glistening along the top of her forehead and headed out of the door. As she left, they heard her mutter 'The aul rip!' and though Emer felt a momentary flash of resentment she couldn't help smiling sympathetically – hard pressed to know for whom she had the most pity – the buxom young girl with her life ahead of her or the bitter old woman who glared in her wake.

As soon as Bridget left the room, Nell came to life. She took the towel from the windowsill and, laying it carefully across her lap, began to fold it exactly corner to corner, smoothing each fold as she went. Over and over the towel halved its size. Then she placed it back on the sill in line with the sill's edge. Having satisfied herself with this, she wiped any damp patches off the woodwork and the arm of her chair. All the time she kept glancing at the doorway. They could hear the voices, muffled, from the other room –Matron Flynn's calm as always, Bridget's annoyed. Emer took a deep breath and stepped down into the room.

35

'Hello, Mam,' she said. 'Are you well?' Ignoring Nell's flinch as she bent to kiss her, she turned to Matty. 'Hello, Matty, fine today, isn't it?'

'Aye, grand,' Matty nodded and reaching out, pushed the chair that stood beside his towards her. She was tempted to sit beside him where at least she would be welcome. With Nell, there'd be no relaxed conversation. Emer would have to do all the talking. Every so often in the course of the monologue, Nell would fire questions at her daughter, terse and aggressive and the answers she gave, regardless of what they were, would undoubtedly be wrong. Her father's face came into her head and for a split second she could see him before he died, asking her in that gentle way of his to look after her mother, explaining, without giving reasons, that it wasn't Nell's fault.

She positioned the chair by the windowsill and started to tell her mother about the week's events in Kildoran. At first Nell didn't appear to be listening. Her brow twitched as she flicked through thoughts then suddenly cleared.

'Is she gone?' Nell suddenly demanded.

'Who, Mam?

'At the funeral – her.'

Emer looked at her, confused. Poor Mother Rosalie – what did she ever do wrong?

'Is she gone, I asked you?'

'Yes, Mam. She's gone, she died and she was buried.'

'Good,' Nell said. 'They shouldn't have taken me there, exposed me to that sort of danger.'

'What danger?'

Nell glared. '*You* know.'

Emer sighed. 'I don't know, Mam. What danger?'

'It wasn't my fault. I couldn't have said anything anyway. It was too late. I won't be blamed.' Nell slumped back in her chair and glared at Emer through half-closed eyes. 'You won't get me to say anything.' Emer waited a minute but though Nell watched her closely, she did not say any more.

Across the room, Matty shuffled uncomfortably and Emer smiled at him to absolve his witness. He'd watched the visits before and though this one was more agitated than usual, he'd known Nell all his life and Emer all hers and she knew he was not sitting in judgement. Instead, he kept checking his watch, waiting for Agnes.

'She's late,' he said simply.

Suddenly, they heard the young nurse open the front door and the sound of someone being shown in and they waited for the familiar tread across the dining room linoleum. Agnes, for all her convent ways, still walked like a farmer's daughter – great big strides that took her to where she needed to go with little concern for grace in the act of getting there. She always walked like that. Matty once told Emer that he could remember watching 'the hefty strap of a lass cross the road to her father's cart, big-boned and big-hipped – her backside like a swaying sack of corn, contained but barely controlled by the cloth which covered it.' As he spoke his voice was full of affection.

They were both glad that she was here now. Emer picked up her bag and carried the chair over beside Matty.

'Here,' she said, 'you'll be needing this.' Then she turned to kiss her mother. She'd go before Agnes settled in for the chat otherwise she'd get caught up in conversation and she wanted to have a word with Matron about Nell's agitation. 'Bye, Mam, see you next week.'

Then she was gone.

Straightening the chair so that Agnes would shield him as he opened the weekly food parcel, Matty smiled to himself. For a minute there he had the terrible feeling that something might be wrong and Agnes wouldn't come. It was probably Nell's edginess that had them all unsettled. Never mind, she was here now. At that, he heard the visitor arrive on the step behind him and was just about to turn and greet her when Nell Byrne looked up. Matty expected her to nod as she usually did. Instead she looked puzzled and there was something else in her expression that Matty couldn't quite decipher. He turned his head and to his surprise, Agnes wasn't there at all. It was a different one. She was poised at the edge of the step, her face in the shadow of her veil, which she kept tilted forward. Her arms were clutched tightly to her chest but he could make out the shape of a brown paper package through her sleeve. She nodded to him curtly in greeting.

'Good afternoon, Mr Hurley. My name is Sister Pius.'

'Afternoon, Sister.' It was an effort to keep the disappointment out of his voice as well as off his face. 'Agnes isn't coming then?'

'No, she isn't'. Pius replied impatiently. She sat opposite him and kept her head bowed. 'She has a cold and was anxious not to pass it on to you. She did, however, feel fit enough to prepare this small parcel.' With a tut that sounded like disapproval, she handed over a bulging package, carefully wrapped in brown paper.

Matty smiled – good old Agnes, she never let him down – and balancing the package across his knees, started to unwrap the parcel. As the untidy sheet unfolded across his lap he satisfied himself that the contents of the parcel were as they should be, then he put them on the table beside him and turned to face his visitor, who had remained motionless, head bowed, apparently waiting for him to start the conversation. *God help us*, he thought, *by the look of that face this'll be an animated visit all right!* He had hardly opened his mouth to speak when Nell sprang forward in her chair.

'You!' She screeched, pointing a gnarled and bony finger at Pius' back. 'Turn around till I get a proper look at that face!'

Matty looked in amazement at the nun. She was deathly white. He realized then that she hadn't been politely waiting to converse with him. She was frozen rigid, a look of absolute terror in her eyes.

'Turn around, damn you!' Nell grabbed the folded tea towel from the windowsill and, hauling herself out of the chair, lashed out at the nun's back. Cursing furiously, she lurched forward just as two nurses came rushing into the lounge to restrain her. They each tried to grab one of her flailing arms before she did herself or anyone else an injury. But they were too late. Nell had the edge of Pius' long black veil in her grasp and, yanking it back, she pulled it, cowl and all, from her head. Pius turned towards the shrieking figure to defend herself and in doing so, came face to face with her assailant. For a moment they stared at each other then slowly, Nell's expression changed. The anger faded and in its place there was fear.

'I knew she was lying. They all lie,' she whispered, 'I knew the minute you walked in it was you. What did you come here for? I thought you were dead – that was the little comfort that was left me – and now you've come back to haunt me. Oh God, is there no end to it?' Twisting the cloth tightly in her hands, her face was contorted in anguish. 'It wasn't my fault. I didn't mean it. It was too late and anyway, I couldn't remember. Jimmy said to forget about it. I only wanted to forget about it…'

and she broke into a wild hysterical wailing. Between them, the young nurses carried her into the other room, muttering rushed apologies for her strange behaviour as they went.

Matty was left alone with Pius.

She stood for what seemed an age saying nothing and, embarrassed and puzzled by the incident, he avoided her eye. Eventually she bent down to retrieve her veil and Matty looked at her properly for the first time. She wasn't really as old as he had first assumed and her hair was not white as he thought it would be. Though peppered with grey, there was plenty of the mousy colour of her youth. As she leaned forward, in the darkening winter afternoon, Matty caught a glimpse of the younger Pius, a glimpse of the girl she used to be and like a chill reaching into his bones, he understood suddenly what had frightened Nell.

She must have felt his gaze.

'I tried,' she whispered. 'I only came today because Sister Agnes needed me to. I tried not to. The Lord knows I didn't want any of this.'

Matty reached out his hand and caught hers. 'I know that.' She was shaking, and her eyes searched his face for comfort. 'There's nothing you could have done. Maybe she'll have forgotten it when she wakes. Go now and in future find a reason if you have to but you mustn't come again.'

Fixing her veil quickly on her head, Pius scrabbled to regain her composure as he ushered her quickly out of the room. She hurried through the front door and banged it behind her, leaving Matty, for the second time in his life, watching as the thin terrified figure ran as if all the hounds of hell were snapping at her heels.

CHAPTER 4

E MER PULLED HER BOOTS OFF and left them on the mat by
the back door. Her mind was still racing after the visit
to St Thomas'. Her mother's increasing agitation was
unsettling and Matron was in a meeting so she hadn't had a
chance to talk to her. Even if Matron was available there was
probably little she would be able to do. Nell had always been a
law unto herself and Emer was no part of it. Stupid really –
every week she came out of St Thomas' feeling worse than
when she went in, yet every week she promised herself that
nothing that happened – or rather didn't happen – between
herself and her mother would upset her.

But it still hurt. The only time her mother ever paid heed
to anyone was when Gareth was there, and then only because
the boy was so like his grandfather. He was the only one she
showed any interest in since her husband died. The greater
part of her died then too and she retreated from the world as if
to be alive still disgusted her. Emer knew that there was no way
her mother would be able to look after herself. She never had.
From the beginning Jimmy Byrne hovered around his wife,
watching her face for signs of anxiety and soothing her when
her moods would suddenly swing and she'd rant and cry in
terror at her invisible demons.

'Well, I'm not one of them, Mam,' she muttered crossly to
herself. 'I have enough demons of my own.' She recalled with
reddening cheeks John's treatment of her earlier – the ritual
humiliation leaving her feeling raw and vulnerable. She filled
the kettle and got herself a packet of Kimberleys from the
cupboard. 'Comfort food.' She ripped open the packet. 'If you

want comfort, Emer Fagan, you can forget it. There's no one to look after you but yourself. Isn't that the way it's always been?'

While the kettle boiled she watched the steam rise and drops form on the tiles above the range. Very slowly they broke away and flowed down and, watching them, Emer was back nearly thirty years, a little girl again.

She could see herself, sodden, on the hill with her friends. They were caught in a downpour and decided to take shelter under a tree until the rain eased. Huddled together in sparse shelter the jostling soon started and Emer slipped, gashing her thigh and covering her dress in mud. She struggled to her feet and, ignoring the blood running down her leg, held out her dress to see if she had torn it.

'Oh Janey, look at your knee!'

'Is it sore?'

'Here, wipe the blood off your sock.' Her friends came out of their shelter and gathered around her to examine the damage.

Emer looked at the hanky being offered. 'Thanks, I'm okay, keep it – I'll never get it off with that.' She held out her skirt to show them the long streaks of mud. 'Here, is it torn anywhere?'

Tilly ignored the skirt and bent instead to take a closer look at the bloodied leg.

'Tilly! Is my skirt torn? Can you see a tear on it anywhere?'

Tilly looked at her impatiently. 'Would you ever give over about the skirt? No, it's not torn and the dirt will wash out, but look at the cut on your leg, it's nearly pumping! We'd better get home and let your mammy wash it.'

Emer appeared not to hear her. Despite the fact that the blood was now pouring freely she was still examining the marks on her clothes and frantically trying to rub them off. 'I'll be killed! Look at the state of this!'

'You're only making it worse. Stop rubbing.'

'I have to get it clean. She told me not to get it dirty – I had it on clean this morning.'

Tilly raised her eyes to heaven impatiently. 'Well, that was stupid, wasn't it? You knew we were going to go up the hill. Why couldn't you just have on what you had on yesterday – that was grand.'

'Mammy washed it.'

'But it wasn't dirty!'

'It was – there was a mark on the front. She said I couldn't go out and disgrace the family in a state like that ... ' Emer felt her cheeks redden she knew there were tears in her eyes that had little to do with the pain in her leg. She looked around at the circle of friends, comfortable in their playing clothes, muddy and almost ragged, and caught the quick glances that flew from one to the other. She knew they were thinking that her mother was soft in the head and that she was a little soft too. 'Are you going to help me clean it or not?'

A few embarrassed whispers and then Tilly smiled. 'Here. C'mon down to the stream with me and we'll see what we can do. If we get the worst of it off it'll maybe only be the wet that she'll notice and you'll hardly get the blame for making it rain, will you?'

Some of the children laughed. Ignoring them, Tilly caught her friend's elbow and ushered her forward. The rest of the children huddled back under the shelter of the tree and the two girls struggled through the tall grass towards the stream.

Neither spoke, just wended their way in silence across the rough uneven surface. The tall grass slid sharply across Emer's cut leg and the throb of it was beginning to register. She looked at her friend.

'Where are we going? I thought the stream was the other way?'

'Nah – it's a short cut if you go this way.'

'But the stream comes down at the back of the church from Dowling's Hill.'

'So?'

'And there's another one on the other side.'

'So … ?' Tilly looked at her impatiently.

'So what are we doing going this way? You said we were going to the stream to wash my skirt and now you're taking me the wrong way and there's no stream here and my leg is sore and—' She started to cry.

'Emer Byrne, would you ever stop fussing? I'm not taking you the wrong way; there *is* a stream here, a small one that joins up with the other two and it makes a pond. It's the nearest. If you'd ever give over and keep walking, I'd have you there in a minute.' She grabbed her hand and pulled her forward. 'Look!'

Tilly was right. Just ahead of them at the edge of the overgrown field three small streams ran together and spread into a pool. The water was so clear that you could see the stones on the bottom. Emer looked at it as if it were a magic place.

'Wow! It's beautiful! How did you know this was here?' She smiled at her friend and, stepping onto a big rock that overhung one side of the pond, peered over into the water below. 'It'd be a great place for swimming.'

44

'Yeah – but my mammy says we shouldn't come up here – it's haunted.'

'Haunted?' Emer laughed, and then noticed the worried look on her friend's face. 'Who's supposed to haunt it?'

Tilly looked around as if it were likely that someone would bother to come up the hill in the rain to listen to the secrets whispered by children. 'A girl,' she said.

'What sort of a girl?'

Tilly took a deep breath. She paused for a moment, casting around the quiet pool for the right word. Then she leaned close to Emer and whispered, 'A mad one.'

'What was she mad for? Did she die here or what?' Suddenly the quiet seemed less peaceful than before and the rain in the trees hummed as if to threaten them in the stillness below.

Folding her arms in front of her, Tilly shook her head. 'That's the whole scary thing about it. Nobody knows. She disappeared. They say she drowned herself but nobody ever found a body and my mam says that when *she* was a little girl you couldn't even ask about it. She said it was a sin to be even thinking about terrible things like that, and when I asked her what sort of terrible things, she gave me a clip on the ear and said I'd get another one if I didn't give over—' she stopped, gasping for air.

'Janey! What terrible thing was it?'

'I don't know, do I? Nobody would tell anyone about it because it was so awful that it'd be a sin even to think about it but I think it was something to do with—' she paused and gestured towards the front of her skirt.

'With what?' Emer looked at her friend's embarrassed face.

Tilly said nothing.

'What?'

Tilly reddened. 'You know...' she gestured again, 'sort of – front bottoms.'

'Front bottoms? What do you mean "front bottoms"?'

'Oh. For God's sake! Do you know nothing about nothing, Emer Byrne? Front bottoms is where girls can do rude things and get murdered or something.' She paused but Emer was still looking at her blankly. 'All I know is that there was a terrible thing done and someone was nearly killed and the girl ran away and they didn't find her for days. Someone saw her up at Mad Morrisseys but she ran off and then someone found her shoes here by the stream. She must have been drowned or taken or something but anyway my mam says it's haunted and we're not to come up here. I wasn't ever going to but you made such a fuss over your skirt that I did and now you keep asking me stupid questions and—' She broke off, seeing the tears well in Emer's eyes. 'Don't cry, I'm only giving out because it's raining and I'm soaked. C'mon. D'you want to wash your skirt or what?'

'No, it's all right. We'll never get it clean and I'm going to get in fierce trouble anyway so we might as well go straight home.' She looked around at the pond. The trees overhanging were so dense that the rain couldn't get through and the water hardly moved. It was as if the place was waiting for her to speak again. 'I don't really like it here anyway. It's a bit scary, isn't it?' She gathered her cardigan around her and started back the way they had come in.

Without a word each child quickened her step. Tilly shot a quick glance at Emer's leg as if she was wondering whether it would be unfair to ask if she could run. She needn't have worried. Before the words had even started to form on her lips,

Emer's step gathered momentum and the two of them shot down the hill without a backward glance. They ran all the way to the bottom where the lane opened out to the road below. By now, both girls were gasping for breath and the exertion made them red-faced and sweaty.

'That was desperate.' Tilly panted, 'Are you all right?'

'Yep,' Emer glanced around, 'Is she still following us, d'you think?'

Tilly didn't look up but there was laughter in her voice. 'Oh, Janey Mac, you're right, she's coming – quick!'

With a whoop, the two girls raced down the road into the village. At the end of the road, Tilly raised her hand and waved, 'Bye! Hope your mam doesn't kill you!'

'Thanks!' Emer stopped running. Her leg was really sore by now and although she doubted Tilly's good wishes would do her any good in the next few minutes, she was glad to be home.

Home was a small, white-washed cottage at the side of a big barn that housed the village bus. As she opened the back door, Emer could hear her parents in the kitchen beyond.

'Late as usual', her mother was grumbling, 'that child has my heart scalded.'

'Now, Nell,' her father replied, 'the rain has been pelting all afternoon and she's probably sheltering—' He must have heard his daughter dropping her shoes by the mat and the sound of wet socks slapping their way to the kitchen door. 'Here she is now.' As Emer came into the room he turned, smiling.

'Hello there, where—? Sweet Mother of God! What happened to you?' In a shot he was out of the chair and by her side.

'I fell, Daddy. We all went up the hill to play cowboys but it started to rain and wouldn't stop. Tilly said it wouldn't last so the best thing to do would be to wait somewhere until it was over. So we did. We were sheltering under a tree and Fergus and Eugene started pucking each other and I got knocked and I fell—.' She caught sight of the look of horror on her mother's face and, thinking she was angry about the state of her clothes, Emer lifted her skirt. 'I got a terrible cut on my leg and there was lots of blood. Me and Tilly had to run all the way home and the pain of it was getting worse and I didn't even cry...'

It didn't work. Her face growing redder by the minute, Nell Byrne pushed her husband aside and stared at her daughter. Her mouth opened as if she was about to say something but no words came out, just a strange choking noise. She had taken hold of the edge of her cardigan and was twisting it fiercely as if to stop her hands from lashing out. When she twisted the fabric as far as it would go, she put her hands to her neck and started to sway. Jimmy stood, catching her just as she was about to fall and sat her back onto a chair. 'It's okay, Nell. She's all right. She's here. You sit down there and don't worry. She's okay.'

He was speaking very loudly but her mother didn't seem to hear. Her face was white and her eyes were huge and frightened. 'Who did this to you? Who did this?' Her voice was no louder than a whisper but it was hard. Her father had his hand on Nell's head and he was stroking her hair gently and crooning to her as if she was a baby. 'Shush now, pet, Jimmy's here and it's all right. Nobody did anything. The child just fell and cut herself –nobody did anything to her.'

She looked so frightened that Emer pulled her skirt as low as she could over her leg to hide the injury. She was puzzled.

Mammy was usually so fussy about keeping everything clean and neat, she'd thought she'd be in fierce trouble over the state of her clothes. Instead it was the blood flowing down between her legs that Mammy was staring at, her eyes all mad and glassy.

'It's all right, Mammy. I just fell. We were sheltering under a tree and I fell – it was an accident.'

But her mother wasn't listening. She had taken the tea towel from the table and was twisting it tighter and tighter. 'He was there, wasn't he?' she muttered. 'He was there, watching. He was just standing there and he knew and he wouldn't stop it. He was just standing there...'

'Who, Mammy?'

'He wouldn't stop it.'

'Nell! Enough!' Jimmy put his arms around his wife's shoulders and lifted her out of the chair. 'Come on with me. You're going up to your bed and we'll call the doctor over to give you something.'

Nell caught Jimmy's hand and the tears poured down her face. She looked at him in desperation. 'It won't go away, Jimmy. It won't go away. There's blood everywhere and he's just watching and he won't stop it.'

'Shush now pet. It's over...' and his voice was lost in the slow shuffling as he half carried his crumpled wife up the stairs to their bedroom. Emer stood in the kitchen looking after them. One minute they were worrying about her; the next thing the two of them disappear, with Mammy in a state and Daddy serious looking and nobody worrying about her at all! She shrugged. It was fine not getting in trouble but with a leg as sore as hers, you'd expect at least a bit of attention.

49

She tilted her head and listened to the sound of her parents in the room above. Their voices were muffled now but it was clear that Mammy was still crying and Daddy was still trying to make her stop. After a minute he came out of the room and Emer heard him in the hallway ringing the doctor. There was a hurried conversation, *Yes, that'd be great if you could come straight away. I'm sorry I caught you in the middle of your day off but she's hysterical and I'm not having any luck calming her …* Then the phone was put down and her father went back upstairs. Her mother had stopped crying and Emer was glad of it. It was horrible when Mammy got upset like that and you didn't know what was after happening even though you were there all the time. But that wasn't any reason to go putting everyone to bed and leaving her standing in the kitchen with her dress still soaked and the pain in her cut leg getting bigger as if someone was taking a hammer to it.

Suddenly aware of the silence from upstairs and filled with an overwhelming urge to fill it, Emer threw back her head and bawled. It worked. No sooner had she paused to gulp enough air for another go, than her father was back in the kitchen and by her side.

'Now, now, pet, don't be crying.' He sat on the chair and lifted her onto his knee. 'Let Daddy have a look at the terrible cut you've got. Oh, dear, isn't that dreadful? It looks fierce all right and you're the bravest girl not to be making a fuss.' He kissed her cheek, 'There's all sorts of dirt in there. We'll have to give it a wash to get the germs out.' He lifted her onto the table and, pulling a clean cloth from the press under the sink, started to wet it under the tap. 'I probably shouldn't be using this but you know how great Mammy is at being enemies with the germs, I'm sure it'll be the very thing,' and he started to dab at her bloodied leg with the cloth.

Emer winced at the cold shock of it but she stopped crying. Daddy was looking at her and smiling as if she was the best girl in the world and even if the Pope walked in this minute he wouldn't have paid any attention to him. Smiling back, she watched as he dabbed at her leg with Mammy's clean white cloth. Every time he lifted it, it was dirtier with blood and mud and sharp little black stones that scratched as he tried to wipe them off.

The throbbing was sharper now and more insistent but still Emer didn't cry. She had Daddy all to herself and if she was a good girl he'd smile and not have that worried look he got when Mammy was upset.

Eventually he stopped and threw the cloth into the sink and then bent his head close to examine the cut. With the dirt washed away her leg looked a lot better but they could see clearly that the cut was a bad one. A deep gash ran from above her knee to the middle of her shin. The edges of the cut were sharp but the centre was deep and angry. Her father peered at it closely and tutted. 'You're a brave little soul. It looks as if you must have caught on something as you fell. Were there sharp stones or what?'

Emer screwed up her face and tried to remember. She could recall the roughened bark of the tree because she tried to catch onto the twig that was sticking out but something tripped her and that was when she fell and she felt the terrible pain in her leg ... .

'The wire, Daddy! That's what I tripped on! There was barbed wire that we'd climbed over and it was nailed to the tree at the back but it had slipped down and that's what tripped me up—' she stopped talking when she realised that her father was looking at her and his face was cross.

'What barbed wire, Emer? Why did you have to climb over barbed wire?'

Too late she remembered the rule about where she was allowed to go. The hill on Dowling's side was fine but time and again her father had warned her that she was never to set a foot on the side beyond Hurley's, the wasteland known in the village only as Mad Morrissey's.

'Where, Emer?' Her father insisted. His tone and the unfamiliar anger in his voice brought tears to her eyes. Daddy hardly ever got cross but when he did his eyes could look right through you and see what you were after doing even if you didn't say. 'I said 'where'?'

'It's just because we were cowboys and Indians and we had to have long grass to hide in...'

'Answer the question.'

'The field at the bottom of M – M—.'

'Morrissey's?' His voice was quiet and Emer couldn't look at him.

'Yes, Daddy,' she whispered and started to cry again. 'My leg hurts,' and she reached out to wipe away the drop of blood that was about to fall onto the table.

Her father shook his head. 'I've told you a thousand times, Emer. If you do a bold thing, bad things happen. You were told that you were never to go onto Morrissey's land and you went. You were deliberately disobedient and so you fell and cut yourself and frightened the life out of your poor Mammy with all the blood. She doesn't know what happened to you at all to give yourself a cut like that.'

'Is that why she's crying, Daddy? Is she sad because I'm hurt and she's worried about me?'

Her father looked as if he had a sore leg as well. 'Of course it is, Missy, so you're to be a good girl and you're not to go places you were told not to go and have the heart scalded in your mammy worrying. Do you hear me?'

'I do, Daddy, I'm sorry. I'll be a good girl.' She reached up and wrapped her arms around his neck. 'Will we tell her?'

In her embrace, she felt her father's shoulders relax. 'What do you think?'

Emer screwed up her face as if the matter warranted consideration before they reached the inevitable conclusion. 'Well, she's very upset with the blood and all and she might only get upsetter if she thought I was bold so—' she looked at him hopefully, 'd'you think it might be better if we said no more about it?'

Her father nodded solemnly. 'It might, all right. But only if a girl promised that she will never, and I mean *never*, go near Morrissey's land again.'

'I promise.'

'Good – and when the doctor comes we'll get him to take a look at that knee. It's deep and it might need a stitch.' There was a knock on the door and the doctor's face appeared around it.

'Is she above, Jimmy? I'll go up. Oh, dear, that's a wicked looking cut you have there, Miss Byrne. Stay there a minute with your daddy and I'll have a look at it.' He shot a quick glance at Jimmy and as if reading something in his eyes, smiled at Emer. 'You must have given your mother a fierce fright; she'll hardly be out of the bed before Sunday! It might need a stitch. You'll be only gorgeous!' And he winked and was up the stairs before anyone could say another word.

Emer smiled back. Dr Rourke was a regular visitor in their house and very good at making Mammy happy when she had one of her bad days. Next to her father he was the nicest man she knew and she had thought she might marry him when she was older. She'd confided this to Tilly who only laughed and said she was an eejit because he was too old and anyway he was married already. Emer shrugged. It didn't matter. He had a son who was nice and was going to go up to Dublin to university when he had finished his Leaving Cert to be a doctor too. Emer wasn't in a hurry. She'd stay with Daddy till she was big and then she'd go to the Rourkes' house and marry the doctor's son and Mammy could have all the medicine she wanted and they'd all live happily ever after ...

Now, in her own kitchen across the road, an adult Emer Fagan smiled at the memory. *Marry the doctor's son, wouldn't that have been nice?* Conor Rourke was a good man and for a while, years ago, it looked as if Emer's ambition might not be such a dream after all. But dreams are fickle things and they can abandon you when bold reality comes lurching into your life. She looked at the photograph on the shelf of the dresser – Emer Byrne, small and white on her wedding day, almost dwarfed by the bulk of her husband. Even then, John Fagan loomed large. Though almost ten years her senior, he was the one who looked full of life and vigour, while she cowered pale beside him.

She was still cowering pale beside him. He called the tune and she danced. It was his pub, his shop and she was just the one needed to run it when he was too tired or too drunk to be bothered. Sometimes she wished she could run away, book herself into the sun lounge in St Thomas' and be looked after.

John's shouts for her to come and help reached her from the store below, and with a sigh she got up and poured the rest of her tea down the sink. There were tears in her eyes as she watched it disappear down the plughole. *Do you see that*, she whispered, *that's your life. Now get on with it.* And she rushed to the store to do what her husband wanted.

CHAPTER 5

THERE WAS NO ONE IN THE KITCHEN when Pius arrived back at the convent after her visit to St. Thomas'. She closed and bolted the door behind her and sat down at the table, her hands flat on its cool surface, trying to calm herself. Shutting her eyes she chanted her prayers like a mantra. *'Mother of Mercy. Pray for us. Mother of Divine Grace—'* The familiar intonations broke through her laboured breathing and she gradually began to relax. So, it had happened then. The past had caught up with her and Matty Hurley had been witness to it. She shrugged. Well, if it had to be anyone, she supposed Matty was the one it should be.

Outside the window, over the bump of the bridge, Kildoran's main street stood to attention, Fagan's Pub and Grocery at the near end and Kildoran Hardware at the other. Beyond lay the houses of the villagers and in the distance, up on the hill she could hear the drone of the builders' machines as they dug the foundations for the new housing estate. By next year the train that thundered through Kildoran on its way to more prestigious places would stop here and the village so long bypassed would finally win its place on the map. Across the road on this side of the bridge she could see the Church of Saints Peter and Paul. It was an imposing granite building, built in the 1840s when the Famine was in full force and three quarters of the population of Ireland starved or emigrated. She smiled at its magnificence. Even in such adversity there were some who held fast to their priorities and she for one was thankful for it.

The convent chapel was warmer but in there, she was easy to find during the day. The parish church was bigger, darker, and more anonymous. Perhaps she should go there now. She could sit there and pray. She would shut her eyes and images of Nell Byrne's blazing desperation would not trespass on her devotions. She unbolted the door and hurried across to the haven of the church's dark solitude.

In her bedroom above, Sister Agnes sat drinking hot lemon, trying to concentrate on the book Pius had left for her to read, *Lives of the Martyrs*, cheery stuff all right when your eyes were streaming and your head throbbed fit to join a jazz band. Defeated, she laid the book on the window-sill and peered out, eager for a sign of life. A movement below caught her eye and she saw Pius quietly cross the street and go into the church on the other side of the road. She glanced at the clock on her little table – a quarter to four – still early and already it was so dark. The day seemed to be over before it was properly begun. Agnes sighed and sat back into her chair again. Pius shouldn't be back so soon. It would take at least an hour to come back now that they were laying the new road on the outskirts of Kilkenny and as she was already late starting out, she surely couldn't have arrived till ages after two. Matty must have thought he was forgotten! Agnes smiled to herself; I bet he had a thing or two to say about that!

Unless he was sick of course and Pius hadn't got to talk to him at all and that was why she was back so early – the thought of Matty being unwell and her not in to see him made her shift uncomfortably in her seat. Maybe she should ask Pius when she came back. Or maybe that would look too much like she was checking up and she knew Pius had been agitated with all the fussing before Agnes has finally waved her off. No, maybe the best thing to do would be to ring the Home and ask to speak to Matron direct.

She straightened her dressing gown around her and tightened the cord. Then, with a warm scarf wrapped around her head, she padded down to the hallway where a simple phone call would confirm that Matty was not ill at all and that if Pius had managed it home in record time there was another simple explanation.

'Goodness!' Fifteen minutes later, Agnes' head was pulsing and it wasn't just the cold that was troubling her. Bridget's description of the extraordinary visit beggared belief. Why on earth would Nell Byrne attack anyone, least of all a quiet nun she couldn't have known from Adam? She pressed her hand to her forehead and tried to sort the jumbled questions that were pounding inside her skull.

'Are you all right, Sister?' The sound of tea trolleys being wheeled into the hallway at St Thomas' crackled down the phone line behind Bridget's voice.

'I'm fine, Bridget, just confused. What can Nell have been thinking about? The poor soul - I'll try to come in and see her if I'm a bit better on Friday. Meanwhile, don't trouble Matron, and don't tell Matty I called, he'll only think I'm fussing.'

Bridget laughed. 'With all due respect, Sister, I don't think Matty could ever think badly of you on a Tuesday afternoon. He's taken his little brown parcel up to his room and no doubt if I were to look in on him now, I'd find him snoozing peacefully in his chair, with the window only slightly open to be sure the smell of malted barley would be well gone by the time he's woken for his tea!'

'Oh, dear.' In the cool of the convent hallway Agnes could feel her face heat up.

'Don't worry. If Matron knows anything about his regular "food" parcel, she knows more about the pleasure Matty gets from having it delivered to him,' She laughed again, 'and the joy he gets from thinking he's having one up on the rest of us!'

Agnes laughed too, till a fit of coughing caught her up.

Bridget waited till the coughs subsided. 'You'd better get back to bed yourself and remember what I said about that chest. I'll say nothing to Matty – he can tell you all himself when you're in.'

'Grand, thank you, dear, goodbye then!'

'Goodbye, Sister, take care.'

And with a click the line went dead.

Agnes stood with the phone in her hand for a minute staring into the growing darkness. By now the pulsing in her head had strengthened to a steady throb and her limbs were aching. Cross with herself for such frailty, she pulled the scarf back over her ears and headed for the kitchen. It'd be grand and warm in there and she could make herself another hot lemon, with maybe a drop of whiskey in it – purely for the medicinal warmth it provided – and then she'd go back to bed. Maybe if she felt better after a little nap she'd come down and have a little talk with Pius and hear all about it from her.

Chance would be a fine thing, Agnes Dowling, the voice in her head said, *that one plays her cards too close to her chest to be confiding her secrets to a countrywoman like yourself.*

'Now you'd never know' she said aloud, 'sure there mightn't be any secrets at all.' There mightn't be, just the strange ramblings of a sad old woman in a home. That might be the start and finish of it.

Somehow Agnes wasn't so sure.

Pius didn't join the other sisters for supper that evening. While they reviewed the day's activities, she crept quietly down the corridor to the convent chapel where she sat and tried to pray.

Our Father, who art in Heaven ... Our Father ... forgive us our trespasses ...

She raised her eyes. At the front of the chapel the figure of Christ on the cross loomed large over the little altar. The crucifix itself was made of wood polished to a high sheen and carved at each side. The details were intricate, fine swirls that wove their way over and under each other as if the craftsman had been working with silk thread and not solid wood. Outsiders who were privileged enough to be allowed into the convent's inner sanctum often remarked on his skill – with much the same passion as the poor unfortunate whose job it was to dust the chapel cursed it. Pius let her eyes follow the swirling Celtic lines of the pattern and wondered if the man who had worked them had any notion of what he was creating. Almost as if the thought had slapped its way into her brain she sat upright and shook her head: *crossed wood to hang a man*. It wasn't right. Using your skill to create beauty so that you can look and admire when you should be looking in horror, horror at the savagery ...

'Are you all right, Sister?' Agnes shuffled, wheezing, in beside her and the smell of soup that accompanied her from the kitchen settled around them.

Pius said nothing.

Agnes waited a while then let her gaze follow Pius' till it settled on the cross. 'It's beautiful, isn't it?'

'Beautiful? Beautiful? How can suffering be beautiful? How can you say such a thing? They took him and they killed him. They—'

Agnes didn't seem to notice the outburst. 'He did that for us. He chose it. It was the most he could do and he did it.'

Pius looked at her in surprise. 'Is that how you see it? He did it because he wanted to?'

'Oh yes,' Agnes smiled. 'I learned that a long time ago, Sister. I learned that you mightn't always like what happens but you have to trust that it happens for a reason and if you could only see through to the reason, you'd be all right. Like that death,' she gestured to the cross, 'terrible, a dreadful thing for a man to have to endure. But what would have happened if he didn't? Would we ever have listened and believed a word if he hadn't got up there and shown us? Would we ever have understood how loved we were at all, how—' She broke off, coughing. 'Listen to me – preaching as if I had a direct line and you with years of learning that *I* spent baking scones! You probably understand it a million times more!'

'I understand nothing.' For a moment it looked as if Pius was about to reach her hand out to Agnes. Instead she tucked it in the folds of her habit. 'Even with all those years of reading and studying, I don't seem to understand anything at all.' Her voice was soft and she was trembling. 'For years I've been looking on that figure with his head bowed and I've thought that the reason his face was turned away was that he couldn't bear to look at me. I sit and I watch him and I'm afraid that some day he'll lift his head and he'll see me sitting here and he'll say, *I know you, sitting there so prim and proper. I know you. Look what you made me do!* '

Her voice was rising and Agnes could hear the panic in it. 'And then he'll hold out his hands and I'll see the blood on them and I'll know it was all my fault—'

'Stop it! Dear Mother of God, do you know who you're talking about at all?' Agnes caught her arm and squeezed it till the pressure got through to Pius and she began to calm. 'He's your friend, not your enemy. He doesn't want you to feel guilty for the size of his sacrifice.' She pulled out her handkerchief and after a fleeting examination, passed it to Pius. 'He wants you to feel special for the size of his gift. That's what it's all about. That's why it's beautiful, can you not see that?'

'I don't know if I can.' Pius took a deep breath and looked at the kindly face. 'I get so many things wrong, you see. Even you.'

'Me?'

'I came here and you smiled, offering me your friendship and I spurned it. You weren't good enough. You didn't study in Rome like I did. You didn't teach in the Mother House. You haven't travelled at all. You just grew up here and stayed at home, baking your scones and drinking your tea and yet you understand more than I can ever hope to learn.'

Agnes blushed. 'Well now, in as much as you under-estimate yourself, I think you over-estimate me. I don't understand it all. I only understand what I'm told – that's all – and I like people.'

'I don't.' The admission surprised Pius as much as it appeared to sadden Agnes. 'I don't trust them. I don't feel part of them and I don't want to.'

'Sounds like a terrible, lonely place to be.'

'It is.'

Agnes gestured to the cross. 'And what about him? Do you like him?'

'Like? I never considered that liking him came into it.'

'Oh, it does. Liking him and trusting him and—' she let Pius' hand go, 'trusting his judgement in liking you.'

Pius smiled. 'I think, Sister, that that is the hardest part of all.' She paused as if she were going to say something else and, shocked that she had already said so much, she reddened. Without another word, the two women looked at each other. Agnes saw something of the fear that Matty had seen earlier: a frightened child in the face of a woman. Pius saw the face of a friend. For a moment she felt as if the easiest thing in the world would be to open her mouth and tell everything, let it all flow out into the candlelight of this quiet place.

But fifty years of secrets weigh heavy and Pius knew that she could not lift them all off in one rush. There was too much and anyway, where would she start? Even as this thought came to her, she knew Agnes could see the lights dim in her pale eyes and the curtains in the lines of her face close.

'Actually, Sister, I think I'm quite tired. I'll go up now and have a rest before Evening Prayer.' She got up and walked to the door of the chapel. At the door she paused a moment and then hurried back. At the edge of the pew she genuflected and without looking at Agnes, whispered, 'I do hope you'll forgive the words I spoke – I don't know what came over me.' She blessed herself quickly and scurried out.

Agnes sat and watched as the door swung slowly closed on its oiled hinge. With a *phut* it shut and she was alone. She smiled ruefully at the figure on the cross in front of her and shrugged.

'What came over her, what came out of her, what's in her in the first place – I don't know what to make of it at all.' She chuckled then at the memory of her preaching. Imagine Agnes Dowling, preaching like one possessed – Pius must have thought she was mad. In fact, poor Pius must think the lot of them were mad: Nell with her anger; Matty with his parcels and holding her hand. She folded her arms over her chest again and looked at the figure on the cross again.

And what do you make of it all?

The figure didn't move but Agnes knew he was listening. He hung silent, head bowed and Agnes watched him, trying to see him as Pius did, angry and accusing, but she couldn't. Not for the first time she cursed her simplicity. It seemed today that so many things had happened but so few that she could understand. She heaved herself to her feet and shuffled wearily to the front of the chapel where she stopped.

'For a full day, thank you. I wish I could understand the half of it – into your hands, O Lord …

In her room she tried to say her Office. Bells that had rung in the chapel during the day took up tolling in her head and it wasn't long before her nightdress was wet with sweat. The throbbing in her head was stronger now and as the waves of heat rose on either side, she drifted into a fitful sleep where the thread of an answer glinted tantalisingly in front of her. As she bent to pick it up it became a snake and slithered off, out of reach into the long grass … .

In St Thomas' Nursing home, Nell Byrne lay on her bed trying to sleep. Unlike Agnes she did not pray - she had given that up years ago. Instead she lay there staring into the darkness trying to free her mind of the pictures that haunted her for as long as she could remember, a clearing in the trees and the shadowy figure of a man waiting. And blood, so much blood. It was on her hands as she held them up to him and begged but no words would come out. And then the angry voices. For a moment it looked like he was going to stop it anyway but he didn't. He just stood there and he looked and it was the look in his eyes that was the hardest to forgive.

In her room in the convent, Sister Pius was awake. Her head was full of pictures too and for her it was the look in his eyes that was hardest to forget.

CHAPTER 6

IT WAS EILISH HENNESSY'S TURN to ring the bell and even though the sound of it caused a collective groan of discontent from the children in the playground and a squeal of panic from those still dragging reluctant feet, or siblings, up the street, it was a job she loved doing. It was the only time in her life that Eilish had the chance to feel important. At home there were too many people; at school, there were too many hard questions. If you said something and it was the wrong thing, Sister Pius looked at you as if you were a worm or something and she squeezed her lips very tight until all the lines on her face seemed to be pointing at the hole in the middle. *That one has a mouth on her as tight as a chicken's backside*, her mammy said. *Don't be frightened of her at all.* But Eilish was.

Settling herself on the step, with her feet wide apart, she pulled her skirt down as far as it would go so that it wouldn't catch the bell as it swung through backwards and forwards between her knees and she relished the moment of power. She raised the bell high into the air and brought it down with a loud brassy clang. All the shouting stopped as the children ran into their class rows, wordlessly nudging and pucking one another for prime position. Eilish smiled and shutting her eyes, wallowed in the echoing chimes of the sounds she had created.

'Enough! What do you think you are doing, foolish child?' Sister Pius' voice was not raised but it still seemed more powerful than the sound of the bell.

Eilish let the bell fall limp in her hand. 'I was just ringing the morning bell to get everyone to come in, Sister.'

'And what is the purpose of the bell?'

'To – to make everyone line up for school.'

'And where is everyone?'

Eilish turned to find the eyes of the whole school on her. Although it was a cold morning and she did not have a coat, she felt as if she was about to burn up. She inclined her head towards the rows of children. 'They're there, Sister.'

'And what are they doing?'

Through her tears, Eilish looked at the faces. *They're smirking*, she thought, *they're laughing at me.* 'They're lined up,' she said.

Pius took the bell from her hands. 'Quite. So I think we can safely assume that there is *no* need for you to stand there like some sort of a savage, making a racket for the sake of it. Go down to your place.'

Head bowed, Eilish crept to the back of the queue. She tried not to catch anyone's eye as she passed but she could hear the soft sniggers. She stood at the back of the line and waited as one by one, the classes were called into the building. When her class was called, she moved forward, trying to blink back the tears. Just ahead of her, Gareth Fagan started to move. Sister Pius was at the head of the line scolding some boy who hadn't wiped his feet and she had taken her eyes off the others for a minute.

Quick as a flash, Gareth turned and caught her hand. 'She's a witch. She likes making people sad – I hate her too!' Then as an afterthought, 'You're a great ringer, Eilish.' He smiled at her then he turned away again. In the classroom she looked at his face but he gave no indication that he had said anything at all. Thirty chairs scraped back – there'd be trouble about that in a minute – and thirty voices joined in prayer, *In the name of the Father, and of the Son and …*

By the time they sat down and Pius finished scolding them about the racket they made with the chairs, she felt as if she had had enough of the day already. Breakfast had been a chaotic affair with Agnes not in the kitchen and Pius hated disorder. Back in Mother House, her day had a routine to it that she considered almost sacred in itself; she prayed and she read and she translated, and the meals she took were quick and without conversation if she could help it. The sisters there knew that she valued her solitude and they treated her with respect. They had no interest in her past and made no attempts to involve her in theirs. Here, they were – friendly – she supposed the word was, though it did little to endear them to her. They seemed obliged to draw her into their lives, almost compelled to find a place for her there. When she shunned their advances, they would look at her, hurt and confused, as if they had offered her something special and she had rejected it. She didn't want to hurt them; she didn't want anything from them. She just wanted to be left alone.

Eventually, most of them had got the message. Individually, they ignored her, in a group they told her things but often she felt it was more for the joy of talking about it than to pass any information on to her. They told stories and reminisced about the past. They talked fondly of people long dead as if it was not enough that she should have to share their present, but was obliged to share their pasts as well. Sometimes they were so passionate that she wanted to jump up and shout at them – she didn't *want* to share anyone's life or memories. She gave no time to her own – they were dead and buried, and all the people in them.

Agnes' face came into her mind and she wondered why she didn't feel the same about Agnes. She was full of sentiment, full of talk about people you didn't know and couldn't care less about, but there was an openness about her, a type of honesty. She would talk to you and not want anything from you. Even her 'favour' yesterday was for somebody else. Pius' cheeks burned at the memory of it – if only Agnes had known. And last night, in the chapel, something about the simplicity of Agnes' vision seeped through and Pius was horrified to realise that she had been on the point of telling her everything! She put her hands to her cheeks – what a thought!

'Are you all right, Sister?'

Pius looked up to see the children watching her and she glared in reply. Nobody was moving. They sat there watching her, waiting for the first instruction, and she had been dreaming. Dreaming! The place was getting to her. She must be more careful. She picked up a ruler and brought it down sharply on the desk.

'Put your hand up when you speak! Is this what you take for manners in this school? Get out your copybooks!'

With a look of collective resentment, the children obeyed and Pius felt her shoulders relax. She preferred their dislike to their concern. Dislike made her feel protected: it kept people at a safe distance and let you get on with your life. She ran her eyes down the rows of bent heads till they came to Eilish Hennessy. Foolish child, throwing her head back in ecstasy as if ringing a bell in an Irish country schoolyard was the best you could aspire to. She had no gumption, that one, always the victim. Little wonder the other children had no time for her cowering timidity. She couldn't even lift her head to look you in the eye … .

But even before that thought had fully formed, Eilish raised her head and looked at Pius. The woman had expected to see fear in the child's eyes but there was none. Somewhere in the defiant gaze there was a look of her mother about her and Pius recalled the amusement on Bridie Hennessy's face when the two had crossed swords on the question of Eilish's father. The memory stung. She had gone there on a mission of mercy only to be ridiculed by a slovenly piece who had been touched neither by soap in years nor evolution in generations. From that day, the memory of Bridie's laughter rankled and dislike for her child grew daily. Where once the sight of the thin body barely dressed in outer garments, hardly in under, might have evoked some sympathy, now it provoked only irritation. She glared more fiercely but the child's gaze didn't waver. They stared at each other for what seemed an age and it was Pius who turned away first.

As the children lined up at the end of lunch break, their silent order was disturbed by the sound of an ambulance driving up to the convent's back gate. Whispers flew down the lines that one of the nuns was ill and was being taken to the hospital. The fourth class quivered in excitement –maybe she might die and they'd all get a day off like they did for Mother Rosalie. That had been great. Nobody really knew her anyway. They'd seen her around but she'd never seemed like a real person – just a thin, powdery shadow who smiled and sometimes touched their faces as she passed them.

There were a few others like that – pale shadows of women with mouths that moved a lot but seldom spoke. You wouldn't see them for months and months and then you'd put on a Christmas concert or there'd be a funeral or something and they'd be wheeled out or they'd shuffle out in huddled pairs for the occasion. Mostly they fell asleep at the concerts – some of them even snored – but they stayed awake for funerals. Peter Rourke, who knew about death and things because his family were doctors from generations back, said it was because nuns are married to God they love dying and so when somebody dies and goes to Heaven to live with God, they all get jealous and they go to the funeral to pray for it to be their turn next. Gareth had seen them, heads bowed, praying fervently and beating their chests slowly with clenched fists. Once he'd even tried to lean close and hear what they were saying but he couldn't.

Peter said he could. 'Honest, it's *me, me, me* only it's a sin to pray to be dead so they have to say that they'd like it to be their turn next, and then they say *Thy Will be done* which means that even though they'd really like it, they can't ask straight out so God had to decide in the end who it is he wants to be next.'

Gareth looked at him. 'Are you sure?'

'Of course I'm sure. Aren't there sick people up at my house all the time?'

Gareth shrugged. It sounded reasonable all right.

And now it looked as if one of them had got her wish. When a girl came back from the convent earlier where she'd been sent to do a message, she'd said that Dr Rourke was there and he was looking real worried. The boys said they didn't believe her, more from habit than conviction, but now it looked as if she'd been right all along. The children jostled to catch a glimpse of the emerging patient, or better still, the body.

'They're coming!' Someone in the sixth class line, who had a better view, called.

'Who is it?'

'It's poo-face Pius!'

A shiver of sheer delight ran through the fourth class. Imagine, she was very alive before lunchtime and now it seemed that she might be nearly dead! Maybe they got fed up of her crabby face inside and someone had the idea to put poison in her lunch! Gareth clasped his hands and tried not to smile too broadly.

He needn't have bothered. No sooner did the prospect of Pius' funeral begin to delight the edges of his consciousness than the prospective corpse appeared on the step. Alive.

'Silence!' Her shrill voice cut through the children's excitement and the six rows were immediately quiet. Gareth glared at the child who had offered her name but the boy shrugged and turned away. 'Move into your classrooms, in silence!' The children shuffled forwards, not daring to give a sideways glance through the gate to the convent door where the ambulance lights could be seen flashing.

Inside, the children bowed their heads in prayer.

For all we have received …

Amen.

For those who prepared it …

Amen.

There was a pause. Sister Pius seemed to be thinking about adding something. She swallowed a couple of times and cleared her throat. Some of the children, including Gareth and Eilish, dared to look up at her. Maybe she was actually going to tell them who it was!

'And now we offer a special prayer for one of our sisters, who is very ill and is, at this moment, on her way to the Hospital.'

The children were about to respond but she wasn't finished.

'—for Sister Agnes, that she will be back amongst us soon.'

Gareth and Eilish looked at one another in horror. Sister Agnes! All hopes of a death and a day off faded into shameful memory and an unfamiliar cold feeling crept over their foreheads. One of the old faded ones dying – that was fine – but Sister Agnes was like part of the family. Each had memories of nights at home when mammy, for some reason they weren't being told about, was sad, and Sister Agnes bustled in with a basket of baking and put her arms around everyone and made it all right again. Now she was the sick one and they had to pray that she wouldn't die – wife of God or not. More fervently than they had ever prayed before, they bowed their heads again.

Amen.

Although that was usually the signal for the children to sit down, today nobody moved. Pius stood looking at them but they stared back, shocked looks on their faces, and didn't even seem to see her.

Eventually, Gareth spoke. 'Will Sister Agnes die?' He was watching her with those clear grey eyes, an expression on his face as if she had just admitted to a crime.

'We all have to die.'

The sharpness of her tone and the terseness of her reply was usually enough to colour the cheeks of even the most impudent child but Gareth was unmoved. 'I know that. It isn't what I meant.'

'It is what you asked.'

Gareth didn't flinch. 'Okay then,' he said, 'can I ask you another question?'

'*May* I ask you another question, *Sister?*'

He ignored the correction. 'Is Sister Agnes going to die sooner than she would have died if she wasn't sick? Might she die tomorrow because of how sick she is today? Is the hospital—?'

Behind him someone sniffed and he stopped and turned around. 'Don't cry, Eilish, she might only have a sickness that you can get better from if you go to the hospital. I'm just going to find out. I'm asking the *proper* question about it now.'

When he turned back to face her, two high spots of colour blazed on his cheeks and his fists were clenched. 'That's what I'm asking you, Sister.'

Pius looked at the small angry figure and the rebuke that was building when his back was turned died on her lips. She looked from him to the other children. They were standing behind their desks in neat rows, hands folded in front of them watching her and suddenly their gaze unnerved her. They weren't politely waiting to hear what she was going to say; they were simply waiting. She knew that she could tell him to sit down and tell the others to get on with their work but she was as sure as she could be that if she did, they would refuse to obey her. Realisation slapped her like a cold cloth – she had momentarily lost control of them. Something stronger than the threat of her ruler was giving them the will to stare her down and Gareth the boldness to stand up. Something tribal.

She swallowed and when she started to speak, her voice came out in little more than a whisper. 'I really don't know. Sister Agnes has an illness that the doctor thinks might be pneumonia, which is very serious if you are a weak person, but as you know, Sister Agnes is a strong person and the hospital will be able to treat her quickly. They're going to do some tests and hopefully she will be back with us soon.' She stopped, breathless.

Gareth turned and looked at Eilish. 'There you are then; don't worry.' Then he sat down and started to open his copybook. The rest of the class followed suit.

Although nothing more was said, there was an atmosphere in the room of disquiet. Pius picked up the sheets of geography work she had prepared earlier and looked around for a volunteer to distribute them. When no one did, she placed the pile on Helen Burke's desk. 'Distribute these, please,' She waited a few moments while Helen went up and down the rows, 'Today we are going to look at the major rivers of Ireland and I want you to pay particular attention to where each river starts, its source, and where it ends, its mouth. Are you all paying attention? Now, look at where there is a one marked on your map ... .'

And so the afternoon continued. She talked and while the children didn't, they didn't seem to be listening either. There was an almost imperceptible hum in the room and though they appeared to be sitting still there was an undercurrent of fidgeting. When she asked a question, nobody volunteered an answer, not even Helen, so she would have to ask again, not just for an answer but also for someone willing to give one.

And Gareth Fagan was at the root of it.

It was hard to define exactly what he had done, apart from repeat his question but his attitude had been hostile and her failure to reprimand him had given the others the wrong impression about what was acceptable in her classroom and what was not. She would have to put a stop to it. Bringing the ruler down sharply on the desk she called for their attention.

'Enough! Children who do not have the good manners to answer questions when they are asked do not deserve to be taught.' She broke off as she caught Gareth's eye. 'You will spend the rest of the afternoon filling in the names for yourselves. I cannot waste my energy helping children who are unwilling to co-operate. Take out your atlases and your geography copybooks. By last bell, I expect every child to have copied the map, neatly, into his book with all the names filled in. Anyone who does not do it exactly as I have said will stay in at break-time tomorrow to do the work all over again. Do you understand me?'

Some of the children nodded and there were a few muttered *Yes, Sisters*.

'I said, do you understand me!'

This time they paid attention and the chorus, *Yes, Sister* was loud and clear.

'Now start.'

After a quick shuffling of desks and banging of desk lids, which she chose to ignore, the class settled down to the task and Pius started on the pile of books waiting to be marked on her desk. The air in the room was striped with the beams of a low wintry sun stretching through the back windows and flecks of dust floated in the rays above the children's heads. Apart from the scratching of pencils and the odd click from the pipes the room was quiet. She surveyed her charges. Thirty small heads were bent in concentration and she had no doubt that if Sister Bernard could see them now she'd be glowing with pride about her *lovely children, God bless them*. Pius didn't think they were lovely. They were foreign to her, aliens bound together by a common heritage and with all sorts of codes of loyalty. They would fight with one another along invisible pre-ordained paths and they could say what they liked but she could not. Agnes was one of them and now that she was ill, they had closed ranks and left her on the outside. Well, that was fine. Outside was where she chose to be and the sooner her term in Kildoran was over and she could get back to her own convent the better. She placed the pile of copybooks in front of her and opened the top one.

My Pet. My pet is a dog caled Spot. He is caled Spot becaus he has a blak spot over one of his eyes—

She opened the next one.

I have a pet called Snowy. She is a cat and I got her for my birthday when I was three. She is white and that is why I call her Snowy—

At least Kathleen Grogan could spell.

The next book was Gareth's.

I do not have a pet of my own but the pet I am going to write about is my granny's budgie. He lives in a cage in the sunroom at my granny's and even though lots of other old people live there too and feed him, he really belongs to my granny. He has a name but my granny calls him Jimmy which is my granddad's name and my granny says that when he sings it is really my granddad keeping an eye on her because he knows how lonely she is …

The florid face of Gareth's vicious grandmother flashed into her head. She looked at the top of Gareth's head and fought the surge of dislike she felt for him ever since she first set eyes on him. True, he had the mark of his mother about him and his manners were no worse than any other and certainly better then some, but she had seen him in the playground too, surrounded by his friends. She had noticed the self-confidence and the way the other boys looked up to him. He was a Fagan all right. A movement on the other side of the room caught her eye and she noticed Eilish pause in her colouring and sneak a quick glance across at Gareth. The look of adoration in her face was plain and Pius' blood boiled. Even at ten boys like him carried all the seeds of the man they would become and Eilish Hennessy was probably aware beyond her years, coming from a home where there were only two bedrooms and a child born every year. She shut the book and stood up. Engrossed in their tasks none of the children paid any attention and she walked slowly up and down the rows, fingering the beads that hung from her belt.

Oh please God, keep me sane till I can leave this place …

From the corner of his eye, Gareth watched the pacing. He had nearly finished his map and he knew it was neat enough. He thought of poor Sister Agnes in the hospital so sick she could die and all they wanted to know was if she might get better soon and how much worrying they would have to do about her first but Meanie Face wouldn't answer the question even though she knew exactly what he meant. She'd probably wanted him to feel stupid the way she had made Eilish feel but he wasn't scared of her. He was glad he'd stood up to her. She was a bully and there were too many bullies. Mammy said you only get bullied if you let it happen but if you stand up to it, the bully can't get you. Well, he was going to stand up to her in future. She'd had her chance to be nice but she wasn't interested so they weren't going to bother being nice to her any more. He finished the last little bit of colouring and put his pencil down. Sister Pius noticed immediately that he had stopped working. He knew she would.

'Get on with your work at once, Gareth Fagan!'

He said nothing, only held the book up.

With the back of her hand she aimed a swipe at the book. 'Put that down, disobedient boy! Did I ask you to hold your book aloft?'

'No, Sister,' Gareth replied calmly. 'You asked me to get on with my work. I'm finished the work I was told to do. I wonder what work you would like me to get on with?'

There was silence while the children held their breaths and waited for the explosion. Gareth knew he'd taken a risk earlier when he had spoken to her as if she was just the same as him, but now he was talking and looking as if he was better than she was and as if he didn't care what she thought about it. He was staring at her and she was holding her beads so tightly that you could see where the bones stuck out on her hands and the veins that crossed over each other on the back of her looked as if they were about to burst. For what seemed like ages her lips stayed pressed together but they moved as if she was having a conversation with herself inside her own mouth. Eventually her lips parted and the words were spit out.

'Put the book down!' She swung her ruler through the air and it landed on the edge of the desk with a sharp *Crack!*

Gareth sat firm.

'I said, put the book down! Or are you going to add the sin of disobedience to the sin of insolence you have already committed?' As she spoke, her voice grew quieter. 'That'd be a wise thing to do all right and you with your hands folded in prayer asking God for favours earlier this very afternoon. Maybe you didn't mean that prayer at all? '

She had him.

All the boldness drained from Gareth's face as he realised what she was saying. He laid the book on the desk.

'Now, I hope we'll be hearing no more insolence from you, Mr Fagan. The rest of you, put down your pencils and pass your copybooks up to the front rows. I do not want a word spoken while your desks are tidied away ... '

She was looking superior again and Gareth bent his head to hide his red face. The other children did as they were told.

Sister Pius had managed to be the right one again.

Placing the pile of books on her desk Pius was thinking much the same thing. There was a challenge open to her this afternoon and she had faced it and won. That was because there was right on her side. She glanced up at the rows of silent children waiting to be told to stand for the final prayer and the strength of dislike in their eyes shocked her for a moment. What was wrong with these people? She was right, the child had been insolent and she was perfectly right to reprimand him. Why should it matter that nobody understood that? Why should it matter that she was alone in this? She was always alone, wasn't she, so why should it be any different now?

She tapped the desk and the children prayed the final prayer of the day in chorus and when the bell went, filed out the door in silence. Nobody looked at her as they left and even when they were gone the room was full of their hostility. Pius opened the top book but she couldn't read a thing. To her horror she found that her eyes were full of tears and the words were swimming in front of her. A drop slipped down her face and landed on the page causing a ragged edge on the already untidy colouring of the Irish coastline. Crossly, she wiped the tear away. What was wrong with *her*? The image of Agnes being lifted into the ambulance came into her head and the look of worry on Sister Kathleen's face as she climbed in beside her. What good would she be? With her fussing and panicking? They'd be far better off if Kathleen had taken the children for a singing lesson or something and Pius could have gone to the hospital with Agnes where she would have been far more efficient at getting the information and seeing to the things Agnes needed. She was a good person in an emergency – she was cool and level-headed, didn't get involved so that her brain stayed clear.

Another tear rolled down her face and another and this time she didn't bother to wipe it away. Didn't get involved indeed. So what was she crying for? It wasn't as if Agnes was a friend of hers or anything.

I like people, you see.

She could feel the warmth of Agnes' hand on hers as she admitted aloud to a gentle countrywoman what she had never even admitted to herself – *I don't* – and then the pressure of Agnes' hand as she tried to convey in touch what she had not the words to express.

Sounds like a terrible lonely place to be.

'It is.' Pius whispered aloud and then louder to the empty classroom, 'It *is* lonely; *I* am lonely. I don't belong and I never belonged and I might be about to lose the nearest I've had to a friend since—' She stood up and walked to the window. Groups of children hurried past on their way home chatting and laughing and outside the school gate a few mothers waited for them. Pius watched as they moved up the street and she stayed watching as they rounded the corner at the far end where Kildoran Hardware jutted out.

In the haze of her tears she thought she could see a little girl being ushered out of the door of the hardware by a woman, both eager to join the commotion on the street. The child was thin, her hair lank and her eyes the palest blue. The woman was big and jolly and round faced and her hair was hoisted back into an untidy bun. A dark printed floral apron criss-crossed her ample bosom and she was struggling with the strings of it so that she wouldn't appear on the street dressed for the kitchen and let herself down. With a flourish, the apron came free, dragging strands of hair with it and the woman turned impatiently to someone behind her. 'Come on – leave the shop a minute, Billy, and come too –' and she caught the little girl's hand to lead her on. Her hand was big and rough and warm and the girl hung on tightly but it was too late. Already the crowds of ghostly figures had begun to claw at her and pull her away. The air was full of voices, harsh, accusing but above them all one whispered plea, Don't Elly, don't, you've got it wrong …

'Noooo!' Pius shut her eyes as great sobs wracked her body. 'I shouldn't be here,' she pleaded. 'I shouldn't.' She thought of the ruler swiping through the air and the crack of it as it landed on Gareth Fagan's desk, and she thought of the way she'd wanted to hit him too only the ruler is too sharp and it swipes through the air and the force of it is over by the time it lands. Like a thing possessed, her sobs turned to laughter as she slowly undid the thick leather belt from which her rosary hung around her waist and let the length of it slip over her palm and return with a *slap* as she repeated the action.

'Nothing like a belt, Eleanor, is there?
Slap.
Sure there's nothing like the taste of a belt to set things right.
Slap.

Outside, Eilish Hennessy was passing the window. The sound stopped her. It was halfway between a cry and a scream and it seemed like it might be coming from their classroom. Oh Janey! Maybe it was the banshee coming to get Sister Agnes! A fleeting hope that the banshee might even be coming for Sister Pius wasn't enough to slow her down. Whoever she was coming for, Eilish wasn't waiting around to find out.

CHAPTER 7

BEHIND THE GROCERY COUNTER Emer was fighting the temptation to throw something – hard. John was in the bar with a few propped up alongside him, discussing world events as if their single opinion was the only one that had any weight to it. And the opinion they held, as usual, was John's. He was pontificating now. Emer could hear the steady drone. Cora was following him around, hanging on to his every word as if it fell from the lips of Solomon.

Yes, Mr Fagan. No, Mr Fagan ...

'Three bloody bags full, Mr Fagan.' Emer muttered to herself crossly. It wasn't the girl's fault; she was besotted. Emer had seen it hundreds of times before. John's self-assurance belied a total lack of actual physical charm. He had pale skin and pale eyes but when he was angry, both would flash red and his voice could fill a room without his actually seeming to raise it. When he wanted to turn on the charm it was a different matter altogether. He would lower his voice to just above a whisper so that to hear what he was saying you had to stand really close to him, close enough to smell his aftershave and be aware of the heat of his body. Women who came into the shop, especially young ones, were treated to this side of him. It was like a game and in the beginning Emer had been amused by it. He would help them to their cars carrying their boxes as if they contained precious ornaments and not groceries. As they drove off or cycled off, blushing and smiling to themselves, he'd come back into the shop and wink at her.

'Another happy customer. All part of the service!'

And they'd both smile.

But that was then and time had dulled his charm. Now his gentle flirting looked more like leering and some of the new customers who came into the shop from the estate were embarrassed as they left. Emer noticed that they made straight for her, avoiding her husband's eye.

Nor were his remarks as gentle either. 'Stuck up bitch – the supermarket in Kilkenny's welcome to her custom,' and then he'd go into the bar and pour himself a quick shot. Other times he'd sit quietly at his end of the shop counter behind the glass screen and not greet them at all. They'd know he was there of course because of the smoke curling over the top of the screen.

If the woman were young and pretty he'd lean back on his chair, just in view and watch her, slowly pulling on his cigarette. Emer could see the colour rise in the customer's face as his mouth opened and he'd push a lazy smoke ring into the air which he'd flick at with his tongue, in and out, in and out. He never said anything but the air all round would fill with the smell of him until Emer felt she would suffocate with the sheer weight of it. There was no point saying anything because he'd just look at her through half closed eyes.

'John, please stop.'

'Please stop what?'

She couldn't explain.

'Smoking? Do you want me to stop smoking?'

'No, it's not the smoking – it's what you do with the smoke.'

'What I do with the smoke? Right. Erm, what exactly is it that I do with the smoke that you'd like me to stop?'

'You know.' It was impossible to explain without sounding stupid and she knew that was exactly why he was asking, 'Blowing rings like that – at the customers.'

'Oh right, I'm not to blow rings. Do you have a pattern of exhaling in mind that would suit you better or maybe a direction I could blow out in that wouldn't offend your own very particular sense of direction? Here, I'll tell you what, maybe it'd be better if I didn't blow into the air at all.' He pulled open the heavy wooden drawer beneath the counter in which the receipt slips were kept, 'I'll blow in here, and I'll be able to try any pattern I like without offending you. Isn't that a great idea?' And he bent and blew hard into the darkness till the smoke came back on him and the mixture of laughter and coughs that followed this performance brought more tears to Emer's eyes than to his.

He didn't wink at her any more either. If there were secret glances to be passed they had long ceased being passed between Emer and her husband. Sometimes she thought she could catch one fly over her shoulder to someone else but when she turned around he'd be rubbing his eye or buried in his paper and not looking up at all. But he'd still be smiling and Emer knew that smile. She knew all his smiles nowadays.

'Is that daughter of mine doing any work in here at all or is she just following your man around like a giggling ninny?' Bridie hauled up the hem of her skirt and sagged onto the chair beside the counter. Shifting her backside so that equal amounts of fleshy thigh hung over either side, she wiped the few drops of sweat from her brow.

'What – oh, right, no – she's grand. They're clearing a space in the store. John wants to move an old desk in there so that he can do his accounts in peace—' she saw Bridie's raised eyebrow, '—it can get busy in here sometimes and he gets distracted, you know, with the customers and that.'

'What! Getting off his fat backside to serve one of them, do you mean?' She threw her head back and bellowed at her own wit.

Despite herself, Emer couldn't help smiling. Bridie had a sharp tongue and as quick as she'd cut you with it, she'd offer to lick the wound afterwards and you took your life into your hands refusing the invitation. 'Bridie Hennessy, do you mind? That's my husband you're talking about.'

Bridie wiped the tears of laughter from her face and looked at Emer solemnly, 'I know it is, pet.'

As the smiles died on their faces, the door of the shop burst open and a terrified-looking Eilish flew straight in and onto her mother's knee. Burying herself deep in the fold between her great breasts, the little girl relaxed and the two women could hear her sobs of relief. She was saying something about bells and Agnes and Pius and banshees.

'Whist your crying' now, darlin' and tell your Mammy what the matter is.' Bridie pulled Eilish out and sat her on her knee. 'Here,' she offered her a clean patch of skirt, 'have a good blow into that and let's have the whole story.'

The child took a deep breath. 'Sister Pius was mean and now someone is screeching in the classroom and I was afraid and I had to run all the way and I—' she stopped suddenly and looked at her mother in horror.

'Oh, yeh little piddler!' Bridie eased the child off her lap gingerly and both women saw the damp patch that was spreading over the knee and down the sides of Bridie's skirt. 'Could you not have gone before you came out of the school?'

'Sorry Mammy, I really am. I wanted to go. I was waiting to see if I could see you coming and then I was going back into the school to go and that's when I heard the noise—'

'What noise?'

'The banshee. I was so afraid and when I saw you it was great and it just all came out.' She started to cry again.

Bridie pulled the edges of her skirt over the damp patch. 'Whist now, don't start your crying. Sure it was due for a wash anyway and it'll be grand. C'mon home and we'll find a pair of knickers to put on you before you die of the cold,' and with a dexterity that belied a woman of her size, she bent and had Eilish's knickers off and in her pocket in a flash. She turned and gave Emer a quick smile, 'I'll be away. Will you tell that Cora to bring home a few rashers for her father's tea and a block of butter? Hang on a minute now till I get the money ...' and she started to rummage around in her pockets. With equal speed, Emer was around the counter, handing a packet of Silvermints to the child.

'Oh, don't worry about that now, Bridie. I'll sort it out with Cora. You hang on there a minute and I'll get you a pair from inside.' She went in to the kitchen and pulled a pair of Gareth's underpants that had been airing from above the range and came back out to the shop with them. 'Here, I hope you don't mind that they're boy's, pet, but they're grand and warm and you won't get a cold.'

Eilish looked at the proffered y-fronts and flushed scarlet. She looked from one woman to the other. 'I can't, Mammy, I can't. I couldn't wear Gareth's underpants—'

Ignoring her, Bridie bent and started to put the pants on her daughter. 'Yerrah, of course you can. The ones you had on you anyway were your brother's and it was a lucky day you had anything on you at all. Here, stop your foustering and help me put these on.'

Emer saw the child's humiliation and understood the problem. 'He won't know, sweetheart. Nobody will know. He has a few pairs the very same as each other and he won't know if one pair is gone. The only people who will know are you, me and your mammy and we aren't going to tell a single soul, are we?'

Bridie straightened up and smiled. 'Of course we won't. Sure a girl's knickers are her own business and nobody else's, isn't that right?'

Eilish giggled. Emer opened the door and ushered the two of them out. 'Go change out of those wet things yourself, Bridie and don't worry about the shopping – I'll give Cora the usual and you can settle with me later.' She remembered the sound of coins jingling in the pocket which was now temporary home to Eilish's wet underwear, 'or maybe Sam could settle on Friday when he comes in for his pint. Whatever – either's grand.'

'You're a decent woman, Emer Fagan.' She turned to her daughter. 'What do you say to Gareth's Mammy?'

'Thanks, Mrs Fagan, sorry I wee-weed in your shop.'

Emer smiled. 'It was an accident, you didn't mean to do it.'

'No,' Eilish's face darkened. 'I was just worried about the noise and all the other things.' Her lip quivered.

'Oh, don't start. Come on, we're away. You can tell me all about it on the way home.' And without another word Bridie tugged the edge of her coat over the wet side of her skirt and pulled her daughter out of the shop.

Emer held the door open for a minute. The shop smelled a bit like the cat's cage at the zoo. They could always heat the place up again afterwards. Down the street she could hear the sound of Eilish talking animatedly to her mother as she struggled to tear open the silver foil and get a sweet out for herself. Poor little mite. Cora Hennessy could be a precocious little madam but Eilish was a dote. She turned to go back inside but no sooner had she reached the counter than Bridie was back at the door, wheezing as if her lungs would burst and her face red with the exertion of her run.

'God forgive us!' she gulped, 'with all our fussing – over a little piddle – we didn't listen – to what the child – was telling us!' She clutched the doorframe and tried to catch her breath.

'What is it? What's the matter, Bridie? What was she trying to tell us?' She put her arm around Bridie's shoulder and tried to lead her back to the chair. Coughing now, Bridie was unable to speak so Emer turned to Eilish, coming back in with her mouth full of mints. 'What is it, Eilish? What did Mammy have to come back to tell me?'

Eilish gave a big suck and swallowed the juice that threatened to spill out of her mouth. 'It's very sad,' she said solemnly.

'What?' Emer could see Bridie, racked in frustration at her own inability to speak, glaring at her daughter to get on with it.

Eilish looked from one to the other. Wasn't it the queerest sort of day after all? She had started off in school where everybody was laughing at her and now she had everyone looking at her as if she was very important. She took a deep breath and savoured the moment. 'I was telling her what all the fuss was about in school. It was about the ambulance and who was in it and if she was going to die or not.'

'Who?' Emer almost shouted at her.

Her tone frightened Eilish and her eyes filled up again. 'That's why I was crying. It's because it is Sister Agnes. Sister Pius told us we had to pray. Sister Agnes is going to die.'

'Cora! Can you come out here a minute? Cora!'

'I'm coming – you don't have to shout at me.' Cora's tone was sullen.

'I have to go across to the convent for a while, Cora. Will you stay in here and keep an eye on the shop for me till I get back? I won't be long.' Emer headed down the steps to the passage leading to the kitchen where her coat was hanging. 'If there's nobody in, you might carry on tidying those shelves for me so there'll be space for the stuff Mr Fagan wants brought up from the store.' She pulled on her coat and came back up the steps.

Cora was still standing with her arms folded and a face like thunder.

'Dunno.' She shrugged.

Emer stopped in her tracks. 'What do you mean you "don't know"?'

'I don't know if that's what *Mr* Fagan would like me to be doing at the moment. I'm actually helping *him* – ouch!'

Bridie's feet didn't touch the ground as she leapt from the chair and aimed a swipe at her daughter's ear. She was still purple-faced but it was more anger than distress that fuelled her now. 'Well! I wouldn't bloody believe it if I was told that a daughter of mine would have the cheek to speak to her boss like that! Little whelp, what have you to say for yourself?'

From the pub door it was impossible to see over the high counter and until that moment, Cora had had no idea that her mother was there. Now she looked in horror at the sight. Bridie, florid and sweating, was ready to hit her again and Eilish was snivelling at the door. Cora shrugged. She was done for now anyway so there was nothing to lose. 'Actually, it's *Mr* Fagan who's my boss and he said I was a great help to him so –

ow!' Her courage deserted her as her mother took a firm hold of her ear. 'Leggo, Mam, I swear you're killing me!'

'I *will* kill you and there won't be time for swearing, Missy. You'll say you're sorry to Mrs Fagan and you'll stack those shelves till she gets back as if your life depended on it and I'll tell you something, madam – it does!'

Cora wiped her nose with her sleeve. 'Yes, Mam,' she turned and glared defiantly at Emer. 'Sorry.'

Emer nodded, absolution as insincere as the apology that requested it. She would really have liked to tell the girl to go home and not come back, and she knew that Bridie would have supported the move – for all the donation Cora was willing to make to family funds out of her wages – but she was eager to get to the convent and find out what had happened to Agnes. She knotted her scarf around her neck. 'Right so – carry on, I'll see you when I get back.' By now Bridie was at the door and the two women left together. As she shut it behind her, Emer could hear John calling Cora. No time to explain now, Cora would no doubt give him a very particular account of what had happened but there was nothing she could do about that – explanations could wait till she got back. With Bridie panting beside her, Emer headed for the convent. Halfway there, Bridie gave up and beckoned her to continue without her. She was wheezing now, so Emer carried on alone.

'Stay with your mammy, pet,' she called to Eilish who followed quietly behind them. 'I'll be back as soon as I find out what's happening inside.'

The convent bell was one of the old fashioned pull types that jangle in the distance. Emer pulled the cord and waited. The sound died away and nobody came.

Impatient for news, she went around to the side, through the schoolyard to the back door. Inside, one of the young novices was busy peeling potatoes.

'Excuse me,' Emer poked her head round the door.

'Oh, hello!' the girl said. 'Can I help you? Come in, come in.'

Emer came in and stood at the end of the table. 'I'm not staying,' she said. 'It's just that I've heard some news about Sister Agnes and I wondered what truth there might be to it?'

'Ah, please God, a couple of weeks in the hospital and a few prayers from the rest of us, and she'll be grand. Dr Rourke said he thought it was pneumonia,' the girl said, letting the peeling knife fall into the sink.

'Pneumonia? How did she get that?'

'I don't know. She was doing gardening all the week and she said she'd caught a bit of a chill. This morning she had a terrible fever and she was moaning so the doctor said she'd have to go to the hospital. They've been gone a couple of hours so I suppose there'll be news when they get back. Oh dear, I'm just about to make tea and I don't know where the new box is kept – I'm sure the one bag will do the job.' She bustled around opening cupboards, looking for sugar and cups while Emer watched her. 'Here, would you like a cup?' Holding the pot aloft, she proceeded to pour the tea into the cups.

Despite her worry, Emer had to smile. It was easy to see the place was in turmoil. With Agnes in residence, tea was served only in cups that were supported by matching saucers and it was certainly never served before it was well drawn and a spoon of sugar added to the pot 'for colour'.

'Thanks anyway,' she said, 'but I'll have to rush it – I have Bridie Hennessy waiting down the street for news and I said I'd let her know.'

'That's all right – I'll go and tell her – you stay there and drink your tea. I'll be glad to get out of the kitchen anyway. The rest are inside in the chapel so I'm chief spud peeler and lowly job do-er for the day! Any excuse to escape for a minute!'

And she was gone.

Emer sat in the kitchen and savoured the quiet, if not the pale brew. The milky blandness of it was cloying on her tongue and she rose and went into the pantry to find the new box of tea leaves. She knew where everything was kept in here. It was a room as familiar to her as her own kitchen at home. Even when she was a little girl, she used to come here. If Mammy was sick and Daddy had to look after her, she had often gone over to the convent for her tea. Agnes and Kathleen and some of the others were young women then but they treated her as if they were her aunties and she was given jobs to do so that she never felt like a visitor here. They had taught her to roll pastry, bake sponges that rose, and make bread so full of wheat and grain that your tummy would gurgle all night in its efforts to shift the fibre. Sometimes they would joke that she wouldn't be long joining them.

'Sure you'd look fine in a nice black habit, wouldn't she, Sister? We'll have to pray for a vocation for you.'

Kneading the dough, Emer would concentrate hard on her task and try to block out the thought. A vocation? All that praying and being married to God? No thanks. She was going to grow up and when she was about seventeen, she would emerge from her plainness and a handsome man would fall in love with her and marry her and look at her the way Daddy looked at Mammy – as if she was the most precious thing he had ever set his eyes on and he would protect her no matter what happened. Sometimes he held Mammy in his arms and stroked her hair and crooned to her as if she was a baby. Emer would sit there, unnoticed by either of them and try to fight the jealousy. At times like that, they were alone in the world and she didn't even exist. If she tried to say anything, Daddy would beckon her to shush.

'Go on up to bed, pet. I'll be up in a minute to tuck you in.'

'Will you read me a story, Daddy?'

'Maybe tomorrow night – Mammy's not feeling so well tonight and she needs me here.'

'Not even a short one?'

'Not tonight, don't pester, Emer. I'll read you one as soon as I get the chance. Be a good girl now and go on up.'

There'd be no point in complaining. Mammy needed the attention and Mammy got it because Mammy wasn't well. Nobody ever explained to her what exactly was wrong with Mammy. One minute she was normal, almost like everybody else's mother, then she would fly into a rage about something and start screaming as if there was a ghost in the room and she would cry and cry and Daddy was the only one who could soothe her. She'd cling to him, begging him never to leave her and he'd say that he wouldn't and there'd be no point in asking him to read you a bedtime story. Over the years Emer learned to stop asking. She would just get up and go. Sometimes, Daddy would find her later and sit and hold her hand and tell her she was the best daughter in the world and that he would be lost without her.

Emer got cross with him once.

'No you wouldn't,' she said gruffly. 'You probably wouldn't even notice.'

'Of course I'd notice, Emer. How could you think I wouldn't notice if my best girl wasn't there?'

He sounded hurt but Emer refused to relent. 'I'm not your best girl. Mammy is your best girl and I'm only the one that has to go to bed and not be getting in the way. If I wasn't here, you'd probably be glad because you wouldn't have to tell anyone to go to bed, you could just mind Mammy and you wouldn't care that I wasn't there at all!' Drained by her outburst, she slumped on her window-seat and glared out of the window. She expected, hoped, that he would respond with denials but there wasn't a sound and when she turned around, the room was empty.

He hadn't denied it. He had said nothing, just walked off.

She sat there for a long time, cold and frightened and lonely – more completely lonely than she had ever felt before in her life. Daddy didn't love her; Mammy wasn't interested in her – she was alone. After a while she got up and went to the door. The house was silent. They must have gone to bed. She crept along the landing and peered in the open door of her parents' bedroom. From the mound on the bed she could hear the steady rhythm of her mother's breathing but her father wasn't there. Where could he be? She hadn't heard him go downstairs and he certainly wouldn't have gone out.

Then she heard a noise in the kitchen. There were people talking quietly. Fuelled as much by curiosity as a desire to escape the desolation inside her, she crept downstairs to find out who it was. At the bottom step, she could make out the voices. It was her father and Dr Rourke.

'—too young to be told – in the past—' her father was saying.

'So what are you going to tell her?' the doctor asked.

'I don't know.' Her father sounded tired and desperately sad. 'I'll have to tell her something. She thinks that we don't want her and that we'd be happier if she wasn't around.'

'It can't be easy for her. Nell's moods aren't getting any better.'

'No,' Jimmy agreed, 'worse if anything. And with Emer coming up to her, you know, growing up I mean, she needs a woman to talk to, to explain things to her.'

'Aye, I know. But before that she needs something else,' the doctor paused. 'She needs you to sit her down and explain how important she is to you. Tell her whatever you like but make sure she understands that much.'

'I will, you're right, Bill. I'll talk to her in the morning.'

'You'll talk to her tonight.'

'I can't – she'll be asleep.'

The doctor laughed. 'Jimmy Byrne, you're a case! Do you know nothing at all about women? You've had a woman cross with you and you think she'll be asleep? Not a bit of it. If ever a breed could brood, it's women! She'll be above in that bed worrying and fretting and angry and upset all at the same time. And you'll be down here working yourself into a state about it. A fat lot of good the pair of you will be to the world tomorrow if you don't get it sorted out tonight!' There was the sound of a glass being put on the table. 'I'm away. Better get back to my own woman, she's trying to teach me bridge if you don't mind. You go talk to Emer, Jimmy. She's a good girl. She only needs to know she's important too.'

Her father's voice was shaky. 'I don't know what I would do without her. Sometimes I think she's the only one in this house who's sane. Poor Nell, she can't help it but she does my head in.'

'I know, so go and talk to that daughter of yours.' And then there was the sound of the back door opening and the doctor was gone. Elated, Emer turned and took the stairs two at a time. In her room, she pulled off her dress, pulled on her nightgown and leapt into bed. She knew her father wouldn't come up till he had washed and put the glasses away. If Mammy came down in the morning and there was anything out of place or unwashed, she would be furious so nothing was ever left untidy. In the bed, she shivered. There was no point trying to understand everything she had heard but it didn't matter. Daddy said that he didn't know what he'd do without her and that was all that mattered. She lay there, waiting for him to come up.

'Are you asleep, pet?'

She held her breath and said nothing.

'Emer – about what you said—'

In his voice she thought she could hear something of the loneliness she had felt earlier although she couldn't have put words to it. 'I didn't mean it really,' she said. 'I know it isn't true.'

Her father sat on the bed and took her hand. 'Do you? Do you really understand that?'

'Yes.'

'Well,' he said, sounding normal again. 'In that case you really *are* the best.' He hesitated and she knew he was looking for words. 'Mammy isn't well sometimes. She has – dreams, bad dreams that frighten her even when she is awake and it's like she can't get out of the nightmare unless I am there to mind her. If I don't stay with her, she can't get the nightmare away, do you understand?'

'I think so, a bit,' Emer said. She had seen her mother's staring terrified eyes often enough. 'What does she have nightmares about?'

'Oh, desperate things, we wouldn't even want to be talking about them. We only have to understand that when she has her nightmares she needs the two of us,' he squeezed her hand, 'the two of us mind, to take care of her. I calm her down and you be as quiet as you can and we'll make her better between us, is that okay?'

Emer smiled in the darkness. 'And I'll take care of you, Daddy.'

'You will,' Jimmy smoothed his daughter's hair, 'until you're a big girl and then some lucky man will fall in love with the best girl in the world and you can live next door and I'll be the proudest daddy in the world.'

'Do you think that will happen?'

He stood up. 'Miss Byrne, I'm sure that will happen. Now go to sleep.'

'Night, Daddy.'

'Night, pet, God bless.'

And in minutes she was fast asleep, dreaming of handsome men who would sweep her off her feet and love her and think her important enough to hold in their arms.

So there was no way Emer Byrne wanted a vocation to the religious life. The nuns could joke all they wanted but Emer was going to have a husband who adored her. Over the years there were a few who took her fancy and as her interest in various possibilities ebbed and flowed, she confided everything in her father.

One night Nell walked in on her husband and daughter deep in conversation. They thought she had gone to bed.

'Oh hello, Mam – are you looking for something?'

'Just wondering where your father was,' her mother smiled. 'I guessed the two of you might be whispering in here.'

'We weren't whispering.'

'It looked like a big secret all the same.'

'No secret, really.'

'What was it then?' Nell was still smiling but Emer could hear the edge in her voice. 'Are you going to tell me? I hate whispers.'

'There were no whispers, honestly.'

Nell looked at her husband. 'Jimmy, tell me.'

Jimmy didn't look up. 'Leave it, Nell. Emer and I were having a harmless chat. There's nothing for you to get concerned about.'

'Why won't you tell me then? There is something, that's why. There's something that you know and you won't tell me. Tell me, Jimmy, tell me why you're whispering about me.' There was panic in her voice now.

Emer could see all the signs. Any time there was a situation that her mother didn't fully understand or have control over, she would become convinced that she was the victim of some conspiracy against her. Usually, Emer was sympathetic but for once, she wished Nell would stay out of it and not be so absorbed in herself.

'Oh, for goodness sake, Mam, do you always have to think everything's about you? Daddy and I were having a conversation about me and it's private and that's all there is to it!'

'Emer! Don't speak to your mother like that!'

'Well, I'm fed up with it! This is supposed to be my home too and I have to pussyfoot around as if I'm not here half the time and the rest of the time I have to watch what I say and how loudly I say it so that Mam doesn't think everything's about her—'

'That's enough, young lady—'

Emer didn't stay to hear the rest of it. She felt abandoned and damned if she was going to stay for a lecture about how she must be considerate to her mother. In a temper she slammed the door and ran, pounding her rage into the ground beneath her feet.

She didn't see his car. He came round the corner of Fagan's without looking and his tyres screeched to a halt within seconds of Emer hitting the wall with a dull thud. In the haze of dust and pain, she heard a car door open and a man's voice.

'Oh, shit! Where did you come out of? I didn't see you. Are you okay?'

Her head was pounding, her back felt as if a buffalo had just kicked it and there was a pain like a flame scorching up her left arm. But she was alive. Blinking into the haze, she tried to see who it was. Then there was shouting and the blackness fell.

When she came to, Emer learned that her collision had been with John Fagan's new car. It was black and shiny and in it he considered himself the hottest thing in the country, never mind the village of Kildoran. Within days of him bringing it down from Dublin, the wary had learned to avoid its shiny front bumper and it was rumoured that the less wary learned more about what needed to be avoided on its shiny back seat. John Fagan fancied himself. His mother, Mary, doted on him and his father, Bertie, kept a close eye on his company. To Bertie's delight, John showed an interest in the business and nobody was surprised when, after his first heart attack, Bertie let it be known that the place was to be signed over to his younger son. Noel, the prodigal, could return if he took a mind to, but there would be no fatted calf waiting for him. It wasn't long before Bertie's second heart attack carried him off, and Mary's death a year after her husband left young John with a business to run and all the power a bit of money in a small village could provide. Eager girls took to shopping in small doses, hoping to catch the eye of Kildoran's most eligible bachelor and equally eager mothers encouraged them. So far no one had been wholly successful. John Fagan's eye was reputedly easily caught but a wedding ring from the same source was not as forthcoming. There were rumours that even a wedding ring from someone else did not keep you safe. You only needed a pretty face or a twinkle in your eye and you'd never need to carry your shopping home again – there'd always be a lift.

Emer was in bed for three weeks after the accident. Jimmy was shaken and threatened to kill John Fagan if he could lay his hands on him but John gave him no chance. Whenever Jimmy was out, John would come knocking, bearing gifts of flowers and chocolates and full of gossip about the comings and goings in Kildoran as reported by loosened tongues over the bar. Nell received the gifts on Emer's behalf but refused to be swayed by John's pampering charm. She'd stand at the door and watch as John regaled Emer with stories that made her laugh but she didn't join in. Once, when he passed her on the way out her face darkened and she glared at him. 'You remind me of something.' She rubbed her hand along the furrows of her brow. 'I can't remember...'

Emer flushed. Lots of people considered her mother to be a bit cracked. John Fagan, with his ready smile and brash arrogance was surely one of them. To her surprise he didn't seem to think anything of the sort. He nodded slightly. 'That happens to me too – a fleeting thought and it's gone before I can catch it. Never mind, I'm sure it will come to you; I hope it was something nice.'

That softened her mother slightly and made his visits easier. Unused to such regular attention, Emer blossomed but even that was not enough to bring any consolation to Jimmy Byrne when he learned, just hours before the story broke to the astounded village that John Fagan had at last decided to take a wife – and that the wife he had chosen was not the usual pretty eye-catcher that graced the front seat of his car, but the quiet, mousy Emer Byrne.

Now, twenty years down the line, Emer hunted crossly for the tea in the convent's pantry. If only she'd known then what she knew now. Her father was furious when she told him of her plans and her mother looked from one to the other, confused and anxious. There was the most dreadful row but Emer couldn't see the genuine concern for her that motivated their opposition; she saw only a means of getting away from the feeling of always being second best and into a home where she would come first. She would be the treasured one. She thought herself so lucky, couldn't imagine what he saw in her. She hung onto his every word and laughed at his outrageous behaviour. She watched him flirt with other women and just when it would begin to make her feel uncomfortable, he would turn and wink at her as if the whole thing had been a game all along and he had been doing it only for her amusement. And she believed him.

She believed him even when, in the throes of her pregnancy she came into the shop and found him holding hands with the feisty Mrs Grogan, newly arrived in the village. They broke apart and Mrs Grogan left without a word. Heavy and aching, Emer challenged him but he laughed off her questions.

'God help her – a little neighbourly kindness wouldn't go amiss and her new in the place, widowed and expecting.'

'Expecting? What do you mean.'

John gestured to Emer's bump.

'But she can't be expecting! I thought her husband die ages ago?'

John turned and started to sort the boxes on the shelf. 'Oh, not so long, not so long. Go on down yourself and stick on the kettle. I got grand cake in today and I'll come and have a cup with you in a minute.' It was obvious the conversation was finished but it left Emer feeling very uncomfortable. When Mrs Grogan gave birth to a daughter two months after Gareth was born and Emer heard the comments about the miraculous length of her pregnancy, considering her husband was supposed to have been dead a year, John didn't comment, only smiled and buried his face in the paper.

It was around the same time that she noticed he was losing interest in her too. He was pleased to have a son but paid little attention to the child and when he would suddenly announce that a man like him needed to have a large family and she would have to endure the weight of his clammy flesh and his

103

groping and grunting, she found her previous admiration of him changing into resentment. She thought she could be mistress in her own home but he made it clear that she had come into *his* home, and if there was a mistress in it – it was not Emer.

'God help us! This exercise is too much for me!'

Emer was startled out of her reveries by the return of the young novice with Bridie and Eilish in tow. With a whoosh of smells and cold air they came into the kitchen just as the telephone shrilled from the corridor on the other side of the kitchen.

'Excuse me – I'll just go and get that,' the girl pushed past and ran out to answer the phone. For a few minutes all they could hear was the odd 'umm' and 'yes, Doctor' and then the phone was replaced with a click and she was back in the kitchen, all smiles. 'Great news! That was the doctor; he says that Sister Agnes is off the critical list. Her temperature is still high but they've started with the medicine and her breathing is easier.'

'Thank God for that!' Emer rose and taking Bridie's elbow, she glanced at her watch – another hour and Gareth would be home from his football match, then tea. The shop was usually quiet on a Thursday evening and John needed no help to keep things flowing in the bar. A warm bath and an early night would be just the thing.

Beside her, Bridie Hennessy puffed and sweated and Emer smiled to herself. Maybe two warm baths …

CHAPTER 8

WITHOUT AGNES' CALMING INFLUENCE there was an air of disquiet about Kildoran. In the convent the nuns found themselves with a few extra tasks that seemed at odds with their usual ordered lives. There were chores to be done; small tasks that lightened the load, which they had never really acknowledged before, though each was aware had been carried out. Across in the Grocery, Emer missed the little notes, which were often included in the convent's daily order inviting her over for a cup of tea, and Bridie was bereft. Unable to drive, she could not make her own way over to the hospital in Kilkenny and she never managed to get herself organised enough to catch the bus. As her pregnancy was now evident and her latest bump protruding well beyond the ones her appetite provided she was increasingly uncomfortable and the fright she got with the news that Agnes had been taken off in an ambulance in the first place had sparked off aches that she didn't seem to be able to shift. They made her tired and cranky with the kids and even impatient with Sam's ambling ways.

'Arrah, for God's sake, can you not come up for your dinner when I call you? It's a mystery why I bother to put it hot on the table in the first place ... '

Sam looked at her in surprise. Bridie was a grand woman but he knew as well as she did that her lack of house pride was second only to her lack of culinary expertise. She could slice and she could boil; and if whatever it was that was to be served up could be neither sliced nor boiled, then you chewed it yourself, raw. He hadn't rushed to a meal in years, relaxed by the knowledge that while it wouldn't be anything worth waiting for, it couldn't get any worse for having waited for him. Now he looked at the soggy grey mound on the plate in front of him and rubbed his head in wonder. 'That's a mystery all right,' he said, 'and tell me now, when it was hot, what was it at all?'

Bridie looked at him crossly. 'What d'you think it was?' She prodded the mound with the handle of her fork. 'Spuds.'

'Spuds.' Sam shook his head. 'Jaysus, that's worth rushing for all right,' He picked his fork up and started to shovel the food into his mouth as if it was a great treat. 'Lovely! You're a great cook, Bridie, I can tell you that. I'll be rushing home tomorrow all right.'

Bridie's temper disappeared as quickly as it had sparked. 'Get on out of that, you shouldn't be laughing at me. I'm terrible contrary.'

'Aye.'

'I must be getting old.'

'Aye.'

'Aye? I'm not as old as yourself.'

Sam pressed a sliver of butter onto the potato and waited for it to react. 'You're right there. Old an' ugly but sure, who's complaining – there's life in the old dog yet.'

Bridie scratched beneath her breasts where they pressed hot and heavy onto her bump and raised her eyes to heaven. 'Should have stayed in you, Sam Hennessy – I wouldn't be half so knackered.' She patted her swollen belly.

'Oh for God's sake. You two are disgusting.' Cora scraped her chair back from the table and stood up. 'You're putting me off my food. I'm going out.'

Sam caught his daughter's arm as she tried to sweep past. 'You'll not go anywhere till you help your mother clear away and put the little ones to bed.'

'I will not.' Cora glared at him. 'They're not my kids. I've been working all day and I need a bit of a rest too.'

Sam's face reddened. 'Is that right now? Working all day, is it? And would you mind telling me what great work you've been up to that has you so tired that you forget who it is you're talking to in your mother's house?'

'I've been helping Mr Fagan clear the store.'

'Clear the store, is it? And it's hard work?'

'Yes.' She stared at him defiantly. 'Yes, it's hard work. So?'

Bridie, silently watching the scene till now, sprang into action. She hauled herself up and stood a head taller than her daughter. 'It's not half as hard as it is slow, would you say?'

The colour was slowly creeping into Cora's face. 'I don't know what you're talking about.'

'You bloody do.' Bridie leaned her face close into her daughter's. 'When I was in that shop a week and a half ago, you were busy helping to clear that store. You were even in there on your half-day; so keen were you to get the job done. And you're telling us not that even with all that time you still haven't the job finished—?'

'It's a long job.' Cora's voice was still defiant but her face was flushed and she suddenly looked like the little girl she had been just a couple of years ago. 'It's taking a while, that's all.'

Bridie folded her arms across her chest. 'It's finished.'

'What do you mean – finished?' Sam looked as shocked as his daughter. Though Cora contributed little to the family funds, the lack of her surly presence around the house while she was working in Fagan's was a blessing. With her wages now she could at least get the bus into the town and look after herself. The idea that she might be slouching around again looking woeful was a gloomy prospect.

'She's finished in the store, that's all. If the job takes her that long and has her that tired that she has to cheek her parents, then it's too much for her.' She nodded to the window where her two oldest sons could be seen tinkering on the tractor. 'I'll send Fergus and Dermot down in the morning. They can explain to Mr Fagan that the clearing job is having a wearying effect on you so they'll give him a hand to get it finished. They're fine strapping lads and as strong as horses. They'll have it finished in the day. You'll be in the following day, all rested, to get on with your job behind the counter as you were taken on to do in the first place.' She glared at Cora and the girl seemed to shrink. 'That's how it will be. I'll be in and out of the place the odd time – to make sure you're all right and there'll be no need for any more "clearing" jobs. D'you understand?'

There was silence for a minute before Cora answered. 'Yes, Mam, but—'

'There is no "but". That's how it is. If there's a problem, I'm sure Mr Fagan would like to have a talk about it with your father and myself – and maybe your brothers. Is there any other "but"?

'No, Mam.'

'Right so. You'll be off to bed because you're very tired and there'll be no more about it.'

For a moment it looked as if Cora might raise an objection but the steady look on her mother's face never wavered and she backed down and left the room. Bridie picked up her fork and stabbed at the cold remains of her food.

Sam was looking at her, bemused. 'Is there something I don't know about? Did I miss a trick there, Bridie?'

She gave him the ghost of a smile. 'Sure, you did all right, pet, but don't worry yourself about it,' she wiped her mouth with the back of her sleeve, 'I didn't.'

Sam took out his pipe and tapped it off the edge of the table, still watching her. 'Is it all right?'

Bridie nodded. 'Aye, I just have to keep a bit of an eye on her, that's all.'

Sam looked down at his plate where the scraping of butter was still wedged, as sharp and firm as when he had first prodded it there. 'John Fagan, is it?'

'Ah, I don't know,' Bridie rubbed the spot between her eyes where a steady throbbing was now threatening to become a full-blown headache. Between that and the aches in her back, she was not in the mood to think. 'I don't know. I just have a feeling that her willingness to help out down below is more for the jobs that *he* wants doing. And there's a cockiness as well shouldn't be there – but maybe it's only me, bad thinking. I don't know, Sam, that's the truth of it, I just don't know.' She looked up and for the first time he could see the weariness in her face.

'Is it too much, will you be able for it?'

'Able for what?'

Sam nodded towards her folds of stomachs. 'The baby.'

'I don't know that either. I must be getting old not having an answer to any of your questions.' Bridie leaned back on the chair. 'Aggie'll be back soon and I'll maybe have a chat with her.'

'You won't wait for Aggie so you won't. For the love o' God, woman, haven't we a perfectly good doctor below who knows the make and shape of you and has a potion to cure everything! You'll go down to see him tomorrow.' He pulled a crumpled note out of his pocket and thrust it across the table at her. 'Here, do it.'

Bridie took the note and stuffed it down the front of her blouse. 'Jaysus, he's throwing money at me!'

Sam didn't smile. 'I'm not makin' light, Bridie. You know what the doctor said before. You're no spring chicken.'

'For feck's sake! Would you ever give over preaching at me! Is it any wonder I have a pain in my head with a daughter who hasn't a civilised word in her head and an old fella who takes up preaching when he'd be far better off keeping his wisdom to himself and getting on with his dinner.'

Sam stood up. 'I'll be off now. And you'll leave John Fagan to me. Eilish, you and the twins help your mammy.' He went out and the house was suddenly quiet.

Eilish, who had been sitting quietly listening to everything came over and stood beside her mother. Neither of them said anything for a few minutes, and then Bridie smiled.

'Sometimes I wish I was stupid, d'you know that?'

The memory of Pius' sneer was still sharp in Eilish's head. She said nothing.

'Come on, Gareth, just put it all in your school bag and get out the door, will you! It's nearly twenty to and if you're late you know there'll be trouble.'

Gareth tried to stuff the rest of the books into the top of his bag but although the pile was a lot smaller than the space he wanted to fit it into, the books stubbornly refused to go. Pencils and bits of paper spilled onto the kitchen table and Emer bit her lip in frustration. That was all she needed this morning,

Gareth foustering and fiddling about when there was so much to be done in the shop. Bill Brady was due in with the deliveries at half past nine. What with John spending his days shifting and sorting and Cora bowed down under the weight of her own importance, Emer was getting no help at all. If she didn't get the child out the door so she could make a start on it, she'd fall behind again and there'd be precious little time to go across to the Home in the afternoon.

John promised he'd be here to cover for her but that was last night when he had come whistling in for his tea in a great humour. Later on there'd been some discussion in the bar when Sam came in with the Hennessy boys and John stayed late drinking and cursing to himself after the last of the stragglers had gone home. When he came up to bed she lay there, pretending to sleep, dreading the brewery stench of him and the way he would haul himself on to her without a word. Usually he just discharged his intentions and was asleep before he had fully rolled onto his back again, but last night she had been lucky. He was well drunk but he ignored her, falling onto the bed and starting to snore immediately. This morning he was still asleep when she got up but she could tell by the look on his blowsy face that when he woke there would be little calm about the place. If he was in a bad humour there was little chance that he would honour his word and she was anxious not to have to spend the day here. She was keen to see her mother who had been refusing to see anyone in case they'd bring Agnes' germs with them. Well, she'd had enough time to get over that particular paranoia and with the hospital just up the road, there was the chance of a quick trip up to see how Agnes was getting on.

'There!' Triumphantly, Gareth held the bulging bag up for her to see.

'Good boy. Go on now, and remember, you're to go to Rourke's after school with Peter and be back here at half past five.'

'Okay, Mammy, 'bye!'

''Bye!' Emer bent to kiss the top of his head but he was already out the door. She heard the shuffle as he struggled with the shop door and the sound of voices as some early customers greeted him. 'Damn!' The table was still a mess of breakfast dishes and a line of Weetabix crumbs trailed across from the big cupboard. 'I'll have to leave this and come back later—' She looked at the stairs. Please God John wouldn't appear before she had time to sort it out. Cora was due in ten minutes but there was little hope she would be much help given as she was too busy getting on with the jobs John had arranged for her the previous day. She pulled off her apron and running her fingers through her hair, went up the steps into the shop.

To her surprise, Cora was early. She was standing sheepishly by the counter flanked by her two brothers.

'Morning, Mrs Fagan!' the boys called in unison.

'Morning.' Cora was quiet but with a quick glance at her brother repeated herself more loudly. 'I mean, good morning, Mrs Fagan.'

'Good morning, Cora, Fergus, Dermot. You're all up bright and early this morning. What can I do for you boys?'

'Show us where you want us to start, if you like.'

'Start?' Emer looked from one to the other. 'What are you supposed to start?' Fergus pulled himself to his full height and nudged his sister forward. There was an authority in his movement that reminded Emer of Bridie and she was surprised that she had not noticed the resemblance before. 'Well, Cora here is helping you in the shop as she was taken on to do and Dermot and myself are going to help Mr Fagan in the store. By all accounts he's doing a great sort out and there's stuff to be moved and shifted that's taking him a long time on his own. Dermot and me are here to help him. We were down last evening with Da and it was all arranged.' He nodded towards the kitchen. 'Is himself about?'

Emer found it hard to hide her surprise. John had never shown any particular liking for the Hennessy boys and Sam Hennessy was little more than a source of amusement to him. Funny that they should now be making arrangements to take a day off from the farm to give John a hand. She glanced across to where Cora had already snipped the twine off the bundle of papers and was starting to write the names on the tops of them. Although her head was bowed, it was obvious that the girl was uncomfortable. 'No,' she said, 'he's still above but I'll give him a shout for you. Are you all right there, Cora?'

'Yes, thank you, Mrs Fagan,' the girl mumbled through gritted teeth.

'Right so, I'll be back in a minute.' As she turned, Emer caught the fleeting glance that passed from Fergus to his sister and she recognised that the girl was being warned. She shook her head. Although the extra help was blessing in disguise, something was not right here. Why on earth would John ask for help from Sam Hennessy and why would the offer of it send him into such a glowering bad mood that he would spend half the night drinking? And what was the matter with—?

No, no, he wouldn't! She's only a child. He wouldn't!

The thought came to her as forcibly as if someone had written it in bold capitals and held it up for her to read.

He wouldn't.

She stopped at the door of the kitchen and held the jamb to steady herself.

Don't be a fool Emer Fagan, of course he would and well you know it. Why else would he be in such bloody good humour taking ages over a job that should only have taken him days? And why else would Cora be looking so sheepish escorted to work by her brothers?

'Oh God!' The cry escaped her as implication after implication piled in on her. What sort of a fool was she that she hadn't seen it coming? She was so pleased when John announced one evening that she was looking tired and that he had decided to hire some help so that she wouldn't have to do the shop all on her own. She was flattered that he'd noticed and charmed by Cora's early willingness to carry out any task set to her. When had it all changed? When had Cora taken to spending all her time helping John and become increasingly surly and unco-operative towards herself?

A noise in the kitchen distracted her and she turned the corner to see him there, already dressed and ready. He was drinking water from a pint glass the way he always did when the night before left him with a tongue that felt like sandpaper and a head full of hammers. He turned.

'Well? What are you standing there for? Have you never seen a man drink water before?' He beckoned towards the table. 'Not that I have a choice and there no tea, only a fucking mess.' When she didn't answer, he glared at her. 'Well, what have you to say to that?'

Emer felt the rage swell inside of her. The bastard! Of course she knew he was unfaithful, she'd known that for years deep down but she'd never confronted him with it. Nothing would be gained by a confrontation. There was Gareth to think of and with her qualified to do nothing more than work in her husband's shop, how could she risk cutting the child afloat?

Because you are a coward, Emer Fagan.

She had watched him smirk at the women who came into the shop, widows and wives alike and she had turned a blind eye to it.

Because you are a coward.

But Cora Hennessy was not a widow or a wife. She was not even a woman. She was a child – and under her own nose, her husband had been trying to seduce a child. She looked at him again and it was not the John she had married that she was looking at but the John he had become, but for his girth the double of his older brother, Noel. Angry at her silence, he made a move towards her but she stood her ground and faced up to him.

'What are you looking at, I asked you!'

'Do you know,' she said, surprised by how calm her voice sounded when inside she was churning, 'I know exactly *what* I'm looking at but I really don't know *who*. It might be John Fagan and it might be Noel Fagan. There really isn't much of a difference.'

Her composure stopped him and he stood with his mouth open, the fumes of his breath filling her with loathing as they gave her the strength to go on.

'You're both disreputable bastards.'

His hand came up with a speed that surprised her and caught her on the cheek, knocking her head against the doorframe. The crack of it blinded her for a minute and when she felt her cheek, she could feel the heat and knew that the print of his hand was there. A small trickle of blood reached her eyebrow on the other side and she didn't bother to wipe it away.

'You shouldn't have made me do that. You shouldn't have said things like that. I'm not like him at all.' Behind the aggression, there was panic in his voice.

'You're cut from the same cloth.'

He made as if to move towards her again.

'Don't! You're not to touch me because this time you hit me in the wrong place. This time it shows and if I walk out of here right now everyone will know what you are and that will be the end of jolly John Fagan. They'll all forgive a drunk, but a wife beater – you won't touch me again.'

His face was now so red she thought he might explode but he said nothing. In silence they glared at one another and she thought they might have stayed there all day but for a movement behind her. She turned to see Fergus peering into the darkness of the passage.

'Are you all right there, Mrs Fagan?' he called, 'only we heard a noise—'

'Who is that?' John hissed.

'Didn't I say? The Hennessy brothers, the two older ones, are here with their sister. It seems they're all a bit concerned about the effort you have to put into your new arrangements so they've come to give you a hand. Seems it was all arranged with you last night, you must have forgotten. Will I go up and tell them that you're on your way?' She was swaying slightly and knew she wouldn't make it to the far end of the passageway but she had already seen the fear in his eyes and it gave her the strength to hold on.

'No, no, I'll go – you hold on – here, sit down.' With one hand he dragged a chair across the floor for her to sit on and with the other handed her a cloth. 'Fix yourself up there. Don't come out.'

'Mrs Fagan—?' The boy was already almost at the kitchen door. John moved quickly to block the view.

'Fergus! Grand to see you here! I'm right glad of the help.' He started to usher the boy back towards the shop. 'Mrs Fagan is fine. Slipped on the mat and gave herself a bump on the doorframe. You go on into the store. Cora will show you where the key is and get your coats off. I'll be along in a minute.'

'Right so,' Fergus headed back, calling his brother as he did.

John came back into the kitchen. Emer was sitting there and she was very pale. 'Are you all right?' He started to mop clumsily at the blood on her forehead but she pushed him off.

'How easily you lie. You're not concerned for me at all. You're frightened because I could ruin your reputation and you couldn't even pretend that I was making it up. Sam Hennessy is on to you too.'

'Sam Hennessy!' John laughed. 'Who'd listen to him?'

From the shop they could hear the sounds of the boys as they clumped down the stone steps at the back of the shop. 'They would, for a start.' She let her eyes travel slowly over her husband's rolling stomach up to where his face was red and sweating heavily. 'Look at you,' she said and she made no effort to hide the disgust in her voice, 'two fine healthy lads like that – I say a start is all they'd need.'

Clenching his fists, he left the room without another word and Emer sat there with only the dripping of the tap and the pounding in her head for company.

That was it then. All those years and fears and she'd finally stood up to him. That wouldn't be an end to it, of course. She'd compared him to Noel and she knew he wouldn't let that lie. Noel Fagan left Kildoran before John was born and only ever showed up when he was broke or desperate. The last time he'd been particularly offensive and aggressive but he wouldn't dare show his dislike of the brother he considered a usurper to John – holder of the purse. Instead he waited till John was out of the room and then Emer got the brunt of it. In the years that had passed since his last visit, Emer consigned him to the far corners of her mind with such determination that she had failed to notice how over those years, his character and his mannerisms were being duplicated in her husband.

And today she had seen it.

Holding the cloth to her forehead she went to the mirror to examine the damage. Her face was distorted and in her eyes there was a mixture of rage and fear. For the first time in her life, she looked like her mother's daughter. She wet the cloth and dabbed at her forehead and as she did the eyes in the mirror caught hers and with them the memory of her father's voice.

'Don't be too hard on your mother, pet. You don't know what she's suffering and you mustn't judge her. She has her own crosses to bear.'

A great rush of love for her mother washed over her. 'Oh, Mam,' she whispered, 'what was your cross?'

As soon as her face was cleaned she took her coat from the back of the door. For all the throbbing in her head she had a feeling of freedom. It was as if by standing up to him she had suddenly grown up and taken control of her life. She would go out right now. As she walked out of the shop, Cora looked up at her in surprise.

'Are you away, Mrs Fagan?'

Emer looked at the girl and her face softened. 'I am, Cora. There are enough of you here to keep things going till I get back. If Mr Fagan asks, I am out to see my mother and do a few other jobs. You'll be well able to cope on your own here for a few hours. I should be back before Bill comes with the delivery. Just leave it at the side and I'll sort it when I get back—' She turned to go, then hesitated. 'And Cora?'

'What?'

'You'll leave when your brothers do, do you understand?'

The girl's face reddened and she lowered her head. 'Yes.'

'Good girl.' Emer smiled at her. 'We both understand so. Goodbye.' And without waiting for a reply, she was gone.

CHAPTER 9

ONCE SHE WAS OUTSIDE, Emer's new-found determination deserted her. The air was cold, the sky overcast and the near empty street desolate. She looked around at houses and buildings she had known all her life and was shocked by how foreign they seemed to her. Even though she knew every occupant in every one of them, there was no door she could go through and be greeted openly, just for herself. She had been born and brought up in this village but there had always been a 'something' about her that stopped her from being the same as everyone else. She could remember having her hair ruffled by strangers outside mass at Christmas, far flung relatives of neighbours who'd loudly demand: 'Aren't you the grand little one – what's your name at all?'

'Emer, Emer Byrne.'

'Well I never, haven't you grown! Jimmy Byrne's young one, is it?'

'Yes—' and then the rest, 'and Nell. My mammy's Nell Byrne.'

Then the voice would change. A polite deference, almost sympathy, would creep in. 'Nell – arrah, the poor soul – how is she?'

As she grew older, Emer grew to resent the question.

How is she? What do you mean? Do you mean is she normal most of the time and ranting more quietly; or is she quiet only some of the time and ranting loudly the rest? Is that what you mean?

But she never said it aloud.

After she married John and moved into the Fagan house, a new type of notoriety attached itself to her. Now she was not so much Nell Byrne's daughter as John Fagan's wife and that set her apart too. She looked back at the shop. Through the window she could see Cora cutting slabs of cheese ready to be wrapped and stacked in the fridge and from the back the banter of the Hennessy boys. *I want to walk out of here right now and never walk back in again,* she thought. *Then I wouldn't be an embarrassment to anyone. Nobody would have to lower their eyes in pity for me, with a bad husband and a mad mother ...*

'Oh God, I feel so lonely!' she said aloud to the quiet street, 'Where can I go and what can I do?'

As if on cue, the school bell rang out and the hubbub from the school yard stopped as the children ran in silence to their lines ready to file in to the school building. Without thinking she started to walk in that direction. As she neared the school, she was overtaken by a couple of white faced stragglers rushing in to face the music and she smiled at the insignificance a couple of minutes late for school held for her while they looked as if they expected little short of execution. *To each his own, I suppose* she shrugged, pulling her coat close around her. Outside the school she stopped and looked at the high classroom windows. Even though they were shut she could hear the murmur of morning prayers and the scraping and banging of desk lids.

The noise stopped suddenly and she heard the singsong of children's voices as they answered the roll call.

Helen Burke.

'Anseo!'

Gerald Cunningham.

'Anseo!'

Moiré Doherty.

'Anseo!'

Gareth Fagan.

'Anseo!'

Gareth Fagan. That was the point of it all, wasn't it? Gareth existed and whatever John was, he was also Gareth's father so of course she couldn't just walk over that bridge and keep on walking. She had the day to sort out everything that was going on her head and then she would turn around and go home again and life would go on. But it wouldn't be the same as before – she wasn't blind now. Turning on her heel, she went into the churchyard and headed for the quiet sanctity of St Peter and Paul's.

The church was even bigger on the inside than it appeared outside. The walls were painted cream and faint lines of damp ran down from the windows to the floor. High up near the ceiling great beams ran across from one side of the church to the other. Above them the ceiling rose high into the roof and was criss-crossed with an intricate pattern of swirls and flows that kept children quiet in Mass just trying to figure out which ones would make a knot if you could grab hold of them and give them a pull. There was one wide aisle up the centre of the church and narrow ones down both sides. Whoever had ordered the long pews years ago had more thought in mind for those who would sit on them than those who would have to negotiate them after Communion. 'Up the middle and down the sides', priests cautioned and it worked, till the first parishioner who was slow on his legs set off on the long trek back to his place. As he hauled stiff limbs from one pew to the next a queue would form behind him, unable to pass. Then the 'Mass walking' as Gareth called it, would start – a long line of people each with joined hands hanging loosely at waist level, swaying their way down the aisle at snail's pace. Now that the new houses were starting to fill with families the crush was even more noticeable. And if the rumour were true, that the remaining section of the hill above the village, Mad Morrisseys, had been sold at last, the building would begin there too and the Sunday congestion would soon reach epidemic proportions. Already there were jokes being made about how the older villagers would have to be speed tested on a Sunday morning and assigned a particular slot ...

Today though, it was practically empty. On the altar, a couple of old ladies were pulling out the flowers which were past their best and dotted here and there, a grey head was bent in prayer. With all the time in the world, Emer crept across to a far corner at the back where she was almost hidden from view by the big pillars. She sat down and rested her head on the stone of the pillar; glad of the way the coldness eased the throbbing where she had fallen against the doorframe. The near silence of the church and the familiar smell of candles and damp wool lulled her so she shut her eyes and concentrated on the sensation. It was so full of memories that she found it hard to focus on anything in particular and before she realised what was happening, had started to fall asleep.

Across in the school, Pius watched the children come in and take their places. There was none of the bustle that had been the norm when she came here first. No desks were thrown open and left to slam noisily when she started to speak; no untidy satchels were left open in the aisles to be tripped over when latecomers made a dash for their places as soon as the prayer started; and nobody spoke. Pius nodded in recognition as each child went to his/her place with a deferential, 'Good morning, Sister Pius.' She smiled at none and none smiled at her.

Later, when the children went out to morning break, Pius sat at her desk and regarded the pile of copybooks in front of her. This was one of the tasks she most hated when she came here first, deciphering illegible script from dog-eared, ink-stained pages, but there was a change in the children's work over the weeks. With constant reminders and threats, lines were being skipped under headings and dates written in the right place. Margins were being drawn with one line along a ruler's edge instead of a series of stops and some of the work actually looked quite neat. Even Billy Doherty was remembering to do his corrections! She lifted the edge of the book on top and gingerly skimmed the latest offering – a composition on *My Family*. It looked tidy enough. She peeped at the next one. That was carefully done too. With a sigh she closed the books. No need to do them just yet. The children were not coming back into the classroom after break but going instead to the hall behind the church to have their first introduction to the Christmas play. That gave Pius the rest of the morning to mark her books and make a start on organising the Christmas reports. Usually there was a supply of report sheets in the ink cupboard on the top corridor but with Sister Bernard away nobody had thought to top up the supply and now they were running short.

'Perhaps you'd see to that, sister, if you have time in the morning?' Sister Kathleen had asked. 'They have to be ordered from Dublin and will take a couple of weeks to arrive so it would be such a help if you would see to it today?'

Pius had nodded, 'Of course,' glad to be doing some useful work that she could get on with on her own without the shuffling of children interrupting her all the time.

'You know where the cupboard is, don't you? It's at the end of the corridor, behind the—'

'Yes, I remember it. I—' She stopped abruptly but Kathleen didn't appear to have noticed, distracted as she was by all the organising left to her now, with Bernard away from the school and Agnes away from the convent.

'Grand, grand – bless you, Sister, I'll leave it to you so,' and touching her thanks lightly on Pius' arm, she was gone.

Pius now stood at the foot of the school stairs and looked up to where a huge painting of the Virgin loomed over the landing where the stairs turned. The painting was ancient and cracked in places but it had hung there for as long as anyone could remember. Some of the children swore that there was a window behind it and that years ago a child had fallen through so the nuns had hung the painting there for safety. Whether true or not, it certainly kept the little ones off the stairs. For all that it was old and dusty, the eyes were as blue and piercing as the first day they were painted. They stared out of the picture, watching as you came up the stairs towards them and rounded the corner to go the last few steps to the top. The little ones, who had their classrooms on the ground floor and were forbidden to go near the stairs, were not tempted to be disobedient. They avoided it completely; not liking the way the Lady watched their every step. Even the bigger children from fifth and sixth class who trooped past her every day to their classrooms upstairs avoided her eye. Only twice in the year did she look approachable; at Christmas when a well-stocked crib nestled at her feet; and in May when the children were allowed to stand jam-jars of buttercups and primroses on the sill at the painting's base. Pius put her foot on the first step and started to climb.

Quick, quick, before the Lady gets you!'

The voice was as quiet as if the words had been whispered by the walls. Pius stopped and looked around. The school was empty. All the children were still out at break and the nuns and teachers either on playground duty or across in the convent kitchen having a cup of tea. She gripped the rail tighter and quickened her step.

Don't let her get you!' The singsong voice urged again. *The lady's going to get you!* and this time it was more familiar.

She shut her eyes and felt her way. *Stop it!* She urged, *It isn't fair.* By now she had reached the top and was out of breath. She took her hand off the banister and wiped it along the rough cloth of her tunic. As she did, the beads hanging from her belt rattled gently against one another and she looked at them in surprise. What—?

'Dear Lord,' she whispered, 'what is happening to me?' She touched the wooden beads gently and then looked back at the Virgin's face; surprised at the fear she had felt only moments before. She thought of the elderly sisters with their notions and their fanciful ways – must be her own age playing games with her. Shaking off the shiver that ran down her spine, she folded the crease of her tunic over where her damp hand had left a mark and started down the corridor.

The upper corridor in Kildoran National School had not changed much since the day it was first built. A heating system had been installed and for a while the huge radiators had stuck out like beacons against the darker walls but their colour faded over the years – with time and the touch of damp gloves on winter mornings – so that they now blended into the walls as if they were part of them. Every ten tears or so, the school was painted and for a while the smell of the glossy paint and the high shine made it all seem fresh and new but it never lasted. You could visit on two days, twenty years apart and swear that nothing had been touched in between. Only the photographs gave the clues.

All along the walls on either side there were photographs. The ones nearest the stairs were the newest, their colours brighter and the outlines sharper. Further back, they faded from black and white to shades of grey and even, at the far end, two sepia prints which dominated the wall where the ink cupboard was hidden behind a rail of abandoned coat pegs. One photo showed the front of the school on the day that it opened, and but for the height of the trees at the gate and the shape of the lamp on the street outside, it could have been taken yesterday. The other photo, placed higher on the wall, showed a group of young nuns, surrounded by smiling children. The habits worn by the women were little different from the ones worn now except for the height of the cowls and the veils that all but covered their faces. Like the other photos on the corridor, their frames had a thin layer of dust on the inner edge and Pius tutted at the slovenly way the cleaning was done. An idea that dusting the frames on the upper corridor might be a useful punishment on two counts came to her as she moved slowly along, reading aloud the small inscriptions beneath each as she passed. *Kildoran National School, 1978, Kildoran National School 1973, Kildoran National School 1952 ...* and at the back reached up to read what was written beneath the higher photo, *Pupils and Sisters at the Opening of the National School* – 'Oh!'

She stopped suddenly and peered into the faces of the children standing around the nuns in the photograph. The picture was faded and the faces blurred. There were only forty or so in all, ages ranging from four to twelve and most of them bare footed. Only one girl at the back had boots and stood proud, looking a world away from the three cheeky-faced little boys jostling for position in the front row. The faces of the two on the outside were most blurred and she could not see them properly in the poor light but the one in the middle was unmistakable. He must have been only about four when the photo was taken. She had never seen him like that before, never known his face so young but she recognised him instantly. Clutching the wall on either side she shut her eyes as much to steady herself as to block out the face, not as it was in the photograph but later, much later. Later and older and pale and full of hurt.

And she shook her head to block out the noise. Outside the bell was ringing and the footsteps of more that a hundred children clattered into place by the outside door but Pius could hear none of it. The sound in her head was the sound of water, the sound of a stream rushing about her ears, and the touch of a finger moving slowly down her body as a soft voice whispered.

Slut.

CHAPTER 10

IT WAS PROBABLY A MISTAKE. Patrick would never do anything bad to her. He'd probably just made a mistake. Forgotten who she was in an excited moment – because he had seemed so excited. His face was red and sweaty and he was breathing funny as if he had been climbing a hill and it was getting nearer and nearer the top. And it had been quite dark too. It was the sort of evening when the sun makes lovely colours on the sky as it goes down and the air is still warm after the heat of the day. You feel as if you're the only person in the world and it all belongs to you.

And she had thought that she was alone. Da had been gone since Tuesday and wouldn't be back till Sunday night. It had been a great week, just herself and Patrick. He'd been lovely to her like he always was – took her down to the village with him when he went for the messages and bought her a drink while she sat in the cart waiting for him. Some of his friends had been there too, drinking stout and shouting rude things across to the girls who went past on the other side of the road. Nobody shouted at her – they wouldn't dare. It wasn't that she wasn't pretty or anything although she knew she'd never be a great beauty. She was too skinny and her eyes didn't have much colour in them. They should have been blue but they were pale and shy. Patrick said she wasn't to mind – he thought she was just gorgeous anyway so what would she want fellas shouting at her for. She was his little sister and he wouldn't let anyone shout at her so she just sat there safe, waiting for him to come out. Waiting and watching. There was plenty to watch. Thursdays in Kildoran were busy because not everyone was able to go through to Kilkenny for the market so they came here – and here was far enough. Patrick told her that.

'Plenty to do, *a stor*, plenty to see.'

And so she was determined to see it all – all the people, the animals, the activity – and she'd tell him about it on the way home. He liked hearing her tell him about what she saw, especially if there was a bit of news in it. Like when Toss Meaney died leaving his childless widow with only the farm and her growing reputation as a skilled midwife for company. Everyone thought she would go back to Kilkenny to live with her sister, but she didn't. She divided the farm into three and sold one part of it on the dark side of the hill to the Dowlings and one part on the sunny side of the hill to the Hurleys. She kept only one small plot for herself. Eleanor heard the old woman announce her decision to the gathering crowd outside the shop.

'Nobody to leave it to,' the Widda Meaney explained. 'So I'll just be keeping a couple a' goats to graze and a few decent chickens, and the babbies'll see to the rest!'

Dan Hurley was really pleased about that and was joking that it wouldn't be so long before he'd be naming the hill after himself when Connie Dowling brought it with her in her bottom drawer, the day she crossed the stream to marry his son, Matty. The crowd laughed at that – except for Connie and Matty Hurley. Connie pretended she didn't hear, just kept her head bowed and Matty had looked shy.

His face grew pink too and he said, 'Ah, would you go away with yourself, Da,' but in a friendly, jokey voice.

They were always joking, the Hurleys, always happy about things that were going on or things that hadn't even happened yet. Dan Hurley's horse was always going to win the race; his grain was going to be cut and baled the quickest; and when Mrs Hurley grew big and fat, his family was going to be the biggest in the land and he was going to provide great farms for all of them. Even afterwards, when his horse fell, and the rain had come hard and heavy and everyone had to go to Hurleys' when they had finished their own cutting to help save what they could, he laughed and said how he'd be better able to manage when they had more children to work the farm with them. And he beamed proudly at Mrs Hurley beside him all big and swollen, and patted her huge stomach as if the new size of her was a great thing altogether. Eleanor didn't think he should be putting his hand on her like that, in front of people, but Patrick didn't seem to think it was wrong. He whispered something to Noel Fagan standing beside him and they laughed – a secret sort of laugh like you didn't want anyone to know what the joke was.

Eleanor wanted to go home then. She hated when he drank with Noel Fagan because it changed him, made him sneering and loud. Noel Fagan always changed things, changed even the air in the room so that she felt she might suffocate and he knew how he was making her feel and he laughed. Patrick couldn't see it – he only thought Noel Fagan was funny. She wanted to take Patrick home where he'd not be laughing and she'd not be lonely as if she wasn't part of his life.

But he hadn't left.

He stayed for a few drinks and afterwards there was a row. Jimmy Byrne, who had been in the same class in school as Patrick, went into the grocery side of Fagans to get some stuff and the crowd in the bar had started to tease him about being boring and Patrick, with a crowd behind him, had teased loudest of all. Jimmy got into a temper and said that he didn't care what Patrick Morrissey or any of his cronies thought – Nell Hannigan thought differently. Then he'd turned away and started to walk out of the pub.

At the door he stopped and said in a loud voice so that the whole village would hear, 'Love to stay and drink with you boys but I have things to be getting on with. My fiancée, Nell, and I have to go and see the priest about a wedding.' And then he walked across the street with a smile so wide it divided his face in half and he greeted everyone, even Eleanor, as if they were best friends.

Patrick stayed in Fagans for so long after that, Dan Hurley had to carry him out to the cart and help him in to it. Dan told her to take Patrick straight home and to let him sleep but Patrick stayed awake. All the while they drove up the hill lane Patrick kept his head down, taking great gulps of air every so often and muttered something about her not being worth the effort and how she was tight anyway, little bitch.

'Who, Patrick?' Eleanor kept her eyes on the track ahead, afraid to let him see the sorrow on her face and the shame in it. 'Did someone upset you?'

'Aye, Elly, she upset me all right but she won't again, little fucking bitch...'' and though his voice was all rough and hard there were tears rolling down his face.

When they got home, he went straight to the pantry to pour himself a large glass of Da's whiskey and Eleanor unloaded the cart herself and put the horse in his stable. By the time she was finished, she was sweaty and hot. The harness and bits were heavy and it took her ages to hang them safely in the barn out of harm's way. Patrick usually did that but he was so quiet and angry she thought it best to leave him alone for a while to relax. She'd go down to the stream for a wash and come back up to cook him a nice supper. That'd cheer him up. They'd finish with some warmed brack smeared with butter and then he'd be back to his usual self. He wouldn't stay angry with just her around. Only Da got angry with her – and Patrick wasn't anything like Da. Not anything at all …

At the edge of the middle field there was a place where the stream widened. Underneath a canopy of heavy trees two other streams flowed into it and made a pool, crystal clear and always cold. You could see the stones at the bottom and in the afternoons she sometimes came here to watch the baby minnows that shoaled around the bigger rocks at the edge. It was a lovely feeling, lying on your tummy with the rock warm beneath you and your hand trailing in the cold water. If you kept very still, the little fish would take you for just another part of the stream and jostle through your fingers, tickling as they went.

Her favourite rock was huge and over hung the stream. It was still warm as it caught the last of the sun and Eleanor was glad to see the cool dappled water beyond. She felt clammy from her exertions and disturbed by the events of the day. She undressed quickly and, laying her dress and slip on the rock, eased herself into the water. It felt lovely, cool and clear. Above her in the trees, flocks of birds sang loudly and if she kept very still, she could hear grasshoppers in the tall grasses on the bank. Eleanor lay back in the water with her eyes shut and, spreading out her arms and legs, let herself float safe and carefree in her own secret world.

With the water lapping in her ears she didn't hear his approach. Nor was she aware that she was not alone till a shout announced his arrival.

'Jaysus! Would you look at that! And she spread out like a hussy!' Patrick's voice was rough and his face red and shiny from the drink. He was breathing heavily and she wondered for a moment if he'd run down from the house over the rutted field. Embarrassed, Eleanor stood and, folding her arms across her chest, started to move slowly towards where her clothes lay spread out on the rock. Not wanting him to see her shame at being found naked, immodest, she didn't look up and was surprised on reaching the rock to find he'd got there first. The rock was quite high, almost to her hip and smooth on the side so for a moment she wondered how she was going to get up onto it without making a complete disgrace of herself. Maybe Patrick would go off, back to the house and wait there till she was decently covered again, but he didn't move away. Raising her eyes, Eleanor saw him crouching over her clothes, arms outstretched to help her up.

'It's – it's all right, Patrick, I'll be able to get up myself here.'

'No, you won't. It's too high and slippery. Can't have you falling and hurting yourself, can I?' The quiver of anger in his voice did not match the concern in his words. 'Here, I'll lift you.'

'But – my clothes are there, Patrick. I haven't got anything on. I was just having a quick dip before I made your supper. I thought you were asleep. I thought I was alone. I didn't mean for anyone to see me...'

'Hush,' he was leaning right down now, his arms around her and with no apparent effort lifted her clean out of the water and stood her in front of him on the rock. She thought he'd let her go then but he didn't. As if in a trance, the tips of his fingers started to trace a line down the back of her arms till they reached her hands. She was shivering with cold and with a sort of fear she'd never felt before. It was like the feeling you'd get if you were about to be told a secret you knew already but had never wanted to be party to in the first place. It was like the feeling she had when she heard them laugh at Mrs Hurley and she didn't like it. She didn't like it at all.

'I'll get dressed, Patrick. I shouldn't stand here in the cold like this.'

'Like what?'

'Like this.'

'This?' He seemed very calm now.

'With my – with no clothes on.'

'Why not, what are you worried about? Sure, who'll see you?'

'You will – you'll see me.'

He opened his eyes very wide and put his face close to hers. 'Me? Sure, I'm your big brother aren't I – what harm is there in me seeing you? There's nothing to be ashamed of in the body God gave you, is there? It's lovely, soft and smooth like a little fruit all ripe and ready to be plucked.' He smiled a little as if he'd made a joke and Eleanor could see his chest begin to rise and fall more quickly as his breathing grew louder and more urgent. His hands started to move again up her arms, across the line of her shoulder and down towards the tip of her small breasts. The fear was like a terrible pounding in her head now.

'Don't, Patrick, don't! You shouldn't do that. It's not right. You shouldn't touch me like that.' The tears started to fill her eyes.

'Hush now, what harm is there? Aren't I only showing you how lovely you are? Don't you know I wouldn't hurt you?'

'But you shouldn't. You know it. You shouldn't!' Her hand was on his arm now but he didn't stop. With a quick movement, he caught both her wrists and, holding them high, continued to follow his line down her stomach towards the small mound of glistening hair between her legs.

'Stop it!' She was shouting now.

'Stop it?' Patrick sounded angry. 'Stop what? I'll stop what I please and when. You're no better then the rest. Flaunting your fare to tease and then protesting that that's not what you meant at all. Only pretending to care. Just like the rest and I never knew it. Just like the fuckin' rest. Slut!' His mouth came down on hers, hot and hard and reeking of whiskey. He began to push her back towards the tree, one hand still holding her wrists, the other pulling at her – trying to force his fingers inside her. Eleanor tried to struggle but it was no use. Patrick was a big fellow, broad and strong from years of working the farm and she was never more than half his size. Suddenly he released her wrists and for a split second she thought he was letting her go but his body continued to press hers and she realised in horror that he was loosening his trousers. As he grappled with the buckle of his belt she knew, without ever having it told to her, what was going to happen next. He'd take her and it would be a mortal sin and they'd both go to hell forever. She had to stop it.

'No!' With all her strength she pounded her fists on his shoulders and threw her weight forward. Struggling with the belt, Patrick was not expecting this attack. He lost his balance and fell backwards, off the side of the wet rock into the stream.

Without waiting to check if he was hurt, Eleanor turned and fled up the field to the safety of the house. The stones along the ridges of the field dug into the soles of her feet but she didn't notice. All she could think of was to get away.

The cottage was dark when she reached it. The last rays of the setting sun lay in orange stripes across the kitchen floor, making the corners even darker – dark enough to hide in. Patrick's jacket was flung across the kitchen table and Eleanor grabbed it and flung it around her shivering body. It was warm and for a moment felt safe – like having his arms around her, around her nakedness – around her, all over her, in her.

In terror she flung the jacket on the floor and rushed up the ladder to her bedroom in the loft. As she put on an old shift dress, Eleanor noticed her feet for the first time. On two toes, the nails had been ripped off and the blood was still wet and ingrained with mud and grit. They looked so dirty. Like she was. Dirty and disgusting like a – what had Patrick called her – a hussy, a slut? She'd have to wash the dirt off, scrub it so that the stains would be gone and the smell of his lust cleaned off her forever.

In the kitchen, the jacket still lay on the floor where she'd flung it. He'd be angry about that. Patrick was always so careful about his appearance.

'They might laugh at the state of the old man,' he'd say, smoothing his hair before the cracked mirror above the basin, 'but they'll not laugh at me. The son is cut from a different cloth, they'll say, all right. What do you think about that, Elly, do I look fine or what?'

And he would look fine, right enough. Patrick always looked fine. Always. A picture flashed into her mind of a face – flushed scarlet with drink and shiny with sweat and lust – but it wasn't Patrick's face. Not really. It had his features but they weren't the same. All flared and angry and full of hatred. He'd never hate her. Not his Eleanor. He was so proud of her and she loved him. Without him, she had nobody. She'd never make him angry or do anything to make him hate her.

Another picture flashed before her. Patrick's face, shocked and frightened as he reeled backwards into the stony stream. He hadn't time to cry out, just a frightened yelp as he lost his footing. There was a splash, then nothing. She hadn't stayed to see if he was all right. He hated the water, had hated it since he fell in the river that day when she was little. He'd been fighting with Jimmy Byrne and lost his footing and fell in and they all thought he'd drowned, till Nell Hannigan's father pulled him out and brought him home. He'd hated Jimmy Byrne ever since too but Nell didn't. Eleanor suspected that Nell didn't hate Patrick either. Sometimes, when she thought nobody was looking she'd smile at him, in that slow way she had. She was nice, small and delicate-looking, and when Patrick looked back at her anyone could see he wanted to keep looking, and if she was climbing into a cart or carrying things he would go up and help her even when he was with his friends and he knew they would laugh at him.

Noel Fagan laughed, 'You're soft, Morrissey. You're like an old woman fussin' over her – bit of skirt!'

Patrick would say nothing, only clench his fists and Eleanor would wish he'd just stand up to Fagan, just once have a big fight with him and then never see him again but he didn't. He stood there and did nothing.

Even Jimmy Byrne laughed at Patrick. He didn't like when Patrick was helping Nell because he was her boyfriend and they often went around together. When he saw Patrick coming he always made remarks about how he wasn't good enough for Nell and the two boys would glare at one another while Nell turned her face to the ground and went pink and looked as if she wanted to cry. When they met in the street one day, Jimmy proudly holding Nell's hand as if he owned her, Patrick ignored Jimmy and stared at Nell as if he could see right into the heart of her. And she stared back so long that Jimmy looked cross and pulled at her hand. Then he shouted after Patrick in the street, 'You're a loser, Morrissey! Nell doesn't want you – you aren't good enough for her! Nobody wants you!'

Eleanor burned with rage at this little speech. What did he mean – nobody wanted him? Patrick had lots of friends. He was always going out to meet this fellow or that and coming home long after it was dark. And sometimes he'd even bring a friend home with him and she'd lie in bed and hear them laughing late into the night in the kitchen below. She always liked the sound of him coming home. It meant he was there to protect her if Da was drunk and angry, or even if Da was away and she was alone. She was all right if Patrick was there to protect her.

But he wasn't with her now. The sky outside was already inky and there was no sign of anyone on the lane. With a shiver Eleanor remembered that Patrick wouldn't be coming up the lane. He'd be coming from the other side, across the field that led from the cottage to the small pool where she'd seen him last, where he'd seen her.

Chimes from the clock on the mantle piece behind her made her jump and Eleanor realised with a shock that it was already eleven o' clock. She hadn't eaten since noon and the gnawing hunger in her stomach made her feel ill and weak. Maybe if she ate something, prepared supper for the two of them the drink would have worn off and he'd come back home and be his old self again and the two of them could forget the terrible thing that had happened, nearly happened, and it'd all be like it was before.

Fuelled with this new hope, she moved quickly around the room, setting the fire and boiling a huge pot of potatoes and onions on the stove. Thick slices of bacon soon sizzled on the griddle and as the smell of it filled the cottage, Eleanor's hopes rose too. If he wasn't home by the time it was ready, she'd leave a great feast of it in the pot for him and have a little bit herself and then she'd sit by the fire and wait for him to come in. When it was cooked, she ate quickly and set the larger portion aside. Then she stoked the fire and settled herself on the wooden bench by the hearth to listen and wait. He'd be hungry when he got home, hungry and cold and glad to see her like he always was and they'd smile at one another and maybe not speak of what had happened because it was probably just a mistake anyway. It had to be. He was her protector, her hero, the one person in the world who really cared about her and he would never, ever harm her.

So that's what it was – just a terrible mistake.

The sound of footsteps in the yard outside woke her but it was too dark to see what time it was. The fire had burned low and the only light in the room was from the few embers that still glowed. In the silence Eleanor listened. The steps outside weren't like anyone she knew. Da lurched noisily when he came in and Patrick's step was always sure and confident. This sounded like neither. The step was uneven as if the person were limping and trying not to be heard. Eleanor found the poker and, holding it before her for safety, backed into the corner at the side of the mantlepiece. The latch was lifted and someone stood on the step, pausing there for a moment as if listening for signs of life. Hearing none, he came into the kitchen and felt his way to the sideboard where there was a small tablelamp. He flicked the switch and light from the lamp filled the room. Then he slumped back into the seat she had just left and Eleanor could see his face clearly for the first time.

'Oh my God! What have I done?'

'Wha—Who's that? Where are you?' Patrick jumped up and peered into the shadows. 'Where are you? Who is it?'

'Here, Patrick. It's me. It's only Eleanor.' She came forward to face him and they stood there, surveying each other in silence.

He was wet still, though not the cold wet of the hill stream but wet with the sweat of exertion. It flowed down his face and his shirt was stuck to his body and smeared with mud and grass. On his face and neck there were cuts and bruises and on the front of his shirt blood, red and purple. His face was white and tear-stained and his eyes bulged, bloodshot and frightened. Eleanor felt the guilt, like a great hammer, pound inside her head.

'Oh Patrick, what have I done? What's happened to you?'

'Happened?' He sounded confused. 'Done? What have you done?'

'Oh, Patrick,' She reached out and gently touched the blood stains on the front of his shirt. 'I didn't mean to hurt you like this. I shouldn't have pushed you. I know you wouldn't have done anything to me. I'm sorry, I'm so sorry – will you forgive me. Will you?'

'Forgive? You did this to me?' He looked down at the blood thick on his shirt for a long time without saying anything then slowly his face cleared. 'You did – yes, you did this to me.' He was looking straight at her now and his expression was more confident.

'I didn't mean it; I swear I didn't mean it. I'd never harm you. Don't hate me, please.' She clutched his shirt, sure he'd push her away and then she'd have nobody, but he didn't. Very slowly, he caught her hands and looked long and hard into her eyes.

'Hush now. Sure don't I know you didn't mean it? It was all a misunderstanding, wasn't it? We always look after each other, you and I, don't we? We should never have rowed.'

Absolved, Eleanor let the tears flow freely. He was so kind, Patrick. She'd pushed him away and he hadn't been about to do anything bad at all. It was just a mistake, a misunderstanding, he'd called it. She pushed him into the water and left him there all scratched and bloody – and run away. She couldn't remember scratching him but she had – it was there all over his face and neck and he was clammy and pulled around.

And still he was going to forgive her for doing that to him.

She was so grateful she wanted to throw her arms around his neck as she usually did but somehow it didn't seem right. Maybe she'd better not. In case she hurt him again.

As if he understood her hesitation, Patrick let her hands fall.

'Right,' he said, 'no more about it. You're sorry and I'm forgiving you, isn't that right?'

She nodded.

'Good. So that's it then. It'll be our little secret, just you and me and we'll not speak of it again.'

She should have known he'd make it all right in the end. She touched his shirt shyly. 'Will I wash this for you, Patrick? Wash all the dirt away?'

'Aye,' He seemed tired now. 'The morning will do. You go on to bed and I'll leave this lot to soak in the bucket. Away with you now.'

Eleanor felt she would burst with relief. She'd never be able to sleep again.

'Goodnight.'

'Goodnight, *a stor*.'

She paused halfway up the ladder.

'And Patrick?'

'What?'

'Thanks.'

He didn't look up but in the half-light she could just see his face. Her Patrick. Despite everything that had happened, he wasn't cross with her at all.

He forgave her.

CHAPTER 11

ELEANOR WAS UP AT FIRST LIGHT the following morning. She had hardly slept. Terrible images flashed through her mind over and over. Patrick was lying in the stream, his arms and legs spread out. There was blood all over his face and it gushed in great torrents into the water around him but she couldn't see where it was coming from. The cuts and bruises were on his neck and there was so much blood. On the flat rock his friends stood, all laughing and nudging each other and she tried to call to him, to warn him about being in the water but it was no good.

When she opened her mouth, only Jimmy Byrne's voice came out, *You're a loser, Morrissey,* Or Noel Fagan's, *You're soft.*

Every so often, Patrick would lift his head from the water and look straight at her. *You did this to me* …. I forgive you … our little secret.

And then the hands were all over her, tracing invisible lines, getting nearer and nearer …

Terrified, she bolted upright. It was no use. She mustn't try to sleep. It was just a stupid nightmare and anyway she'd be better off up and doing something so she got out of bed and padded down to the kitchen. The bucket was by the front door, the water black and gritty. Beside it, Patrick's boots lay covered in mud. Rolling up her sleeves, Eleanor set to work. First she cleared the remains of yesterday's fire and lit a fresh one, setting on top a cauldron of water to wash the clothes in. Having scraped the mud off his boots, Eleanor placed them, open and inwards on either side of the fire then, armed with the old washer board and a slab of soap, she started to scrub the stains from his shirt. At first she worked cautiously, expecting from the dirt that it would be torn but it wasn't – just mud and grass and blood. Backwards and forwards she rubbed, backwards and forwards, watching as the small lines of bubbles, which collected and fell from each of the glassy ridges turned from grey to clean white. Eleanor smiled to herself. She'd have his clothes cleaned and hung out to dry and then go and get herself tidy before he got up and Patrick would be pleased with her. She finished the shirt and left his trousers to soak in the soapy water while she spread his shirt to dry on the bushes at the side of the yard. Before the sun rose much higher his trousers were there too and Eleanor went inside to make herself something to eat.

Patrick's supper lay untouched in the pot, so she took one of the cold potatoes and started to pick off the white floury crumbs that clung to its edges. Swallowing was difficult despite her hunger. Her throat was raw and the food rasped off angry skin as she tried to force it down so she gave up and, pouring a glass of thick buttermilk, drank that instead. Through the window she could see the clothes lifting slightly in the early morning breeze, clean and unmarked. It was as if yesterday hadn't happened at all.

But it had. The empty bucket was still sitting beside the sink and as she turned to walk back to the table she knocked her foot against it. The pain made her cry out and she fell into the chair with angry tears in her eyes. Her feet were still muddy and bruised, one toe swelling from the cut where she had torn the nail off in her flight from the stream. Struggling to her feet she limped over to the sink. There was a little clean water at the bottom so she siphoned it into the bucket and cautiously lowered her throbbing foot. The water was still warm so it did little to help. Eleanor shrugged helplessly. She'd be better off with the cold clear water of the stream.

That's what she should do. She'd bind her foot and go down to the stream and sit on her rock and the cool clear water would wash the pain away.

Unbidden, Patrick's voice came into her head, *It's too high and slippery. Can't have you falling and hurting yourself, can I?* and she could see him there, his face red and shiny, his arms outstretched.

And suddenly she understood that the tepid drop of water lapping around her feet now would have to do.

There was no sign of their father all day. By early evening Eleanor was reading by the fire when Patrick came in holding a chicken by the neck.

'Here,' he said, throwing the lifeless bird on the table. 'What do you think of that one, is she fine or what? What do you say to me plucking her and the two of us having a grand dinner for ourselves before himself gets back to disturb us?'

Eleanor looked at him doubtfully. Then she reached out her hand and touched the bird's feathers. They were a rich autumn brown, sleek and shiny and still warm from their owner's last frantic flight. She said nothing.

'Well, what do you say? You like chicken, don't you?'

'Yeah.'

'So – what's up with you?'

'It's just—' Eleanor fought to keep the quiver out of her voice, 'it just seems a pity. She was real pretty, that one. It just seems a shame to kill her.'

'Aren't you the soft one?' Patrick pulled a chair, seat forward, towards him and sat straddling it, watching her closely. 'It's only a chicken, Elly, for God's sake. Chickens aren't meant to be pretty.' He lifted the bird's head and kissed the tip of its beak gently. 'You aren't meant to be pretty, my little one, are you? You're meant to be—' he pouted as if searching for the right word '—consumed!' And he started to laugh.

'Don't do that!' Eleanor jumped to her feet. 'Don't tease me. I only said she looked nice when she was alive, that's all.'

'Well, she'll taste a damn sight nicer now she's dead.' Patrick sounded annoyed and the red colour was coming back into his face.

Eleanor moved to the sink. 'I'll get the bucket for you, will I? And some paper to put the feathers in – would that be a help to you?'

'It would,' his voice began to soften again, 'there's a good girl. I only thought a bit of chicken would be good for the two of us – build us up again after our—' he looked at her closely '—little accident. I still feel weak, you know.' He touched his chest lightly and winced as if in pain. 'There's nothing like a good stew to build you up.' Then he stood and, turning the chair around, sat himself close in to the table and began to pluck.

Eleanor stood and watched him in silence for a couple of minutes. With his head bowed like that you couldn't see the marks on his neck. He was concentrating on his task and as he did, he stuck his tongue out at the side and was biting on it the way you do when you don't want to get sums wrong or something. He was beautiful.

As if he sensed her thoughts, Patrick looked up at her and winked. 'Thirsty work this, *a stor*, why don't you make the two of us a cup of tea? Go and get the fresh water from the pump.'

'Right, I will. I'll just go out and fill this.' And she was gone.

In the yard outside, two large buckets stood side by side beneath the stone wall, cool in the shade. Lifting the lid off one, Eleanor was just about to fill the kettle when she heard a commotion from the house. Someone was shouting and chairs were being thrown around. She dropped the kettle and ran.

Back in the kitchen, chaos had replaced the companionable calm she had left only minutes previously. There were chicken feathers everywhere and the air was full of the smell of those that had landed on the fire. Patrick was backed up against the wall facing their father who was swaying in the centre of the room, one hand clutching a half-empty bottle of whiskey, the other flailing aimlessly.

'What in the name of Jaysus is going on here! I leave the two of you for a couple of days and come back to find the kitchen like the inside of a fucking pillow! And where's that useless slut? She supposed to keep this place tidy – where is she?' He lurched angrily towards the table and clutched at it to support himself while he looked for her.

'It's not Elly's fault, Da. It was my idea to pluck the chicken in here. Elly and me, we thought you'd like a nice stew when you came home. Isn't that a good idea, Da, wouldn't you like a stew?'

'A stew?' Jim Morrissey looked at his son thoughtfully through narrowed eyes. 'What are you playing at ? "*Me and Elly thought you'd like a stew?*" Since when did you two ever think?' And he threw his head back at laughed at his own great wit. Then he lifted the bottle to take another swig and losing his balance, knocked both himself and the bird to the floor. Patrick rushed forward to help him up; Eleanor picked up the chicken.

When he was back on his feet, Jim Morrissey looked at his daughter. 'That's about right,' he said, swaying dangerously in her direction. 'That's about fucking right. Your father falls and nearly kills himself and you save the fucking dinner! Where's your respect, bitch? I'll teach you some respect. Come 'ere to me, you!' And pulling the belt from his trousers, he lurched forward, arm upraised to beat her.

'No!' Patrick grabbed his father's arm. 'Don't you touch her!'

Surprised by his son's action, Jim fell backwards onto the chair. Patrick pulled the belt from his father's hand.

'Leave her alone! She didn't do anything wrong. Just leave her alone, will you?'

'I'll do what I fucking please in my own house—' Jim tried to stand but Patrick pushed him back.

'You'll not touch her. Elly, go to bed.' Father and son stared at each other angrily, Jim squeezing the chair's arm, Patrick slowly rolling the belt. Neither spoke – just stared – then slowly the interest and anger left the old man's eyes and he turned to Eleanor. 'Right so – you're not worth the effort, either of you. I couldn't be bothered.' He pointed a tobacco-stained finger in Eleanor's direction. 'You got off lightly this time, I can tell you. Lucky for you that you have this hero to fight for you – but you'd better watch your step, missy. I've got my eye on you.' Then he slumped back in the chair and started to snore. The bottle slipped from his hand and its contents spilled onto the floor.

'It's okay – he's asleep. You go now and I'll sort this lot out. Go on – go now.' Patrick bent down and picked up the empty bottle and stared at it. Then as if all the spirit had been poured out of him too, he moved slowly around the kitchen, picking up the chairs and setting them straight.

Eleanor watched him. He'd stood up for her like he always did. He wouldn't let Da hurt her. He'd protected her. She'd been right about him all along. She walked over and, perching on tiptoe, kissed him lightly on the cheek.

'You're great, Patrick Morrissey, do you know that? You're really great. I love you,'

He smiled but his face was flushed and his eyes filled with tears. 'Ah, go on out of that, Elly, go to bed.'

She skipped to the foot of the ladder. 'I do, you know.'

He shook his head angrily and the tears splashed on the cold floor. 'Yeah,' he whispered, 'I know.' And he sank onto his knees in the mess of whiskey and feathers, tears coming now hot and furious.

Eleanor shrugged helplessly then turned and glared at their father who was lying, head thrown back, belching whiskey fumes into the thick air. 'I hate him,' she said. 'He ruined our evening and he's made you cry.' She climbed the ladder slowly. 'And I'll never forgive anyone, Patrick,' she swore, 'who makes you cry.'

The kitchen was quiet next morning when Eleanor came downstairs dressed and ready for Mass. Patrick was up already, sitting at the kitchen table, sewing a buckle onto his old leather belt. The room was tidy and Da was nowhere to be seen.

'Is he up?' She asked, pulling a chair up to sit beside him.

'No – he's still out cold. I shifted him inside – the old bastard.' And he beckoned to the door of their father's bedroom. His voice was weary and his eyes were bloodshot. His face looked very white and the marks on his neck more livid for his ghostly pallor.

'Did you sleep at all?' She touched his arm gently.

Patrick flinched. 'I didn't – couldn't trust the bastard to stay asleep. Anyway, I wanted to sort the place out after he made a right mess of it. And I wanted to finish that.' He nodded towards the sideboard where the chicken lay gutted and ready for the pot.

Eleanor looked at it. 'You think it's okay then – he won't get mad again if he sees it?'

'No,' Patrick sighed. 'Nor do I give a damn if he does get mad. I'll sort him.' He looked at her then as if he might read the answer in her face to the question as yet unasked. His mouth opened and closed but no words came out.

'What?' She said. ' What do you want to ask me?'

'Nothing.' He lowered his head again.

'Yes, you do,' she teased him gently. 'You were going to say something.' She picked up the bird and carried it over to the table. 'Was it about this, did you want me to stuff it or something?'

Patrick laughed. 'No, Elly, it wasn't about the bloody bird.'

'Well, what was it about then?'

He said nothing.

'Go on,' she tried to coax him. 'If it's bothering you, say it.'

He lifted his head and the look on his face disturbed her. It wasn't the red, angry look that made him look like someone else; it was pale and frightened and in his eyes she could see herself.

'It's him, Elly. Am I—' he twisted the belt in his hands and took a deep breath. 'Do you think I'm like him?'

Eleanor opened her mouth to say, don't be stupid, but an image flashed through her brain of Patrick's hand undoing the buckle of his belt. Was that what it was? Was he going to hit her with it? She tried to remember where his other hand was but

151

the memory wouldn't come. 'You'd never hit me, would you, Patrick?'

He looked as if he'd been slapped himself. 'Nooo.' The word came out in a long breath.

Of course he wouldn't. Eleanor laughed in relief.

'Oh, Patrick Morrissey – you're a funny one all right. You're kind and nice and you take care of me. He's drunk and cruel and he hurts people. How could you be like him?' She kissed the top of his head and went off to get water for the kettle, humming to herself.

Patrick pulled the collar of his shirt up to cover the angry marks on his neck. 'Kind and nice – how could I indeed?'

A short while later, after they had eaten breakfast, Eleanor went to the door and started to try and fit her shoes over her swollen foot. Patrick had gone outside to put another hole in the belt, which had long since become too tight for him.

'What are you up to?' He asked, coming back into the kitchen.

'Trying to get my shoes on – they're tight.'

'Well, leave them off so – you're not going anywhere.'

'I am,' she looked at him in surprise, 'and so are you. It's Sunday. We have to go to Mass!'

Patrick clicked his tongue in annoyance. 'Damn! So it is, I forgot.' He looked around him as if he was searching for something. 'Look, Elly, leave the shoes off. We can't go today, we'll have to miss it.'

'Miss Mass?' Eleanor was horrified. 'We can't miss Mass, Patrick – it's Sunday. It'd be a mortal sin.'

He snatched the shoe out of her hand, 'You'll do as you're told, my girl. We can't go today and that's the end of it,' and he threw the shoes across the room.

Eleanor started to cry. 'But Patrick, we'll go to hell – we have to go.'

'We're not going!' He was shouting now.

'Why? Why aren't we going?'

As quickly as it had flared, Patrick's anger subsided. He sat beside her and his voice was slow and steady. 'Because we can't – look!' He pulled down his collar and pointed to the marks on his neck. 'See these? It's a fine day, Elly. What happens if I get hot and loosen my collar without thinking and folk get to see these? Heh? What'd happen then, do you think? They'd probably ask me about them and I'd have to tell them, wouldn't I? Because you know I couldn't lie – and then everybody would know what you did. Is that what you want to happen?'

Eleanor shook her head.

'No, it isn't, is it,' and now he was holding her hand and stroking it gently, 'because we don't want anyone else to know. It's just for you and me. So we'll stay here together today and soon it'll all be healed up and we can go down to the village. Maybe even by next Thursday, what do you think?'

She began to nod and the fear was easing from her face.

'And maybe a picnic today? We'll cook the feckin' chicken and you and me will go for a grand picnic and stay out of the old man's way. Would you like that?'

Eleanor smiled.

'Good girl, now don't you worry about it. It'll be okay about Mass – I promise you – it's the right thing to do. There, see? This old thing fits me again now.' He stood up and threaded the belt through his trousers. 'I'll go outside and make sure everything's fed and watered and you get that chicken cooked. Himself won't be fit before noon and we can be well on our way by then. Where do you think we should go?'

'I don't know really.' A picnic was a rare treat. She could hardly remember the last one or even if there had been one before. It sounded great – eating your tea outside with no-one else around. Just her and Patrick – and no-one else around. She caught sight of the marks on his neck and stopped. 'Not too far from home, I think. Maybe we could just go down by—'

'What about the hill above Dowlings?' He pulled her out of the chair. 'That'd be a fine spot. We'd be on top of the world and not a sinner could touch us.'

'The hill,' Eleanor dropped her hands, 'yes, that's exactly right. We'll go to the top of the hill.'

'And I won't hear any more about Mass?'

'You won't.'

''Cause I've said it's okay?'

'Yes.'

'Good girl,' he patted her head, 'and if I say it, then that's the way it is. Now, shift yourself.'

'I can just wear the old sandals then and not bother with shoes?'

'You can – and be quick about it.' He winked at her. 'You can't be hanging around when you have a picnic date with the best looking' fella in Kildoran!'

Eleanor laughed. Suddenly life seemed to be sunny again. Patrick had looked after her with Da and now he was making sure no one else would have cause to criticise her either. Wasn't he great all the same?

And to think he had asked her if she thought he was like Da! Honestly!

The picnic was great. The chicken was ready just after eleven and Patrick lifted it straight out of the pot and wrapped it in a cloth. Then he emptied the juice out onto the yard outside. She wondered at the waste but Patrick just laughed.

'Well, we're not leaving any evidence for him.' He jerked his head towards the house. He was so far gone last night, he won't remember on his own and I'm not for leaving any hints!' He rinsed the pot and left it back inside. He picked up the basket. 'C'mon, you – let's be off!' And away they went, down the lane and over the stile.

It took ages to get to the top of Meaney's Hill and they ran most of the way – or Patrick ran and Eleanor hobbled in his wake. By the time they reached the top they were panting hard and her foot was throbbing, but she didn't care – it felt so good to be there. They sat together, hugging their knees and surveying the world around. Across on the lower hill, they could see the distant figures of Dan Hurley and his son standing looking down onto their farm. Beyond them, far below, the village shimmered and the chimes of the church were blown away by the breeze. Nothing looked real and even here on the hilltop everything was moving. Patrick lifted out the bird while Eleanor buttered bread. It had been too hot to bring milk so they drank water from a spring in the rocks – cool and clear in their cupped hands. Afterwards they lay back in the grass and Patrick told her stories of what it had been like when Mammy was alive, how different it had been then. He had never spoken much about her before but now he talked and talked. His voice was soft and full of love and his eyes looked far away, lost in a dreamy place where children were smiled at and Da was happy. Eleanor never knew her mother and had always pictured her only from the dusty picture beside Da's bed. She looked severe in it – pale and solemn – but the picture Patrick painted was different. In it she was tall and elegant with soft eyes and a great love of learning.

'Da used to tease her about it, you know, when he'd come in and I'd be on her knee and she'd be reading to me. 'Filling the lad's head with dreams, Mrs Morrissey. What good will that be to him, and he a farmer's son' – that's what he'd say, but he'd be only kidding her. He was mad about her, you know—' his voice grew quieter and quieter, '—and then she died.'

'Is that what went wrong?' Eleanor propped herself up on one elbow.

'Aye, I suppose it is.' Patrick was beginning to fall asleep. 'Filling the lad's head with dreams, that's what he'd say, and he a farmer's son.'

'And do you still have dreams, Patrick?'

There was no answer.

'Patrick, do you?'

But he was already asleep.

They both slept and it was cool when they woke. Together they picked the cold meat off and threw the bones for the foxes to find. Then they finished the bread and, picking up the basket, headed for home. As they passed by Hurley's land on the way back, Eleanor noticed a small square of black cloth flapping on the gate. She wanted to go and see if there was anything wrong but Patrick urged her to hurry.

'Come on, Elly, we can find out all about it on Thursday. We'll have to get home now and do the cows before Da gets cross with us again.' And so she'd put it out of her mind and hobbled quickly after him, still warm from the food and sleep.

It had been a perfect day.

CHAPTER 12

THE SKY WAS OVERCAST WHEN SHE WOKE on Thursday. Eleanor dragged herself out of bed and picking up her old cardigan, flung it round her shoulders and went downstairs. To her surprise, both Patrick and her father were already up and dressed.

'Come on then, lazybones, it's nearly seven o' clock. You'll have to be quicker than that if we're to get to the market today.' Patrick smiled at her.

'The market! D'you mean all the way to Kilkenny?'

'Will you whist with your questions, girl and make yourself decent! 'Tisn't a hotel I'm runnin' here with you as Lady Muck lying in the bed half the day!' Her father glared at her.

'Yes, Da,' Eleanor's feet barely touched the rungs of the ladder. Kilkenny! Imagine! They hardly ever went through into the city – it was ages since they'd been there before. Only Da ever took trips that long and she and Patrick went as far as the village.

She pulled on her best dress and found a pair of white socks. Her toe still hurt and the sock felt tight around it but she wouldn't have to walk far. Probably Da would let her sit and watch while he and Patrick did the jobs and went for a drink. The thought of it made her pause. She hoped they wouldn't go for a drink for too long. It always made Da angry and Patrick went quiet and sometimes he laughed a bit too long and hated people and said it. She shook her head. She wouldn't worry about it now. Maybe it'd be great and they'd come straight home. Maybe if they stayed in good humour with her. That's what she'd do. She'd stay very quiet and hope for that.

'Eleanor Morrissey, will you shift yourself! Da's already loadin' the cart.' She grabbed her cardigan to ward off the early morning chill and rushed down to the kitchen. 'C'mon, will you? We've all the jobs done and you're still dolling yourself up,' he tweaked her hair, 'typical woman!'

Something in his voice sent a shiver across her forehead. Eleanor turned on him with a passion that surprised even herself. 'I'm not a woman, Patrick Morrissey – I'm Eleanor. D'you hear me? Just Eleanor.'

He took a step back, his hands held up in submission. 'Jaysus, don't eat me, Eleanor - I'm only teasing you. You're not a woman; you're just Eleanor.'

'That's right,' she said, then seeing his expression, smiled, 'your Eleanor though.'

'Oh aye, none other,' and he brushed past her and out into the yard where their Da and the cart stood waiting.

The journey to Kilkenny took ages. The rain had long stopped but the roads were rutted and muddy. Da cursed when the wheels juddered on the slippery stones but Eleanor and Patrick said nothing. She was sitting in the back; her knees held up close to her face while Patrick sat in the front beside their father. Despite the fact that the clouds cleared early and the day already had a clammy warmth to it, he had on his jacket, the collar pulled high against his face. Around his neck he had a coloured 'kerchief and he looked like one of those heroes you'd see in a book. He didn't look very happy with himself though. His shoulders were hunched and he watched the road very closely as they drove along. When they passed through the village, he didn't shout greetings to the few folk they met as he usually did, just kept his eyes on the road ahead. Eleanor wondered at this but she was glad really. Maybe if Noel Fagan or one of that lot came out, they'd be tempted to go in for a drink 'to set themselves up for the day' and then they'd stay too long and the day would be ruined. Fagan's was the rougher of the village's two pubs and it never seemed to be closed, even in the early hours of the day. Noel Fagan drank enough to keep the place afloat on his own and though Eleanor had never been in the pub side of it, she'd seen often enough what came out and she knew it must be horrible. As the horse neared the pub, she kept her head bowed, her eyes tightly shut and prayed they'd keep going.

Clip, Clop! Clip, Clop! The sound of the horse's shoes changed and her step became hollower. Eleanor opened her eyes and smiled. Hurrah! That meant they were on the bridge and Fagan's was behind them. On they went, past the church and the convent school and out to the open countryside. Patrick seemed to relax a bit more now and even Da was brighter than usual. He was whistling a tune to himself and Patrick turned and winked at her. She smiled, then leaned back her head and dozed the rest of the journey.

Kilkenny was throbbing with activity when they got there. The sun was high now and the corrals of damp sheep steamed in the heat. The air was full of the smell of animals, people and cooking. Da stopped the cart and thrust the reins at Patrick.

'Here,' he said, pulling some notes off a roll he had taken out of his pocket and handing them to Patrick, 'get what lime we need for the whitewashin' and find Benny Faraday and ask if he'll see to mending that roof before the winter comes. Put down a deposit to him and get the lazy bastard to set a date. Make arrangements at the mill for collecting the corn and see if that fella in the office has any more idea about taking you on part-time after the harvest. You'll know yourself what else is needed at the store and you can keep what's over. I'll meet you back here when Murray's closes for the Holy Hour.' He turned to go.

'Hey, Da!' Patrick took the notes and stuffed them into his pocket, 'what about her?' He nodded towards Eleanor.

'What about her?' Jim Morrissey looked at his daughter as if he had forgotten she was there.

'She'll be going' back to school soon, Da. She needs new shoes and stuff.'

'Back to school, eh?' He laughed scornfully. 'New shoes? Fuckin' Lady Muck, I ask you! What does she need with schooling – filling her head with dreams and nonsense. I tell you, the sooner she's wed and off my hands the better. Earn her keep then. Back to school—' He caught his son's eye and sighed, 'Jaysus wept.' And unrolling another note, thrust it towards Patrick, 'I'll want the change of that one, mind.' Then he disappeared into the crowd.

Patrick folded the notes carefully and put them into his shirt pocket. He rubbed his hands gleefully together and winked at Eleanor. 'Right so, Lady Muck, are we off? Shoes first – what do you say?'

'Great!' Eleanor climbed down from the cart and together they headed for Flanagan's, the huge Drapery Store that dominated Kilkenny's busy streets.

Eleanor spotted the shoes in the window as they walked towards the shop, standing proudly at the top of the display stand. They were lovely – black and shiny, with laces and heels that would make you look taller. The price ticket had slipped and was lying face down. Eleanor bent this way and that trying to read it.

'Now what are you doing?' Patrick watched her, a smile playing around his mouth.

'I'm just looking at those shoes. Oh God, Patrick, aren't they gorgeous? D'you ever think they'd be my size? D'you think I could get those ones?'

He looked at the shoes as if considering her questions. 'They're grand shoes, all right. Ma used to have a pair like that. I remember them.' He was quiet for a minute, his face dark and sad-looking. Then it cleared and he turned to her, smiling, 'Imagine you picking out a pair like that! Maybe they'd fit – we can only ask. Come on.' And he opened the door and led the way inside.

Inside, Flanagan's was huge and Eleanor looked around in amazement. Wooden shelves and glass cabinets reached from the floor to the ceiling, stacked with every sort of treasure imaginable. There were boxes of socks, boxes of gloves, handkerchiefs, hats and bicycle clips. There was fabric – bright cottons, soft linens, and rough tweeds that looked and even smelled of country hedges. In large brass containers, black umbrellas jostled for position with wooden walking sticks that were polished to every shade of brown. Eleanor held her breath and looked around. She would have been happy to stand there all day but Patrick was impatient to get on. He ushered her through into the back where steps led to another room, its walls lined with shoes and boots. A small, stern-faced woman sat there. Eleanor looked at her shyly and smiled; Patrick walked straight over.

'There's a pair of shoes in the window,' he said, 'black ones with laces, on the top shelf. My sister here would like to try on a pair.'

'Um,' the woman looked at the boxes high on the shelves overhead. Slowly her eyes scanned the labels on each one and she tutted to herself as she came to the end of each row. Eventually, she turned to Eleanor with an air of finality. 'We have no more of those. They're sold out and the ones in the window would be too big for you. You'll have to try another style.'

Eleanor's shoulders sank.

'She won't.' Patrick's voice was very sure. 'She likes the ones in the window and she'll try them on. If they're too big, she'll not be long growing into them. You get them for her now, please?' And before the woman could say another word, he had sat Eleanor down and instructed her to remove her shoes.

The shop assistant tutted again, disgruntled, and disappeared into the front of the shop, returning a minute later with a shiny black shoe in each hand. 'So what size *is* she?'

Patrick looked at the shoes. 'Oh, about that size, I'd say. What do you think, Elly?'

Eleanor smiled at him nervously, 'Probably,' she said, 'hold on now, I nearly have these off - they're awful tight.' And giving a last pull, finally managed to wrench her reluctant feet free. The onlookers saw what was emerging before she did and gasped. Her left sock was dirty and damp with sweat but the right was a complete mess. It was stuck to her foot and stained with blood. Embarrassed, she tried to hide her foot under the chair but it was too late. The woman clutched the shoes even tighter to her and started to insist that Eleanor take the sock off till they'd have a good look at what was causing all the blood.

'Ah no, it's fine, Missus, really. I only knocked it getting out of the cart.' She looked at Patrick helplessly. 'That's right, isn't it, Patrick?'

He was watching her very closely. 'That's right. We'll be home soon where we can give it a good soak and it'll be grand.'

'Well now,' the woman looked doubtfully at the dark stain spreading over the girl's foot. 'It certainly looks as if there's a lot of blood.' She held up the shoe. 'I don't know that it's a good idea to be putting that into a new shoe.' She looked at Patrick. 'I mean, in case you don't buy it, like.'

Patrick took the other shoe from her before she could object. 'She can try on the left one so. If that fits, then I'm sure the right one will be fine once we've sorted her foot. Here, Cinderella, hold out that other one to me.' And he knelt in front of her.

Eleanor stuck out her foot gratefully and slipped on the shoe. It was lovely - stiff and shiny with room at the top where the cotton wool could go till her feet grew bigger. Patrick pulled the laces tight so that her foot wouldn't slip and then, holding her arm, he pulled her to her feet in front of the long mirror so that she could see how grand she looked. 'They look just fine – what do you think, Elly?'

Eleanor regarded herself very seriously. Even balanced on one foot, she was taller, almost to his shoulder and it felt just right. She beamed at him in reply.

'Right so. Parcel them up, Missus, we'll take the two!' And he handed the shoe back.

The woman shrugged. Leaving the shoes on the counter, she pulled an empty box from under the counter and read the label. 'That'll be one pound and sixpence ha'penny'.

Eleanor and Patrick looked at each other. Then Patrick pulled a note out of his pocket.

'Patrick!' Eleanor whispered anxiously. 'We can't afford those ones. It's okay – I can get another pair.'

'You will not. You wanted those and those are the ones you will have.'

'But Da will kill us!'

The woman was watching them.

'Da won't say a word.' He sounded very certain. 'You'll get your new shoes and you'll look grand and I'll be dead proud of you.' He winked at her. 'Sure wouldn't you be only proving him right, Miss Morrissey – Lady Muck indeed in her fine footwear!' And he held the note out to the woman.

She looked at it. 'I said *and sixpence ha'penny*.'

'You did,' Patrick agreed, 'but that is the price of a new pair, in a box – and you have none of those. These have sat in a window and they're the last pair and they'll maybe not fit the next woman who comes in here and you'll be stuck with them. And you could have had the pound.' He leaned over and put his face very close to hers. 'And I know that Mr Jake Flanagan will be right cross when he hears about that, won't he?'

The woman glared at him and her face was red. Neither of them moved nor said anything. After what seemed ages, Patrick's lips started to curve into a smile while the woman seemed to shrink a little.

'Right so,' she said, her fingers pressing the high brass keys of her till though her eyes didn't once move from Patrick's. 'That'll be a pound to you then.'

'You're a decent woman,' he flashed his brightest smile. 'We'll shop in here again, won't we, Elly?'

Eleanor looked from one to the other. 'Yes, Patrick,' she whispered and she turned to leave. She was at the door before he caught up with her, the shoes in a neat brown paper package under his arm.

'Hold on,' He caught her elbow, 'what's the rush? Don't you want to have a look around?'

'No – no thanks.' Eleanor looked up at the high shelves. Suddenly they seemed to be looming over her and she just wanted to get out as quickly as she could. If she stayed there she thought she might cry. Patrick saw her blink.

'What's the matter?' he asked her gently, handing her the parcel.

'I didn't like it.' She brushed a tear away. 'That woman was cross with you and I didn't like it.'

Patrick said nothing for a moment.

'She was not honest,' he said eventually. 'I saw the price label on that box, Elly, and it was only a pound. She would have kept the sixpence ha'penny for herself. And that would have been stealing, you know.' He shook his head ruefully. 'I'd have been wrong too if I'd let her get away with it. It would have been a sin. You don't want me committing sins, do you?'

She turned to him; he looked worried.

'No, of course not. I'd hate you to sin.'

'There you are then!' He rubbed his hands happily. 'I did the proper thing so!'

Eleanor thought about it. It certainly made sense. If he'd let her, the two of them would be after committing a sin – and Eleanor and her fine shoes at the bottom of it. He did the right thing. And hugging her parcel close to her, she limped across the square after him.

Wasn't he the clever one to spot it, all the same? That woman had been trying to cod the two of them and but for Patrick, Eleanor would never have known.

She would have thought the woman was telling the truth all along.

CHAPTER 13

IT WAS WELL PAST THREE O' CLOCK and still there was no sign of Da. Leaving her in the cart, Patrick said he'd go and have a look in the window of Murray's to see if he was still there. Eleanor pulled off her shoes and stretched out her legs, glad of the opportunity to relax before the bumpy ride home. Lifting her precious parcel onto her lap, she carefully undid the twine and took out her new shoes. She held them aloft and admired them this way and that. No doubt about it – they were the grandest shoes she had ever—

'That's a grand pair of shoes, all right!' A familiar voice broke through her thoughts.

Eleanor turned to see the Widda Meaney standing there, smiling at her. Crooked on one arm she had a basket full of parcels and on the other a basket in which lay a tiny pup.

'The runt,' the Widda said, 'looks too small to live, but that wasn't the only fight he had to put up. Seven in the litter and not a teat to feed this wee lad at all.' She stuck her finger into the pup's mouth and he sucked on it greedily. 'See that? That's all the wee soul needed – the will to survive.' She looked at Eleanor sadly. 'If you don't have the will, then there's no reason for you to be here at all. Poor little Rose.' And she wiped a tear from her eye.

'Rose?' Eleanor peered into the basket. 'I thought you said he was a boy – why have you called him Rose?'

The Widda cackled, 'Oh don't pay heed to me, Alana.' She pulled a strip of rough sacking over the pup to protect him from the sun. 'Not him – Mel Hurley's babby.'

'Mel Hur— oh! Has Mrs Hurley had the baby then? When? A little girl, was it?' Eleanor warmed at thought of a baby to visit but the Widda only shook her head.

'Aye, she had a girl all right, Sunday, but the wee creature wasn't intended for this world at all. Her poor mother had a hard fight to bring her out but the babby had no will to stay. She was barely warm in her mother's arms before her poor father buried her cold in her grave.'

'That's terrible!' Eleanor sank back into her seat. 'Are they fierce upset?'

'They are – broken-hearted. She hasn't spoken a word since and Dan has the life drained out of him into that wee grave. In all my years, I've never known a man to fall so sad and yet, to tell you the truth, we could all see it coming. I've been up to that house every night for the last month keeping a eye on her and Dan knew it.' She shook her head.

'And Matty?'

'Ah, the lad doesn't know what's going on at all. Dan's sent him over to Dowling's till his mother gets her strength and maybe some of her spirit back, God help her. He's hoping the company might cheer the lad up.'

Eleanor nodded. She could still see Matty's face when his Da teased him about Connie Dowling. She smiled, 'Connie will cheer him up anyway – he's going to marry her when they grow up, you know.'

'Oh, please God he will. That'll be a grand day for us all!' The Widda perked up at the thought of a good party. She was as well acquainted with the unholy spirit as Father McMahon was with the Holy one. She patted her skirts and turned as if to go.

'Well, there *is* a wedding coming up soon, anyway. I heard about it last week in the village.' Eleanor was keen to keep the old woman there. She didn't usually mind being alone but Kilkenny was big and milling with strangers. Da and Patrick were taking ages coming back.

'There is?' The Widda turned back. 'Who?'

'Nell Hannigan! She's to wed Jimmy Byrne. I heard it last week in Kildoran. Isn't that great? I don't like him much but she's nice – and she's awful pretty.'

The Widda's face darkened and she leaned close to the cart and looked around as if she feared someone might be listening to their conversation. 'She *was* awful pretty,' she said, 'but she's not pretty now. Lying there with her eyes shut and her body all bloody and broken. I saw her. I tell you, child, I've seen some queer sights in my time but I've never seen the like o' this. That poor lass's future was in her bonny face and there she was – broke – and not only her face lost—' She broke off suddenly, realizing the youth of her audience.

The child was frozen in horror. 'But – how can that be? She was planning to get married last week.'

'That was last week,' the Widda said, still locked in her reveries. She shook her head and looked at Eleanor. 'Where were you since then? The village was full of it and Father McMahon talked long of it at Mass on Sunday. *Evil in our midst*, he said, *though God knows such a crime can only have been committed by strangers.*'

Eleanor opened her mouth to speak, and then shut it again. An image flashed into her mind – they hadn't gone to Mass on Sunday. They'd gone on a picnic. She tried to recall why but somehow the reason slipped just beyond her reach.

'We didn't go to Mass on Sunday,' she said slowly.

'Didn't go to Mass! Good Mother of God, child! What would keep you from the church on a Sunday – were you ill?'

'I—' Eleanor searched for an answer. It took a long time in coming and she became aware suddenly of the throbbing pain in her right foot. Her face cleared. 'I fell, you see, just as we were setting out to go.' The words were coming easily to her now. 'The horse backed onto my foot and there was a lot of blood and Patrick had to get down and he carried me into the house—' she took a gulp of air '—and he tried to fix it but it was very sore and I felt faint and he said I should rest. That'd be the proper thing to do, he said, so I did and it was, wasn't it? The proper thing to do?' She looked at the old woman hopefully.

The Widda Meaney didn't say a word. She watched Eleanor's face very closely for a minute, then she said, 'Oh aye, that'd be the thing to do all right, what Patrick said.' She beckoned towards the cart. 'And is your foot all right now?'

'No,' Eleanor was glad of the chance to be truthful. 'It's not and it won't stop bleeding. There's a pain in it that pushes hot and then goes away and then pushes hot again – look!' She undid the latch and the back of the cart fell open. The Widda put her baskets down and climbed in. Very gently, she lifted the girl's throbbing foot onto her lap and slowly peeled off the sock. When she saw what it contained she looked closely at Eleanor again and nodded. The toe was badly swollen and its tip congealed with blood and pus. She touched it gently and as Eleanor winced, she could see that there was a lot of grit embedded in the mess. 'God spare you, child, and you say this happened last Sunday?'

Impatient with pain and uneasy with questions, Eleanor nodded crossly.

170

'Your brother looked after it for you?'

'He did.'

'He washed it well, did he?'

Eleanor looked up and stared at the old woman. 'He couldn't. He wanted to but I wouldn't let him. It was too painful. Then he said I must, but I cried and promised I would so he fetched the water for me and I tried but I couldn't. I covered it up and pretended. He didn't know. He was trying to do the right thing but I am the one who was to blame.' Now she knew she was talking too much again so she stopped suddenly and shut her eyes.

Without a word, the Widda Meaney climbed down from the cart. Eleanor didn't know where she had gone to and she didn't care. She was glad the old woman with her piercing eyes and searching questions was gone. She knew what she had been trying to do. She had been trying to say that Patrick hadn't looked after her properly, that he wasn't good to her, that he didn't take care of her.

Well, it wasn't true. He had stood up for her with Da and bought her lovely new shoes. Unbidden, a picture came into her mind of a face. It was the face of the woman in the shop and it was full of fear and Patrick's voice was whispering softly, *what harm is there*. Behind him, the water of the stream glinted in the evening sun and it looked very deep …

'No!' Eleanor shot up to find herself sitting in the cart. She must have drifted off to sleep. The Widda was climbing in carrying a small bundle of herbs and a basin of water. She looked at the girl and nodded. Then she lifted the pup out of his basket and laid him in Eleanor's lap.

'You keep him,' she said. 'Don't worry about your Da – he'll agree to it. Now, I'm going to fix your foot and there might be pain. Hold the pup and stroke him gently. He has a great will to survive. If you care for him, he'll give some of his strength to you.' And then she bent her head down and started to work.

For a long time she washed and scraped and though it was painful, Eleanor did not suffer. The pain seemed to be happening somewhere else. All she could feel was the rise and fall of the little animal's breathing and the touch of his fur as she stroked him backwards and forwards, backwards and forwards; all the while the old woman applied her thickened potions and crooned soft words to the angry wound. When she finished, she handed Eleanor a paper in which some leaves were folded and told her how to apply them. Then she climbed down from the cart again. She reached over and with her hand under Eleanor's chin, lifted the child's face to hers.

'Don't be afraid, Elly – you aren't alone,' she said. 'I can do no more for you at the moment but you won't be alone, I'll see to it.' And she was gone.

Eleanor watched her go and shrugged. She was a strange woman all right. Still, she had fixed the leg and given her a pup to own. And she had believed her about Sunday.

And that was the important thing.

The journey home was quiet. Da was in a mood because Mrs Murray said he'd had enough and wouldn't serve him.

'You've had yer fill, Jim Morrissey. It's well past the holy hour and I'll not serve you another drink. Away home with you now. Have you no pubs in Kildoran?' And she stood at the door with a scowl on her face that invited no objections.

Da offered none. Ma Murray had been known to send grown men flying by the seat of their pants and he had no wish to join them. Muttering angrily, he caught the sleeve of Patrick's jacket. 'I'm goin', I'm goin' and aye, we have grand pubs in Kildoran but they're not like this one.'

'No?'

'No,' he said, making sure he was well clear. 'In Kildoran they serve decent drink!' And he laughed loudly at his own great wit as the door slammed just as loudly in his wake.

Eleanor was pleased to see them coming. Da didn't look too far-gone and Patrick was chatting away with him. He nodded when he saw her.

'Hello there! Are you all right? It took a bit of time – things to do – but we'll be on our way now.' He flung a large sack onto the back of the cart, catching sight of the pup as he did so. 'What's that?'

'It's a pup – a present for me. I can keep it, can't I, Da?'

Her father looked at the pup nestling in her lap.

'Another mouth to feed? What do I need another one for?' He looked at the pup more closely. 'Oh, Jaysus, the fuckin' runt! Here, give it to me. It can go in the stream on the way past. We don't need another scrounger.'

Eleanor held the animal tight. 'But Da – the Widda said you'd let me keep it!'

'The Widda?'

'Aye, the Widda Meaney. She said I could have it and that you'd be agreeable. Please can I keep it, Da? Please?'

'What was the Widda doing' here?' Eleanor could see he was losing interest in the pup already. She thought about her new shoes. 'She was just walking past and she stopped and had a look at my foot and she ... '

'Yer foot? What's she looking at that for?'

'I hurt it.' So many questions. Eleanor could feel the panic rising in her again and she looked to Patrick for support.

He was quick to come to her rescue. 'Aye, she stubbed it, Da, tripped. That's why she needed new shoes – couldn't walk in the old ones.' He winked at her. 'And we got a grand pair all right – and cheaper too.'

'Aye, aye, well, enough of your talk.' Da climbed into the cart and turned his back on his daughter. Patrick climbed up beside him and Eleanor breathed a sigh of relief and nestled her pup closer to her. Da seemed to have forgotten all about him for the moment so she was determined to be as quiet as she could and then maybe she'd stay out of trouble.

As the cart reached Kildoran Da's mood began to pick up. Handing the reins to his son, he fumbled around in his pockets and began mumbling to himself.

'Have you lost something, Da?'

'Not at all, I'm just puttin' my hand to a few bob. It's light enough yet and I might pop into Bertie Fagan's for a jar. Are ye havin' one?'

Eleanor held her breath. If Patrick joined Da for a drink, she could be left there half the night and it looked like it might start to rain. But he shook his head.

'I'll not have one yet,' he said. 'You go on and I'll drop this lot home and feed the beasts and the like. Will I call down for you later?'

'Indeed and ye needn't bother.' Da was already halfway to Fagan's door. 'I'll just look after myself. Sure that's all a man can do these days—' and his voice faded as he disappeared inside.

Eleanor watched him go, and then climbed over onto the front seat beside her brother. 'Are you not going for one, then?'

'No – I'll take you home.' He nodded at her foot. 'You'd best get that rested.' He clicked his tongue and the horse started up again.

'It feels fine now.' Eleanor smiled at the neat bandage. 'It's not hot any more and she gave me herbs and stuff to put on it when the bandage comes off. And the pup too. He's great, isn't he? I'm going to call him Finn.'

'Finn - that's a grand name.' Patrick was watching the road ahead. 'And had she nothing to say for herself?'

'Who, the Widda d'you mean?'

'Aye.'

'Em—' Eleanor tried to recall the details of her conversation. Suddenly she grabbed his arm. 'Oh, God, yeah – I nearly forgot! She had a lot to tell - you'd never guess the half of it! Something terrible happened last week.'

'Is that right? What was that now?'

'Well, two things really. One was that Mel Hurley had her baby but it was born dead and the other thing was even worse!' She paused a minute. Though relishing the thought of having so much of the current news to break to him, Eleanor dreaded what Patrick's reaction might be. He always seemed fond of Nell. She took a deep breath. 'Thursday, the very day we heard that Nell Hannigan was after getting engaged to Jimmy Byrne, you'll never believe what happened to her?'

Patrick said nothing.

Eleanor waited for a minute for his curiosity to get the better of him, but when he continued staring at the road ahead, she could hold it no longer. 'She was attacked, that's what! The Widda said her poor face was destroyed with the beating and there was more too – something awful – but she wouldn't say what it was.'

Patrick shook his head. 'God help us, isn't that terrible all right. And she said it happened – when?'

'Thursday, Thursday night.'

'Oh aye. We were at home that night, the two of us.'

Eleanor tried to remember but found she couldn't. The events of last Thursday were all confused in her mind and she didn't want to talk about them. She turned to find Patrick looking at her.

'Well?' he said.

'Well?' Eleanor looked at him blankly.

'Isn't that right? We were at home, the two of us, don't you remember?'

'Em—' Pictures were flashing across her mind but they were moving so fast that she couldn't focus on them very clearly and there was a hammering sound in her ears. 'That's probably what it was all right – I'm not really sure – it keeps moving.'

'What's moving?' His voice was calm and very soothing. 'You're tired, *a stor*. Sure you're hardly able to remember all you have to tell me from today, never mind last week. I'll do the remembering for the two of us. Would you like that?'

'I would.' She was tired all right. Only that this part of the lane up from the village to the farm was very narrow and bumpy she'd be asleep in no time. As it was, she was being jostled around and she kept sliding on the seat and nudging into him. She wished that wouldn't keep happening. He didn't seem to mind – but sure, wasn't he as kind as could be? Still, she wished she'd stayed in the back all the same. She kept her head down and tried to concentrate on the pup in her lap.

After a while, the lane widened a bit and the ride became less bumpy. The two of them rode along in silence for a while, and then Patrick spoke again.

'Is she okay?'

'Who? The pup?'

'No.' He cracked the whip and the horse picked up speed. 'I mean your woman – what's her name – Hannigan, Nell Hannigan.'

'Oh,' and she had thought he had a soft spot for Nell and there he was, hardly able to remember her name. 'I don't know. She didn't say whether she was dead or alive. She only said that Father McMahon called it a terrible evil, or something like that, so she might be dead I suppose. Oh! And I forgot – another thing.'

'What?'

'That's where everyone heard about it – at Mass. Father McMahon talked about it and she was surprised that we didn't know and I said it was because we weren't there and she was wanting to know why.'

'And what did you tell her?' Even in the low evening light, Patrick's face was pale and drawn.

'I told her my foot was hurt and I wasn't able to go and you stayed at home to look after me, 'cause Da wouldn't have been able to, would he?' She reached out and caught his arm. 'That was the right thing to do, Patrick, wasn't it? That was the right thing to say?'

Patrick relaxed his grip on the reins and the horse slowed to an amble. 'Exactly right. Sure your poor foot has been a terrible bother to you. Aren't you a great girl all the same not to be complaining about it?'

Eleanor smiled. She supposed she was. And now her foot would heal up in no time. She tried to remember why she hadn't cleaned it herself properly when she noticed it first but she couldn't.

It didn't matter now anyway. It had all been ages ago and it was over and that was the end of it.

Back at the house, Patrick unloaded the cart and saw to the animals while Eleanor started to cook the supper for the two of them. She was just cutting the bread when he came into the kitchen. He looked tired and strained. Without a word, he slumped into the chair and sat there, staring into the fire. Eleanor poured him a strong cup of tea and handed it to him.

'Here,' she said, 'give me your boots and jacket and I'll put them away for you.'

He eased off his boots and kicked them towards her. Then he leaned forward and pulled off his jacket. She handed him the cup and once he had started drinking, poured milk into her own and sat at the table watching Finn. He was sniffing at a saucer, in the centre of which she had put a thick slice of bread, soaked through with warm milk. Once he realised that there was food to be had, he started to nudge the slice happily with his nose, licking as the drops fell on his waiting tongue.

'He's a grand little fella, all right,' Patrick said, following her gaze. 'As soon as he gets a bit of strength and a bit of sense, we can train him to help around the place. Shep is growing stiff and Da won't begrudge a new mouth to feed if it saves him the price of a sheep dog.'

Eleanor nodded. 'But he'd still be mine, wouldn't he? The Widda said I was to look after him.'

'Oh, he's yours to look after all right.' Patrick looked at her. 'Wasn't the Widda in a generous mood all the same – why did she give him to you?'

'I don't really know. She was cheerful enough in the beginning but then she got into a queer mood. Probably to do with the Hurleys' baby.' She put her cup down and tried to recall the old woman's exact words. 'She said Mrs. Hurley had the baby Sunday and it was a girl and it didn't have the will to live. Then she gave me Finn because he did and she said I'd get the strength I needed from him – I don't know what she meant by that.' She smiled at her brother. 'She's a little bit queer herself really, isn't she?'

Patrick said nothing. He was staring into the fire.

'Isn't she?'

He looked up but he wasn't paying attention.

'Isn't who, what?'

'The Widda Meaney, isn't she a bit queer?'

Patrick nodded slowly. He hooked his thumbs behind the buckle of his old belt and sat forward in the chair, stretching himself. 'A bit queer, Elly? Oh, she's that all right—' And then he was silent.

They both sat there as the light faded outside, lost in their thoughts and not a sound in the room save for the greedy slurping of the pup and the snapping of flames on the hearth behind him.

CHAPTER 14

ELEANOR SAW LITTLE OF HER BROTHER for the next couple of days. Da arrived in, late and steaming as usual and it was as much as she could do to stay out of his way and occupy Finn so that he stayed out of trouble. It wasn't until Sunday morning that she had a chance to talk to Patrick again. Usually they went to the eleven o' clock Mass and often she would have to sit and wait for him while he and his friends went into Fagan's for a jar afterwards. Or she'd get a lift back with the Hurleys and get the dinner ready and he'd catch up later. Those times he'd arrive well merry and often in company. Eleanor hated the raucous laughter and jeering comments of his friends and the way Noel Fagan would brush against her when she was putting the food on the table. He'd step back and pretend to be upset when she glared at him.

'Oh, do excuse me, Miss Morrissey.' And he'd bow to her.

Eleanor would say nothing but the others would laugh as if he'd been really clever and wasn't after doing that a million times already. She tried to avoid him but he had sneaky ways of always being near her. Like the time Patrick told her to sit down and stop fussing and when she went to her chair, Noel Fagan had put his hand on it, palm up, as if he had put it there for a rest and forgotten all about it. She looked for a moment, waiting for him to take it away.

'Sit down, will you!' Patrick's voice was gruff.

The hand didn't move but lay on the chair, the middle finger erect, waiting for her. Nobody else could see what was going on, only herself and Fagan and he was pulling the skin off a potato with the other hand and pretending not to notice.

'Sit!'

'But – he's got—' Eleanor looked at her brother in despair.

Very slowly, and without taking his eyes from the plate in front of him, Noel Fagan brought his hand to the table and slowly rubbed his finger all along the length of it and nodded towards the chair. 'Are ye not keen to sit beside me then, young Miss Morrissey? God, I'm terrible offended.' And he pretended to sob.

They all laughed, even though they knew he didn't mean it and Eleanor sat down, cheeks burning. *I hate you, Noel Fagan*, she thought to herself, *I'll get you back some day* and she stabbed her knife into the meat on her plate. Blinking furiously, she kept her head down and hoped they'd leave her alone now but they were talking and laughing and paying no heed to her anyway, now that they'd had their fun. When she eventually lifted her head, only Patrick was looking in her direction. He gave her a quick wink and nodding towards Noel Fagan, raised his eyes to Heaven. Eleanor smiled. That was okay then. Obviously Patrick realized that the creep had been annoying her and he was on her side. As usual.

But this Sunday they didn't go to the eleven o' clock Mass. Patrick called her early and told her to get her chores done as quickly as she could as they'd be going to the eight o' clock. Eleanor was surprised at how busy he was round the farm these days – hadn't gone out for a drink at all which was maybe why he was in such a bad humour, but at least it meant that he wasn't coming in drunk with his friends. She had neither sight nor sign of Noel Fagan for ages.

'The eight o'clock? That's terrible early! Why can't we go to the eleven o' clock like we usually do?' When he didn't answer, she continued, 'I wanted to see Mrs Hurley and say to her sorry about the baby and all and see was there any news on Nell Hannigan.'

Patrick stopped tying his laces and glared at her.

'Nell Hannigan? What d'you want to know about her for?'

'Because of what happened, you know. Maybe she's still alive and she might be getting better and anyway, the Widda said Father McMahon knows who must have done it—'

Patrick was on his feet. 'Who knows? What d'you mean *Father McMahon knows who must have done it*? How does he know?'

'It was—' Eleanor screwed up her eyed and concentrated as hard as she could. 'Well, she said that he said that it was a stranger in our midst because nobody from around here could ever do anything that bad.' She looked at him. 'D'you think that's right, Patrick? D'you think a stranger came and did it?'

Patrick laughed. 'Begod I do!' He slapped his knee the way folk do when they figure out the answer to a question that has been bothering them. 'I'd say that's the very fella, all right. A feckin' stranger in our midst!'

Eleanor couldn't see what was so great about that. If there were an evil stranger around, maybe he'd come up the lane and if Da and Patrick were out, she'd be here all alone and he might get her. What could she do then? For all that she was quite strong, she was still small and Nell Hannigan was grown and she hadn't been able to fight him off. And what if the stranger came in the night—

Patrick noticed her change of expression. He pulled on his jacket and straightened his tie and went to the mirror to check himself. 'What's up with you now?' he asked, turning his face from side to side.

'The stranger -' Eleanor was nearly too scared to put it into words. 'What'd I do if, if he came here? What'd I do if he decided to come here and beat me?'

'Oh, now,' Patrick straightened the front of his shirt so that it looked smooth and neat. 'Nobody will lay a finger on you, Elly, even if I'm not here. Honest. I'll put the word out that you're Patrick Morrissey's sister and that anyone who lays a finger on you will have to deal with me first. That'll do it – there'll be no stranger bringing his sins to this house so don't you be worrying about it at all.'

'Are you sure?' She was glad of his confidence even if she wasn't fully convinced.

'Absolutely sure. Now, come on and get ready and we'll go.' He turned to face her. 'What d'you think, am I decent?'

'You're grand.' She looked him up and down. 'Except—'

'Except what?'

'Where's your proper belt? The black one you got at Christmas? The leather on that old one's very cracked looking ... '

Patrick cut her short. 'I lost it.'

'When?' Her voice sounded very far away from her. There was something about his belt nudging at the sides of her memory and a picture of his hands on the buckle ...

'Jaysus, Elly! Have you nothing to do but ask stupid questions? If I knew where I'd lost it, it wouldn't be lost, would it?' He ran his fingers through his hair. 'Kilkenny probably, last week – I was trying on some trousers and I must have put it down and some bastard walked off with it. Yep – I think that's the very place. God, you couldn't trust anyone nowadays...' He turned to leave. 'Now would you come on. I don't want to be late. The eight o' clock won't be full and we'll look like a right pair of eejits clattering in if Father McMahon has already started.'

Eleanor shrugged and went to get her mantilla. Shame about the belt. It was a nice one – made him look like a cowboy. She fixed the mantilla to the front of her head and went to get her prayer book from the mantelpiece. They'd better hurry all right. It'd be a divil to be late for mass even if there'd hardly be a soul there to notice … .

She smiled as she came outside and saw him sitting in the cart already waiting for her. Typical! It wouldn't matter to him that there'd be hardly anybody else there. He was always doing everything properly.

Always particular about that.

Mass was sparsely attended as expected. Only a scattering of grey heads and aged shoulders hunched under thick black coats. A heavy blanket of mutterings dulled the priest's voice as it rose and fell with the singsong Latin prayers. Sometimes, his words were completely drowned out by the clacking of Rosary Beads and the murmuring intonations of the old women who hardly raised their eyes to acknowledge his presence at all. It wasn't until Communion time that he seemed to notice Eleanor and Patrick. She slid up the aisle self-consciously, her agility, despite the slight limp, seeming to mock the laboured shuffling of the rest of the congregation.

'Corpus Dei.' Father McMahon whispered, placing the thin white disc on her proffered tongue.

'Amen.' Eleanor remained on her knees to wait till Patrick rose and led the way down the aisle ahead of her. When the old priest said no more but walked back to the altar she looked around, surprised to find that he was not beside her as she had thought, but was still sitting below on the bench, head bowed in prayer. She rose and hurried back to her place, conscious that Father McMahon was watching her. Feck it! He'd be sure to wait for them outside afterwards and start asking loads of questions the way he sometimes did and Patrick would be bucking and it'd put him in a bad humour for the rest of the day. She buried her face in her hands and prayed furiously for a quick escape.

God mustn't have been listening. As the priest gave the final blessing, Patrick and Eleanor stood and waited for him to pass out of the church before they quickly made for the door. As she expected, he was waiting there for them.

'Well now, good morning to you, young Mr and Miss Morrissey. You're not often with us this early of a Sunday?'

Patrick smiled at him. 'Indeed we're not, Father, and it isn't by choice that we're up so early today!' His voice was friendly and jokey. He took Father McMahon by the arm and turned him gently as if he feared others might overhear the conversation. 'It's the da, Father; he's not at all well. You know yourself what the problem is.'

Father McMahon nodded.

'Well, he's been gettin' worse just recently, coming in late in a blaze of drink and fury and then having to sleep it off till the morning is well gone. He was terrible bad last night. It took me an age to settle him and I was worried, I don't mind telling you. He's asleep just now but I don't want him waking at eleven and finding the house empty – or with just herself there to bear the brunt. I thought it best that the two of us would come down now and be well home to look after him when he wakes.' He stopped and looked the old priest steadily in the eye.

If Father McMahon was surprised by the familiarity of Patrick's manner or the unusual show of devotion to his inebriated parent, he gave no sign of it, only smiled warmly and patted Patrick's arm. 'Ah, sure God bless you, son. Aren't you a good lad all the same? Indeed, there aren't many sons would have the loyalty the Good Lord blessed you with.' He smiled at Eleanor. 'You're a lucky lassie, all right, to have a fine brother like that to look after you.'

'I am, Father, thank you.' Eleanor gave a little curtsey. It looked like they could go now. She was just about to take her leave when a thought struck her. 'It's a pity Nell Hannigan didn't have a brother to look after her last week, Father, isn't it?'

The priest's face darkened and he nodded sadly. 'A terrible pity indeed, child.' He wrung his hands in torment at the horror of it all. 'What's the sense in a thing like that happening to a lovely young girl in a Christian land?'

He looked so upset Eleanor didn't know what to say. They stood in silence for a minute as the old folk shuffled out of the church behind them and seeing the priest's downcast eyes, abstained from their usual greeting and went on their way. It was Patrick who broke the silence and his voice was steady and calm.

'She's dead then?'

Father McMahon looked up in surprise. 'Oh, not at all! No, no, she's not dead – though God knows she probably wishes she was.' He crossed himself at the heresy of it. 'Sure what sort of a life can the poor girl hope for now, her face battered and the honour taken from her for ever?'

'What does that mean?' Eleanor looked from her brother to the priest but neither offered an answer. Father McMahon was staring at the ground again and Patrick's face had grown pale and hard. Eventually he spoke.

'And what of the fella who did it, the stranger who came and attacked her? Have they a notion where he might be at all?'

The priest lifted his head and now his face was red with anger and his eyes blazed. 'The very devil himself – whoever he is! He'll burn forever – and 'tis the only justice the poor girl can hope for – for there's little chance the blackguard will be caught this side of the grave!'

'What do you mean, Father?'

'They'll never find him.'

'Why not?' Patrick voiced the question for the two of them. 'Surely she'll be able to tell what happened?'

Father McMahon looked at him sadly and shook his head. 'Indeed she won't, son. God forgive me for calling him so but the blackguard took more than the good of her body. She was unconscious when they found her and though she's woken fitfully since there's not a word of sense coming from her lips. She can't remember a thing, only that she was to be married and she had to tell him something but then he just watched and he wouldn't stop it and she can't remember anything else. She won't say who he is. Her mind is gone. Sure who'd marry the poor girl now? She'll have trouble to bear a child after the damage that was done and Jimmy Byrne is that angry and broken he can barely look at her. No, she's done for and the fella that did it the only one who knows who or why.'

'That's terrible all right.' Patrick took Eleanor's hand and made to move towards the cart. 'And he gets away with it.'

'Oh, he won't get away with it.'

187

Patrick stopped in his tracks and turned to look at the priest.

'God knows who he is. You can't hide from God.'

Patrick smiled. 'You're right there, Father. God knows.'

'And He can't tell us.'

'He can't.' Patrick squeezed Eleanor's hand. 'Well, we'd best be off, Father. Good morning to you now.'

'Good morning to the both of you and my greetings to your poor father.' He raised his hand. 'Say a prayer for her, won't you?'

'Oh, we will all right.' Patrick helped Eleanor over the step and into the cart. 'And I'll make sure this little lady stays well clear of strangers.'

'You do that – it's the best you can do. Say your prayers and look after your own.' He waved them off.

'Say your prayers and look after your own,' Patrick winked at her. 'We'll do that, won't we, Elly?' He was smiling at her and he looked quite happy.

Eleanor didn't feel happy but she answered him all the same. 'Yes, Patrick. We'll do that. It's what the priest said. That's all we can do.'

CHAPTER 15

ON MONDAY THERE WAS NO SIGN OF PATRICK when Eleanor got up. It seemed like he was staying out of her way. Instead of the usual chats while they went about their chores, he was very quiet, busying himself with a million jobs around the farm and keeping Da happy. He worked so hard on the whitewashing that even Da was moved to comment.

'Jaysus, would you look at that,' he said, more to himself than to her, as he wiped a moustache of creamy buttermilk off his top lip, 'he's a worker all right.' He glared at his daughter. 'And a pity more of it wouldn't rub off on you, isn't it? Standing around the place dreamin'. Get on with your jobs, girl. I'll be glad when the holidays are over and the nuns find something to occupy your mind instead of having you standing around my kitchen occupying space.' He laughed at his own little joke. 'That's a good one, all right, occupying your mind instead of my kitchen! Heh! Heh! Wait till I tell himself that one.' And off he went, still chuckling to himself.

Eleanor watched him as he bent over Patrick and told him his great joke. Patrick laughed; he had to. That was one of the unspoken rules in this house: Da made up a joke and everyone who was invited to, had to laugh. He'd never tell her any of his jokes but she didn't care. She was usually the butt of them and anyway they weren't funny. He was too stupid to make up anything that was really funny. Ma had been the clever one – Patrick told her that. She used to read and sing and was a great one for making up jokes. Da could only listen and Patrick said too that Da used to be proud of his clever Mrs Morrissey. You'd

189

think then that he'd have a bit of time for her daughter but Da didn't think of Eleanor like that. She didn't even look like Ma. Ma had had fine features, Patrick said, and her skin was dark and her hair black, like Patrick's. Eleanor's hair was light brown, like what was left of her father's, and her skin pale and dry. She would never be pretty but she was clever – even Sister Teresa down at the convent grudgingly admitted that - and she wasn't one for praising any child in case it made her proud. But nothing Eleanor could do would ever make up to him for the wife he lost at her birth. Especially not her cleverness anyway. Da said that was what killed her mother.

It had been a couple of days before her eighth birthday and it was Christmas. She'd just been given her first proper school report and it said that she was first in the class at sums and spelling and handwriting. Sister Rosalie had sent Eleanor up to the top corridor where the reports were kept in the ink cupboard. She'd dreaded the task as it meant passing the huge painting of the Virgin where the stairs turned and trying to avoid the eyes, which followed you everywhere. Once, Noel Fagan had come into the school and hidden under the stairs when she'd stayed late to help and he knew she'd have to go up to the top corridor so he whispered scary things at her. She'd become so frightened that she ran off and forgot to finish the job. Later he'd come to the house and said she couldn't tell on him because the nuns would be cross with her for being frightened of the Virgin – that was a sin and she'd go to Hell for it. This time, though, he wasn't there. Sister Rosalie told her she was a credit and that she was going to get the best report of anyone in the school. As she handed over the report she told her she was a very good girl and that her daddy would be proud of her.

'Will he, Sister? Do you really think he'd be proud of me?'

Sister Rosalie smiled at her. 'Sure of course he will, child. Haven't you the very gift of your mammy's brains and that must be a great comfort to him. Away home with you now and show him that report you've worked so hard to earn.'

Eleanor was bursting with excitement as she waited outside the Christian Brothers for Patrick to come out. She knew she wasn't supposed to wait there – the nuns would murder her if they found her but today it was worth the risk. Patrick was doing his Little Inter and his exam would be over in a few minutes. He'd had to stay back a year when he failed the Inter last time but he was sure to be all right now. Some of the other boys laughed at him and said he was bog stupid but they were the stupid ones. Patrick only missed a lot of school 'cause of Da and he had to do all the work. He was always telling her that she had to do her best at school and nobody would ever laugh at her and she could be anything she wanted when she grew up. And now she had this wonderful piece of paper that said it was true. She was the best. Patrick was sure to be dead proud and Mother Clement said even Da would be dead proud too.

Eventually Patrick appeared. He was taller than the other boys in his class and always had a little gang with him that liked to listen to his great ideas. They were obviously talking about one now with their heads together and lots of laughing. Patrick was the first to look up and see her.

'Jaysus, Elly! What are you doing over this side of the road? You'd be in fierce trouble if the penguins see you.'

'They won't if you come here quick, Patrick!' She held up the envelope. 'Look at what it says in here! It's a report to do with the tests we had to do last week and I'm after coming first in the class!'

'What! First in the class! Well, aren't you a great girl?' He picked her up and turned to face his companions. 'Did ye hear that now, yeh bunch of bog men. This here is the best girl in the third class at Kildoran National School. And she's a sister of mine. I'll tell you what – there's brains in them Morrisseys, all right!' Then he swung her around and put her on the crossbar of Noel Fagan's fancy bike that was propped up against the wall. 'Here, Fagan,' he said, 'ye can have your bike back later. I can't be tiring my sister's great intelligence making her walk three miles up a hill in the dead of winter.' And he threw his leg over the bar and with a push forward, started to pedal as fast as he could up the street.

'Hey, feck off you, and gimme back me bike!' Noel Fagan tried to grab them as they flew off but his short legs were designed for padding and not for speed and he hadn't a hope of catching them. Eleanor smiled as she saw his face grow redder and she laughed aloud when she noticed Brother Benny come running after him to mete out fitting punishment for saying rude words out loud in front of the Christian Brothers' School.

They were both laughing when they reached the house, though Patrick was red in the face himself by now and could hardly catch his breath. He threw the bicycle down in the yard and went inside with her to see where their father was.

He was in the kitchen, sitting by the fire, staring at a photo of Ma. He often did that at this time of the year 'cause it was nearly her anniversary and he had fallen into the habit of

192

drinking his way through it. He was very quiet and didn't look up when they came in. Eleanor saw the flush on his face and the bottle on the floor beside his chair. She stopped in her tracks and Patrick nearly knocked her down as he rushed in behind her.

'What's up? What are you stopping' there for?'

'Shusssh!' Eleanor whispered. 'He's been having a few drinks. Maybe we'd be better showing it to him later.'

'No, no, it's great news. Show it to him now – maybe it'd cheer him up!' He nudged her forward.

Eleanor looked back at him pleadingly and held out the envelope. 'Here,' she said, 'you give it to him. He likes you better anyway.'

Patrick smiled. 'Eleanor Morrissey, you big coward. It's your report and you'll show your father. Go on!'

'Show your father what!' Their father's voice lurched at them from the depths of the chair. 'Shut the fuckin' door and keep a bit o' heat in the place, will you! Christ, can a man not sit by the fire in peace in his own house at all?' He glared at Eleanor standing in front of him, the envelope clutched in her hand. 'Well, you, what have you done? What are the old bitches complaining about now?'

'They're not complaining, Da. It's my report. I was just going to show you my report.' She held it out to him.

For a minute he didn't move, just sat there trying to focus on her.

'Go on, Da,' Patrick urged him gently. 'It's a great report. Our Elly is after coming first in the class. Open it for him, Elly.'

Eleanor opened the envelope and, unfolding the precious paper, held it out for him to read. Even upside down she could see the line of firsts in the column headed 'place in the class'. He was going to be delighted.

He said nothing. He leaned forward very slowly and let his eyes wander down the page. Then he belched and fell back in the chair. Eleanor smelled the foul whiskey-sodden breath of him and for the first time, felt a terrible anger begin to bubble up inside of her. She stood there waiting for him to say something but he was silent, save for the heavy rasping breath that came on him at the end of every bottle.

'Well?' she said.

'Well what?'

She knew he wasn't going to be happy for her, as Patrick had done. 'Well, can I have it back so?' She held out her hand. 'It's mine. I earned it. Sister Rosalie said so.'

Da's face grew even redder. 'She said so, did she, your Sister Rosalie?'

'Yes, she did.' Eleanor knew she was growing redder too, but she didn't care.

'It's very good, Da. Would you not read it again? Everyone is saying what a brainy girl Eleanor Morrissey is.' Patrick sounded like he was pleading.

Jim Morrissey cleared his throat and spat his venom onto the fire. Eleanor heard the hiss of it and knew that he really wanted to spit it at her. 'Oh I know she has brains, all right,' he said, 'but she didn't get them from us Morrisseys, son. Look at these.' And he held out a pair of huge hands, palms etched deep with anger and fingers calloused. 'This is what you'd get from the Morrisseys – working man's hands. Doers not dreamers.' He sat back again and picked up the report from where it had fallen onto his lap. 'No, she got her brains from her mother,' his voice rose and it was trembling with fury, 'took

194

them with her when she came, the little bitch.' He spat again but this time he didn't bother to turn his head towards the fire.

Eleanor stood staring at him. She could feel the spittle run down her leg but she didn't dare to wipe it off.

'You didn't know that, did you? 'He was shouting at her now. 'But I know all about it because I was there. There wasn't even time to call for Ma Meaney to come and give your mother a hand. Oh no, Miss fuckin' head full o' brains here chose her own time to come and nothin' was going to stop her. All fuckin' night she pounded away and in the morning I was a widower with a young son never gave me a day's bother and a useless screaming daughter with her big head all covered with her mother's blood!' He stopped suddenly as if he had spent his passion and turned to his son. 'D'you see, Patrick? If she'd been stupid she'd maybe have come easier and it'd be different.' His voice was growing softer and he sounded nearly as young as Patrick now. 'Cause it was different then, wasn't it? You remember, don't you?'

Patrick came forward and put his arms around his father. 'I do, I remember, Da. It was very different.' And he was crying too.

Eleanor watched them for a couple of minutes and she knew they had forgotten she was there. Her report lay crumpled at her father's feet and she bent quietly and picked it up. For a moment she wondered what to do with it, then she knew. Crushing it into a ball, she wiped the spittle from her leg and threw both her achievement and his anger into the fire. For a moment the hissing flame rose and then sank and the paper was gone.

'Goodnight,' she whispered, almost to herself as she turned to go up to her bed. It was still broad daylight outside

195

but in her head the sun had already set and there was no more to be done today. She didn't expect an answer but Patrick caught her skirt as she passed him.

'Night,' he whispered, '*I'm* proud of you.'

'Thanks,' she whispered back.

But it didn't matter now anyway.

So now there was Da bending over Patrick and telling him things and letting on he was a great fella. He wasn't. He was just a drunk and a fool and it was little wonder half the village laughed at him and the other half looked away embarrassed when they saw him coming. Eleanor didn't actually care about that. In her mind this foul man had nothing to do with her at all. His features were similar – and only then when he was sober enough not to have distorted them. And he was hardly ever sober enough for that. She heard them laugh again and saw her father slap his son on the back. Acting like he was Patrick's great buddy!

A sound behind her made her turn around to find Finn groping his way into the pot she had left down to wash. He was trying to get at the scrapings of porridge he could smell. Behind him a trail of warm urine indicated those places he had already succeeded in reaching.

'Finn! You little devil! Da'll kill you if he sees the mess you're after making!' She picked up the little pup and shoved him into the makeshift basket Patrick had rigged up for him. Then she started to mop up the mess. If Da saw this he would be only delighted, give him another excuse to rant and rave at her. She was just finishing when the door opened and the two of them came in.

'Eleanor! Come here and make us a bite to eat!'

'I'm here Da, I'll get you something now.' She hid the soaking newspapers under her apron and scuttled to the sink to fill the kettle.

'What's that you've got there?'

'Nothing, Da, I was only clearing away the old newspapers –to tidy the place, like.'

'About bloody time.' He sat heavily on the chair and turned his back to her. Patrick sat beside him but said nothing. He hadn't spoken a word to her since Mass yesterday. They left the church with him in a cheerful mood but by the time they reached home, he was silent and thoughtful again. Da was up, eating a crust of bread when they came into the kitchen and if he was suffering any of the hangover Patrick had spoken of to Father McMahon, there was no sign of it now. He was just his usual self, barking orders at her and urging the two of them to get on with their jobs.

'I didn't realise Da was fluthered last night, Patrick. I thought he had already gone up when we came in from the milking. Did he go out again?'

'Who?'

'Da – did he go out again after I went to bed?'

'No, he didn't. What are you talking about?'

'Father McMahon – you told him Da was fluthered and we had to look after him.'

'Oh, for God's sake, Elly. What are all the questions for? Father McMahon is just a nosy old busybody who wants to know everybody's business.' He pulled his good shoes off angrily. 'Leave off, will you?'

'Get on with it, you two! Out gallivanting half the morning and then coming in here bickering. Give me a bit of peace!'

Da's voice woke the little pup who started to yelp. 'And get that fucking mongrel out of here before I wring its neck.'

Eleanor scooped up her pup and took him outside. Her ears were burning and angry tears prickled behind her eyes. That wasn't fair. Patrick *had* said that Da wasn't well and would be in bed half the morning. He *had* said that he'd been really bad the night before. She'd heard him say all of that and now he was acting like she was the one who was saying it and it wasn't true. She kicked a stone angrily across the yard, remembering too late that her foot was still only healing, and grimaced as the memory was brought forcibly home to her through the hot pain that shot up her leg. Well, she'd show him. If he was going to be mean to her she would just ignore him. That would show him all right. Patrick hated being on his own with nobody talking to him. He'd even admitted to her once that he was still a little bit afraid of the dark.

She stroked Finn's back. 'Well, they can just go and talk to each other, can't they, Finn? You and me will keep one another company and we'll ignore the two of them – see how they like it then!' Her voice sounded very brave but she wasn't sure if she was quite convincing herself. Ignore them. Make them do without her. It sounded like a great idea all right, but in her heart of hearts she doubted if either of them would even notice.

Nor did they seem to. The days passed with hardly any conversation and by Thursday she was dying for a break. She woke early and listened for sounds down below. Outside it was just light and the trees were full of activity but the house was quiet save for the distant rumble of Da's snores. She turned over and tried to go back to sleep. Might as well make the most of it – next week she would be back at school and there wouldn't be time for lie-ins. It took over an hour to walk the distance and now that Patrick wouldn't be going in that direction, there was little hope of a lift. She was just drifting back to sleep when she heard the back door open and someone come quietly into the kitchen. There was a bit of shuffling around and then it went quiet again. She lay listening for a bit until a faint murmuring reached her ears. Whoever was in the kitchen was either not alone or didn't want to be heard. Eleanor lay very still. Who could it be? Da was obviously in a deep sleep and there wasn't anyone for Patrick to be talking to. She froze. The stranger! She slipped out of bed and padded quietly across the room to where the top of her ladder rose from the open hatch. Lying on her tummy, she craned her neck to try to hear what was going on.

In the kitchen below, Patrick was sitting in Da's chair, Finn nestled snugly in his lap, and he was stroking him.

'Well,' he crooned softly, 'you're a grand little fella, aren't you? How do you like it here?' He lifted the pup and holding his head close to his face, moved it from side to side.

'Yerra, 'tis a queer aul household,' he answered himself in a high girly voice. 'The aul fella is nearly always givin' out and the young wan is nearly always givin' in – and there's yerself in the middle doesn't know what end is up.' Then he put the pup back down.

'I think you're right there – how a chap is to stay sane is such a household is a mystery all right.' And he sat back in the chair and started to stroke Finn's back again.

Eleanor came down the ladder. 'Are you talking to yourself, Patrick Morrissey?' she asked him, relief mixed with laughter in her voice.

Patrick jumped and quickly put the pup back down into his basket. 'I am not,' he said crossly.

'Yes you were – I heard you.'

'I wasn't and you shouldn't have been listening. What are you doing up at this ungodly hour anyway?'

'I just woke up,' she said. 'I didn't think there was anyone else about.' He didn't say anything. The two of them sat for a few minutes listening to the noises from the yard. The house was silent; Da must have turned over.

'Patrick?'

'What?'

'D'you ever wish you lived in the town?'

He looked at her, surprised. 'That's a funny question. What'd I want to live in the town for?'

Eleanor shrugged. 'I don't know – I just think it might be nice sometimes to have other people around. Not coming in and asking your business, like, just – there.'

'And what would be the point of that? What would you want them to be around for if you didn't want them coming in?'

Eleanor stood and walked over to the window. She looked out for a moment then turned to face him, arms outstretched. 'Well, listen to this place!'

He listened. 'What am I supposed to be listening to? I can't hear anything – except birds.'

'That's it.' She dropped her hands. 'That's all there is sometimes – birds. Wouldn't you like to be able to hear people on their way to places and things? Just so that it wouldn't be so quiet – with just birds?'

Patrick looked at her and smiled. 'Ah ha! So that's what you're on about! Little Miss Morrissey is done with her sulking and now she wants someone to talk to. Is that it?'

'No, it isn't – and I wasn't sulking either. I just wasn't in the humour to be talking to you, that's all.'

'And you are now?' He was still smiling and despite her best intentions, Eleanor found herself beginning to weaken.

'I might be.'

'Well, I'm honoured. Does that mean there'd be a chance of a pot of tea and maybe an egg or two?'

'Oh, all right then.' It was great to be friends again. She knelt down and started to set the fire. 'And I suppose you'd be expecting toast to go with it?'

Patrick stretched and rubbed his stomach. 'Indeed I would.' He sat back in the chair. 'I'll tell you what – if I had a feed like that inside of me I'd be so full of energy I might even be tempted to take the cart down into the village later. Da wants me to finish the whitewashing and I'm out of lime. They'll probably have a bit they could let me have below and you can buy yourself pencils and stuff for school next week. What day is you go back?'

Eleanor threw her arms around his neck. 'Tuesday – oh thanks, Patrick. I'd love a day out. Will Da be coming with us?'

He pulled her arms away. 'Not if you stop your dithering and get on with the job of making my breakfast. Go on. Get yourself started before he wakes up.' He looked at the clock. 'I'll go out and finish the jobs and we should be away out of here by ten.' And he was off.

Eleanor followed him out into the yard to get water for the kettle. The sun was up by now and, despite the light autumn breeze it was looking like a lovely day. She held her face to the sky and smiled into the light. It seemed an age since they were in the village last. So much seemed to have happened since – and it was really only two weeks ago. She shook herself. Better get on – if everything was done and tidy before Da got up, he would just drink a pot of tea and be off and not bother them and she'd have Patrick to herself for the day. She'd buy her bits and then sit and listen to all the talk and be able to tell him about it on the way home. She smiled at the yard around her. With the early morning sunshine lying on it like that, it looked quite nice. Maybe it wasn't so bad living up here. Nothing ever happened really but at least they had nice days out – and with the prospect of a trip into Kildoran, today was sure to be one of them.

CHAPTER 16

WHEN THEY EVENTUALLY REACHED THE VILLAGE, Kildoran looked as if it was ready to fulfil all Eleanor's expectations for the day. The bus going into town was an hour late and a crowd was gathered outside Fagan's waiting for it. As the sun was hotter than would have been expected so late in the season, most of the women looked hot and overdressed and the men comfortably dishevelled, jackets flung over shoulders and sleeves rolled. Everyone was grumbling about how you couldn't trust the young fellows nowadays and where was the bus? Old Mick Byrne, who had been the bus driver for as long as anyone could remember, had dropped dead of a heart attack a few months previously and the job taken over by his grandson, Jimmy. Normally, Jimmy Byrne was the model of efficiency, especially on Thursdays when folk were keen to get into Kilkenny, but not today. Today, for almost the first time in living memory, the Kilkenny bus was late and everyone was furious about it, except for one.

Noel Fagan's father, Bertie, was in his element. Usually his clientele could be predicted to a man, but today he seemed to have half the village at his door, hot, bothered and, thank God for it – thirsty.

'There yeh go now, Missis. Sure you couldn't be standing there in all your finery and not a drop to keep the heat down! Lemonade, is it? Right so, grand, a lemonade it is … ' and he bustled off, whistling to himself. If the bus didn't come soon, there'd be no point in going to Kilkenny at all. They might as well stay here, dressed to the nines and their pockets rattling with money to spend – and all outside his establishment!

'Mary! Mary!' He called to his wife. 'Come out here, will you – there's people dying of the thirst!'

He was out again minutes later, his face shining and a bottle of whiskey in his hand. Pushing his way to the front of the crowd, he held the bottle aloft and cleared his throat.

'Never mind the lemonade!' he called. 'That's only for drowning thirst and there's more than that to be drinking for today!'

The small crowd looked at him in surprise.

'Ladies and gentlemen,' he announced, savouring every moment. 'You all know I'm no spring chicken?' Ignoring the vigorous nodding, he continued. 'But I'm not past it yet. Here – fill up a glass and we'll drink to the safe arrival of the second Fagan.' There was a gasp from some of the listeners. 'That's right,' he said. 'I've only just found out why me missus is leaving the work to me. She's expecting – there'll be another young one in this house come Christmas.'

'Christmas? That'd be about right – another miracle birth!' a voice called out and the crowd started to laugh.

But Bertie's good humour was not to be quenched. 'Oh, now, stranger things have happened.'

'Maybe so,' the voice continued – I suppose you mean by that that the whiskey's on the house!' And there was a fresh burst of laughter.

It was to this scene that Eleanor and Patrick arrived. They heard the laughter first and saw Bertie Fagan pouring his drink out liberally to all the men – and the women standing around the bus stop, forgotten.

'Ah, young Morrissey! There you are!' Bertie hailed him as if he were an old friend. 'D'you know where that son of mine is?'

'I don't,' Patrick replied and his face was set and hard. 'I've not been down for days – whitewashing – the da has me hard at it.'

'Like yourself so!' One of Bertie's companions nudged him knowingly and the two of them laughed.

Patrick looked from one to the other questioningly.

'Did I miss something big?'

'Yeh did,' one of the men said, 'but herself didn't!' And the laughter started afresh.

Patrick and Eleanor looked at one another. Whatever was going on here, it looked as if a session was on the way. Already some of the women had drifted off, realising that if the bus did arrive, there'd soon be little hope of persuading their menfolk to get onto it – especially as Bertie Fagan was pouring whiskey as if a drought was coming. Eleanor watched them go and prayed Patrick would not join the drinking. She looked at him hopefully.

'Noel's not around so, will I go with you to get the lime? I could help you carry it?'

Patrick nodded reluctantly. 'Yeah – I suppose we'd better get hold of it first.' He jumped off the cart and helped her down. 'Come on, you can get your bits as well.'

'Great!' Eleanor was surprised he agreed so easily but she wasn't about to question it. Maybe he didn't like to go in when it was only the old fellows around. They were in a loud mood. Anyone who was anyway decent was drifting off and the crowd that was left was the hard set. They'd be there all day and not even Father McMahon would be able to shift them. Patrick was better off staying away from it. Together they walked down the street and into the small hardware shop at the far end.

Carmodys looked empty. Patrick opened the door and they stepped into the cool darkness. Old Billy Carmody sat on his high stool at the counter reading a paper. His face was wreathed in smoke from the Sweet Afton hanging from his lip and he looked up and smiled as the two of them came in.

'Customers – and on a fine day like today! That's great – I thought everyone was leaving on their holidays with all the commotion going on down the street.'

'I don't know what it is – Bertie Fagan's celebrating something and the crowd is hanging around to help him.' Patrick smiled at the old man. 'Maybe O'Shea's is closing up and moving out and he's celebrating the prospect of no competition!'

Billy nodded. 'You're probably right there. Now what can I do for you?'

'Lime,' Patrick said. 'I have only a bit of whitewashing to finish and I've run out. Have you any?'

'I might. Come out here with me till we see if there's enough for you.' As they went out the back to get it, Eleanor wandered around the shop looking at the neat boxes of nails and screws lined up on shelves. Some of them were made of brass and shone like jewellery in the shop's dim light. She put her hand out and ran her fingers through the small boxes.

'Are yeh all right there?' a voice called from the gloom.

Eleanor swung around and peered into the darkness. 'Yes, I am, thank you. Patrick and Mr Carmody have just gone to get some lime and I'm waiting.'

'Oh, it's yourself!' Eileen Carmody came up from the back of the shop. She had radishes in one hand and scallions in the other. 'God, it's desperate dark in here – was just out the back pulling a bit of lunch. I can't believe this weather. I thought this lot would be well spent by now but a few cool days, a drop of rain, and then the sun comes up and we're off again.' She smiled at the girl. 'Hungry?'

Eleanor thought about it a moment and nodded. She had been rushing around since breakfast trying to finish before Da came out and she had hardly paused to eat. She rubbed her stomach.

'I am, actually.'

'Well, come on with me so.' Eileen held out her arm. 'If I know my Billy, he'll be using the opportunity to show your brother the details of the crock of an engine he's working on. He has a great idea he can rig the thing up so we could use it! God help him – can you imagine the sight of us clatterin' down the street to go to Mass of a Sunday? Sure he'd be that scared anyone would touch it, he'd never take it anywhere else!'

Eleanor smiled. Eileen Carmody was a kind woman who always had time for her. She'd been a friend of Ma's years ago and she was kind to Da as well, though, like everyone else, she had long ago stopped visiting because if Da was drunk, he'd shout and swear and send the visitors away, she was ready to admit that he was not at all the man he had been when Ma was alive. She was always also a fount of information on every event in the county. Eleanor walked across the shop towards the door at the back.

'You're limping,' Eileen announced as is it was something that Eleanor herself might not have noticed.

Eleanor nodded. 'I hurt it. The Widda Meaney fixed it for me and it's nearly better already.'

'Ah God bless her, isn't she a gifted woman all the same. I have stuff here she gave me for Billy's chest the last time he was bad and it had him right in a day.' Eileen held the radishes under water in a basin and started to shake them vigorously. 'Sit yourself down there for a minute, pet, and I'll get you a bite to eat. It'll be grand for you to have a sandwich you didn't have to make for yourself. Isn't that right?'

'It is.' Eleanor settled herself comfortably in the chair and watched the woman as she worked. She was a big woman, grey-haired and heavy-breasted. Although she had a large floral apron wrapped around her, her clothes had spatters of paint and oil on them. Her face was rosy and framed by wisps of soft grey hair, which she had tied into a careless bun. Eleanor liked it in Carmodys' kitchen. It was cool with the backdoor flung open and all sorts of noises floating in from the street beyond – the distant shouts of the men outside the pub at the far end and the odd tap of footsteps going up the street. Eileen hummed as she worked, snatches of tunes Eleanor didn't know.

Eventually, Eleanor spoke. 'That sounds like a nice song,' she said. 'I don't know many songs myself – only the ones we learn at school – and most of those are hymns.'

'I bet they are – sure there's nothing like a wee song to cheer you up.' She looked at Eleanor. 'Do you know your father is a grand singer? Or at least he was.'

'Da? My da? Was he?'

Eileen laughed at the astonished look on the girl's face. 'Indeed he was. Does he not sing at all now?'

Eleanor thought for a minute then shook her head. 'No, he only shouts a lot.'

'God help him. He was never a strong man.'

Eleanor looked at her, puzzled. What did she mean by that, never a strong man? Sure Da could lift two full sacks when he was sober and not seem to mind at all. She opened her mouth to point this out, but Eileen was humming again. 'Patrick's very strong,' she offered instead.

'He is, thank God.'

'He does nearly all the work, you know.'

'Well, isn't that grand for you? He's the very spit of your ma.' She set a platter of sandwiches in the middle of the table and handed Eleanor a plate. 'There you are, pet. Eat up a good feed of those sandwiches and you'll be the height of your brother in no time. The ones this end have cheese and the ones that end have ham.'

Eleanor picked up a sandwich and bit into it gratefully. Eileen was right. Even though they were only sandwiches, they tasted lovely when you didn't have to make them yourself. She ate the first one quickly and took another. Relaxing back into the chair, she prepared to take this one at her leisure and enjoy it.

'Right so, now is there anything else?' Billy Carmody's voice broke through her reveries from the front of the shop.

'Nope – that's it. How much do I owe you?'

There was a muttering while Billy totted up the bill and fussed around looking for bits of paper to wrap the various odds and ends. Eleanor was about to go and tell Patrick where she was but Eileen got to her feet first.

'She's in here,' she called out to him. 'She's having a bite to eat and resting the poor foot.'

Patrick looked closely at her then he nodded. 'Right so, she's not being a nuisance, is she?'

Eileen laughed. 'Would you listen to the aul fellow! She's grand company for me while you two whitter away your day looking at things no busy man has time for! Will you have a bite yourself?'

Patrick took his change and put it in his pocket. 'No, thanks, Missis. I'll do a few more jobs and then maybe wander down to Fagan's to see what the commotion is all about.'

Eileen smoothed her apron and winked. 'I think I could tell you that myself.' She took a deep breath and prepared herself to enlighten a captive audience. 'Mary Fagan was in here the other day looking for some kerosene and I was pouring it into the bottle for her. I was watching what I was doing very carefully – seeing as there's a chip on the side of the funnel that nobody has mended though he's been promising to for six months now—' she shot her husband a quick look. 'Next thing, what do you know, but I heard the most almighty thump and when I looked around, wasn't the poor woman on the flat of her back in the middle of the floor! Fell right over! Well, I didn't know what was after happening to her. I went over and helped her up and I don't mind telling you, she was a desperate colour. *Are you all right there, Mrs Fagan*, says I to her. *Ah sure, 'tis only the smell of that stuff – I'm grand*, says she to me. *Well now, you don't look it – if you don't mind me saying so*, says I. *Indeed and I don't*, says she, *seeing as I have a reason for it*, and she was smiling like the cat that got the cream. *And what's that? Says* I. *Well*, says she, taking her time about getting to the point—' she took a breath.

'Unlike yerself!' Her husband interjected. Eileen ignored him.

'—*the fact is*, says she, *I'm pregnant!* Well, you could have knocked me down with a feather! Imagine – sure she's nearly as old as myself!'

'She is not,' Billy laughed. 'She only looks it sometimes, having to put up with a blackguard the likes of that son of hers!' he shot a glance at Patrick. 'I hope you're keeping away from that fellow – he's no good, I tell you.'

Eileen interrupted the awkward silence that followed. 'And I suppose it's putting up with you has me so fresh and beautiful?'

'It might be.' He winked at Patrick. 'Remember that now you, for the future.'

'I will – thanks.'

'Would you leave the chap alone, sure he has enough to be doing without gettin' involved with young ones at his age.' Eileen was game for any argument with her husband.

She wasn't going to get one.

'You're probably right. Look at the state of that young Byrne after what happened.'

'The state of Jimmy Byrne!' Eileen didn't give up easily. 'The state of that young Hannigan girl is more to the point.'

'Sure that's not his fault. I'm only saying he's terrible upset about it.'

'And why wouldn't he be?' She looked at Patrick. 'Wasn't it a desperate thing all the same?'

Patrick nodded.

'Desperate.'

There was another silence while the three of them considered the event, and then Eleanor's voice broke in.

'They didn't catch the fellow yet, did they?'

Billy shrugged then, going over to the window, peered out at the crowd at the far end of the street. 'I don't know, all the same,' he said. 'There a queer notion in the air today. Jimmy was here in the morning before he took the early bus into the

211

town and he said that Con Hannigan was after calling him with a bit of good news about the girl. Jimmy was going to call in on her before he took the bus back for the eleven o' clock run and it's nearly one o' clock now and he's not back ye—' He suddenly became aware of his wife's face staring at him on horror '—Oh!'

'Billy Carmody! You useless excuse for a man! Do you mean to tell me you've known a thing like that since the start of the day and you didn't have the common decency to tell your wife?'

'I don't have to tell you everything!'

'You bloody well do, you're a terrible gobshite – oh, excuse me, pet,' she shrugged apologetically at Eleanor.

'That's all right.' Eleanor was enjoying the conversation. She loved it here in Carmody's. Eileen and Billy Carmody were well known for their arguments. They never had a good word to say about one another and most visitors to the shop were treated to a list of the others failings – but it was woe betide anyone who agreed that anything on the list might be valid. She smiled at Billy. 'So, do you think they might have caught the fellow then?'

'I don't know, Jimmy wasn't too hopeful. But maybe if she's improving there might be something to go on all the same.'

'That'd be great, wouldn't it?'

'Indeed it would, pet.' Eileen put her arm around the girl's shoulder. 'Come on with me now till we have a cup of tea. We women can't be wasting our days standing out here gossiping!'

'God, no, go waste them inside – where you'd be more comfortable!' Billy gave a guffaw and winked at Patrick. 'Isn't that right?'

Patrick wasn't smiling. He was fiddling with the package of screws Billy had wrapped for him on the counter. He looked up. 'What?'

'I said the women should go and waste their time inside where they'd be more comfortable – isn't that right?'

Patrick gave a weak smile. 'Yeah – it's best to keep the women inside all right.'

He sounded sad. Eleanor felt sorry for him. There she was, sitting chatting while he did all the work. The poor thing. She wished they'd not go on about bad news and stuff when it'd only be worrying him like that, with him having to look after her and all, but you couldn't help wanting to know if they'd caught the fellow. A shiver ran down her spine. Didn't bear thinking about. She shook herself. Please God they'd get him soon and Nell would come home and be better and everything would go back to normal. She smiled at Patrick. 'Do we need to go now?'

Patrick looked at her thoughtfully. Then he shook his head. 'No – you stay here and finish your lunch. I'll put this lot in the cart and pick you up in a minute. I'll maybe get wind of the news, if there's any.'

'Oh, thanks! And will you tell me about it on the way home?'

Patrick was already at the door. 'I might,' he called back, 'if there's any for you to know. Behave yourself now and I'll see you in a while. Thanks Billy, Mrs Carmody!'

'You're welcome, pet.' Eileen ushered Eleanor towards the kitchen. 'Come on till we have that cup of tea – I suppose you'll be expecting one?' She raised an eyebrow at her husband.

'I will – and a grand high sandwich to mop it up with!' Billy was still pleased with his little coup in having a spot of news his ever-vigilant wife had not yet heard about. 'Is there a chance I might get one?'

'Oh, now, there might be,' Eileen said grudgingly. 'And aren't you lucky that I'm a sight more generous with my sandwiches than some people are with their information?'

'Terrible lucky. Sure I'm a terrible lucky man indeed!' Flattery was a great weapon and Billy Carmody was nothing if not well armed.

Eleanor looked from one to the other happily. It was lovely here. And this was an unexpected treat, Patrick letting her stay for a while. She could happily stay here forever. She sighed. She had been right. Wasn't it turning out to be the loveliest day?

Lunch took ages. First the sandwiches had to be eaten, and then thick slices of buttered brack washed down with a fresh pot of tea. As they ate, Eileen filled her in on all the gossip she could think of. Apparently, poor Mrs Hurley was in a terrible state over the baby she lost and the Widda reckoned that she'd not be likely to carry another one.

'That's a shame all right – them Hurleys are decent people. I've known them for years. Dan even has two brothers priests.' She leaned forward and took another mouthful of tea. 'That's the sort of decent those Hurleys are – grand people altogether. Young Matty was in here with his father yesterday buying paint – yellow – thought if they did the place up it might cheer herself. He's a grand fellow.' She looked at Eleanor questioningly.

'He is,' Eleanor said, 'though I don't really talk to him much. Sometimes they give me a lift home from the eleven o'clock Mass on a Sunday but it's Mr Hurley who does all the talking. He's very funny. He's always looking forward to something.'

Eileen nodded. Then she thought for a minute. 'That's kind of them all the same but what'd you be getting a lift for? Does your brother not take you back?'

'Sometimes, but sometimes he goes for a jar with Noel Fagan and that lot and he doesn't get back till later.'

Eileen's face darkened. 'They're a bad lot, that lot. That young Fagan is a gurrier. This village hasn't seen like of him since his uncle was alive.'

'I heard something about that once,' Eleanor tried to remember what it was. 'Didn't he drink too much and fall into the river or something?'

'That's right. Oh a bad one – God forgive me for speaking ill of the dead – but I can tell you, I didn't feel safe going around with the like of that fellow there if he'd been drinking. It was a tragedy for his family but there were a few of us felt safer in our beds when that fellow came to his watery end. Nearly killed his father, of course, but at least the business stood some chance of surviving being run by the younger brother.' She paused, lost in the memory.

'D'you mean Bertie?'

'Aye – he's a bit of an eejit but he's harmless. All the more pity then that young Noel is the spit of his uncle, he has a temper on him ... '

Eleanor thought of the quiet way he would lay his hand along her chair so that she would be forced to sit on it and then of his face the day Patrick took his bicycle. There'd been a blazing fight but they soon made up and now only she bore the brunt of it.

A fresh shout of laughter reached them from the open window. 'And now there's another one of them on the way! God help us! We'll have to say a prayer it's a wee girl – or if it's to be a lad, please God he'll take after his mother's side of the family.'

'Were *they* nice?' Eleanor took another slice of brack and started to pull the raisins out of it.

'To tell you the truth, pet, I don't know!' Eileen started to laugh. 'There can't be much to tell about them if I don't know it! She's a blow-in from Galway. Friend of a cousin or something, met at the Galway races when Bertie was sent over on his holidays to improve his Irish.' She winked. 'Weren't they hopeful, all the same, that fellow can barely put two civil words together in English sometimes and they were getting him to speak Irish!' They both laughed.

'Eileen! Come out here and have a look at this! The bus is here!' Billy's voice was loud with excitement.

The two of them ran into the shop and peered out the window at the scene at the far end of the street. The bus had finally arrived and only Jimmy Byrne and Con Hannigan were getting off it. The crowd who had been gathered waiting for it earlier were rising to their feet or easing themselves off their comfortable perches on the wall outside Fagan's. Bertie was there, hands on his hips, ready to do spokesman for the delay though everyone present knew he had enjoyed every minute of it. Wives, who had found a niche in the shop, or the kitchen of a friend's house were making their way towards the bus to read the riot act over Jimmy, who would be held personally responsible for the drunken snoring which was sure to keep them awake that night. Betty Flaherty, chest preceding her like a mighty Boadicea, was first in line to do battle.

'Oh, God, would you look at the walk of yer one?' Eileen could hardly contain herself with the excitement. 'She's going to kill the poor lad. I've seen her fell grown men simply by standing close to them and swinging sideways!'

'Eileen! The child!' Billy did his best to sound shocked but they both knew he was as amused as she was.

Eileen grabbed Eleanor's hand and started out the door. 'Come on – we'll go up and see what happens. If Betty gets her hands on young Byrne before we get there, there'll be nothing left to look at! Leave the shop a minute, Billy and come too.'

With a flourish she had pulled the apron from around her generous waist and was trying to tug her hair free of it. She was still holding Eleanor's hand tightly as she flung the apron behind her and rushed up the street, Billy following behind her. They made their way to where the crowd had gathered and the air was fizzing with tension. Eleanor looked around for Patrick but he was nowhere to be seen. The door of Fagan's was swung open and Mrs Fagan stood there, arms folded, looking a bit green. Eleanor smiled at her as she went past.

'Hello, Mrs Fagan. We heard your great news – congratulations.'

'Thanks!' Mary Fagan raised her hand in acknowledgment. 'Your brother is in here if you're looking for him.' She nodded her head towards the dark shop behind her. 'He's had a few. I wouldn't be hoping for an early lift home tonight – I think he might be doing a bit of celebrating himself!' And she laughed and went back inside.

'Right,' Eleanor shrugged. What was he up to – starting so early? She'd be as well off to go back down to Carmody's and wait for him there. Damn! If he was going to be drunk she didn't want to go back with him anyway, not if he was going to be all red and shiny faced and not acting like himself. She felt the anger bubble up inside her. Bloody Fagan's! She hesitated a minute, wondering if she could go inside and try to get Patrick to come out now. Eileen smiled at her.

'Come on; don't waste your energy bothering about that now. Let's see what's going on.'

They pushed themselves into the back of the crowd that was now gathered around the two who were standing on the lower step of the bus. Even with her back to Eileen's soft stomach and her nose pressed into Monica Dillon's back, Eleanor could hear the sound of a voice holding forth with great strength and authority. Being considerably shorter than the others who pressed around her, Eleanor couldn't see who it was. It might be Jimmy or Con – it certainly wasn't Betty. Whatever Jimmy's excuse for bringing the bus back so late, it must be a good one. She started to squeeze her way towards the front. If she could get a good view, she'd know it all and be able to tell Patrick on the way home and that'd put him into good humour with her and maybe it wouldn't be such a bad evening – with him having spent the afternoon drinking and all.

She pulled her shoulders close to her sides, lowered her head and made for the nearest gap.

CHAPTER 17

A T THE FRONT OF THE CROWD, the air was thick with tension. Bertie Fagan was there, hands still on hips, his shiny red face nodding furiously as, swallowing back his belches, he clung onto every word that was being spoken. Betty Flaherty was there too, arms crossed, waiting for an opportunity to hold forth on her own grievances. She was going to have to wait for a long time.

Facing the crowd, Jimmy Byrne's face was stony. From the back his voice had sounded loud and full of authority but up close it didn't sound like that at all. He seemed to be speaking very quietly and his words were clipped and cold. He spoke slowly, each word set in anger. Eleanor craned forward to hear what he was saying.

'—Scars *slap*. The hospital said they could fix the wounds *slap* but they'll never be able to fix those scars *slap*.'

There was a gasp of sympathy from the listening crowd. Somebody asked him a question.

'No *slap* she didn't say. She can't bear to say *slap*. But that doesn't matter at all *slap*. I love her and I'm going to marry her *slap*. No murdering bastard is going to take that away from us *slap*.'

There was another question from the crowd.

'I don't know his name *slap*. But it won't take me long to find him *slap*.' He paused, 'I'll find him easy enough *slap*.' He was quiet then but the slapping noise continued like water dripping cold into the darkest corners of her mind. Slow and steady, *slap slap slap slap* … Eleanor wished he'd stop. She tried to push forward to see what he was doing, what was making the noise. She wanted to ask him to stop. She put her hand on Betty's back and whispered, 'Excuse me.'

Mesmerised by the force of his rage, the usually immobile Betty stepped aside and Eleanor found herself in the front, facing him. He was looking down at his hands.

'You see, *slap* I don't actually need her to tell me what he looked like *slap* or even what his name is *slap*. I have all the evidence I need right here *slap*. He'll not get away with it *slap*. I'll see they hang the bastard!' And he held his hands high above his head. Eleanor peered up to see what he was holding but she was peering straight into the sun. All she could make out was his arm, shimmering in the light and held aloft, something dangled from his hands.

It was long and black and shiny and made of the smoothest leather.

Even in the heat and with the crowd pressing at her back, Eleanor could feel the fingers trace invisible lines down her body, dripping cold from the water of the stream. Someone was screaming in her ears and his hand was on the buckle as it glinted in the sunlight in front of her.

'Jimmy Byrne,' she whispered. 'What are you trying to do?'

There was silence. Jimmy leaned forward and spoke to her very quietly.

'What is it, Eleanor? What is it you want to know?'

The water was rushing into her brain and tears coursed down her face. She opened her mouth and tried to speak. 'I want to know what you're doing—'

In front of her, Jimmy's eyes glinted in triumph and she could feel the crowd part behind her. Without turning round she knew that Patrick was standing there.

'Don't, Elly!' She heard Patrick cry. 'You've got it wrong!'

But it was too late.

The waters of the stream were swirling madly around in her head now and she had no control. Her mouth opened and out the words poured and this time they were loud and strong and everyone could hear them.

'I want to know,' they said. 'I want to know what you're doing with my Patrick's belt.'

CHAPTER 18

'HERE, BILLY, QUICK! I think she's waking up!'
Eileen Carmody's words came to her out of the thick fog that was swirling round in her head. Eleanor tried to open her eyes but they were weighed down and a dull pain throbbed in her forehead.

'Don't touch her – just call the doctor and let him have a look...'

There was a sound of people walking round but it didn't sound like home. None of the boards creaked and the footsteps were sharp and rang in her head. Slowly and painfully, Eleanor opened one eye, the other one stayed shut.

'Eileen?'

'Hush now, pet. You're safe here. Billy and I are looking after you and nobody is going to lay a finger on you now.'

'Safe?' Eleanor tried to focus. Eileen didn't look right. Her face was usually pink and cheerful looking but now it was blotchy and her eyes were red. 'Are you all right?'

'Am *I* all right? Ah, God love you – do you not remember?'

Remember? What was she supposed to remember? Eleanor shut her eye again. Sounds and pictures flashed into her head but it was hard to make sense of them. *Slap!* There was a crowd; there was a noise. *Slap!* She tried to see who it was. She was pushing – *Slap!* Jimmy Byrne.

'Oh!' As the full memory came flooding back, Eleanor shot upright. 'Where is he? Where's Patrick? What have they done with him?' She looked at Eileen and Billy in panic but neither of them moved. Eileen looked as if she was going to cry again. 'Where is he?'

Billy's face was hard. 'Gone.'

'Gone? Gone where?'

'The Gardai have him.'

'Where? What are they going to do with him?'

Billy shrugged. 'God knows – hang him, I hope.'

'Billy!' Eileen stared in amazement at the harsh tones of her husband then turned to look at Eleanor. The girl had lost all colour and was thrown back on the settee with her mouth open. Her lips were working furiously but no sound was coming out. 'Not in front of the child, for God's sake.'

But Billy didn't soften. 'She's no child, Eileen.' He looked at Eleanor and his face was as hard as if he were looking at a stranger – and an unwelcome one, at that. 'You knew, didn't you?'

'Knew?' Eleanor looked from one to the other. 'I didn't know anything.' Neither of them moved. They were like a pair of statues. As if someone had taken people she had known all her life and had made statues of them but had left the expressions off their faces. Everything was wrong. 'I didn't.' She started to cry.

'Shush now, whist your crying.' As if they had suddenly come to life again, Eileen and Billy were at her side. Billy was rubbing her arm awkwardly and Eileen was trying to dry her eyes with the hem of her dark apron. 'Of course you didn't know. He's bad, that one and you'll be better off without him. You just stay here with Eileen and me till your Da comes for you.'

'Da? Why's he coming?'

'To take you home – you're not in a fit state to be taking yourself home at this time of night.'

Eleanor looked around her for the first time and realised why the footsteps had sounded so sharp and hollow. They weren't in the kitchen at all. They were upstairs in the Carmodys' front parlour above the shop. Unlike downstairs, where the floors were covered in matting, the floor here was bare wood and shining with polish. The only covering was a small Persian rug that lay in state in front of the fire. It had been a wedding present from Eileen's rich auntie – she could remember being told that. And it only lay in front of the fire for show. As soon as the fire was lit and there was a chance that a spark might jump the three feet and attempt to land on it, it would be carefully lifted and laid on the piano stool for safety. *And God help the fellow who'd take a notion of sitting in the stool to play an old tune!* Patrick's voice laughed in her ear and she jumped at the nearness of it.

'Patrick?'

'Don't mention that name in this house.'

'Where is he gone, Mr Carmody?' Eleanor caught his hand and tried to make him look at her. 'They won't hurt him, will they – it's all a terrible mistake, you know.'

Billy shook his head. 'It's no mistake and there's no use you trying to cover for him any more.'

'I wasn't!'

They were both looking at her closely now. Eileen's voice was little more than a whisper.

'Then what did you tell him?'

'Tell who?'

'Jimmy – you said something to him and he knew then that your brother was the one he was looking for. You must have told him who it was.'

Eleanor felt the room swimming around. 'But I couldn't have told him anything – because I didn't know anything.' She shook her head and tried to make everything go back to its proper place so that she could focus.

'Then why did you push through to the front? Why did you want to talk to Jimmy?'

It was a bit clearer now. 'I didn't,' she said simply, 'I didn't want to talk to him at all. I didn't even want to hear what he was saying. I only wanted to stop him making that noise.'

'What noise?' She was aware that Billy and Eileen were looking at each other over her head and she felt as if she were up there too, looking down. Her voice seemed to have detached itself and was telling the story all on its own and she didn't even know what it was going to say until she heard it.

'You know,' it said, 'that noise – *slap* – the sound it makes when you let a belt land in your hand and it slides off slowly. And you have to lift it up and let if fall again and when it falls, that's the sound it makes – *slap*—' The voice trailed off. Eleanor felt as if she should step back into herself before it said anything else and caused more trouble for everyone but it started again. 'I know the sound, you see. He sometimes takes his belt off and he does that with it as if he likes the feel of it and it's always when he's really angry. You get to wishing he'd just stop making that noise and get it over with, but he doesn't hurry 'cause the more he makes you wait, the more you know he's going to enjoy beating you in the end ... '

'Jesus Christ!' Their voices in her ear brought her back to life. 'Are you saying your brother's been beating you?'

'My brother?' It was so silly she nearly started to laugh. 'Patrick wouldn't beat me! Patrick looks after me! Da's the one who beats me! He comes in drunk and he finds something that annoys him, something I've forgotten to do or haven't done right, and he gets angry. Patrick always stands up for me and stops him. If Da's *really* mad and doesn't stop on his own, Patrick even goes and takes the belt out of his hand and gets a beating himself. But he doesn't mind that. He says that as soon as he's able, he's going to take me out of that house and the two of us will get a place of our own and nobody will ever touch me again and he'll look—' She stopped suddenly, breathless, as the full realisation of what had happened hit her. She looked from one to the other.

Billy and Eileen were staring back at her, their faces pale and their mouths open.

'I had no idea,' Eileen whispered.

Billy shook his head.

'Was our Patrick the one – the one that did it?' Eleanor held her hands out to them. 'Was he the stranger?'

The desperation in their eyes offered her no answers, no comfort.

'There won't be a place of our own at all, now, will there? It'll be just Da and me – and there won't be Patrick to stop anything 'cause he's gone?'

The clock on the mantelpiece ticked slowly and the question hovered hopelessly over the three of them.

'He isn't really bad,' she whispered. 'He wouldn't mean to hurt anyone. It must have just been an accident. Maybe she slipped and hurt herself and that's why she was so—' She stopped. But there was no point trying to convince anyone. She didn't believe it herself. In her mind she could clearly see Patrick's face as he traced his finger down her body; and smell the drunken smell of him. And she could see the hopelessness in his face when he asked her, *It's him, Elly, do you think I'm like him?* And all the time he knew he was – the very same. Nell Hannigan had been beaten nearly to death with a belt. She shivered. Even though it had been such a hot day and she was lying here with a blanket over her, she was very cold. The coldness was even in her head.

'Can I get you anything, pet?' Eileen's voice was soft like it usually was but Eleanor looked at her as if she had never seen her before in her life.

'I don't want anything,' she said, 'I can look after myself. I'll have to now anyway.' She tried to get up but her legs were shaky any wouldn't hold her weight. Falling back on the sofa she pulled the blanket close to her chest. 'I'll just lie here a while till I'm ready to go then I'll be out of your way.'

Suddenly, down in the street, she heard the sound of her father coming to get her. He was ranting but she wasn't afraid. There was no Patrick to protect her any more so she would just have to protect herself. She looked at Billy. 'You can send him away – I'm not going with him. I'm too tired and my head's too sore. He'll have to go and look after himself too. I need to sleep now.' And she lay down with her back to the two of them and shut her eyes.

Billy and Eileen Carmody looked at the small figure curled in a tight ball on their good settee. Apart from the bruise that was welling over her eye from when she had fallen as the crowd surged round her to grab her brother, she looked like any other little girl, asleep and dreaming.

'You were right there, all the same, Billy,' Eileen whispered, 'she's not a child.' The sound of banging on the door of the shop reached them. Curling herself tighter, Eleanor shuddered and turned over. 'She can't go back with him. What are we to do with her?'

Billy shrugged. 'We'll do nothing. She can stay here till a place is found for her then she'll have to go.'

'We can't send her away, Billy. We're probably the only friends the poor child has in the world.'

'Aye, and we'd be no friends to her keeping her here after what happened today. Think about it, Eileen. If we hadn't pulled her out, the lot of them would have gone for her too.' The banging below was growing louder. 'Ignore it. He'll have the whole village on him in a minute. He's tarred with the same brush – and he'll get what punishment he deserves.'

Eileen tucked the blanket around Eleanor. 'But she doesn't, Billy. She's never had a chance.'

'And she won't get one here.' He held up his hand and Eileen knew that the discussion was nearly over. 'No, a stor, there's no point in talking about it any more. If that child is to have any sort of a future, she's not going to have it here. She has to get as far away as she can and find a new life for herself. If she has any sense, she'll understand that. Folk have very long memories and something like this won't be forgotten or forgiven for a long, long time. You mark my words – the Morrisseys are finished in Kildoran.' He helped his wife to her feet and together they went down to the kitchen to make a pot of tea and maybe a sandwich and then wait.

They wouldn't have to wait too long, with the racket that fellow was making – all they had to do was sit quiet and say nothing.

And that was what they did.

For two weeks Eleanor was closeted and cosseted in Carmodys' warm parlour. Billy and Eileen were careful not to let anyone know she was there and so she was not allowed to talk to anyone or even go to the window to look out at the street below. At first it had felt safe but the feeling soon turned sour. Slowly the warmth of her haven became stifling and she felt that if she didn't escape she would suffocate. She'd asked Eileen if she could go out the back for a minute but Eileen had turned a worried face towards her.

'Ah God pet, I don't know if that's a good idea.'

'Why not?'

Eileen looked uncomfortable, unwilling to upset the girl any more then she was upset already. 'It just might be a bit soon – folk might want to talk to you – you need to get your strength up a bit more yet.'

'Why would they want to talk to me? I didn't do anything. Why can't I go home? I have to check on Finn, make sure he's all right. I've been away ages and Da could have done anything to him by now.'

But Eileen just looked at her hopelessly. 'I don't think it's a good idea for you to be out and about at all yet. Will you not stay a wee while more – till your Da calms down or we can be sure he's in Kilkenny for a while and then we'll go and get your pet or anything else you need?'

Eleanor shrugged. There was no point anyway. Finn was probably long gone by now, maybe even back to the Widda's. She hoped so but as the days passed even that hope faded. Billy and Eileen were so kind and probed her with questions. What would she like to do now? Where would she like to go? Did she have any relatives she could think of that might be able to help? The last question filled her with surprise. Relatives? She'd never thought of relatives. There was an auntie, a sister of Mammy's who used to come a long time ago but Da got cross with her for something and sent her off. And there was a man, a tall man who came once and he and Da stayed up late and talked and laughed about 'them days' but in the morning he was gone and she hadn't seen him again either. And then there was only herself and Patrick and Da – and now Patrick was gone and there was only Da.

Da. Her father, the only person she could think of who was related to her and might be wondering where she was. She looked at Eileen. What if Eileen was wrong and Da was only in a state 'cause she was gone as well and she was all he had left? Maybe he would be glad to have her home now that there was only the two of them. Maybe ...

'What are you thinking about, pet? Don't be worrying yourself about anything now, sure you won't? You just stay here with Billy and me till we sort out what's best for you to do.'

Eleanor looked at her blankly. She lay back in the chair while Eileen fixed a blanket over her knees as if keeping out the cold would be the solution to all her problems! She nodded meekly and shut her eyes.

Eileen stood and looked at her for a few moments until, assuming she had gone to sleep, she crept out of the room and shut the door behind her. Eleanor listened to her heavy step on the stair then she threw back the stifling cover and opening the door quietly went to the top of the stairs to listen.

In the kitchen below, Eileen and Billy were discussing her in hushed voices. It was impossible to hear the whole conversation but snatches of it reached her. First Billy's voice *can't do any more here ... have to go*. And Eileen, sounding less certain *convent ... send her away*. Then there was the clatter of teacups and Eileen pottering around looking for her coat and umbrella. Eleanor heard her boots on the stone shop floor and the tinkle of the bell as she opened the front door and went out. She sneaked back into the parlour and watched Eileen bend into the rain as she made her way towards the convent to arrange to send her away. Well, that would be grand all right! She'd be stuck into the convent as a servant like one of those poor abandoned children they were always collecting money for in school and she'd have to live on charity and second-hand clothes for the rest of her life. She looked at the dress Eileen had so carefully ironed for her early this morning. It was nice. It was green and had a pattern of little yellow flowers on it. It was her best dress. Patrick bought it for her when he won lots of money on the horses once. *There you are now, aren't you the finest young one in the village! All the fellows will want to take you out now!* And he had offered her his arm as if the two of them were real swanky and not just ordinary.

And not just ordinary.

That was the very saddest bit of all, wasn't it? Then, just ordinary was all she was; now, just ordinary was more than she could ever hope to be.

The sadness of it swept over her in a great wave and for the first time since she had come here, Eleanor felt free to cry. Big tears rolled down her face and fell in splashes on the front of her dress and onto her lap. Through her tears she watched the patterns they were making and made no effort to stem their flow. For what seemed to her like ages she sat there and cried. She cried for Patrick and all his pride and stupidity; she cried for Da and all his raging anger; and she cried for herself – poor little Eleanor Morrissey who never really stood a chance since the day she came into the world with her dead mother's blood on her big brainy head. And now she'd end up in other people's cast-offs, because there was no one wanted her and no one she belonged to.

Eventually, the tears stopped all by themselves. Eleanor screwed up her face but nothing else came. She felt dry inside. A shudder shook her body and the last of the tears fell off her cheek. That was it then. There was nothing left to cry for and nothing anyone could do to her any more. From the shop below she could hear Billy sorting out his boxes, counting out his stock and tearing the neat little squares of brown paper he used to wrap the smaller orders. Dan Hurley was there too – looking for bits to mend an old dresser that he and Matty were going to do up.

There was no noise from the kitchen so Eileen mustn't be back yet. Eleanor went to the window and looked out. The sky was still gloomy and it was raining heavily. The clock in the parlour hadn't been wound because Eileen had been worried its chiming would waken her in the night, so it was impossible to tell how long she had been sitting there. She got up and, taking the blanket from the chair, threw it over her head. Even if it didn't keep her dry for long, it would make it harder for anyone to spot who she was, if anyone was bothered to be out on a day like this. Creeping down the stairs, she could hear Billy muttering to himself as the wind caught his swinging sign outside and threw it on its face. She knew he'd stuff his glasses into his top pocket to keep them dry before shuffling blindly outside to fix it up again.

As soon as he opened the front door, Eleanor made a dash for the back one. If she could get to the end of the lane behind the shop without being seen it would be easy enough to make it to the road. After that it was just a case of staying behind the hedges and out of sight of any travellers. She'd be able to travel for miles that way. Pulling the blanket tight around her head, she pulled the latch, the door swung open and she was off.

She was on the road at least ten minutes before the realization of what she had done hit her. The rain lashed in her face, and though she was cold and wet she was glad of the feel of it. She had run away. She had run away from the prospect of being sent away and now she was on the road to somewhere. She needn't have worried about being seen. The rain was so heavy there wasn't a soul in sight so there was no need for her to stay behind the hedges. The blanket was soaked through and growing heavier by the minute so she shrugged it off into the ditch and walked on, unhindered. Although it was still early autumn, there was one of those winds that blows straight into your bones and finds any last bit of warmth that's hiding there. Eleanor knew she was cold but she didn't actually mind. It was great to be free. There wasn't anyone looking after her and no one she had to be grateful to. There was just herself. With a shout she started to run.

'I'm free!' she shouted to the rain, and splashed into the deep puddles that littered the road. This was the life.

Suddenly, Eleanor saw someone walking down the road in her direction. They were still at some distance so it was hard to see who it was. Eleanor jumped into the cover of the hedge and crouched there, waiting. For what seemed like ages, the figure moved slowly towards her. It was short and hunched and didn't seem to have noticed her at all. As it came closer, Eleanor realized who it was – the Widda Meaney! Of course. She was the only person who'd choose to be out on a day like this. She had all sorts of ideas about the best time to pick herbs and wild flowers for her 'pagan potions' as Da called them. Eleanor smiled to herself. Maybe he was right about that anyway. You'd have to be mad to go out in this unless you had to. Slowly, the Widda moved away and Eleanor crept out of her hiding place and continued on her journey. She was almost at the Hurleys' gate and then it'd only be another hundred yards or so before she reached the lane that led up the hill to the house. She ran as fast and as low as she could past the gate and kept running till she reached the turning for the lane. Made it! She looked up and down the road to check but there was no one in sight. It was growing darker so she'd have to hurry.

The lane was pitted and full of muddy puddles but Eleanor hardly noticed. 'Come on, come on,' she urged her freezing feet. 'If you two don't lift yourselves, it'll be night before we're there and then there'll be trouble.'

Her feet made no response. As if propelled by a force outside of herself, they just kept on walking, *left, right, left, right*, on and on up the hill to where the house was waiting for her, *left, right, left, right*, got to get there soon, *left, right* ...

And then she was there.

With the chill of the rain and something close to terror, Eleanor stood looking at the house she had called home for as long as she could remember. For no reason that she could fathom, the place didn't look familiar to her at all. She had always assumed it was a small house, neat and sturdy but it didn't look small now. The rain was lashing hard on its windows and even from the gate she could hear them rattle in protest and there was a low sort of hum in the air all around her. She walked slowly around to the yard and felt a moment of surprise to see that the back door was closed and there was no light from inside. There was no reason why it should be any different really, seeing as she and Patrick had been away, but for a moment she had thought that the door might be opened, waiting for her, and there might be a light on inside and maybe the fire lit.

But there was nothing. The house was dark and empty and there was no sign of life anywhere. So that was it then. Da was away and Finn must have left and gone back to the Widda's. Now that she had got here she was too tired and cold to do any more. She didn't want to be on her own but it was too far to walk back down to the village tonight. And anyway it was growing dark. She'd be as well to go inside and light a fire and change into something dry. Then she'd maybe have a bite to eat and go to bed. It should have stopped raining in the morning and she could get a bag packed with her own things before she headed back down to whatever future the convent might offer. Pushing her hair out of her eyes she started to walk towards the door.

As she neared it, the humming was louder like a warning inside her head. By the time her hand was on the latch, it was roaring in her ears. Deafened by the force of it she pushed the door open and stood on the threshold and stared at the sight. She wasn't sure what she had expected to see – her father maybe, but not this.

The walls of what had once been the kitchen were charred and where there had been a ceiling the rain fell mocking on blackened beams. She thought she could hear laughter but there was no one there and she knew if she looked hard enough, she'd find what was left of Finn. A pile of cloth was still smouldering in the fireplace and from the ragged pieces that had escaped the flame she could recognize her clothes. Every stitch, destroyed as if she should never have existed.

At the end of the lane below, Matty Hurley was the first to hear the screams. He had gone out to the gate to look out for his Da coming home from the village. It was growing dark and he was hoping they'd get a chance to work on the dresser before the light failed. As he came out of the house, he thought he saw something flash past the gate. Funny that – not like a fox to be out in this sort of weather. Before he could give it another thought, he heard his da shout to him and turned to see him in the cart with two others. The man was Billy Carmody and as they came closer, he saw that the other was the Widda. She was holding a sodden blanket.

'Did you see her?' His father called to him.

'Who?'

'Eleanor, Eleanor Morrissey. She's been at the Carmodys' but she ran away. She's fierce upset still and we have to find her.'

'No, I haven't seen anyone, I—' Then the picture of the fleeting figure flashed into his mind again. Of course – it wasn't a fox. It was a girl. 'Hang on! I did – a few minutes ago I saw something, or maybe someone flying past the gate. I thought it was a fox but it might have been her trying not to be seen.'

'Good lad yourself!' Dan jumped down from the cart and helped the Widda down behind him. 'You go on into the house and tell Mel to put the kettle on. There's no point taking the cart with us in this mud so Billy and I will go and get her.' He handed the reins to Matty. 'Here, son, take the horse up to the stable and dry her off. We'll be back in a minute.'

'Can't I go with you, Da? Elly knows me. I might be able to help.'

The two men looked at each other and nodded. 'Right so, but remember, she's very upset and probably confused so say nothing unless you're told to.'

'Right.' And Matty started off up the road ahead of them. He had just reached the lane when he heard the screams and beckoned to the others to hurry. 'Come on quick! There's terrible screaming going on up there. It sounds as if someone's being killed!'

'Jesus Christ, Billy, come on!'

The three of them raced up the lane as fast as they could with Matty, having neither age nor flesh to hinder him, in the lead. As he rounded the corner of the yard, Eleanor flew past him, arms outstretched. For a moment he thought she was being chased but there was no-one coming behind her, only the darkened empty house with its back door swinging open. He stood where he was, watching as she ran straight into the waiting arms of the two men behind.

'You'll be all right now, Elly,' he called and for a moment she paused and turned to look at him. The screaming stopped and she shook her head. Then she ran again, away from her invisible devils with nothing at all behind but the rain and the hounds of hell snapping at her heels.

CHAPTER 19

THE CONVENT IN KILDORAN was a forbidding looking place with its high granite walls and stone steps leading to a solid oak door. Although it faced onto the street and its brass knocker was polished to a bright shine, the front door was seldom used. Mostly it was kept shut and opened only to the very important or the very desperate. No spy hole gave indication that the building's inhabitants had any interest in the outside world, yet there was little that happened in Kildoran, or indeed any of the neighbouring villages, that the nuns did not know about, or have lengthy opinions on. So it came as little surprise to Mother Clement, the convent's superior, when one of her young postulants knocked at her parlour door and asked if she was able to see Mrs Carmody, from the hardware shop, at once, without an appointment. Mother Clement wiped the corners of her mouth with her linen napkin and nodded.

'Mrs Carmody, is it? Fine, fine, I'll see her – and Moira—'

'Yes, Mother?'

'Another pot, if you please. For two this time.' She indicated the tray, which was perched on the side of her table.

'Yes, Mother.' The little postulant bowed her way into the room and removed the tray. She was alive with excitement. Today was turning out to be one of the most exciting days she had had since she arrived in Kildoran.

Moira Flanagan had been in the convent only six months yet it seemed like forever. She'd grown up in the West of Ireland, in a house with six brothers and never a moment's peace. When the notion of a vocation to the religious life first entered her head she had paid little heed but as the years passed and she saw herself being sucked into a life of servitude on the farm, with a husband, children and possibly an impoverished brother or two to look after, the notion crystallised into something ever more attractive. Unable to decide for herself, she offered it up.

'Dear Lord, are you listening? I don't know what I want but I know I don't like the way things are going round here right now. I'm not sure what your plans are but I'd be very grateful if they involve a bit of peace and quiet. Thy will be done. Amen.'

So here she was, in the Convent of Mercy in Kildoran, up to her ears in peace and drowning in it. At first it had seemed wonderful, the steady chanting of women in prayer and the long polished corridors smelling of lavender stretched out before her. She loved the calm of it all, the order and the elegance. She was going to have a great life. God had saved her from a life of slavery to the men in her family. She had sat in the chapel on her first evening and thanked him for it.

'I'm no one's slave but your servant now, O Lord. You brought me here and with your help I'll be the best servant you ever had!'

Her enthusiasm and spirit quickly endeared her to the older sisters and they held her up as an example to the other postulants, some of whom seemed to regard their vocations as the curse of the younger or less attractive daughter. *Put a bit of life into it, child! Can you not be a little more like our Moira here, always with a spring in her step and a smile on her face and she about the will of God?* While such comments pleased Moira more than she cared to admit, they did little to endear her to her fellows and she found herself increasingly isolated. When she sought company in her free moments, she often found them otherwise occupied or unwilling to spend the time with her, and this she found very difficult. She'd never wanted for companions at school as she'd always had talk of her brothers to use as currency. Here, nobody knew of her fine handsome brothers or would care if they did. Slowly, the novelty of her peaceful life wore thin and, while she didn't regret her decision for a moment, she longed for a bit of excitement, something she could use to get the others to take an interest in her.

Now, she closed the door of Mother Clement's parlour quietly and hugged herself in excitement. Imagine! Mrs Carmody from the hardware was here and she had come to the front door and asked if it were possible for her to speak with Mother Clement on a very private matter. Only Moira had been in the front hall so only she knew that Mrs Carmody was here. And she was to bring a pot of tea! Maybe she might get to hear a little of what the conversation was to be about! She turned into the hall and held out her hand to the pale woman sitting there, wringing her hands in worry.

'Mother Clement says she will see you right away, Mrs Carmody.' Moira said, keeping her voice low.

'Thank you,' Eileen rose and started to follow her down the corridor. 'It's very good of her to see me. I don't have an appointment or anything. I don't even know if I've come to the right place.' Her voice shook and she caught Moira's arm. 'I just didn't know what else to do. We have to sort it out and there isn't anyone else we could go to.'

Moira looked at her. She could make a fair guess that whatever was troubling this usually cheerful woman was something to do with the Morrissey girl. They'd heard the commotion that day a couple of weeks ago and there was a lot of whispering amongst the older nuns that the girl had told on her brother and after the Gardai got hold of him, the girl had disappeared. There were reports of sightings in the woods where the streams met at the edge of Morrisseys' land and even some suggestions that she had drowned herself. The father had gone crazy, banging on every house in the village demanding his daughter back but nobody would open their door to him, and eventually he had taken himself off to Kilkenny and hadn't been seen since. The young postulants and novices were dying to know what the rest of the story was but nobody would discuss it with them.

Such avid interest in the sordid affairs of the outside world is tantamount to taking part in them! The old nuns threw their hands up in horror. *You would be better off showing as much interest in your prayers!* So Moira kept her head down and went about her business. The fewer people noticed she was there, the more likely they would be to say more in her presence than they intended her to hear – and any information was grand currency!

'This is a very private place, Mrs Carmody.' She said now, giving Eileen's hand a quick squeeze of support.

Eileen smiled and looked at her as if only now seeing her properly for the first time. 'Thank you – you're very kind.'

'Not at all,' Moira was dying to ask her a few questions but they had reached Mother Clement's parlour. Conversing with lay folk was strictly forbidden and she wasn't about to blot her copybook after six months. *You're welcome*, she whispered, and then in a louder voice, 'Mrs Carmody, Mother.'

Eileen was ushered into the room and Moira shut the door and picked up the tray she had left on the table outside.

Carrying it to the kitchen, she smiled to herself at the thought of the news she'd have to tell. *I won't say anything straight away* she thought to herself. *I might just remark that it's a wet day indeed for visitors. And then anyone who cares to be nosy will have to ask all the questions herself and I'll only be obliged to answer as truthfully as I can.* She passed the statue of the Blessed Virgin who seemed to be watching her reproachfully, *because I wouldn't want to be guilty of gossiping,* she shot a guilty glance at the figure, *honestly I wouldn't.* And thus absolved, she hopped down the steps to the warmth of the convent kitchen, hoping there would be somebody there so that she could make her remark in innocence, and really not intend to tell anyone anything at all.

In Mother Clement's parlour the air was very still. The two women sat on either side of a low polished table and waited for the tray to arrive so that they could pour tea and butter scones and avoid the conversation they both knew must follow. Eventually, Mother Clement broke the silence.

'Mrs Carmody,' she said, fingering the heavy wooden beads hung from her belt, 'you have a matter that you wish to discuss with me?'

'I have,' Eileen said, still looking at the table. 'I have a matter of the gravest importance and—' she swallowed hard and tried to control the quiver in her voice.

'Take your time, my dear,' the nun said, 'perhaps you will feel more ready to explain when we have a cup of tea in our hands. I always find a nice cup of tea helps me to get things straight in my mind, don't you?'

'I do, Mother,' Eileen said gratefully. 'I'm a great tea drinker myself. My Billy says I'm probably keeping an entire community alive in India with all the trade they get from me!'

Mother Clement smiled politely and Eileen settled back more comfortably in her chair. Perhaps this wasn't going to be so bad after all; maybe the nuns would be able to help. She folded her arms and fixed her eyes on the raindrops that were racing down the windowpane. Funny places, convents. For all that there was one in nearly every town and most decent villages in the country, they still seemed like worlds apart. She knew there was a late summer storm raging outside but in here you couldn't hear a bit of it. The only evidence was the medley of raindrops that painted their respectful stripes down the windows, but didn't dare make a sound. She shot a quick glance at the woman sitting across from her and wondered if she should start talking again.

Mother Clement didn't seem to be bothered. Her eyes were lowered and she was looking at the heavy crucifix at the end of her beads. *Right so* Eileen thought *you're not bothered so I'll wait for the tea to fortify my next words.* She smiled to herself, Billy would be surprised, and she could almost hear him now. *What! D'you mean to tell me there was a gap in the conversation and you didn't rush to fill it? God help us, Eileen Carmody, what is the world coming to at all!*

A knock on the door broke her reveries. The door was opening slowly and the little postulant who had shown her in was entering with a tray laden with tea and scones and cake and pots of blackcurrant and gooseberry jam.

'Your tea, Mother,' she said, placing the tray on the table.

Mother Clement looked at her in surprise. 'Why thank you, Moira – you have surpassed yourself!'

Moira blushed; perhaps she'd overdone it. She'd forgotten that the new term was in full swing across at the school and that the other novices were engaged in helping to cut the squares for Sister Breda's sewing class and help the new Infants to draw the lines in their copybooks. The kitchen was empty and in annoyance she aimed a kick at the pantry door. Her action brought two jars of jam crashing to the floor and though neither had broken, both had spilled some of their contents. In desperation, Moira cleaned up the mess and scooped two generous spoonfuls into the little dishes kept in the cupboard. If anyone asked, she would apologise for her presumption in opening both but confess that since Mother had an unexpected visitor and had expressly asked for tea for two, she hoped she had done the right thing. Now it looked as if she may not have.

She smiled apologetically at Mother. 'It's very damp out today, Mother. I thought maybe Mrs Carmody would be better for a shivery bite.'

Eileen beamed at her. 'A shivery bite! God bless you, pet, I haven't heard that expression around here for a while! You're not local, are you?'

'No,' Moira was conscious of her Superior watching her and uncertain how much she should say. She would probably be best to go but the thought of a bit of a chat, no matter how short was too much, 'I'm from Mayo.'

'Moira is one of our new postulants,' Mother Clement cut in on her. 'She has been with us for six months.' She paused a moment and looked closely at Eileen as if a thought had just come into her mind, 'and she will soon be taking the next step to become a novice of our order – perhaps in a different house. We're very far flung, you know.' She heard Moira's gasp of surprise and smiled at her. 'I shall miss her terribly, of course. She's one of our brightest stars. You may go about you tasks now–' And she waved the girl away with a polite but dismissive hand.

'Yes, Mother. Thank you, Mother.' Moira almost skipped out of the room. Imagine! She was to travel! Coming here from Mayo had seemed the greatest adventure and now she was to travel again. She wondered where she would go. Sure the sisters had houses all over Ireland – and outside too. She stopped. England! Maybe they'd send her to England! Oh please God, wouldn't Mammy be dead proud if she ended up teaching in England.

Sent to civilise those heathens, my Moira.

All thoughts of Eileen Carmody and the recent events in Kildoran swept clean out of her mind by the latest news, she rushed to the Chapel to offer up a prayer. God had made all the right decisions for her so far so maybe he could give a bit of thought to this one. The world was a busy place and she didn't want to be taking up too much of his time with deciding what to do with her so she'd give him a hand.

She knelt on her cushion at the back of the chapel.

'Good afternoon, Lord,' she said, crossing herself, 'it's me, Moira Flanagan again. I might be leaving here soon and going to another house. If the decision isn't made yet – and I promise to accept with humility whatever is chosen for me – could it maybe be in England? Thank you, Lord. Your will be done, Amen.'

CHAPTER 20

'OH, THAT'S A GRAND CUP OF TEA ALL RIGHT,' Eileen drained the last drop reluctantly and set the cup on the table. Then she settled back in her chair. Right so, she'd had her tea and her couple of scones and if she didn't get on with the matter in hand soon, Mother Clement would wonder what she was up to at all. Probably think she was some kind of madwoman.

Mother Clement thought no such thing. The window of her parlour, where she spent what time she didn't pass in the chapel, had a bird's eye view directly out on to bridge where the road turned slightly and led along the main street of the village. She watched the faces the day little Eleanor Morrissey fought her way into the crowd and stunned the whole village with her words. She watched the brother, as he stood ashen and frozen when the crowd parted and Jimmy Byrne walked towards him. She heard the scream of the child as the crowd surged forward, baying for his blood. Then she let the curtain drop and went to the chapel to pray. She stayed there the rest of the day. Now perhaps, there might be an answer to her prayer.

'It's been an eventful few weeks in Kildoran, Mrs Carmody, God help us.'

'It has,' Eileen put her feet together and started to straighten the pleats of her skirt.

'It was a very sad thing, a very sad thing indeed.'

'Yes.'

'Such crimes tend to bring out the worst in people. They condemn the criminal for his savagery, but can find no Christianity in themselves to forgive him.'

246

Eileen looked at her in astonishment. 'Well, I don't think—'

'—or those that belong to him.' Now Mother Clement raised her head and looked at Eileen directly. 'Did she know?'

Eileen folded the last pleat and smoothed it carefully over her knee. 'She did not.' she whispered. 'Or maybe she could have but she didn't dare to. He was all she had, you know. He was her home, her protection, and her hope for the future. If she lost him, she lost everything. She couldn't risk that.'

'Then what happened?'

'I don't know.' Eileen shook her head. 'Who's to say what got into her? She just saw the belt that young Byrne was holding up and something inside her snapped. One minute she was desperate like the rest of us to hear the latest, next she was standing like in a trance staring at her brother's belt as if at the very devil himself.'

'And how is she now?'

'God help her, Billy and myself are heart-scalded with the creature. We can't get a word of sense out of her. She keeps asking us when her brother will be back to get her and then she remembers and insists that she has to go up to the house to get her pet. Her pet, I ask ye!'

'Does she have a pet?'

'Well, none that me nor Billy's ever heard of. She insists that the Widda Meaney gave it to her to take her pain away but she'll not explain what pain she's talking of and me and Billy can't do anything for her. If we let her go, the whole of the village will be on her like hounds after a rabbit and we can't keep her with us much longer because if they find out where she is, they'll do for us too – oh!' She stopped, breathless, and looked at the old nun in horror. 'You'll not say a word will you, Mother? She's only a child and me and Billy – we're too old to

247

uproot and make a start elsewhere. A story like this would never be left behind. It'd follow us wherever we went.'

Mother Clement got up out of her chair slowly and went to the window. 'Of course.' She was silent for a minute and then she turned around and looked at Eileen. 'And what is it exactly that you wanted from us?'

Eileen's face flushed pink and her hands played furiously in her lap. 'That's the problem. I don't know what it is I want. I only know what I don't want and I seem to be powerless to do anything about it.'

'Let's start there then, shall we? Tell me what you don't want.'

Slowly, Eileen started to arrange the pleats again in neat folds over her knees. As she straightened each one she spoke slowly as if the very action would get the jumble of thoughts in her mind into some sort of order. 'I don't want the child to suffer any more. I don't want me and Billy to suffer. I don't want the child blamed for her brother's wrongdoing. I don't want me and Billy to be blamed for being associated with them. I don't want—' her hands shook and the quiver in her voice grew stronger. 'In the name of God! What do you want me to say? I don't want any of this to have happened but it did, and somehow me and Billy are in the middle of it and I don't know what to do next!'

There was silence then. Eileen slumped, horrified at her own disrespectful outburst and exhausted at the fierceness of her own emotions. Mother Clement said nothing. She stood looking at Eileen. Eventually, she took a deep breath and moved across to her desk. 'In that case, Mrs Carmody, as you are so obviously a soul in need, we shall have to help you, shan't we?'

'Help me, Mother? What can you do?'

Mother Clement smiled. 'To be perfectly honest, Mrs Carmody, I really don't know. For the moment I shall pray and you—' she stood up and gestured towards the door '—you will go home and pray too. Pack a travelling bag for the child and both of you return here at the same time tomorrow. By then I will have made arrangements.'

Eileen's confused state was little relieved at the nun's words. 'What sort of arrangements? What can you do for her?'

'Help her start a new life. The Lord has many friends and friends are what she needs now. Bring her here and say goodbye. Do you understand?'

'Yes.' Eileen said, though she didn't. She got up and started to walk to the door. 'Well, thank you for your help, Mother, I—'

Mother Clement held up her hand. 'Any help I can give you has yet to be given, Mrs Carmody. You tell the child not to worry.'

'I'll tell her,' Eileen said, shaking the proffered hand, 'though I doubt she'll take any notice. We've tried everything, me and Billy.'

'That was before,' Mother Clement's voice was warm and confident, 'now we have God on our side and you are no longer alone.'

'Aye.' Eileen smiled at the novice who appeared at the door at the sound of her superior's bell, 'we have God on our side now – sure we should have an answer to it in no time.' And shrugging her shoulders in resignation at her own lack of faith, she bid the two of them goodbye and headed for the turmoil of her own home at the far end of the street.

Moira and Mother Clement stood looking after her, Moira holding her breath.

'Not a word about this visit, my dear.'

'Of course not, Mother,' Moira cleared her throat. 'Will you be able to do anything to help her?'

'I don't know. I presume you mean the child?'

Moira nodded.

'We can get her into a safe place for now, but as far as the future goes—'

'What'll happen to her?'

Mother Clement shrugged. 'God knows and that's a fact.' She pushed the door shut and ushered Moira back into the dark hallway. 'In the meantime, my dear, we have work to do.'

'We?'

Mother Clement smiled. 'You, if you like.'

Moira held her breath as the elderly nun ushered her into the parlour and motioned her to sit down. She waited while Mother Clement sat opposite her and watched her, her forehead creased as she formulated her plan. Eventually, she spoke.

'What we are dealing with,' Mother Clement said, 'is a child who has had all the rights of childhood stripped away from her: the love of a family; the security of a home; and even, God forbid, the innocence which should have accompanied her far beyond her present age. Kildoran can offer her none of these now. People are too angry, too shocked and the child is too closely involved – she must leave. I will arrange for her to go to our sister house in Dublin as soon and as inconspicuously as possible and I would like you, my dear, to accompany her.' Ignoring Moira's gasp, she continued. 'Only God knows what the future holds for Eleanor Morrissey but it will hold no hope for her until she can put the past completely behind her. When she is older and has found her way in life, she will be able to look back and see that this was not her burden to carry, but for the moment we can only do our best to help her start anew.'

'What will she do in Dublin?'

Mother Clement shrugged. 'I don't know. Perhaps she will be found a family who could offer her shelter and some hope of a normal life. We will have to pray and hope.'

'Can't I keep I touch with her for a while, for company?'

'No.' Mother Clement shook her head firmly. 'She must make a fresh start and she cannot do that while you are there as a reminder.'

'So I'll come back here?' Moira sounded disappointed. She had hoped her adventure was going to last longer than a return journey to Dublin, whatever the charge.

'I don't think that would be such a good idea, do you?' Mother Clement smiled. 'With the weight of such a secret? Would you be able to keep that to yourself with all the gossip that's being whispered around here at the minute?'

Moira blushed. 'Probably not.'

'Well then, in that case I think the best thing is for me to request that you be transferred to one of our sister houses as you enter your novitiate. It will be good for you to have a broad range of experience – I sense that you have a bright future ahead of you in our order.' She could see Moira's fists, clenched in anticipation. 'Perhaps we might send you over the water?'

Moira threw her hands in the air in delight before flinging herself at her Superior. 'Oh, thank you, Mother! Thank you so much! England – imagine that – I've never been further than Galway and Kilkenny in my life and now Dublin and England in one go! Wait till I tell – oh!' She stopped suddenly and pulled herself together. 'Sorry, Mother.'

Mother Clement straightened her tunic where Moira had crumpled it and smiled. 'Quite. So now you know why it's best that you are not here while your secret mission is fresh in your mind. You will not tell a soul, Moira, and when you go to another house you will have so many new experiences to occupy you that you won't have time to think about Kildoran or anything that happened here. Now—' and she stood up '— away with you. The bells for prayer will ring soon. You may be excused for this evening – occupy yourself till supper when you will sit beside me.'

'Yes, Mother. Thank you, Mother.'

'And Moira?'

'Yes, Mother?'

'Not a word.'

As Moira shut the parlour door behind her, her hands were shaking. She was bursting with the excitement of the day and wished there was someone she could tell. But she was in that uncertain place where the past was to be closed off and the future unknown and she didn't know where she'd start. She wanted to go into the chapel but that'd be filling up soon so she made her way to the garden. It was quiet out there and she decided to walk around and stay out of sight for the minute.

She lasted only the minute before the quiet got to her. In frustration she threw her head back and whispered her prayers aloud towards the stars.

'Well, Lord, did you hear all that? Thank you so much – I can't believe you agreed so quickly. I don't know how I feel about it but I

think I'm probably terrified. I know it's your will and your will be done, but if you don't mind, could I ask you another couple of favours?'

She took a deep breath.

'Eleanor and I are supposed to be leaving Kildoran, maybe for ever, but I quite like it here and I'd like to come back some day. That's the first thing. The second's about Eleanor. We don't know what'll happen to her and that's maybe the best thing – but if you don't mind, could you arrange for me to find out sometime? Anyway, as I said, Your Will be done—'

At the back gate of the convent garden the Widda Meaney moved quietly. When she heard Moira's whispered prayer she smiled to herself and shifted the basket of herbs she was carrying to her other arm. Pulling her shawl more closely around her, she opened the gate and moved quickly to the girl's side.

'… Amen.'

EMER WASN'T SURE WHAT WOKE HER but for a couple of minutes she lay still, head resting against the pillar, the remnants of a dream trailing away out of reach. With an effort she pulled herself upright and lifted a tentative hand to a large swelling on the side of her head. It was cold on the surface, but there was a steady hot throb from its base that she knew would stay with her for days. Slowly, the events of the morning came back to her: the argument with John; her realisation of what he had been up to with Cora Hennessey; the recognition of her mother's face in her own. She wondered how long she had been there. She was so full of resolve when she walked out but now she was tired and cold and hungry and she wished she could just crawl home to bed and forget that today had ever happened.

Sniff.

The noise was very faint. Emer was aware that she had heard it already. That's what had woken her but the church appeared to be empty.

Sniff. It was there again and it was close.

Gingerly, keeping her head as steady as she could, she leaned forward to see who it was.

At first there was no one to be seen. The noise was coming from the other side of the pillar a little further back but it was impossible to make out where. A low winter sun shone straight in through the door at the back of the church and left the seats in shadow. As she squinted to see better, Emer could just make out the shape of someone sitting on the other side. Her clothes were dark and she was hunched over so it was impossible to see whom it was. From the distance and in the poor light it appeared to be a girl with long dark hair flowing down her back. For a while Emer sat, leaning forward, wondering what she should do. Should she respect her privacy or would the girl welcome a sympathetic ear?

The figure moved and as Emer saw the flash of white above her face, she realised that it was not a young girl but a much older woman and what she had taken to be long flowing hair was not hair at all but a veil. It was one of the nuns.

Wishing to spare her any embarrassment, Emer stood up and pulling her scarf over her head so as to hide the swelling on the side of her face, tried to leave the church as quietly as possible.

She did not notice that the other woman had risen also and both reached the heavy swing doors at the same time. Sunlight shone through the old stained glass and colours played on their faces as they stood facing one another.

'Sister Pius?'

'Mrs Fagan.'

There was nothing more to be said. Pius was half a head taller and had always appeared lofty and forbidding but now her face was tear-streaked and she was hunched and frightened-looking. Her hands played nervously with the heavy beads that hung from her belt and a thin line of sweat had seeped into the edge of her cowl so that she looked dishevelled. As if in slow motion, she raised her hand and gently touched the side of Emer's face.

'You are hurt,' she said simply, as if it was to be expected. 'Your husband did this?'

'Yes.' The answer was out before she had time to think.

As if reminded, the dried blood on her cheek started to pull at her skin but Emer could think of nothing more to say.

'You must clean it.' Pius pushed the door open and Emer followed her outside into the glaring light. In silence, the two of them walked towards the side gate of the convent and went through together. When they got to the back door, Pius opened it and stood back to let Emer pass. If either thought it strange that she should find the other in such a state, or herself in such company, neither gave any indication. Emer sat at the table and slowly peeled off her headscarf while Pius went to the sink to wet a cloth. Then she opened a drawer and took out a small mirror. She handed both to Emer. 'It's quite nasty.'

She was right. There was a thin gash running along the side of Emer's face and the skin on either side was puffy and angry looking. The blood that had trickled earlier had dried and was flaking along the length of her cheek. On her other cheek the imprint of a hand was clearly visible. Her eyes were puffy too, though she couldn't remember crying.

'Oh dear.' With a smile, Emer handed her back the mirror. 'I'm surprised I didn't frighten you!'

Pius laugh was low and there was no amusement in it. '*Your* face does not frighten me, Mrs Fagan.' She appeared to be about to say something else but she stopped and even though her back was turned, Emer could see that her hands were shaking.

'Are you all right, Sister?'

'Perfectly all right, thank you.' As if the question had snapped her back to reality, Pius' back straightened and her voice was firm and steady again. 'Do you need a cup of tea – I'm afraid that I can't stay as the children will be returning any moment and I must go back to my classroom.'

Emer stood up, recognising the dismissal. 'No, no, thank you. I must be away myself.' She held the stained cloth awkwardly in her hands. 'I'll take this with me and wash it.'

Pius looked at the cloth. Her lips were tight and her expression anguished. Emer had the impression that she wanted to say more but she was fighting with herself for control. Eventually, she nodded. 'Yes,' she said, 'I imagine that would be the best thing.'

Despite the situation, Emer nearly smiled openly. Here were two women, united in anguish and mutually aware and yet Pius could not bring herself to bend even a little. Agnes would have whipped the cloth out of her hands with a *Would you give that here to me! What would you be doing walking the streets with an aul damp thing like that!* but Pius was obviously keen that the whole episode be over as soon as possible. Emer pulled her coat closed and arranged her scarf over her face. 'Is there any news of Sister Agnes? I thought I might call into the hospital to see her.'

'That won't be necessary, thank you, Ms Fagan. Our sister will be coming home this afternoon.' Before Emer could open her mouth to say something, she continued, 'I imagine she will be terribly tired for the first few days; she may not be able for visitors.' She ushered Emer to the door with trembling hands. 'Perhaps you might like to 'phone first?'

Emer felt her dislike for this woman surface again. The cheek of her! Biting her lip in annoyance, she turned to leave, 'Goodbye, Sister Pius.'

'Goodbye, Mrs Fagan – oh, and Mrs Fagan?'

'Yes?'

Pius looked unsure again. 'If you need, I mean—' She gestured at the mark on Emer's face.

Emer smiled, 'I'm sure it will be all right, but – thank you.' The other woman nodded and stood looking after her.

Outside, Emer stood at the back convent gate with her head in a whirl. What on earth was that all about? The woman was a nutter! One minute she was all concern and insistent that she have her cut seen; the next practically shoving Emer out the door making it quite clear that unsolicited visits to the convent will not be welcomed. Between faithless husbands, flighty shop assistants and mad nuns, she was beginning to believe that the whole world was going crazy – and she in the middle of it!

From the kitchen window, Pius watched her walk away. Her heart was breaking for the small figure in the well worn coat with her determined walk and bright head scarf pulled close over her face to hide where her husband had – did she say he had hit her? Pius couldn't remember – only that she was hurt and it had been his fault. For a moment in the church, when they stood face to face, she understood exactly what was in the other woman's head - the fear, the pain and the anger – but she couldn't admit to that. Fifty years of solitude were her defence against the pain that almost tore her apart and she could not risk feeling that pain again. All those memories of her own betrayal – Eleanor Morrissey, Patrick, her father, the Fagans – they were all dead and now she was Sister Pius and she belonged to no-one and no-one belonged to her. And that was the way it had to be.

Only Emer Fagan wasn't no-one. She was as much a part of Pius' life as Pius was of hers. She saw her reflection in the window, a tall, lined woman with a forbidding emotionless face and she remembered Reverend Mother's words the day she sent her here, *You will go to Kildoran, Sister, not because of what you have to teach. You will go to Kildoran because of what you have to learn.* Well, she'd been here for a few months now and what had she learned? That you are trapped? That the past is more powerful than the present because the present constantly moves on but the past is always there, always the same, ready to pounce on you?

She remembered another conversation, some weeks before she was sent here. Mother Mary had just arrived and was getting to know the sisters. Talk turned to progress and how one might achieve it. Someone had offered the opinion that 'we cannot grow towards the future unless we acknowledge the importance in our lives of the past, much as a plant cannot grow without roots.' Pius felt angry at such sentimental nonsense.

'Ridiculous! We do not need our pasts – they're over and done with. Why else would we be called upon to confess our sins and move on, cleansed, towards a better future?'

'So our pasts are of no consequence, Sister?' Mother Mary looked at her in that half amused way she had.

'None. We forget our past and we move on.'

For a moment it seemed as if Mother would make no reply. She had her head down and she was studying the folds of her tunic as she searched for the right words. 'No,' she said eventually, 'we do *not* forget our past. We remember it, we learn from it, *and then* we move on. Is that not the case, Sister?'

'That is not the case with me.' Pius closed her prayer book and stood up. 'That is not the case with me at all.' And she had believed that to be the truth.

BRRRRRNG! In the school yard the bell was being rung vigorously. Any minute now, the children would stream back from the hall and the school would fill with the sound of heavy winter shoes clumping and trooping on the wooden floors. Pius straightened her veil and smoothed her skirt.

'Well, Mother,' she whispered to the empty room. 'Are you happy now? You sent me here to face my past and what did I learn from it? Nothing – except what I always suspected, that I'm trapped in it. Are you happy now? I hope you're happy now.'

She walked across the narrow passage to the school building, to be ready for the children when they came into the classroom. At the end of the stairs she paused for a moment, then carried on, head high, ignoring the piercing blue eyes of the painting at the window, which watched her every move.

As she knew it always had.

CHAPTER 22

'EMER! WE DIDN'T EXPECT YOU TODAY!' The young nurse stood aside and held the door open, ushering Emer into the warmth. 'God, it's perishing out there – will I bring you a drop of tea?'

'Thanks, Bridget, I'd kill for a cup.' Emer stamped her feet and started to take off her scarf. Keeping the side of her face to the wall as best she could, she gestured into the sun lounge, 'Is she inside?'

Bridget held out her hands to take the scarf. 'Your mother's upstairs. She's not had good nights this last week, waking up bothered and not able to go off again. Matron gave her something to help about six this morning and she's had a good sleep but she doesn't want to come downstairs. She says she's safe in her room and that's where she's staying. The rest will do her good. The last I saw she was reading – go on up and see if she wants to get dressed and come down or what. I'll follow you up with the tea in a minute.'

Emer waved her thanks and, keeping her head turned, started up the stairs. Outside her mother's room she paused, taking a deep breath. Then she knocked gingerly and waited for a sound from inside. When none came, she pulled her hair over where make-up camouflaged the mark on her face and opened the door. 'Mam?'

Nell didn't look up. A *Woman's Weekly* lay open in front of her as she sat nervously twisting the cuff of her bed jacket. She glared suspiciously at Emer.

'Close the door!' she whispered, crossly. 'Quickly! Before she gets in!' She gathered the bedclothes higher around her, knocking some of the magazines to the floor.

Emer picked them up and left them on the bedside table. 'What's wrong, Mam? Did you have an argument with Bridget?'

'Don't be stupid!'

Despite the old woman's obvious agitation, Emer felt her temper rise. 'All right, then, not Bridget – is it the matron?'

Nell looked at her as if the question didn't warrant an answer.

'Oh, look; I can't play guessing games with you today, Mam. You don't want someone to come in – who?'

Nell leaned forwards and clutched Emer's arm tightly. 'Her!' she whispered, all the time keeping her eyes on the door.

'Her – who?'

Nell's voice was weak and her face full of fear. 'Don't you know anything? Her! I told them I didn't want to see anyone! She might come back. She knew about it, you know. And he knew too – 'cause he was there. I saw him. He was there and he wouldn't make it stop—' her voice was rising and the note of hysteria grew louder with each word.

'Make what stop, Mam?' Very gently, Emer took Nell's hand into her own and held it tight. 'Tell me, Mam, who was there and what wouldn't he stop?'

'Patrick Morrissey.' She spat the name out and then wiped her mouth with the back of her hand. She sat upright and pushed back a lock of hair. 'He told me he loved me once, you know. Said he'd marry me and build us a house on land that his mother left. Only he'd have to bring her too 'cause she couldn't do without him. He seemed nice sometimes—' her voice trailed off and she was staring into space. 'There was even a time I thought he might do but he was tied to that place. Jimmy said he was no good but he was only jealous.' She winked at Emer and her voice was high and girlie. 'He didn't need to be. He was the one I had my eye on all the time – ha ha. Though they were all keen. I was the belle of the place – could have had my pick of any one of them.' As suddenly as the bright mood had come over her, it disappeared and she slumped back on the pillows. 'But that was before—' She caught Emer's arm and brought her face close. Her mouth was working furiously as she struggled for the words. 'He was supposed to love me but he hadn't the guts. I could see him taking off his belt like he was going to stop him but he hadn't the guts. He stood there and when the other was finished and he could see the blood, he ran away. He just ran away and left me there—'

She was crying quietly now and Emer didn't know what to do. She bent and caught her mother's eye and as she did, Nell slowly pushed the duvet back and lifted her nightdress. Emer wanted to turn away, break the spell but it was already too late.

'Look!' Nell's hands were shaking. 'Look what he did to me!'

Emer looked where her mother indicated and gasped in horror. Along the length of her thighs, from her knee upwards, there were scars, not the smooth silver lines of motherhood but angry jagged scars etched deep into the loose folds of her skin. They ran the all the way to the top where the skin was pulled together and there were bald patches where no hair could grow. Even in her most intimate folds there were scars and mutilation. For a minute neither woman spoke but Nell must have registered Emer's sharp intake of breath because she suddenly pulled her night dress down quickly and smoothed the duvet neatly over her knees. Taking a handkerchief from her pocket, she started to fold it corner to corner, taking meticulous care to meet the sides exactly.

'He had a bottle, you know, and when I wouldn't go with him he said maybe I'd like the feel of a bottle on my lips. *Come on, come on,* he whispered from his hiding place in the darkness.' She looked at Emer slyly. 'But he never put the bottle to my mouth. I tried to run away but he caught me from behind and he bent me down and pushed it into me.' Then she paused. 'It was the kicking broke the bottle.'

As the horror of what she was hearing washed over Emer, Nell started folding again. 'He wore boots, you see, that's what he kicked me with and that's all that I could see – big shiny boots. My Jimmy could never afford big boots like those. I thought I was going to die. I was so frightened I couldn't remember his face. But I could remember the boots.' She stopped, peering closely at the handkerchief where the bias of the material wouldn't let the sides meet exactly.

Emer waited for her to continue and when she didn't, prompted, 'Did you remember afterwards, Mam? Did you know who it was?'

Nell looked up at her crossly, 'I did not. How could I? I'd have had to explain about Patrick and the arrangement. I couldn't tell and then *she* came ...'

Without warning the door burst open and Bridget came bustling in carrying a tray laden with cups and cakes. 'Here we are! A pot of fresh tea! Shall I leave you to pour, Emer, or will I do the honours? There's a grand bit of brack there as well and butter if you'd fancy—' When there was no response, she looked from one to the other. 'Emer, are you all right?'

264

Emer was looking at her mother as if seeing her for the first time 'Grand – grand, thanks, Bridget. The tea's fine, leave it there and I'll pour it in a minute.' Bridget opened her mouth as if to say something but Emer ushered her away. 'Really, it's fine, thanks – I'll come and talk to you in a while.'

Bridget's face registered the disappointment of the frantically curious when banished from a place where something was obviously going on, but she put the tray on the dressing table and went to the door. 'Right so, call down when you're ready. 'But Emer was not listening. As Bridget closed the door behind her, she leaned towards her mother and asked, 'Tell what, Mam? What wouldn't they let you tell? And who was she?'

Nell pulled the bedclothes close again and looked around the room as if she was frightened that someone might be listening. 'It wasn't my fault. I didn't say because I couldn't remember. When they took him away everyone was so glad that he had been caught and they could feel safe again and that's what Jimmy kept telling me – I had to believe that, don't you see? If I thought that he was still around, I'd have gone mad, can't you understand that?' She was beginning to panic again, clutching the covers and shivering. 'I was afraid to remember, afraid of how cross Jimmy'd be, and afraid that one day *he* would come and get me and punish me for not telling them the truth.'

'Who would come and get you?'

Nell's mouth worked furiously as she struggled to get out the words. 'Don't let them get me, Jimmy. I didn't mean it to happen like that. Make it stop.'

Emer put her arms around her mother's shoulders, 'Hey, Mam, it's okay. No-one is going to get you.'

Nell pushed her daughter away. 'You were always stupid,' she said. 'You don't know anything. I have to get out of here before she comes back.'

'Who, Mam, who comes back?'

But Nell had her eyes closed and she was muttering crossly to herself.

'Mam! I can't help you if you don't tell me! Who is going to come back?'

Nell opened one eye. 'She is not *going* to come back. She's back already. She was here and I knew her and she knew me. She's come to get me for not saying that it wasn't him – he was only there watching. It was the one with the boots, the big shiny boots...' She opened her other eye and glared at Emer. 'And you needn't think I'm telling you any more either because you probably knew all along ... '

'Oh, for goodness sake, what am I supposed to know?' Emer's head was spinning and she didn't know what she was hearing any more or what she was supposed to believe.

Nell shook the handkerchief loose from its tight folds and blew her nose loudly. 'I saw you,' she said, 'up there on the altar in the dress I had the day I married your father. Set up for life, a business like that, never be short of a penny for clothes to put on your back.' She lay deep into the pillows again and shut her eyes. 'And no worry that anything like that would happen to you with a husband to take care of you. A big fellow like that with a prosperous stomach and boots on his feet. Big shiny boots.' From between squeezed eyelids two tears rolled over her cheeks and soaked into the pillow.

Emer leaned over to kiss her but at her touch, Nell flinched. 'You were supposed to protect me. ' And she pulled the duvet over her head.

For what seemed like hours, Emer sat staring into space. Whether Nell was asleep or not it was impossible to tell. Wearily, she pulled herself to her feet. 'Sleep well, Mam – and try not to worry. I'll find out what it is and I'll make sure you'll be safe here.' Nell made no response so she picked up the tray and went out, closing the door quietly behind her. What a day! It was as if clouds that had been gathering forever had suddenly converged and the most almighty storm was breaking out over her head: first John and Cora; then Sister Pius; and now her mother and some man who failed to save her from another's shiny boots.

From the lounge downstairs, she could hear Bridget and one of the other nurses laughing. On shaky knees she headed for the light.

Matty sat by the door of the sun lounge and watched Emer as she came into the room, pale and dishevelled. She looked as if she could do with a drink – a strong one. He could do with a drink himself. It seemed like forever since Aggie went into the hospital and meantime he was trapped in here with only the whittering of old women who'd probably killed off their unfortunate husbands by chit-chattering them to death, and the clicking of knitting needles for company. He glowered at the corner where Nell should be sitting. Contrary old thing. She wasn't much company anyway but at least she wasn't looking to knit him a jumper he'd never wear or bleed compliments from him for hairdos he hadn't noticed in the first place.

Emer and Bridget were having a long talk and Matty hoped Emer would stay a while afterwards and maybe come and have a chat with him. Bridget was shaking her head and looking puzzled and the other nurse was shrugging. Then Bridget pointed over to him and Emer looked and waved. Lifting his hand in recognition, Matty hoped he didn't look too grateful. If any of the others realised he was lonely for a bit of company the whole knitting brigade would have their chairs moved into the sun lounge and he'd never get a minute's peace at all.

'Matty, hello! Are you well?'

'Ah, as well as can be expected.' He shifted himself on the chair. 'Here, sit yourself down there a minute. I could do with the company of a woman who's *not* out to either mother me or smother me.'

Emer laughed. 'Is it that bad?'

Matty gestured towards the inner lounge. 'God help me, Emer – there's women in there would put the heart crossways in you! Eighty years of age and they're still desperate, if you'll excuse me saying so!'

'"Blessed art thou amongst women" isn't the case, then?'

Matty smiled, 'How's your mother? Have you seen her today?'

'I have,' Emer looked at him. 'She's not well, Matty.'

'Is it her chest?' As if in sympathy, he patted his own and managed a few feeble coughs.

Emer smiled sympathetically. 'No, physically she's fine as far as I can see. No, whatever's up with her is in her head. I've just been hearing the most disturbing things and I don't know whether it's something she's read in one of the magazines she had heaped on the bed or—'

She sat wringing her hands in confusion and as Matty watched her, he knew that he could lean forward and say, 'Don't fret yourself with it – she's only rambling.' And because he was old and steady she might believe him. On the other hand, it wouldn't be true and while she was obviously innocent to all the things that had gone before, she might find out from someone else anyway. And then who would you trust?

'What sort of disturbing things?' he asked her gently.

'I couldn't begin to tell you, about someone doing something to her and he wouldn't stop it and he had big shiny black boots and there was some woman who has come back to get her revenge on Mam for not telling what really happened. Does that make any sense to you at all? '

Matty shook his head. 'Did she say who the woman was?'

Emer shook her head. 'She said only one name. What was it – Patrick Morrissey.'

It was such a long time since Matty had heard the name spoken aloud that he felt a shiver down his spine. After he had been taken away, nobody would mention him in case the very sound of his name would bring back the fear that had stalked the community in the couple of weeks before he was caught. He shook his head; sad that at this stage of her life, the old woman couldn't put her ghosts to rest. 'He was an evil bastard, begging your pardon for the language.'

'No,' Emer stopped him short. 'I don't think he was. From what she was saying – and she was rambling away – there was someone else. Patrick Morrissey was there, watching, and she was calling to him to do something. He took off his belt and she thought he was going to help her but then the other fellow must have seen him or something and stepped back, and when Morrissey saw all the blood that was on her, he panicked and ran off. I think that's what she was saying. Does that make any sense to you, Matty? Matty? Are you all right?'

Opposite her, Matty felt as if he had seen a ghost. 'Matty, what is it?'

'Sweet Mother of Jesus!' Matty breathed, 'and she never said?'

'Mam? Do you mean Mam? She said it all happened while she was sick and afterwards it was too late and anyway Dad would be cross about some arrangement. Matty, talk to me, is this real? Is there someone upsetting Mam?'

Matty shook his head. 'Well, I can't say for sure.'

'What do you mean – you can't say? Either it is or it isn't!' Emer was angry now, 'Come on, Matty, I'm not a child any more who has to be kept in the dark about "grown up things". I'm a grown up myself, with a child of my own, and a husband and a mother who is convinced someone is out to get her!'

'Well now, you can rest assured on that bit,' he said, in the infuriatingly slow way of the elderly when they find the story they have to tell is at the centre of everyone's attention, 'Nobody means your mother any harm.' He paused and sat back in the chair, ready to savour the hearing of what he had to say. 'A long time ago, before your parents were married, your mother was attacked one night after the fair. She was on her way across the middle field late at night – God knows why. There was nothing nearby save the stream and beyond, the lane to the cottage of a woman known locally as the Widda Meaney. She was a grand woman, a healer, she—'

'Mam, Matty? What happened to Mam?'

'Your mother, as I said, was attacked, horrific, left for dead.'

'Oh, my God!'

Matty shifted uncomfortably. While it was dramatic as stories go, he wished he could have had a different audience. 'But she was fine, fine. You father was helping out with the buses at the time and he was just locking up and ready to go to his bed when he heard the Widda shouting. She'd been out gathering her herbs to make a tonic for my mother who was having troubles at the time. She was on the lane down by the stream when she heard a cry and found Nell there, covered in blood, looking for all the world as if she was found too late.'

Emer was sitting still, listening to every word so he continued. 'She was alive all right, but she wouldn't wake up so the Widda came screaming into the village for help. Jimmy fetched the doctor and they got her to the hospital. She was unconscious for the better part of two weeks and not a sign of the fellow that did it but for a belt that Jimmy picked up at the place. I was only a lad at the time but I remember the way your father went around with that belt, praying for your mother's life and swearing what he'd do to the fellow when he was caught.'

'And was he caught?'

'Well now,' Matty rubbed his forehead and shook his head. 'From that day to this, I'd have said he was but I don't know now.'

'What do you mean?'

Matty looked around at the listening walls then, without taking his eyes off her face, told Emer the story of the Morrisseys and their downfall, from the day Nell Hannigan was raped to the day he watched Patrick Morrissey's terrified sister fleeing from the burnt out ruins of her home. In a rage of drink old man Morrissey set light to the place and took himself off to Dublin to try and save his son. Got no further than to be kicked out of the first pub there before he staggered out in front of a cart and was killed stone dead in an instant.'

'And was she all right then, did she stay with the Carmodys?'

'Well, some said the Carmodys sent her off to relations in Cork but they wouldn't talk of it – even denied she ever been with them – and some said that she drowned herself—'

'The stream at Mad Morrisseys!'

'That's it. That's where she was to have thrown herself in and floated down to the river and out to the sea, never to be seen again.'

'And is that what happened, do you think? '

'Who's to say?' He paused and looked at Emer, uncertain whether he should say more but she was watching him.

'Matty,' she said and her voice was slow and steady. 'I've lived with whispers and secrets all my life. They might have been there to protect me but at the end of the day, they're all lies. And I'm fed up with them. My Mam, after years of torment has suddenly decided to tell me what she's not told a soul before, not even my father, because something or someone has frightened her – and I want to know who. Now if there's anything else I should know, I'd be very grateful.'

'Yes, Mam.' Matty saluted her. 'Aren't you as bossy as your father was all the same?' When she smiled at him, he continued. 'I didn't know, no more than anyone else, what happened to the Morrissey girl. She could have gone to Cork; she could have been dead. Then, she turned up here and your mother recognised her.'

'What! Why did nobody tell me?' Emer was white with rage.

'Calm yourself! She didn't come here for your mother at all – didn't even know she was here – and I can tell you, she'd not have set foot in the place if she had known.'

'What did she want then?'

For all that he knew her anger was justified, Matty was not in the mood to be spoken crossly to. He had had enough of women, even if they were fine young women like Emer Fagan. 'Sit down and calm yourself and I'll tell you.' He waited while she settled. 'She was here to do a good deed, coming to see someone else altogether. She didn't choose to come, she was sent.'

Emer's head span with it all. 'Who did she come to see? Who sent her?'

Matty pulled himself upright and tidied the front lapels of his jacket. 'As a matter of fact, it was Aggie who sent her and it was me she came to see.'

'Why?'

Questions, questions, questions. Matty was tired. He spoke very slowly as if to a child, 'She was sent by Agnes because Agnes couldn't come herself and the reason she came was to bring me a bit of brown bread and a few other things, which I haven't had since. You were here yourself, do you not remember? You were going out when she was coming in? You must have passed her in the hallway?'

'I did?' She sat back and Matty watched her brow fuss and furrow as she replayed the day's events in her head. She'd left quickly so as not to get drawn in to conversation with Agnes but it wasn't Agnes – her face cleared. 'Oh, my God!'

Matty nodded calmly. 'That's who she is and now you know who she was - I think her name was Helen, or Ellen or no – what was it – Eleanor Morrissey, that's who she was!'

'And that's who she is now.'

Matty nodded. 'Sister Pius.'

CHAPTER 23

THOUGH IT WAS STILL EARLY IN THE AFTERNOON when Emer came out of the home, it was overcast and the wind had blown heavy clouds across the sky. Sister Pius, Eleanor Morrissey, poor soul. Little wonder she was as cold and angry as she was – losing everything she had and probably thinking she was somehow to blame. And what if she had known nothing after all? What boy is going to boast of his cowardice to a sister who idolises him? He'd be more likely to act as if he had.

She got into the car and drove slowly down the Home's long drive. At the end she paused a while, considered her next move and then turned left towards the main road to the city. As she came up to the crossroads a tractor pulled out in front of her and the farmer leaned out and offered a friendly wave but not a space to pass. Emer sat tapping the steering wheel impatiently. In the dim light he wouldn't be able to see into the car so he probably thought it was John. Come on, come on, she willed him, as the huge wheels sucked a pattern of mud off the narrow road and flipped it over in front of her, this isn't the time for me to be dawdling along country roads when the day has a momentum of its own and I'm only just able to keep up with the speed of it.

Without warning, the tractor pulled into a gateway and Emer was about to overtake when she saw the ambulance coming in the other direction. The lights were flashing and the siren sounded shrill and alien in the dusky air. She pulled in with a screech and watched as it went flying past, barely skimming the side of the car. The car cut out and when she tried to restart it, she found that her hands were shaking so much they wouldn't obey her and turn the key. Damn, damn …

'Are you all right there, Mister Fa— oh! Is it yourself, Missus?'

Emer turned to see a ruddy face pressed up against the window. She wound the window down and smiled at him. 'I'm grand, thanks Jack – I wasn't expecting it.'

'No, I'd have warned you only I didn't see it meself tearing around like that at this time of the afternoon.' He took off his cap and scratched the top of his head. 'Where do you think it's off to? It's in a terrible hurry.' He slid his cap back on and peered down the empty road as if he might pick up some clues.

Emer followed the direction of his gaze. 'I don't know. It could be Kildoran or if it turns right at the top of the hill it could be for Ballyfee. No doubt we'll hear soon enough anyway.'

Jack wiped his nose and nodded approvingly. 'You're right there. Well, whoever it is, they'll be in time – they should the way that feckin' lunatic was driving!' He threw his head back and laughed at his own joke. 'That'd be a fine thing altogether – ambulances collecting their own patients be causin' accidents!' And giving the top of his cap a token scratch, he climbed back onto the tractor and drove off.

When she pulled into the hospital car park later, a light stinging drizzle had started. Emer parked near the exit and sat a while gathering her thoughts. The arrival of other cars eventually heralded the start of visiting hours so she headed up the steps towards the lights of the front door.

Inside, it was bright and the walls shone with the sickly cream of washable paint. Emer removed her scarf and ran her fingers through her hair. There were two people ahead of her at the desk so she pulled her compact out her bag and took a quick look at her face in the mirror. A pale version of herself looked back. Her eyes looked huge and dark and her cheeks were bright in the white face. She looked like a ghost. Dabbing a bit of powder over her cheeks and onto her nose to try and even out the effect, she rummaged in her bag for a lipstick. Amongst the tissues and receipts at the bottom was a shiny gold lipstick that had lived in this bag for years. 'Pink Promise' was more like 'Lurid Insult' in the flesh but at least it would give her a bit of colour. Hooking her bag onto her elbow, she lifted the small compact mirror close to her lips and tried to apply the lipstick.

Just as she put it to her lips her elbow was jostled as the side doors burst open and a trolley bed was pushed quickly to the sliding emergency doors. Doctors and nurses adjusted tubes and stood ready to receive the patient who was being lifted out of an ambulance newly arrived outside. Emer moved over to the corner out of the way and lifted the mirror again to see how much colour the jostling had streaked across her face. There was a line of lipstick all the way across her cheek and she looked worse than when she had started. She was rummaging in her bag for a tissue when the group moved past, through the doors, and by the time she was fixed up again they had moved inside. The waiting area was calm again. The person in front of her in the queue was handing over a form she had been filling and Emer moved to the front. The receptionist behind the counter looked at her expectantly.

'Oh, hello,' Emer stuffed the tissue and compact untidily back into her bag and smiled. 'Sorry, I'm not very organised – I got held up by a tractor and then an ambulance—' The woman barely stifled a sigh and Emer realised she was whittering but she was too weary with the day to care. 'I wondered if I might see Sister Agnes Dowling for a few minutes, please? She's in Ward Four?'

The woman looked at her for a few moments before exhaling slowly. 'Um,' she said, as if the matter warranted great effort on her part. She flipped the pages of the large book in front of her and ran a manicured finger down the list of names, 'Who was it you wanted to see?'

'Sister Agnes Dowling, from the convent at Kildoran. I think she's due home soon. I wondered if there's any—'

'Sister Agnes Dowling? Ah! Here we are – no, I'm afraid you can't see her at the moment.' The woman lifted her head and there was a trace of a smile on her perfectly painted face. She turned back the pages of her book with a flourish. 'Sister Agnes has left already. She was taken home today, left just before lunch. I'm afraid you've had a wasted journey.'

'Oh!' Emer didn't know whether to be pleased or disappointed. It would have been nice to have a few quiet moments with Sister Agnes but it was good that she was well enough to go home. She nodded at the woman. 'I see, well, thank you anyway.'

'Not at all.' The woman turned her attention to the next person, Emer's existence already forgotten.

All that for nothing. She was cold, she was tired and she wasn't in the mood for the drive back along dark muddy roads but there was no point hanging around here. Might as well go home and see what had been going on there while she had been out having her life turned upside down. She didn't relish the thought of 'home' just yet or facing John but she would have to sometime. He didn't usually stay angry with her for too long – she didn't interest him enough for that. He could blaze at her in the morning and reduce her to tears and come in at lunchtime with the paper tucked under his arm and not even notice her tear streaked face or care enough to remember that he was the one who had caused it. Usually that indifference crushed her but today she was glad of it. She didn't have the energy for another confrontation. She shook out her scarf into a triangle, swung it round to the back of her head and was just about to tie it under her chin when somebody caught her elbow and a familiar voice said: 'Emer! Thank God! How did you get here so quickly?'

She turned around to see Dr Rourke looking at her anxiously. 'Conor? What do you mean? I'm too late, aren't I? Agnes went home at lunchtime.'

He looked puzzled. 'You're here to see Agnes?'

She nodded. 'Why – who else would I be here to see—' Suddenly the picture of an ambulance speeding past her in the direction of Kildoran flashed into her mind and her forehead went suddenly cold. 'Conor, who is it? What's happened? Gareth?'

He put his arm around her and sat her onto one of the hard chairs arranged by the wall. It seemed a long time before he spoke and all the while she could feel how her elbow was jostled as she applied the lurid lipstick and she could hear again the commotion as the trolley bed was pushed quickly past with someone on it – someone the doctor thought she had rushed here to be with—

'Not Gareth, Emer, Gareth's fine – he's in our house and Helen will keep him for you till you get back.'

She felt the wave of relief wash over her.

'It's John.'

John.

The doctor was waiting for her to say something but she only crossed herself and then turned her face to him. She was very calm as if she had all day to hear what he had to say so he started slowly. 'Apparently, John was in the shop tidying the shelves. One minute he was on the ladder, the next he keeled over and hit his head on the side of the counter as he came down.'

'Then it's a bump to the head? It's not so serious, is it?' She was now clutching his sleeve and there was a kind of quiet desperation in her voice.

The doctor took her hand and held it tightly. 'The fall's not the problem, Emer.' He cleared his throat. 'John's had a heart attack. It's been coming for a while now and anything could have sent him over the edge. Whether he stretched too quickly or whatever, it happened today and it was that which made him fall. The knock on the head was incidental.'

'What does that mean – incidental? It's dangerous to knock your head. What do you mean, it's incidental?'

She was shaking now so he held her hands and made her look at him. 'Listen to me, Emer, it's incidental because it happened but it didn't make any difference. John's been living on the edge and he wouldn't take advice. Today he tipped over.'

Through the haze and the wild buzzing in her ears, Emer saw the concern in his eyes and heard the words he wasn't saying. 'So what are you telling me, Conor Rourke? Are you telling me he could have hit his head as hard as he liked because he was already—'

'No, I'm not saying that. The ambulance was there within minutes and he's very weak but he's still alive. They're working on him now, we'll just have to wait.'

He had barely finished the sentence when the doors behind them opened and without turning around, Emer could feel someone standing there. She saw the glance, which passed from one man to the other, and then the dark cloud come over him as he looked down at her. He opened his mouth to speak and seemed about to tighten his grip on her hand but she pulled it away.

'Shush,' she whispered, putting a finger to his lips. 'Say nothing. I don't want to hear it. You don't need to say it. I know.' She stood up, aware that she shouldn't feel so calm but somehow this fitted in with the day she was living. It had started with John and her whole life had been thrown into turmoil and it had ended with John and now there was nothing she didn't know and she should go home. She tied another knot in the scarf under her chin and started to walk towards the door.

'Emer.' The doctor caught up with her. 'Do you want to see him, to say goodbye?'

'No,' she said and she was cold inside now as well. 'I don't want to say goodbye. I just want to go home. But I don't want to drive. Will you take me home?' She asked the question as if she were stating a fact.

He picked up her bag where she had dropped it on the floor and beckoning a nurse who was watching them, said quietly, 'Nurse, can you sit a moment with Mrs Fagan, please. I will be back as soon as possible.' Then he followed the other doctor through the doors. He might have been gone for moments or hours – Emer could never remember afterwards.

She only remembered that he came back and then they were driving through the dark roads back to Kildoran.

All the way home he kept his eyes on the roads ahead and said nothing as she recounted in a steady voice all that had happened that day, all that she had learned. And when she was finished telling him that, she told him that there were no secrets in her life any more. She told him that she'd spent her whole life holding her tongue and that the one time she'd stood up to her mother, she'd had to stand alone. She told him how angry she's been and how she had rushed out and fallen under the car of the man she had later married. And now she must bury him. And then she had fumbled in her bag again and when he offered her his handkerchief she pushed it angrily away and instead took out a frivolous lipstick and tried to put it on her lips. The roads were muddy and rutted and as the car moved over the bumps, her elbow was jostled and an angry line of colour streaked her face. She took out her compact with a *tut* of impatience and examined it.

And it was only when she tried to wipe it off with the back of her hand that she eventually started to cry.

CHAPTER 24

AGNES CALLED THE FOLLOWING MORNING, accompanied by Bridie. 'Oh Emer. How are you?'

'You should be in your bed!' Emer ushered Agnes into the chair by the fire. ' I don't know what the doctor will say if he comes in here and finds you.'

'Arrah, stop your fussin'. He won't be able to get in here at all unless he can make it past me!' Bridie turned sideways to show how effectively she was qualified to fill a doorway and despite herself, Emer couldn't help smiling at the sight of so much human flesh being wielded as a weapon on an unsuspecting village. Agnes tried to stifle a chuckle, which turned into a cough. All eyes were on her.

'Oh, Agnes, you're great to come but you mustn't get ill again.' Emer smiled at her friend.

'I'm grand. I'm grateful to be out of bed for a change though it's a sad reason for coming across. Are you all right?' She patted Emer's hand and looked into her face for the answer.

Emer nodded. 'I'm fine, Agnes. I don't think I feel anything really, just numb at the suddenness of it.'

'Is there anything we can do?' Bridie started to collect the cups that were scattered across the table. 'I'll wash these for you for a start.'

'No, leave them.' Emer caught her arm and held her there, 'I need to keep busy at the moment. I know it's all going to hit me soon and I need to be ready.' Bridie seemed about to move again. 'Really, it's kind of you but I'd prefer to be occupied.' She got up and took the cups from Bridie's hands and started to wash them. The women watched her back for a moment and noticed together how the water went on running long after the basin was full and the cups lay in the flow of it, untouched.

Bridie nodded to Agnes. 'Here, Sister,' she said, 'you stay in the heat and I'll pop up and help Cora outside. There's all sorts coming in and some of them from the country haven't heard the news yet.'

For a while neither woman left in the kitchen spoke. Agnes sat, looking at the array of cups and plates still left on the table and Emer with her hands in the sink, immobile. Eventually, Agnes spoke. 'If you don't turn that tap off, we'll have to start praying for rain.'

Emer turned the tap off and sat down. Her face was composed and her eyes were dry. She smiled at the empty doorway. 'Poor things,' she said, 'Bridie's been here half the night and Cora and the boys were here at the crack of dawn, working away. I don't know what I'd have done without them.'

Agnes watched her but said nothing. The tap, not fully shut, dripped loudly and the sound of it was like a metronome to her still-laboured breathing. Emer played with a bit of fluff on the sleeve of her jumper till she could no longer pretend to have any interest in it and when she spoke, her voice was quiet. 'I should feel sad, shouldn't I, Agnes? I should feel sad because yesterday my husband had a heart attack and died.' She rolled the fluff into a little ball and let it fall onto the floor. 'But I don't.' She lifted her head and looked straight at her friend.

Agnes could see the change in her face. Unlike that morning when they had last spoken, there was no timidity there now. Her eyes were clear and her mouth was set and determined.

'Mostly there's numbness but no emotion except maybe—' she paused and swallowed as if she was about to make a confession '—except maybe relief.' Then she let out a sigh as if it was a relief in itself to have made such an admission. 'Is that terrible? Am I a bad person? I am, aren't I? I'm unnatural. I shouldn't be saying things like that ... '

Her voice rose slightly and Agnes heard the edge of hysteria. She also saw the swelling on the side of Emer's face that had only gone down a little since the previous day. Leaning forward, she traced a line gently the length of the swelling and brought her fingers round to rest for a second on Emer's lips.

'Shush, now, pet,' she said. 'You're not bad.' She caught Emer's eye and held her stare. 'Listen to me. I have known you for all of your life. I knew you when you were a little girl sitting across in our kitchen peeling apples and I knew you when your father died and you were left to look after a mother so beside herself with grief that she couldn't see the living for the dead. I knew you the day you married and I have known you since. You are not bad. You are not unnatural.' She touched the swelling. 'And if you feel relief, maybe it's only because you no longer have anything to fear.'

Emer looked at her in amazement. 'Did you know, then?' she gestured to the marks, 'Did you know what he did?'

Agnes shrugged. 'I suspected but I wasn't sure. I tried to get you to tell me but you were always a secretive one.'

'Secretive? God help us – that's the last thing I need to be.' She leaned forward and held Agnes' hand tightly. 'That's part of it, you see. Part of what makes it all so unreal. Even if it hadn't happened, even if John hadn't – you know, today would have been different.' Behind her she heard someone come to the door then turn and go up the passage again to the shop. Then Bridie's voice boomed out. 'I'm afraid she's busy at the moment. You carry on there and I'll tell her you called.' Taking a deep breath, Emer started to tell Agnes the story of all she had learned. She left nothing out, the argument with John, the meeting with Pius in the church, the ranting of her mother and the calm way Matty had listened and filled in the story of Nell's life. She stopped then and sat back.

Agnes waited till the story was over before she nodded slowly. 'Well, I never!' she said. 'I knew part of it but never the whole. I remember being told the story of 'Mad Morrissey' and the drowned sister but there was always a doubt about that part of it. My older sister Connie used to say that the girl was taken away by the nuns – claimed someone had confided that to her– but she never dwelt on it and then she was gone herself so the story died and became another local legend.' She shook her head, recalling Pius' anguished face as she stared at the crucifix that night in the chapel. 'The poor soul, having to come back here after running from it all those years ago and everything that was dear to her lost and gone. And your poor mother!' Suddenly the implication of what Emer had heard hit her. 'Does she really believe that Sister Pius – Eleanor – has come back to get her?'

Emer nodded.

'God help her.' Agnes crossed herself. 'What can we do?

'I don't know. My head has been full of it all night. Dr Rourke gave me something to help me sleep but I might as well have taken Silvermints. It raced around in my head and I kept thinking that John is dead and that should be the biggest thing but somehow it all seems to tie in and I can't separate it. That's why I can't feel sad – only confused – and that's making me numb.'

'Um—' Agnes rubbed her forehead to clear the niggling worry that was there.

Mistaking her gesture for headache, Emer stood up. 'Listen to me, loading all this on you and you barely a day out of the hospital. I haven't even asked you how you are.'

'I'm fine.' Agnes chuckled, 'mind you, I'll think twice about falling ill in the future. When I went in this was a steady sort of a place and I come back to find a right state of chaos!'

'You're right. And I'm in the middle of it and I don't know what to do.'

'What to do?' Agnes looked at her friend sternly. 'You'll do nothing about this for the minute. There's enough that needs to be done first. The rest can wait. It's waited nearly fifty years; it can wait a few more. You have a husband to bury and a child to rear and that's what you'll do.'

Emer looked at her and the reality of her situation suddenly flooded in on her. From out of nowhere she remembered John as he was when she met him first: big and brash but attentive too, and generous. She remembered how important he made her feel when he took her places and while he might spend the time flirting with every other woman in the place, it was to her side he returned at the end of the day. She remembered the smile on his face as she walked up the aisle towards him, feeling beautiful for the first time in her life; and the way she had felt protected as he took her from her father's arm and linked her to his. For once, she was the main woman and she loved it. There were other times too, when Gareth was born and he had come into the room to be handed his son. She could still see the pride on his face.

She didn't realise she was crying till Agnes pushed a handkerchief into her hands. She took it without a word, grateful for Agnes' kindness as well as the tears that prompted it. All night she had tried to cry for John but the memory of recent years and the gratitude that she would never have to relive them blanked out all sorrow and she had been left feeling cold and unnatural.

So when the tears came she was glad of them. She wept quietly for the life they hadn't had together and the person he had become and when she was done, she wiped her eyes and got up. Agnes nodded off to sleep as Emer pottered around her, tidying things that didn't need it and listening to the sounds of people coming into the shop and hearing the news from a hushed Cora and Bridie in full flight. And when they were done they came down to the kitchen. Bridie winked at her when she saw Agnes.

'Now,' she said, rolling her sleeves down. 'That's enough of that for you, my girl; I have decided how we can help. This kitchen is fine for a few but you don't want the whole country traipsing in here after the funeral and you certainly don't want to open the bar.'

Emer opened her mouth to object but Bridie stopped her. 'Not a word! You'll look after yourself and Gareth on Wednesday next. I'm over to the convent to arrange that the sisters and I will look after everything else. The convent parlour is big enough for the mourners and every other gurrier who likes to find himself drowning his sorrows at the passing of a publican. You try to do it here and you'll be pulling pints till the cows come home.'

'She's right.' Agnes muttered sleepily from the depths of the chair. 'She's completely right, as usual. You come to us and we'll look after it for you.'

Emer smiled but said nothing. She had given little thought to the funeral, knowing that it would mean hours of listening to condolences from men she didn't know, men whose faces were not familiar to her, only their voices late at night in the bar below, laughing. And the rough edge of her husband's voice laughing loudest of all and she would lie there waiting for him to come up to her. And now he was gone and she would not have to face those men alone.

She looked at the women now willing her to agree. 'You are good to me,' she said, 'and I appreciate it. That's what we'll do then. Thank you.'

Bridie and Agnes were stalwarts in the week before John's funeral. Agnes grew stronger by the day, declaring her goal to be full fitness by Tuesday so that she would be ready for the sandwich making on Wednesday morning. Every day one or other of them came into the shop and stayed just long enough to be company and just short enough not to be a bother. Cora poked her head in a few times but she was pale and withdrawn and eventually, Emer told her to go home.

'You're not sacking me, Mrs Fagan, are you?' The girl's voice was full of panic.

Emer looked at her in surprise. 'Sacking you, Cora? Of course I'm not sacking you!'

'Don't be cross with me then.'

'I'm not cross with you either, what gave you that idea?' Emer put down the boxes she had been stacking and turned to face her. Cora wouldn't meet her eye. She played with the hem of her cardigan and opened her mouth to speak but nothing came out. 'Cora?'

'I didn't do anything – it wasn't my fault, I swear it, I didn't even hear him coming.'

The doctor's voice came back to her *One minute he was on the ladder—* and Emer suddenly realised what had happened. 'What was he helping you with, Cora?'

Cora raised her head slowly. 'I didn't need any help; I said I didn't. Fergus was just below in the store and I could hear him and I said I didn't need help and he said a pretty girl like me—' she started to cry, 'And then there was a bang and he was on the floor and Fergus came up and said he was having a heart attack and his face was all purple.'

Emer looked at her calmly. So that was it – John was true to form even to the end. She exhaled slowly and, taking a handkerchief from her sleeve, handed it to the girl. 'Here, wipe your eyes. I'm not cross with you. Mr Fagan had a bad heart and he knew himself not to go climbing ladders. That's enough crying now. We'll be shut from Wednesday for the rest of the week so there's lots to be done and I need you to help me.' Cora wiped her eyes and offered the handkerchief back. 'Keep it. I'm just going back to the kitchen for a while – you carry on here, I'll be up later.'

'Yes, Mrs Fagan. Thanks and—' Emer waited while she struggled for the words '—I'm sorry about before. You know, cheeking you and all. Mam was right, I was losing the run of myself.'

Emer smiled. 'You were a bit – but sure we all did that when were young. I gave a bit of lip myself.'

'Did you!' Cora couldn't hide the amazement

'I did – but only a bit, mind, so don't go getting any ideas!'

'I won't – and I'll have this place so tidy you'll be dead proud. Oh, sorry, I—'

'Don't, it doesn't matter. And listen, if anyone comes in, say that I'm having a rest and maybe they'd call later, would you?' Picking up a packet of fig rolls as she went past, she went down the steps to the peace of the kitchen beyond.

The kitchen was warm and still smelled of breakfast. After a lethargic weekend, Gareth was keen to go to school and Emer was glad. He had enough of his sadness for the moment and school offered a welcome respite. He was packed and ready before Peter arrived to get him.

'Bye!' She wanted to kiss him but he was gone. Soon after, Bridie came, her daughter trailing after her. They looked after the shop while she toyed reluctantly with account books before giving up. Next week would be soon enough. Now only Cora was left and Emer was glad of the quiet. All her thoughts were on the past and the immediate future. Anything beyond next Wednesday didn't exist. She knew that she was still living in a daze and it wouldn't be till afterwards, till all the excitement died down that it would really hit her but she couldn't cope with that for the moment. For the moment all she wanted to do was sleep. She sat back and let her mind wander. She must have fallen asleep because suddenly it was the afternoon and Gareth was standing in front of her, breathless.

'Mammy, I didn't do anything bold in school today.'

Well used to ground being prepared, Emer rubbed her eyes and looked at him closely. 'And why might I think you had?'

Gareth's eyes flicked to the door. In the shop the bell rang and there was the sound of hushed voices. 'I don't know what she wants but it wasn't me.' Emer recognised Pius' voice.

'I'm sure it's me she's come to see, Gareth, about Daddy.' He breathed a sigh of relief, 'Why don't you go to Peter's for half an hour. See the kittens and you're allowed one biscuit – if it's offered – and then straight home.'

'Oh, thanks. I'll go out the back.' And he was gone, just as Cora turned the corner into the kitchen.

'Mrs Fagan? There is a visitor here for you.'

'That's all right, Cora, thanks.' She made to get up from the chair but Pius gestured her to stay where she was.

'Please don't get up on my account, Mrs Fagan. I have come to offer my sympathy.' Her voice was very steady and her manner stiff. It was as if she had read what words were to be used when offering condolences and had memorised them.

Snatches of what her mother and Matty told her the other night flew around Emer's head but she couldn't quite focus on them. Maybe afterwards when things settled she would give time to it but for the moment she couldn't be bothered. She pointed to a chair.

'Thank you, that's very kind. Won't you sit down?' Pius looked as if she might refuse but Emer stopped her. 'Please do, really. I must have fallen asleep and I'm about to wake myself up with a cup of tea. Have one with me.'

Pius perched awkwardly on the edge of the chair. 'That would be very nice, thank you.' she said, in a voice which suggested that it was anything but. Emer ignored it. Whatever the woman's story, there was a link between them whether Pius would be prepared to admit it or not. It made Emer feel safe. Maybe the links of the past are tougher than she imagined and things unresolved hang on until someone comes along to break the spell. They would have to talk later and this might prepare the ground. 'I have coffee, either, if you'd prefer?'

'Thank you, tea will be fine. You mustn't go to any bother.'

'To be honest, I'm glad to be doing something. I don't seem to be able to concentrate on anything at all for any length of time at the moment so making a cup of tea is about the limit.' She realised she was rattling on but Pius didn't seem to notice. She was looking all around her slowly, lost in her own world, till her eyes came to rest on a photograph of Emer's parents on the dresser. It was old and faded but taken when they were newly married and both looked so happy. Pius stared at the photo for a minute and then her face started to redden. Seeing her discomfort, Emer busied herself with the pot and finding a plate for the biscuits she had brought down earlier. She hoped she'd given her time to compose herself but by the time the pot was on the table, Pius was still fixed on the faces.

'They're my parents,' she said.

Pius said nothing.

'My father died some years ago, before his time – a weakness in the lungs. Apparently he's always had it but we didn't know.'

'No,' Pius said quietly, 'you'd never know.' Then, as if hearing her own voice brought her to her senses, she corrected herself, 'I mean he looks like a fine man.'

Emer smiled at her.

'And your mother was a pretty woman.'

Emer peered closely at the photo. 'Yes, she said, 'I suppose she was.' She saw the surprised look on Pius' face. 'Oh dear, that sounds awful. I meant that you don't really think of your mother as pretty or not, do you, you just think of her as your mother.'

'I wouldn't know.' Pius picked up a biscuit and took a tentative bite from the corner of it. 'My mother died before I knew her.' She lifted her hand to ward off sympathy. 'I didn't know her.' She might have said more but the bell at the shop door rang again and they could hear a man's voice. Unlike the usual hushed voices of those who had come for a drink or a pound of rashers, this man was loud. He headed into the bar where they could barely hear him and within a few seconds, Cora was in the kitchen. She was flustered and embarrassed. She stood at the door rolling her cardigan hem.

'What is it, Cora? Is that a customer for the bar? Will you tell him that we're not serving there at the moment? Fergus will be down at seven and we'll open then for a while but at the moment there's no one serving.'

Cora looked as if she was going to cry. 'I already told him that. I said we were shut, except for groceries and that the bar was shut but he said it wasn't. He said he wanted a drink and I told him there was no one there to serve him, and about Mr Fagan, and he said it didn't matter because he knew already and he could serve himself. I couldn't stop him—'

From the bar they could hear the sound of someone pulling aside a stool and then the steady *clop, clop* of someone throwing the rubber rings at the ring board. Sister Pius stood up. 'Would you like me to come with you while you remove this person from the premises?'

Emer shook her head. 'It'd take more than the three of us, I'm afraid. Cora, would you run across and see if your father is across at the hotel? He might be there by now because your mother said he'd pick you up on the way home. If he's not, find

293

me a man who'll come over a minute.' The *clopping* from the bar had stopped. 'He won't stay too long if there's a man here to shift him.'

She crept up the steps and peered through the side of the door into the bar. The lights were off and it took a while before her eyes became accustomed to the gloom. When they did, she could see his profile in the dim light. She crept back to the kitchen. Cora had let herself out the back door and Pius was sitting there waiting. 'You don't have to stay, Sister, Cora will be here in a minute and I'll be rid of him. He's only pushing it because he knows John's not around. As soon as a man stands up to him, he'll be gone.' She held the back door open for Pius. 'I should have known he'd turn up—'

About to leave, Pius paused.

'—looking for his inheritance.'

A loud belch came from the bar and the two of them shuddered at the sound. Even in his vulgarity the voice was unmistakable. For Emer it had been – maybe ten years; for Pius more like fifty, but it was still a voice neither of them would forget.

They both had every reason not to want to remember Noel Fagan.

CHAPTER 25

B Y THE TIME CORA ARRIVED BACK with her father in tow, Noel Fagan had left the bar. He finished his drink and left the glass back on the counter with a bang. Then, pushing the stool back noisily he stood up and hitched the front of his trousers. With both palms he smoothed his hair back, all the while watching his reflection in the mirror at the back of the bar. He seemed to be considering his next move while the two women outside held their breath and waited. They both felt rooted to the spot, though each knew that if he came around the counter to pour himself another drink he would see her there. He didn't. Another ineffectual attempt at tucking an unwilling shirtfront into his trousers and he was off. As he passed the hoop board he kicked the ones that he'd missed into the ashes in the fireplace and strode out without a backward glance.

Frozen in the blast of cold air from the street the women stood. From the step there was only half a glimpse of the doorway but the sight of even half a back and the sound of that step was enough. Emer felt a rush of bile rise to her throat and she swallowed hard to stop herself letting go. Behind her she could hear Pius exhale slowly and she wondered who would speak first. As it happened, neither needed to, the back door opened and Sam shuffled in with Cora in the shadows behind him.

'Ye're all right now; the cavalry's arrived! Where is he? Evenin', Sister.' He doffed his cap and started up the step but Emer stopped him.

'It's all right, Sam, he's gone.'

'Gone! Well, would you credit it and me all ready to take on the blackguard? Do you know who it was at all?'

The two women looked at one another but neither said a word.

'Just someone passin' through, do you think?'

'No,' Emer said, 'though I hope he might do that. Come down and have a cup with us – we were just about brewed when he came in.' She ushered the three of them in front of her and continued, 'It was the brother, Sam,'

'Jaysus! I though that fellow was gone for good! What's he doing back here! It must be – what – ten years since he was in the place.'

'Something like that – I haven't been counting. He must have read the announcement in the paper and he's here to see what's in it for him.' She sighed. 'Sit down – I'll make a fresh pot, this is cold.'

As she poured the tea, Pius stood fiddling with her beads and before the second cup was filled, she held up her hand. 'I can't stay. I really must be off,' and she got up and nodded her goodbyes to Emer and was out the door before either of them realised what she was doing.

They heard her shoes clipping across the floor of the shop and then the sound of the bell over the front door. A blast of cold air swept into the kitchen and Emer shivered. 'Don't ask me what that was about, Sam. She's the oddest I ever met. She stands looking as if she has a lot to say, then she's off.'

'Aye,' he started to chuckle, 'that's women for you. Will I finish these?' He took another biscuit and bit into it.

'Do, please, they'd never keep.' Emer smiled to herself. The poor divil probably never got to a full biscuit in his own house with all those children, or if the children didn't get to them first, there was always Bridie's journey up the lane home to be survived. 'Pour yourself another cup as well, will you? I'll just nip up the road and collect Gareth. I don't want him walking down on his own in this light.'

'Nor with that fellow about; he's a dangerous bastard when he's had a few. Would you like me to walk you?'

'Not at all, it's only down the street – there'll be plenty about. Look to the shop for me, Cora, will you?'

'Right-o,' Cora went up the steps in front of her. 'He's terrible like him, isn't he?' she whispered as soon as they were out of her father's earshot. When Emer said nothing, she continued, 'I mean, he doesn't look that like him, what with being older and all, but he has the same way of standing and when he walks, he sounds the very same...' Her voice trailed off as she realised that she was talking too much but Emer was already out and on her way to Rourke's to collect Gareth.

As she approached the bridge on the near side of the convent, Pius could see him sitting on the wall. He had his head turned away and was looking at something in the water so he didn't see her coming. Even if he did, she was sure he wouldn't know who she was. It was almost fifty years since they had last set eyes on one another and she was not then in the anonymous disguise of a nun's habit. She quickened her step as she approached him, aware that if she turned and walked in the other direction, she would only draw more attention to herself as her steps rang out in the frosty evening air. Anyway, where would she go? The parish church was huge and there would be a few in there, making their peace before making their way home for tea, but he might still be there when she came out and then what would she do? She bent her head and kept walking.

At the top of the bridge the road narrowed and the path was worn so that you had to step onto the road to pass anyone. If nothing came from the other side, she'd be fine. The bridge was not high and as soon as she reached the top she would be able to see the lights of the convent and she'd be safe. All she had to do was keep walking. Keep walking and keep calm and he wouldn't notice her and it would only be a minute. She quickened her pace and stepped off the pavement as she neared him.

She was so intent on getting there that she didn't see the bicycle coming up from the other side. With a swish of tyres the cyclist swerved to avoid her and almost knocked Noel Fagan off the wall at the same time.

'Whoa! Look where you're going for Jaysus' sake!'

'Sorry! Ah, hell – would you look at the state of my coat.' Muttering to himself, the old man picked his cap off the road and slid it back on his head. He brushed the bits of grit from his coat and turned to face Pius. 'What were *you* doing in the mid— oh, sorry Sister, I didn't see you what with the black and all – are you all right?'

'I'm fine, thank you, I hope your bicycle is not damaged?'

'Fuck the bicycle – you could have knocked me into the river, riding around without a light like a feckin' lunatic.' Noel Fagan's voice came out of the darkness.

The old man picked up his bike. 'Watch your language, would you! What sort of an eejit would be sitting on a bridge on a night like this anyway?' He moved closer and peered up into Noel's face. 'Be the love o' Jaysus, Fagan! Back to look for your inheritance, is it?' He started to laugh as he eased his leg over the crossbar. 'I wouldn't hold my breath if I was you. Goodnight to you, Sister!' And he wobbled off, still laughing.

Noel muttered to himself and fumbled in the pockets of his coat. When he found the cigarettes he glanced to where Pius was still rooted to the wall on the other side.

'I don't suppose you have a match on you?'

She shook her head, still avoiding his eye.

'Or a spare candle, neither!' He threw his head back, pleased at his wit.

His laughter followed her as she almost ran off the bridge towards the convent. He watched her go, skinny old bag; hardly have use for a candle that one. He heard the sound of a box in the depths of one of his pockets and fished it out. The first match wouldn't light nor the second one so he cupped his hands round the third and inhaled deeply. He looked around. The bike was gone and the nun was just at the door of the convent. He took the cigarette out of his mouth and called after her, 'Hey, Sister, any chance of a cup of tea!' He thought she'd ignore him but she stopped and turned around on the step. From the distance he couldn't see her clearly or hear her but she appeared to be saying something to him. He moved a step closer to hear what it was. As he came abreast of the convent gate he stopped. She had opened the door and now she was framed in the light from the hallway beyond. What was the silly bitch saying at all? He took a drag from his cigarette and shuffled towards the light. The damp from the wall had seeped into the back of his coat and he was cold and uncomfortable. Maybe he should go back to the pub – he'd not be welcome but at least he'd be dry - that's if he could get in. The tarty young one had probably gone fretting by now and the door would be locked; he hadn't the strength to go back and demand to be let in. Maybe the convent would be a better idea …

Pius stood framed in the doorway unable to move. It was freezing out and she knew all she had to do was push the door to but her arms wouldn't move. She was watching him as if he was on a screen in front of her and now he was coming this way and any minute he'd be right up in her face and she have to look at him properly. The edges of the door pressed into her palms but she still couldn't move.

'The Lord between us and all harm, would you shut that door!' Agnes voice preceded her down the hallway as she came around the corner at the back of the stairs. 'You can feel the draught back here in the kitchen. Oh, it's yourself, Sister, are you coming in?'

The normality of her voice flicked a switch in Pius' brain and she was about to swing the door shut but Noel called to her from the bottom of the step, 'Hold on there, Sister, what about that cup of tea?'

'Who's that? Have we a visitor?' Agnes came to stand beside her and peered out into the darkness. 'Who is it?' Noel came up the steps and into the light. 'Well now – would you look at who we have here!' Her voice was cold and unwelcoming. 'Did you want something?'

'A grand warm cup of tea's what I was offered and what I was expecting.' He smiled from one to the other. Pius wanted to say that she hadn't offered him anything but no words would come out. 'And a nice warm welcome from good Christian ladies wouldn't go far astray either.' There was a sneer to his voice as if he was well used to others' dislike but not at all affected by it.

Agnes pulled her woolly shawl around her shoulders and looked surprised at Pius. She wasn't usually given to offering anyone a cup of tea, let alone bedraggled strangers out of the dark. Pius had her eyes cast down and, for a moment, Agnes wondered at the conversation which must have gone on outside. She didn't know Noel Fagan as well as she knew of him – and there was nothing in that knowledge that encouraged her to like him. It was a few years since she's seen him so she stood now and stared into his face. Time had etched the lines deep and his pallor was sickly. Although there was a sneer playing about his lips, he looked as if he hadn't eaten a proper meal for ages.

'Right so,' she said. 'If it's a cup of tea you're after, you'd better come through.' She turned and started to walk towards the kitchen. 'Follow me – and wipe your feet. We don't want you leaving your mess on our floors.' She beckoned to Pius, 'And yourself, Sister, you look perished with the cold.' As she passed the bell board she pressed the little black button that rang out the bell in every corridor of the house. *Dring dring, dring*! The one-two sequence was the signal for Sister Kathleen to come. 'Maybe Sister Kathleen might join us too – seeing that we have an unexpected visitor.' She opened the door and stood back for the two to go into the kitchen. 'Sit down, I'll have you warmed in a minute.'

'I don't—'

'Sit!' Agnes' voice was so sharp that the two of them jumped. Noel sat while Pius stood at the end of the table motionless and watched as Agnes bustled around, her energy belying her still laboured breathing, filling the kettle and getting cups. She arranged a cup and saucer in front of each and then sat there as if waiting for something. Just as the kettle began to whistle, the door opened and Sister Kathleen came in.

'I heard the bell – was someone looking for me?'

Agnes pulled herself up slowly and gestured to the old man at the far side of the table. 'We have an unexpected visitor, Sister.'

Kathleen nodded but didn't appear to be any the wiser.

'This is Mr Noel Fagan.' Agnes said. 'He is the older brother of Emer's John, the Lord have mercy on his soul. He wants a cup of tea.'

Kathleen looked even more confused. 'Well, that's grand.' She held out her hand to him. 'Sister Kathleen, I'm pleased to meet you, Mr Fagan, and sorry for your troubles. I'm surprised we haven't met before.'

Noel said nothing but took her hand and gave it a cursory tug.

'Have you been over to see Emer? She's bearing up well, God bless her.'

'He's not going to see Emer, Sister,' Agnes cut in. 'He's having a cup of tea and a bite to eat and then he'll be on his way.' Her voice was firm and Kathleen looked at her in amazement. Gentle Agnes, sending a grieving brother on his way? But Agnes only set the teapot on the table and started to cut slices off a loaf of bread with gusto. 'Isn't that right now, Mr Fagan?'

Noel shook his head. 'It is not. My brother is dead and his widow will need a man about the place to give her a hand. There's no one better than myself to do it – wasn't I reared in the business – sure, I know it like the back of my hand.'

Agnes stopped cutting and pointed the blade of the knife at him. 'I'm not one for gossip, Mr Fagan,' and she sent a quick prayer up for pardon, 'but by all accounts, you're not the only one who was ever familiar with the back of your hand. You'll not go near Emer – she has enough trouble to cope with and she doesn't need you now. So you'll eat up and be on your way.'

Kathleen's mouth was open in amazement. She looked from one to the other.

Noel Fagan was not bothered. This one wasn't anyone. He had a vague notion who she might be – one of the Dowlings from outside the village. He tried to remember the family but they were all a lot younger than he and never amounted to anything worth his time or interest. The one who'd just come in was soft enough and a bit simple – he couldn't be bothered with her – so he turned his attention to the skinny one who'd been out in the street. She hadn't said a word all the time they'd been in here, just stood there with her head bent.

'Well, that's not a nice way to talk to an old man in out of the cold, now is it, Sister, and you the one who invited me in the first place.' He took another mouthful of his tea and nodded towards the chair. 'Won't you join me?'

As if in slow motion, Pius came around and stood beside him. He had pulled out the chair for her to sit but she just looked at it. There was something odd in her expression and though his eyesight was poor he was sure he knew her from somewhere. She peered at the empty chair and mumbled something to herself.

'I beg your pardon, Sister?' Agnes leaned forward to catch what she said. 'Did you say something?'

Pius repeated it but still half to herself. It sounded like 'nothing there'. Then she started to laugh softly and raised her head. 'There's nothing there! You weren't quick enough, were you? I could have sat down and there would have been nothing there because you forgot, didn't you?' She leaned her face very close to his and he stared. She was so bloody familiar but he couldn't for the life of him remember who she was. 'So you can't do anything about it. You didn't remember in time and—' and her voice was high and sing-song, *'I'm not keen to sit beside you.'* She straightened up then and looked at the others triumphantly. 'I didn't invite him in at all, Sister. He was out on the bridge trying to cause an accident and he invited himself.' Her voice grew higher and more tremulous with each word. 'I didn't invite him. I didn't want him.'

'That's all right so,' Agnes put a hand on her arm to calm her. 'We'll pack him the few sandwiches and he'll be on his way. And you,' she said, glaring at him, 'will not go near Fagan's tonight or any night. I'll ring the Gardai if needs be and make sure that you don't. Have you money on you?' He shook his head. She went into the pantry and returned with a small leather purse from which she pulled out a couple of notes and thrust them towards him. 'Here, 'she said, 'there's a bus along at half past and you'll be getting on it. It goes into Kilkenny and you'll have no problem getting the train from there back to Dublin or wherever you came from.'

Noel finished his tea and took the notes and the bag of sandwiches held out to him. Bitch! Who did she think she was, talking to him like that? Ignorant farmer's daughter putting on airs because she had a habit on her – tight bitch. He wanted to hit her with the bag but he was hungry. The journey had cost him all the money he had but he'd considered it money well spent for the award that was at the end of it. Or could have been at the end of it if he'd only stayed in the bar and not come out. But he'd wanted to come outside to do a bit of thinking.

He hadn't stopped to think since he'd read the death notice in the paper and he knew the wife wouldn't welcome him. And now this stupid cow was giving him marching orders. The other one was sitting with a face on her like a stunned mullet not knowing what was going on and the skinny one – she was a fucking lunatic! *Not keen to sit beside you, there's nothing there.* What was she on about at all? He looked at her again and the notion that he knew her from somewhere pressed in on the sides of his head but he couldn't think straight. He needed another drink. He looked at the two notes in his hand. A bus, did she say? Right, that's what he'd do. Get the bus into Kilkenny. There was more than enough for a train fare but he wasn't going anywhere. A nice quite evening in Mooney's if it was still there, or another if it wasn't and he'd be right as rain. They could fuck off if they thought he was going all the way back to Dublin now. The spoilt little bastard of a brother was dead and there was a grand pub sitting there. No mousey blow-in was going to get her hands on it. He was Bertie Fagan's blood as much as his brother and now his brother was gone, he had an inheritance due him and he was going to claim it. He'd contest the will. See if he wouldn't.

Agnes had opened the back door and was standing there holding it. Without a word, he passed her and out into the dark night. As he went by the window he glanced in at the three women inside. They were moving around the room slowly, clearing the table and not even looking at one another. He peered again at the mad one, sure she was someone, but the fat one looked up so he offered her his fist and kept going.

He reached the bus stop at the same time as the bus. There were a couple of others waiting so he followed them on and sat hunched at the back. With a loud judder, the bus pulled off, down the street to turn at the end before doing the loop and coming back up across the bridge again. He looked at all the familiar shop fronts and some new ones. There were a hundred things he could remember about this place if he could be bothered to, but he was tired and cold and the motion of the bus was lulling him to sleep.

Coming back down the street from the doctor's house, Emer saw the bus pull out and noticed the man hunched into his big coat at the back. So he was off then. She held Gareth's hand tightly and breathed a sigh of relief. It wasn't going to be easy, but it was going to be okay.

From the small window at the side of the convent's front door, Pius watched the bus trundle over the bridge. It was picking up speed now that it was clear of the main street but she could just make out the shape of a man sitting alone at the back. In her head, a million thoughts raced around and chased each other and she felt as if all her life was coming to a head and any minute now she might explode with it all. Part of her knew she was here and now and the other part of her was like an intruder peeping out from the inside, taking over. She had to get out of here before she went mad altogether.

A hand touched her shoulder and she jumped.

'Come back into the kitchen, Sister, it's cold out here and you could do with a bit of heat.' Agnes' voice was gentle and familiar and Pius was tempted to refuse and go to her room but the look on the other woman's face was firm. She sighed and let herself be led into the kitchen where Kathleen had already set out a sheet of paper and was sitting, pen in hand.

'Well now,' Agnes said airily, as if the events of the past half hour had not happened at all. 'Hadn't we better get on with the task of planning the food for this funeral? We agreed we'd have it all sorted and we haven't given a minute to it. Have you books to mark, Sister, or would you be free to lend a hand here?' She didn't wait for an answer but pushed the sheet towards Pius. 'Here, Kathleen will have a look in the pantry and call out what's needed and if you write it down, I can go and get the shopping tomorrow. What's the first thing you need there, Sister, have we anything to make sandwiches at all? Write it down there, Sister, we'll need a good two pounds of sliced ham ...'

So Kathleen called out and Pius wrote; and Emer breathed a sigh of relief and Noel slept; and Agnes watched it all and wondered. She watched it all but she didn't know what she was seeing. There was a lull about the place but she knew enough to know that it wasn't over at all. Whatever the storm was, it hadn't blown over.

It was quiet but it was brewing and the worst was yet to come.

CHAPTER 26

O N THE DAY JOHN FAGAN WAS BURIED, Kildoran was covered with frost. The ground in the churchyard was steely and the mourners found it hard not to hop from foot to foot to prevent themselves from losing all feeling from the knees down. As soon as the last prayers were said, and the first clod of earth thrown onto the coffin, Emer turned Gareth away and started to walk back along the narrow road to the main street. Her right hand was still warm from the heat of those who had shaken it, muttering their condolences and ruffling Gareth's hair – as if their friendliness to the child would somehow alleviate the seriousness of the occasion. Behind her, some of the older villagers, well used to the ritual of funerals, directed the would-be stragglers in the direction of the convent. They had been surprised (and some not a little disappointed) when Father Martin announced that the tea was to be at the convent and not at Fagan's but a hot cup of tea was a hot cup of tea and they were freezing.

There was tea all right, gallons of the stuff and enough sandwiches to feed an army – though a very genteel one. The nuns surpassed themselves with the presentation and there was not a crust in sight. Some of the older people, who had come over straight from the church, were now sitting around the edges of the big parlour waiting for the signal to start. As soon as Emer came in, young girls appeared with huge pots of tea and some picked up the plates and started to hand round the sandwiches. No crusts meant no chewing and it was grand to be able to just sit and suck on a cold day. Those who had come from the graveyard accepted cups of tea gratefully but wished for mugs, anything to wrap frozen hands round. The convent's bone china saucers felt cold and brittle in their clumsy hands and they drank quickly so that they could put them down before they snapped.

But the girls had been primed and as soon as one cup was drained, it was refilled. Soon the effects of the warm tea, the cold graveyard and the long church service began to take its toll on the collective bladders of many of the men who drifted towards the door waiting for a decent opportunity to make an exit. There was surely a toilet in the convent but it was hardly likely to be a gents and somehow it didn't seem decent to go in the nuns' one, improper somehow. Leading the shuffling posse was Sam Hennessy, as desperate for physical relief as he was to avoid being seen by his wife as he made his escape. He watched as a girl approached Bridie with a laden platter and as soon as she had stuffed another sandwich into her mouth, he made a bolt for it.

'Sam Hennessy! Where do you think you're off to?' Bridie's voice, only barely muffled by mashed egg and half chewed white bread stopped him in his tracks.

For a second he debated pretending he hadn't heard but that might encourage her to repeat the question, only louder this time. He turned and tried to signal her to pipe down. It was already too late. Growing bored by the tea-fuelled sobriety of the occasion, the other mourners were glad of the entertainment and it seemed every eye in the room was on him.

'I'm—' he pointed towards the door. 'I'm just across the road for a minute, I'll be back.'

'You won't – you'll stay here and give me a hand keep control of these two. Come out of there before your father gets

309

a hold of you!' She bent over and tried to grab the backside of her youngest as he crawled under the table. Around her, a few people smiled, some in sympathy and some in amusement. Bill Brady's mother raised her eyes to Heaven and tutted her disapproval.

'*Bridie, I'll be back in a minute!*' Sam's voice was lower and his tone more urgent.

'Back from where? What do you need to go across the road for now?'

The look of desperation on his face made his predicament obvious to practically everyone in the room except his wife. Emer, who was sitting beside her, leaned and whispered quietly, '*Let him off, Bridie, I think he needs to go to the toilet.*'

It was the wrong move. With a dramatic flourish, Bridie put her cup on the table and hauled herself upright. 'Ah, for the love a' God, are you making all that fuss over a piddle? You don't need to cross the road for that, do you? Agnes, is there a toilet in this place at all a man could use?'

The silence that followed provided an instant cure for those who had intended to follow Sam. As if by magic, their bladders dried up and they drifted back to their wives' sides leaving him standing alone, mortified, his needs exposed. Agnes, who was standing near, caught his elbow and ushered him out of the door. As soon as they were in the hallway, the chatter started up again and now there was almost an air of merriment about it. Sam looked at Agnes in despair.

'What am I going to do with her, Agnes? She's desperate.'

Agnes smiled, 'Don't worry, nobody pays any attention and by the time you get back there'll be something else to distract the audience.'

The sound of Bridie shouting at one of the children followed by the chink of bone china breaking seemed to confirm her prediction and the two of them exchanged a shrug.

'Here's the cloakroom.' She tried to open the small door at the back of the stairs but it was locked from the inside. 'Oh, there's someone in there. Do you want to wait or what?'

'I'll wait – don't worry. You go on ahead back and I'll be up in a minute.'

'All right.' She turned and headed back to the big parlour and Sam was glad of the peace and the dim haven. From inside the politely named cloakroom there was the sound of someone running a tap and voices. The door opened and Nell Byrne came out with a nurse. With the light behind her and the dark hallway in front, she stopped and glared into the gloom. 'Who is it? Why are you sneaking out here? What do you want? Go away! Tell him to go away!'

'It's okay, Nell, it's only me.'

'Who are you? Make him go away!'

Sam stepped backwards, aware from the blast of cold air that someone had come in the front door and down the passageway behind him. But as he was keen to get near the lamp on the phone table so that Nell would be able to see him and calm down, he didn't turn around. 'It's Sam, Sam Hennessy, you know me.'

She came up close and peered into his face. Slowly a smile appeared and she touched his shoulder playfully. 'Of course I know you, you don't live here?'

'I came for the funeral, you know, Emer's John.'

'He's dead,' she said simply.

'Yes, I'm sorry about that.'

Nell straightened herself. 'I'm not,' she said, ignoring the gasp from the young nurse behind her, 'I'm glad. He was a bad man. He was not kind and he didn't make her happy.'

'Whist now, don't be saying things like that. It's not good to speak ill of the dead.'

'I'm not speaking ill – I'm saying what's true. He was bad. I know him, I saw him, I know what he was thinking, I know what was—' Her voice was lowering to a mumble as she shuffled past and let the nurse usher her toward the parlour. The nurse looked apologetically at Sam and nodded at the person who was standing at the foot of the stairs to let them pass. Sam waited till they were clear and then made a run for the cloakroom. He swung the door shut behind him and revelled in the glorious relief of the next few seconds. God help us – women would be the death of him today! If they weren't saying the wrong thing out loud, they were saying the wrong thing on the quiet. Still, he couldn't really disagree with Nell. John Fagan was not a good man, God rest his soul, and Bridie had always maintained that Emer suffered at his hands. Though it was a desperate thing to be left a widow so young, she was well rid of him. He fastened his zip and crossed himself guiltily. Imagine, thinking ill of the dead and in a convent toilet as well!

When he opened the door he was surprised to see that there was no one there. The other person must have tired of waiting and gone elsewhere. As he rounded the foot of the stairs he saw that the fellow had not gone away but was sitting on the steps waiting. 'It's free now – go ahead,' he called to the figure as he passed.

The man stood up and pulled his coat straight. 'Thanks,' he muttered. Sam looked at him and for a minute his heart stopped. Had John Fagan, like Lannigan, decided to enjoy the company at his own funeral? But no, this man was slightly shorter and a good deal older.

'Noel Fagan, well now, there's a turn up for the books!'

Noel nodded, 'You got it in one. That's exactly what I turned up for – the books – and not a moment too soon. By the look of things this place is being run by women.' The sound of a heated exchange between Bridie and Mrs Brady could be heard from the parlour and Noel laughed. 'My little sister-in-law will need a strong man about the place. Now if you'll excuse me, I need a slash. I'll be along to join the celebration as soon as I've made my mark.' And he walked away.

Sam looked after him and felt uncomfortable. This fellow would do Emer no favours and the sooner she was warned he was here the better. He could hear Bridie's voice, now fuelled with sandwiches and a few decibels louder and he smiled to himself. Never mind Emer, maybe he should set Bridie on the blackguard. If she didn't manage to scare him away, nobody would. Her earlier aberrations forgiven, he combed his hair through with his fingers and turned into the parlour to prepare his ever-capable wife for the battle.

There was no need to say anything to Emer. As soon as Sam turned into the parlour Agnes was by his side, cheeks flushed and her voice was low and urgent, 'What does he want, did he say?' She pulled him to a chair by the side of the door, 'Here, sit a minute so we can keep an eye on the hallway.'

Surprised by urgency in her tone, Sam sat. Agnes was usually one of the calmest women, sensible enough to be nearly not like a woman at all and here she was fussing and fretting like the worst of them. 'Right, right, what's the fuss. Sure, he's only coming to pay his respects to a dead brother.'

Agnes fixed him with a look, 'Sam, he didn't have respect for his living brother, he'll hardly find it in him to feel anything for a dead one. I don't want him bothering Emer – she's had enough to carry and the weight of that fellow is more than she needs to add to it.' Her voice offered no room for compromise and years of experience had taught him not to look for any. He shifted his backside so that he was perched on the side of the chair facing the door.

He needn't have bothered. Seamus, carefully avoiding his mother's eye, had managed to grab a handful of custard creams and was making a bolt for the door when he landed headlong in the folds of a long dark coat.

'Whoa there, what's your hurry?'

Seamus looked up at the stranger and then at his father. 'Sorry, Mister,' and then he was gone, through the hall and out the front door before he could be stopped. There'd be hell to pay later but for the moment he had a fistful of biscuits and no school for the afternoon – it was a price worth paying.

Noel Fagan stood in the parlour doorway looking after him and inside the room there was quiet. The few who hadn't noticed the great escape had noted a change in atmosphere and all eyes were on him. He straightened the lapels of his coat and, rubbing his hands together, looked around the room for his sister-in-law. He saw her by the window, flanked by the soft-faced nun and another woman and was conscious of all the attention he was attracting as he made his way towards her.

'Emer!' he said, his voice soft and respectful, 'Emer, I'm so sorry. I came as soon as I heard.' She opened her mouth to say something but he held up his hand to stop her. 'Not a word now, you mustn't worry about a thing. I'm here to give you any help I can.' He smiled at the nun, 'Afternoon, Sister, is there a cup of tea in the pot?'

A girl approached him with a cup and plate.

'That's very kind.' He took the cup and the sandwiches. As he bit into the first one, the chatter in the room started up again.

The few who had heard that he'd turned up and had been seen getting on to the bus surmised that he had not been made welcome so they expected a bit of a reaction when he turned up again. And here he was, drinking tea and eating sandwiches and nobody bothering at all.

The older ones who remembered the young man he had been, watched him and noted how time had not been kind to him. But for all that, he was still a presence. He was no longer portly and his coat, long and heavy, hung loosely on him. The clothes beneath were shabby and, looking at the greedy way he was gulping the tea and holding out his cup for more, it was clear that thirst was still more of an affliction to him than hunger ever would be. Those who had spent the afternoon recalling his brother now had the opportunity to compare the two and the rush of affection that filtered through into the reminiscences of the onlookers would have surprised even John Fagan.

Ah sure, God help him, he's not a patch on the brother ...

... looks more like his father if you ask me ...

He does not! Sure the father was a fine figure of a man – that fellow was always a blackguard ...

Divil the bit of help she can expect with that fellow sniffing around ...

His brother would turn in his grave ...

He would, God rest him ...

God rest him, indeed, he was a grand man …
He was.

Emer said nothing. Like the others she watched him but unlike them she didn't wonder what he was here for. She saw Agnes' face as he came in and knew that they had already met. She sighed. It had been a relief to see him on the bus but it was too much to expect that he'd go far on it. All through the Mass she had been watching for him to turn up and was pleased when he didn't and when he wasn't at the convent either she had started to relax. And now here he was. She'd have to deal with him but at the moment she didn't have the energy. She didn't even have the energy to talk to him. She just sat and waited for what came next.

Sam waited too. For the first time that day he had a chance of a sit down and there wasn't anyone telling him to get up or come here or go there or whatever. Bridie was well distracted with Mrs Brady who had made one of her usual snide remarks as Seamus escaped and any minute now there would be fists flying. Father Martin was edging his way gingerly towards the pair of them. Good luck to him – he had God on his side, Sam had only distance – but that was good enough for him.

In the corner of the room, quietly enjoying the tea and the change of scenery, Matty watched the faces. He had insisted on coming here today despite Matron's insistence that it would do his chest no end of harm. *Traipsing around in the damp and the cold*, she warned. *You'll end up in the bed and have to stay there for the Christmas!'*

That was what decided it. The thought of the Christmas festivities filled him with dread – the long table groaning with food and all around it, eighteen old ladies giggling in

316

merriment as they sucked a turkey to death. There'd be crackers to pull and not a body in the place with the strength to pull them. Then there'd be the arguments and the frustration as jokes waited to be read and nobody willing to whist a minute and listen. And if it was anything like last year – he had been just about able to cope when that young fool of a nurse produced the mistletoe – oh no, if coming to John Fagan's funeral was going to land him in peace and quiet until the whole bloody show was over, so much the better for it.

Anyway, he liked Emer, always had. She was a timid wee thing, always a step behind but there was maybe a chance that now she might be able to have a life for herself. She had a good head on her – just never had the chance to show it. He'd watched her, week after week, sitting there with her mother. There were times when she turned up and any fool could see from her face that things weren't right and she was struggling to hold herself together and Nell would not even give her daughter a second glance. Emer never complained. Matty watched the hard set of her mouth and understood why she let herself be treated like that. He knew Jimmy Byrne had asked her to look after her mother and he knew that she wouldn't break a promise. When she sat in front of him last week and asked for his advice he felt great affection for her. She was like the daughter he never had, never would have, but she had come to him for help and he had done his best to give it. Looking at her now, he hoped he had done the right thing. He'd always wondered how much she knew and was surprised that so much could have been kept from her all these years. Still, it was hard to know how reliable Nell's recollections were after all this time. Like everyone else, he always supposed Patrick Morrissey to be the culprit. He was a blackguard all right, but he could be decent too – a show-off who needed everyone to think he was a great fellow.

Even at fourteen, Matty was surprised when it turned out to be him … .

It was Gareth who broke the spell. He was sitting beside his grandmother, holding her plate when his uncle came in. Granny finished her sandwiches and was insisting on wiping all the crumbs into a napkin, which she was now folding. She liked folding things. It made them tidy and you always knew where things were, she said. Now she was bending over the napkin on her lap, carefully positioning the edges so that they were just perfect. She would fold and press, fold and press till it was exactly to her satisfaction. Then she'd put it back on the plate and in a minute, if she had a biscuit or anything, she'd open it all out and start again. Getting near the end of her task, the folded edge was unyielding under her stiff fingers. Any minute now she would start muttering crossly to herself and having seen before how she could fly into a rage when things were out of her control, Gareth was pleased to find a distraction for her.

'Granny, look!' He pulled at her elbow. 'There's a man after coming in and I think he might be one of Daddy's relations! Who is he, Granny? Look!'

CHAPTER 27

E GG SANDWICHES WERE NICE. She always liked the egg sandwiches. Messy though – you had to be careful not to put too much on or the bread would go sliding around and you wouldn't be able to get a good hold of it and after all your work there'd still be a bit of crust left. And if you put on too little, it'd look mean and Jimmy would hate that. *Better wearing than wanting, Nell,* he'd say. She smiled to herself as she folded the last corner over and it was all perfectly straight. It was nice when it was all perfectly straight. She was aware of the boy tugging at her sleeve. She wished he wouldn't do that. She hated people pulling at her.

'Who is he, Granny?'

She shrugged a little as she brushed his hand off her arm. Who was who? She didn't know who people were. She never knew who people were, didn't know any people.

'Look!'

That's when she noticed that the boy wasn't being loud; it was all the other people who were quiet and into the middle of it the boy's voice, and him tugging at her and making her hand shake and now the napkin had all come loose again …

'Gareth!' For a man crippled with arthritis Matty Hurley had a last lap left in him. At the very moment that Nell gave up ignoring her grandson and decided to see what he was bothering her about, Matty had a sudden premonition that he must stop her. He was out of his chair and across the room. 'Did I ever tell you about the day the sheep got stuck in the bog and we had to pull it out? Will you come over to me here till I tell you about it?'

Gareth was no less surprised than the rest of them. Of course he'd known Mr Hurley all of his life but never before had the old man volunteered a story. Usually he just said 'hello' and he might pull a toffee out of his pocket for you, but he never got out of his chair and offered to tell you something you didn't ask about.

What was he thinking of, jumping up like a jackass and grabbing at the boy like that? What was he talking about – a sheep? Did somebody lose a sheep? Is that what the people were there for?

Nell looked slowly around the room but it was hard to focus on the faces. Some of them were so near that they were all fuzzy. Better that way. Some of them were turned in her direction and she wondered if one of them might be going to get her another sandwich. They were nice, those sandwiches.

She shook the napkin on her lap loose and tutted as a few crumbs escaped onto the floor, making a mess. She hated that, messes, things not being where they should be, not clean. She tried to push the crumbs with her foot but they were too soft and instead stuck to the underside of her shoe.

Oh!

She felt the familiar panic rising inside of her. Now there would be a mark wherever she walked and there would be a stain on the rug – someone would have to come and sweep it up straight away, one of the nurses, they must come, she would have to call them.

Someone was standing in front of her and for a moment she thought it might be Bridget with the dustpan and she tried to point to where the crumbs were but the person did not bend down to look.

'There,' she whispered, 'I dropped some, there's a mess, it's not clean,' but the person still did not answer and she was forced to lift her head to look up instead.

At first she thought it was one of the nuns, all dressed in black, but she could see now that it wasn't a woman at all. It was a man in a long dark coat. He was standing very still in front of her, not saying anything and she wondered why he was there if he had not come to help. Squinting into the poor light of the convent parlour she tried to make out who it was.

'Crumbs,' she said, by way of explanation, 'I can't hold a plate and reach the table from here and the boy was supposed to be helping me but now he's gone to look for a sheep or something. Bridget! Where are you!'

'All right, Nell, here you are.' Bridget put down her plate and rushed to Nell's side. 'Let me help you with that.' She bent down and started to wipe up the few crumbs with her handkerchief. 'There you are! It's all fine now, not a crumb in sight. Did you want me to get you another sandwich, ham or egg?'

'Egg,'

'Right you are.' She turned as she rose to pass the plate across to Nell, 'there's a whole plate of them here. Excuse me, Mr Fagan.'

Noel moved slightly to the side as Nell's hand stopped in mid air. 'Mr Fagan?' she said, 'Mr Fagan? He died you know.' She leaned forward and her whisper could be heard all around the room. *'Wedded my daughter but he was never properly committed to her. I was worried the day he took her to the altar that it was just to keep him looking respectable and it turned out I was right. But she didn't notice a thing and as long as she was happy ...* but I don't think he made her happy ...'

'Ahem—' Bridget cleared her throat and tried to get Nell to concentrate on the plate that was being offered to her before she could say any more, but the hush that had fallen on the room was warning enough for Nell. She could see Gareth's shocked face and Emer's angry one and she knew she should stop but it was the truth and it wasn't a secret and she'd had enough of secrets.

She stood up slowly and addressed the room. 'He was, you know – bad – he was bad and now he's gone and I'm not going to pretend she's not well rid of him.' She turned to face Emer. 'You're better off on your own - you and the boy. He's not one of them – he has no badness in him. He—' As if she felt his eyes, she suddenly stopped speaking and the fire went out of her.

Noel Fagan was staring as if he was seeing a ghost. He had not set eyes on Nell Hannigan for fifty years and time had not been kind to her face. Where once she had been the prettiest girl in Kildoran, she was now wizened. Anger etched the lines deeper than time alone would have done and left her with a permanent scowl. If she had not spoken, he might not have known who she was. There was nothing of the young Nell in her; nothing about her face that he could remember from the last time he had seen her.

Nothing except the fear.

For what seemed an age the two of them stared at one another and everybody in the room waited. To most of them, it looked like an embarrassing encounter between two old people who shared no more than a mutual dislike but to one couple it was as if the lights had gone on in their heads and all the pieces suddenly fitted into place.

Emer looked at her brother-in-law. She had been right in what she said to John that last morning. He was like him: like him in manner, arrogant and rude; like him in appearance, heavy and overbearing – from his blowsy drinker's face right down to his big shiny boots. Matty saw her look at the boots and the conversation he had with her in the Home came flooding back to him. At the time he'd been saddened by the knowledge that had been forced upon her and had hoped that in time they could put it away as the history of an confused old woman but the look on Nell's face now told him that that was not the case. Still holding Gareth by the hand he stood up and put his arm around Nell's shoulders as Emer came to stand at her other side.

Together they faced Noel Fagan and in a voice that was barely more than a whisper Emer said, 'This is my mother. Are you surprised to see her? Did you think she was dead?'

Regaining his composure quickly, Noel held out his hand. 'Not at all, how good to see you, Nell, it's been a long time,'

Nell said nothing and the onlookers wondered at how none of them moved while the hand was held in mid air. Emer could feel her mother begin to tremble beside her and she motioned to Bridget to come and help. Together they eased the old woman into a chair and Matty winked at Agnes that a small drop of brandy might be just the thing. As Agnes fetched the brandy the murmur of voices in the room started up again. By the time the glass was drained, the conversation was flowing freely and if there was confusion about exactly what had happened, nobody was going to ask too much about it at the moment. As if the incident had been a signal to them, young girls appeared and started to clear plates and cups back into the kitchen. 'Goodbyes' were muttered and as they passed out of the room, people touched Emer gently on the hand and ruffled Gareth's hair. *Be seein' you, Emer* .... call us if you need anything... I'll be in in the week to give you a hand with things ... take care, pet ... mind yourself ... One by one they shuffled out and while a faint smile acknowledged their condolences and good wishes, Emer's mind was not with them at all. She looked at the faces, old familiar, friendly faces and she shivered. Today she had buried her husband and seen her own mother come face to face after nearly half a century with the man who had raped her and left her for dead.

And that man was her brother-in-law.

As the last of the well-wishers left the room, she realised that there was only Matty, Agnes, Bridget and her mother left. Gareth had been taken into the kitchen by Sister Kathleen with the promise of a treat from the larder and somehow, in all the exodus, Noel Fagan had gone too. She shrugged slightly and looked at Matty. 'It was him,' she said, 'and I've had him in my house and fed him at my table. And I never knew.' She shook her head. 'I never even knew.'

'That's right,' Matty said, 'you never knew. If you had it might have been different but nobody told you and so you never knew. None of us knew the full story, until now.' He inclined his head towards Nell who was fussing with the collar of her cardigan and muttering to herself. 'She probably didn't even know herself – not all of it anyway.'

Emer looked at her mother's face. 'Do you think she knows now?'

Matty shrugged. 'Who's to tell, pet? She's spent most of her life not looking at the things she doesn't want to see and mostly she manages it.' He patted Nell's hand. 'Are you all right there, Nell?'

Nell pulled her hand away crossly and glared at him. 'I am not all right! How could I be all right! I am cold and I am hungry and I asked for a sandwich and all you can do is sit there and ask me if I am all right. How could I be all right, surrounded by fools?' She pulled her cardigan tight over her chest and started to button it, muttering angrily as she fumbled with the buttons. 'Take me home, Bridget. I do not like this place. I want my tea.'

With more than a little reluctance, Bridget helped her to her feet. 'Are you coming, Mr Hurley, will I take you back now?'

Matty was still looking at Emer.

'It's okay,' she nodded at him. 'You go back. Agnes and I will finish up here and I'll be over in a couple of days when things settle down a bit.' Seeing him about to object, she touched his sleeve, 'Really, Matty, it's okay. There's no more to be done today. Look, it'll soon be dark and it's damp outside. Get yourself home – and thanks.'

Matty pulled his coat over his shoulders and wrapped his scarf round his neck. 'Well,' he said, 'there I was in my perch in the corner thinking I'd seen it all and I hadn't seen the half of it!' He gestured towards the door. 'Where do you think the blackguard's gone?'

Emer shrugged. 'I don't know. He's gone anyway. I don't think we'll be seeing any more of him.'

Agnes was helping to get Nell's coat fastened and watching the old woman's face as she tried to follow the conversation. Nell was looking from one to the other of them.

As if she could sense her gaze, Emer turned to face her mother. 'What is it Mam?'

'Is he really gone?' she whispered. 'Will he come back?'

'No, Mam, we'll take care of it and he won't come back. You're safe now and we'll look after you. You can go home with Bridget and have your tea and Gareth and I will come and see you soon.'

Nell almost smiled. 'Will you? That would be good. And now there's no more secrets and you're not cross with me?'

'Why should I be cross with you?'

Nell giggled to herself. 'Your father never knew that I had gone to meet him, you know. He never liked him, said he was a bad lot but I liked him. Even loved him a little, I suppose. And he was always sweet on me. He wanted us to get married – wanted me to tell Jimmy about us and in the end I had to choose.' Her voice softened. 'I knew he'd be sad. I wanted to tell him myself and I wanted it kept a secret till I told him myself.' She paused, smiling at the memory.

'What did you want to tell him, Mam?' Emer prompted her.

'About Jimmy! I wanted to tell him myself that it was Jimmy I'd chosen and I said not to tell anyone until later. I wanted to see him and say it myself but I couldn't get him on his own. He went into Fagan's and heard it for himself and after that there wasn't a chance. That's why I went to our secret place.'

'Good God! Is that why you were up there? You were hoping to meet Patrick Morrissey by the pool so that you could explain to him yourself that you were going to marry Jimmy?'

'That's it!' Nell's eyes were bright. 'It wasn't such a bad thing, was it? I knew he'd be sad so I had to tell him myself and

I was going to – only when I got there—' her voice trailed off '—*he* was there already!'

'Noel? Patrick came later?'

'Too late. He was drunk and he stood there, swaying and crying, *You've killed her, you bastard, you've killed her. I'll do for you, you bastard* and he took off his belt and he looked like he really would but the other one was stronger. *What'll you do, you fucking coward? You could have had her years ago but you were too fucking scared. Go on then, hit me* – but he just stood there and he couldn't even get up a fist to hit him, lurching and crying with scratches all down his front. *I'll kill you* he said but the other just laughed and said, *You won't. You won't even tell because nobody will believe it wasn't you. It might as well have been because you just don't have the guts* and then the two of them scrapped. I tried to call out to him that I wasn't dead but the words wouldn't come and then there was blackness and the Widda's voice crying out to me but I couldn't reach her—' She stopped suddenly and looked at her amazed audience. 'And the awful thing was that I couldn't remember who the other one was. I wanted to remember everything, really I did but I'd only barely managed to survive it the first time and if I'd let all the memories come back, then I'd have had to live through it all again, wouldn't I? So I pushed it away.'

'Till today,' Emer whispered.

'Till today.' Nell caught Bridget's arm and the light went out of her eyes as quickly as it had come into them. 'Why are you standing there?' she said. 'I told you I want to go home for my tea! Take me home for my tea.' And with Bridget on one side and Matty on the other, she allowed herself to be led out of the room. Nobody moved as the shuffling procession made its way to where the car was parked at the side of the front door and only when they heard the engines start did Agnes dare speak.

'The poor creature! She must have felt she was in some way responsible for it all along.'

Emer's heart was racing. 'And then when Patrick Morrissey was taken away, she knew it wasn't him but she was so angry with him for not helping her that she let him take the blame. What a horrible mess!' She looked at Agnes and her face was like the sad little girl who used to come to the convent kitchen looking for a friend. 'And she could never tell Daddy because she would have had to admit she'd been two-timing him.'

Agnes shook her head at the intricacy of it all. 'So they were both victims – and they were both punished for it. You mustn't blame her.'

'I don't – I just wish she could have told someone, anyone. Daddy loved her so much he'd have forgiven her anything.'

'By the time she was well enough to tell him, she must have felt it was already too late.'

They looked at one another sadly, so many lies and so many secrets and the waves of it touching even fifty years down the line. Agnes held out her arms and wrapped them around Emer as if she was a child again. 'Well, that's an end to it now, pet. Now we know and your mother is all the better for being able to let it go.'

'But what about him?'

'Him?' Agnes snorted. 'Noel Fagan hasn't got long to go in him. He gave up on a future the day he looked for it in the bottom of a bottle. He won't come back here now. By the look of him he'll be getting his justice from his maker before too long. It's too late to do anything about it tonight anyway. Let it go.'

Emer shrugged. 'You're right.' She shook herself as if to clear her head of the events of the day. I'd better get Gareth home. Thank you so much for everything – I couldn't have coped without my friends today.'

Agnes smiled, 'You don't have to – today or any day. Get you home now and God bless.'

Emer smiled and headed for the kitchen to collect Gareth. Agnes stayed where she was and watched as the two of them walked up the street towards the shop escorted by a much more lively Sam Hennessy who had somehow managed to shake off his wife in all the commotion and find a more sympathetic ear in the kitchen. She could hear Kathleen below, talking animatedly to some of the others as they got the tea ready and she sent up a prayer of thanks that it was all over. She wouldn't go in for tea herself – the day's events were altogether too much and she was still weak. She'd get a hot bottle to take up and say her prayers and go to bed. She shuffled towards the chapel at the far end of the corridor and pushed the door open quietly. After all the comings and goings she was glad that there was an end to it. Wouldn't it be just grand in the morning to have everyone back to normal?

Taking her Office book from the pile she was about to sit down when a movement at the back of the chapel caught her eye. Oh, Good Lord Above! How could she have forgotten! Of course there wasn't an end to it yet. There was still one person yet to be told the whole story – someone she and everyone else assumed was dead for the last fifty years. She bent her head and prayed for guidance.

Who was going to tell Eleanor?

CHAPTER 28

I T TOOK A WEEK FOR THE PRAYERS TO BE ANSWERED – a week during which Pius seemed to be deliberately avoiding contact with everyone. She went about her business quietly, ate her meals in silence and spent the rest of her waking time in prayer. Because of this, she missed the news that Sister Bernard was coming home sooner than anticipated and that she would not be travelling alone. No sooner had the two women arrived and had a cup of tea than Agnes asked the Mother General if she could have a private word.

Mother Mary looked at her for a minute. 'Is it about Sister Pius?' she asked quietly.

Agnes nodded.

Mother Mary smiled. Taking Agnes by the elbow she ushered her into the front parlour and having ascertained that they would not be disturbed, sat back with her eyes shut while Agnes recounted as accurately the events of the last few weeks and all that she had found out.

'—and so, you see, in the end, she was responsible, albeit innocently, for getting him punished for a crime that he never committed. I think – *we* think – that *that* is why our sister finds it so hard to be among people. She lost the only person she ever loved, had him taken away for a crime that she can't let herself believe he ever actually committed. His crime, if you can call it that – personally I think it's more a weakness than a crime – is that he *was* weak and—' Agnes realised that she was prattling on at almost the same moment that she realised that Mother Mary was smiling at her. She stopped talking and slumped back in the chair, her arms raised in despair, 'so you see, I don't know what to do. I had thought to tell the whole story to Sister Bernard but as you were coming, Mother, I though it best to come to you. After all, it was you who sent her here for the while but how could you have known—'

Mother Mary raised her hand and she was still smiling. 'I *did* know.' She rested her hand on her knee and smoothed the folds of her habit slowly. 'Sister Pius was not sent here because she was the only person who was available to come – in fact her presence has been greatly missed. We have struggled to find someone with her qualifications to fill her post while she was away. But we have managed. I only pray to God that she has.'

Agnes looked at her in amazement. 'What do you mean, you *did* know? Are you saying that you knew all along what coming here could do to her? Did you not know how unhappy she would become?'

Mother Mary shook her head. 'She did not become unhappy when I sent her here. She was unhappy already – unhappy and unsettled from the day she left Kildoran as a child with only a postulant she hardly knew for company and not a soul sad to see the back of her.' Seeing Agnes' mouth slowly fall open in amazement, she continued. 'Eleanor Morrissey came to this house, to this very room, a broken child. She brought with her only the clothes she stood in and the prayers of the two women who accompanied her – Mrs Carmody from the hardware store and our own Mother Clement, God rest her soul. Mother Clement, who was then Superior, decided that the best, the safest thing, for the child, was that she be taken away from this place as soon as possible. A change of clothes was found for her and as soon as it was dark, she left and that was the last she saw of Kildoran.'

'Till she came back here in August.'

Mother Mary nodded. 'That's right. She left Kildoran nearly fifty years ago but Kildoran never left her. It has haunted her day and night and the pain of it has her twisted.' Her confidence seemed to falter and she looked at Agnes as if she was pleading for understanding. 'I had to do something. As you know, our sister is a very private person and she does not reveal her pain easily. It has become a burden that she insisted on carrying alone. I tried to get her to talk but she would not and all the while she became more and more troubled. I could not help her alone so in the end, I had to hand it over to the Lord and trust that he would find a solution.' Then her face brightened again. 'Within days two letters arrived from Ireland; the first a request for a permanent replacement for our dear Sister Rosalie and a temporary one for Sister Bernard – and there you are! The answer to our prayers!'

'But—' Agnes' head buzzed with questions. She opened her mouth to ask at least some of the questions but Mother stopped her.

'Shush, don't trouble yourself, Sister. You have been very kind and by all accounts a good friend but it is out of your hands now. Concentrate on getting yourself fit and leave Sister Pius to me. Go now,' she raised her hand again before Agnes' rush of questions reached her mouth, 'and kindly send Sister Pius in here to see me. I will talk to you later.' Then she lowered her head and Agnes was dismissed.

As soon as she opened the chapel door, she saw her, huddled as usual in the far corner; head bowed as if she was afraid that the figure on the cross would raise his head and start to berate her for her guilt and sins. The poor creature! Agnes padded

332

softly down the pews and tapped Pius on the shoulder. Pius raised her head, startled, 'Sister?'

'It's Mother General, Sister. She's here and she wants to see you in the front parlour.'

Pius breathed a sigh of relief. Mother Mary was back which could only mean that she would leave here soon. Upstairs, her bags had never been properly unpacked and she was ready to go now. Mother Mary had only to give her the word.

Mother Mary didn't seem to be in a hurry at all. 'Sit down, Sister,' she said, 'I want to tell you a story.' She breathed deeply a couple of times as if to collect her thoughts, then she began.

'It's the story of a young man and what happened to him one summer's evening a long time ago in this very village.'

Pius shifted uncomfortably but the soft voice continued.

'He was a confused fellow, torn between how hard it was for him to stay good, as he wanted, and how easy it was to go the other way. There was plenty to lead him the other way as well. His mother was dead, his father was a drunk and the farm would have gone to ruin if it were not for the work put into it by him and the sister for whom he was responsible – a child eight years his junior who adored him as much as their father loathed her.'

In her lap, Pius' hands were clenched and the whites of her knuckles pressed tightly between angry veins.

'He might have managed to hold it all together too – he was his mother's son and had her charm but he had also his father's weakness. Torn between the loyalty he felt for the father he saw destroyed by grief at the mother's death, and loyalty to the sister whose birth had caused it, he took to drinking and found no solution. He was only nineteen and already he was slipping down the path that would be the ruination of him, of all of them—' and as Pius sat rooted to her chair, Mother Mary recounted the story of Eleanor Morrissey.

Pius heard the words but they meant little to her – until she learned that it was not Patrick who raped Nell Hannigan and left her for dead.

'He didn't do it?'

'No, he didn't do it.'

'He didn't do it …'

Pius' voice was little more than a whisper. 'What happened to him, afterwards?' She could barely breath.

'He was brought up to Dublin to wait for the trial and when it happened, he was found guilty and put away.'

'But he was innocent!'

Mother Mary shut her eyes. 'He was innocent, Sister, of the crime for which he was punished. But *that* was not the crime he committed that night.' She kept her eyes shut and though Pius stared hard and willed her to react, she did not move.

When the silence in the room was almost unbearable, Pius spat the words at her. '*What do you mean by that? He was innocent!*'

Mother Mary opened her eyes. 'He was not.'

Pius felt the words like a slap. There was a ringing in her ears and the sound of a stream whispering into the air around her. She put her hand to her neck where already a cold finger had found its way, tracing its line gently, ever so gently …

'He was innocent!'

'He was not.'

Again the silence – while the two women stared at one another before Mother eventually continued. 'When he was drunk there was badness in him that would never have left him innocent. He—'

'He wasn't bad! He wasn't! He was innocent and he had to pay for something he didn't do and it's my entire fault! I should have trusted him!'

'You shouldn't. He was drunk and he wasn't to be trusted.'

Pius glared at her, standing there so calmly talking about Patrick as if she knew him, as if she knew anything about him, as if she knew anything about any of it. Then she realised. 'How do *you* know?' she asked. 'How could *you* possibly know any of this? You weren't there!'

'That's right,' Mother Mary said, 'I wasn't there – I was here. I took my final vows in England, Sister, but that's not where I started.' And for the first time Pius heard a softness in her accent, the faintest remnants of a voice that had learned to speak in the west of Ireland. 'Don't you remember anything of your last evening in Kildoran? Can't you remember anything about that night?'

Pius squinted into the flecks of dust that were floating in the wintry sunlight from the parlour window. She tried to remember the day she had first come into the convent but it was very dim. It had been misty and the street was empty as Eileen rang the bell and then stood behind her to shield her from anyone who might pass. For an age they had stood there, holding their breath and only breathed again when the sound of footsteps echoed from the hallway on the other side of he door. As quietly as possible, the great door had swung open and a soft country voice of a little postulant had beckoned them to hurry inside …

'That was you?'

335

Mother Mary nodded. 'That's right. And I was in the front of that car accompanying you to Dublin. I was the one who brought you to the house there and handed you over to the care of our sisters ... ' She stopped then and the two of them looked at one another.

Waves of half-remembered faces washed over Pius and she tried to see the face of the girl in the dark habit who had smiled at her.

Mother Mary looked too. She saw in the face of the woman opposite a child betrayed. She remembered as if it was yesterday how the Widda arrived in the convent garden the night Moira had been told that she was to accompany Eleanor to Dublin. She brought with her a basket of herbs and Moira accepted the gift gratefully. Expecting the Widda to leave then, she had been surprised when the old woman caught her arm and pulled her away from the convent lights into the shadow of the trees.

... *At the sound of the bell the Widda started. 'What's that for?' she asked.*

'Prayers, we're supposed to go to the chapel now but ...' Moira peered out into the darkness beyond the old woman's head. 'Thank you for these. It's very dark out there, isn't it? Will you be all right going home on your own?'

The Widda nodded. 'I know every stone on the roads, even on the paths of Kildoran and every bump in the fields beyond. I like the dark.' She looked out into the night. 'I often walk around at night.' Then she turned and looked at Moira. 'That's how I know that they're wrong.'

'Who's wrong? Wrong about what?'

The Widda shrugged. 'About Patrick Morrissey. About Eleanor.'

'What do you mean, they're wrong? He's a rapist, nearly a murderer and now he's caught.'

The Widda fixed her with a look and Moira shivered, as the old woman's eyes seemed to pierce right through her. 'Eleanor Morrissey thinks that her brother raped Nell Hannigan and left her for dead - I don't think he did. I think he knows about it but he wasn't the only person wandering around the hill that night.' She linked Moira's arm through hers. 'Come walk a little of the way with me,' and as they walked, she continued her story. 'When I left Hurleys it was late and I took the short cut through the copse. There was someone waiting by the stream there, waiting for somebody and it wasn't for me. He hid as I went past and I thought it might be Morrissey. I've seen him there with Nell Hannigan and I supposed he was meeting her there again,' she flashed a furtive look at Moira. 'But it wasn't Patrick. As I came up to cross over the lane at the end of Morrissey's land I heard him coming, drunk and very upset from the field on their side. He was crying and talking to himself and though he was drunk I supposed he was grieving the loss of his love. Not wanting to let him see me, I stayed in the shadow and he went past. I couldn't hear all he was saying but it wasn't anger, it was apologies, and it was not to Nell that he was apologising.' She paused.

By now Moira was fully engrossed in the story. 'Ah, don't stop now. Who was he saying sorry to?'

The Widda looked at her as if it should be obvious. 'To Eleanor,' she said simply. 'He was apologising to his sister.'

' What was wrong with his sister?'

The Widda ignored the question. 'I knew then that something terrible had happened so instead of staying on my own path, I crossed the wall and went over the field in the direction he had come. It led me to the stream and the air there was bad. There was a feeling about the place and I feared I would find the child but she wasn't there. The pool was as still as it ever was and I wouldn't have known that there was anything wrong—' She took a deep breath. 'On the bush beside the stream, a child's dress and slip hung as if the child had left them there when she got in to swim. But there was no child there.' Her voice was low and angry now and Moira had to strain to hear her. 'There was a light on above at the cottage – just the light of a fire and there was someone moving about inside. I knew Jim Morrissey was away so it couldn't be him. I took the clothes and went up – but I made no noise. Inside the child was alone. When you looked at her first, she seemed normal but as I watched her, I knew.'

'Knew what?'

'She was rushing around the room, fixing the fire, preparing the meal with the sort of frenzy you'd have if it was someone very important coming. She'd rush here and do this and rush there and do that and stop to fix her hair and check the potatoes and then rush again—'

'I don't understand, what's not right about getting ready for a visitor?'

'The Morrisseys didn't have visitors, not ones the child would be involved with anyway. She wasn't getting ready for any visitor, she was getting ready for her brother.'

'And you saw him leave the house.'

'I didn't see him leave the house. I saw him come from the field. He'd come up from the pool where he'd been alone. Where he'd been drunk and crying and apologising to his sister and her not there—' she looked at Moira as if she didn't really want to spell out the rest'—only her clothes.'

Moira thought of her own brothers and the way they teased her most of the time. They were big and burly but they were good and they'd never really upset her or – oh no! She clapped her hand to her mouth and looked at the Widda in horror. 'He couldn't! Surely he wouldn't! That's–' there was no word she knew. 'You must be mistaken ....'

338

The Widda said nothing. She'd lived long enough and seen enough of people in their rawest moments to have a sense of what they were, and when they would not tell you with their mouths she had only to look into their eyes and she knew. She had looked at Eleanor that day in Kilkenny and she had seen her brother and she had known. She shook her head. 'I'm not wrong.'

Moira felt cold and sick. 'That's the worst thing I've ever heard. He's an animal – he'll have to be stopped.'

The Widda touched her face and she could feel the warmth in the wizened old hand. 'He has been. Even if I could prove that it was not him who was waiting by the stream below that night, it would do no good. He has been tainted with the blame of it and she would not be safe with him. She's better off where she's going – under the protection of good women.'

'Ah, God love her!' Then the thought struck her. 'Hang on now, if he didn't harm Nell Hannigan, who did?'

The Widda shrugged. 'I'm not certain – but whoever he is, he won't stay around here for long – he won't risk it.' She sensed the argument in her companion, 'You can do nothing about him but I need to ask you do help me with someone else.'

'Who?'

'The child.'

'What can I do for her? Apart from see her safely up to Dublin.'

The Widda caught her face and looked into her eyes for what seemed to Moira to be a very long time. Then she touched Moira's lips gently and whispered to her. 'Take her to Dublin and go on your way. You'll lose track of her for a while but if it's meant to be you'll find her again. Maybe by then she'll understand why she couldn't stay here. Maybe she'll even understand her brother and what he did to her but if she doesn't, if she's still carrying those demons around, you must see to it that she is brought back here. She won't want to come but she must, and she must stay long enough to lay those demons down.'

339

Moira felt a shiver down her spine as the old woman intoned her instructions and though she knew such thoughts were forbidden, she felt as if a spell was being cast on her. As quickly as she felt it, the air around her shifted and she realised that the other sisters would be out of chapel soon and she would have to get back before she was caught. Kissing the Widda quickly on the cheek she started to run back towards the convent. 'Don't worry,' she called as she ran, 'I'll do it. I promise ....'

Mother Mary smiled. 'How easily the young make promises.'

Pius was slumped in the chair as if all the energy was drained out of her. Tears gathered at the corners of her eyes and she blinked them back. 'All this time you knew who I was and you never said.'

'I didn't. I got to Dublin, handed you over and then got on with my life. I had no idea you would come back in to it.' Mother Mary reached over and placed her hand on Pius' shoulder. 'Are you all right?'

'I don't know. I don't know what I feel. The Widda knew all along that Patrick did not harm Nell Hannigan but she let him go to protect me. His crime was against me, not against Nell – he came there too late – wait!' Suddenly she realised that she had not been told the whole story. 'The Widda only saw Patrick in the lane. How can she have been able to tell you what happened afterwards?'

'She didn't, he did.'

Pius sat bolt upright.

Mother Mary sat down again. 'It wasn't till years later. I was teaching in London and helped out some nights in a soup kitchen. One night, just before Christmas, it came up in conversation that I had started out in Kildoran and when I was putting on my coat to go, one of the other helpers came up and asked if he could have a chat with me. We found a quiet corner and he told me the story of who he was and what he was and what and who he had been. Then he asked about you.'

There were tears in Pius' eyes. 'Was he angry with me?'

'No'

'I betrayed him.' Pius took a deep breath. 'He was the only one who ever really loved me and I betrayed him.'

'You did nothing of the sort!' Mother Mary stood up crossly. 'Are you still not able to see? Patrick was not angry with you. He wasn't angry with anyone. He had done his time, paid his price, if not for the crime he didn't commit, then for the one he did. You trusted him and *he* betrayed *you*. He made his peace with God and man and only wanted to know that he would make his peace with you.'

Pius was now crying openly. The tears ran down her face and with them the years of hurt and pain. 'But why didn't he come and find me? Why didn't he come and say? He only had to say.'

Mother Mary shook her head. 'He didn't know where you were and neither did I. All I knew of you was that the nuns in Dublin had educated you and found you to be a good pupil.' She smiled at Pius but there was no response. 'I supposed that you had left and gone on to make a life for yourself. Patrick said he'd find you himself and I wished him well. My own life was rushing along and I trusted that if you were to reappear it would be in your own time – as the Widda predicted. It wasn't till my appointment to the post of Mother General that I was privy to all the files and as I read through them, I realised that Eleanor Morrissey hadn't left the convent at all. '

Pius sighed deeply. 'He never found me.'

'No.'

'I loved him, you know. He was my whole world and I'd have forgiven him anything if he'd only said.'

'I know.'

'And now it's too late...'

Mother Mary watched her closely, her hands now folded in her lap. Under the thick fabric of her habit she could feel the second letter she had mentioned to Agnes. Its sharp edges seemed to prompt her to speak but the pale face opposite, drained with shock, and the eyes made paler by the tears that swam in them, stopped her. She placed her hands, palms down on the desk in front of her but could not bring herself to dismiss Sister Pius just yet.

'Is there more?' Pius' voice was no more than a cracked whisper and she looked as if she had been opened up, scooped out and left raw. Mother Mary didn't think she could take any more tonight.

That decided her.

'Enough now, my dear – you must rest. We have a busy few days ahead of us.' She rubbed her hands together. 'I have business to attend to in Kilkenny tomorrow but I'll be back in the afternoon and I would be pleased to have you come and talk to me. Four o'clock, here, if you would.' Her voice lost its lilt and she sounded efficient again.

Pius stood. She'd had her whole past laid out and she felt so exposed. She would go to bed and pray to sleep and in the morning she would start again. She didn't know what the future held and she didn't care – at least the past was behind her. 'Thank you, Mother.'

'Goodnight, my dear, God bless.'

As she watched the door shutting, Mother Mary raised her eyes to the crucifix on the wall above her desk. 'Did you get all that, Lord? The poor soul – gone off to say her prayers thinking she's heard it all now. Today's been very hard on her and only you and I know what we have to do for her tomorrow. Let's hope she's strong enough for it. I'm not looking forward to it but I pray it'll go well. You'll be there so we can trust in that. As always, Your will be done. Amen.'

At four o'clock the following day, Pius knocked on the door of the small parlour, which was always used as Mother Superior's office. It had been a hectic day with the children as high as the wind on the street outside and she felt unbearably weary. Whatever Mother General wanted her for, she hoped it would be brief and uncomplicated. All she had learned yesterday left her drained and though she supposed that she ought to feel better, she didn't. All the secrets she had kept locked up inside her for fifty years weren't secrets at all. The Widda Meaney had known, Moira Flanagan had known and she herself had only known the half of it. There were so many questions still hanging in the air around her head and she knew that later, when she was well away from here she would think of them, but for the moment she was too weary, too weighted down with everything that had happened.

'Come in!' There was a fire flickering in the grate in the parlour and Mother Mary's face was flushed from her outing to Kilkenny. She was rubbing her hands briskly and there was an energy about her that made her seem nervous. 'Sit down, Sister, sit down. Make yourself comfortable. Are you warm enough there? Pull your chair closer to the fire.'

Pius looked at her, surprised. Mother Mary *was* nervous. She was fussing around moving things and humming to herself.

'Mother?'

'Yes?' She was looking at Pius as if she'd forgotten that she had summoned her there.

'You wanted to see me, Mother.'

Mother Mary stood still, resigned. 'I did.' Then she took a seat opposite Pius and smiled. 'I did.'

They both waited for what seemed an age before Mother Mary started. 'When we spoke last night, Sister, I told you that the Lord has a knack of answering my prayers very quickly. For this reason I have never questioned his methods – or his timing. I knew where you were fifty years ago; I knew nothing of your brother. I lost track of you then and met your brother. For years after that I lost track of both of you. I supposed, hoped, that he had found you. Then, last year, I found you again and knew by your sorrow that he hadn't.'

She paused and Pius struggled to contain her impatience. She was exhausted: physically, mentally, emotionally and didn't want to have to sit here listening to her superior's preamble.

When Mother Mary didn't continue, she said, 'Mother, haven't we done with all this? It's the past, it's over. It's too late to do anything about it now. Can't we just pack up and leave here and get on with what's left of the rest of our lives?' Her voice was almost drowned by the loud rumbling of a builder's truck as it thundered over the bridge outside on its way to the development site on the hill.

Mother Mary clapped her hands. 'Did you hear that, Sister? Isn't the Lord's timing wonderful? I think he's agreeing with you, telling me to get on with it! A builder's truck! Imagine!'

Pius was almost ready to hit her. The woman was rambling. She caught the sides of her chair as if she was going to rise but Mother Mary stopped her. She slowly pulled a rumpled letter out of her pocket and held it up. 'Shortly after I discovered where you were, I received two letters, as I told our Sister Agnes last night. The first was from the convent here, and concerned Mother Rosalie's passing. The second was also from Ireland, and posted in Kilkenny.'

Pius leaned forward and peered at the envelope. On the side of it was the name of Kilkenny's oldest firm of solicitors. She looked questioningly at Mother Mary. 'Phillips and Sons? What do they have to do with me?'

'Plenty!' Mother Mary sounded almost triumphant. 'Tell me my dear, on the day when you entered the convent, how old were you?'

'Eighteen.'

'And what did you bring with you, what dowry?'

'Dowry? I had no dowry – you know that. I left Kildoran at eleven with only a change of clothing and apart from a few books, owned nothing more the day I entered.'

From a file on her desk, Mother Mary pulled a yellowed sheet of paper and handed it to Pius. It was a will, short and succinct and as she read, Pius' heart beat furiously. 'It's my mother's will! Where did you get this?'

'From your mother's solicitors in Kilkenny. Your parents' home was known as Morrissey's, but only since your parents married. Before that the land belonged to your mother's family and it was her wish that after her death and your father's, the land should be shared between you and your brother. She knew your father was fond of drink and I suppose she wanted to safeguard your future should anything happen to her and she not be around to keep your father in check herself. Your father never changed the will.'

'But I don't see—'

'When you and your brother left and your father died, the farm lay abandoned for years. What with stories of ghosts haunting the place, nobody went near it – nor bothered with it at all till the developers came to Kildoran and started to buy up the land on the edge of the village for their new estate.'

'I still don't see what that has to do with me.'

Mother Mary was unruffled by Pius' impatience. 'Sister Agnes' family had already sold the land and the Widda Meaney's estate was available. Matty Hurley was finding the work too much and glad to sell off Hurleys' to pay for his comfort at St Thomas'. That left only Morrisseys'.

'They could have had that too – if there was no-one living on it.'

'Living on it wasn't the issue. They could do nothing with it until they bought it and they couldn't buy it till they found the owners.' She sat back as if that explained everything.

Opposite her, Pius was very still though her mind raced. What was she being told? That she still owned the land? That developers were looking for her? 'What do I have to do?'

'Only what you want to, my dear. Only what you want to.'

'Am I to sell land? Is that it?' She sounded like a child, lost in a grown-up world.

'No, it is not yours to sell.' Mother Mary reached across the table and picked up some more papers. 'When you entered the convent, your dowry, your share of Morrisseys' land, became the property of the convent. It has belonged to us for forty years.'

'And?'

'And we have sold it.'

'So then? That's all there is to it? Why do I need to know any of this? It has nothing to do with me, hasn't had for forty years. Why do I need to hear about it now? Let them build castles on it if they want to – I don't care.'

'They don't want to build castles – only housing estates – and for that they didn't just want your share of the land. They wanted all of it.' She waited to see if Pius realised what she was saying. 'They wanted to buy Patrick's share too.'

Pius said nothing.

'And before they could do that, they had to find him.'

Pius' mouth opened but no words came out. Another truck thundered over the bridge and with it Agnes' words the day she wrapped up her little parcel to be taken to Matty in the home, *And now that the developers have managed to buy up all the land* ... She found her voice but it was trembling. 'When was it sold?'

'The final papers were signed this morning. In Kilkenny.'

'Signed by whom?'

'By the owners.'

'This morning in Kilkenny?'

'Yes.'

'You signed for my share because you own it now.'

'Yes.'

'And my brother ... ?'

'And your brother owned his.' Mother Mary watched as the implications of what she had been saying finally dawned on the woman sitting opposite her. Pius' hands were trembling and to still them she was clutching the wooden crucifix that hung from the rosary beads on her belt. The knuckles on her hand were sharp through the opaque skin and as she clenched and unclenched, Mother Mary could see where the crucifix was leaving its imprint deep in the reddening palms. Pius' lips were working furiously.

'You signed for my share ... ' she whispered.

Mother Mary leaned forward and caught her hands, letting the crucifix fall. 'As I said, my dear, you need do only what you want to do. And yes, in answer to your question, yes.' She waited until the trembling stopped and then she said very quietly. 'Your brother signed for his.'

CHAPTER 29

HER SUMMONS BELL RANG OUT THREE TIMES and still Sister Pius did not move from her pew in the chapel. Even old Sister Celia, with her hearing aid turned off, knew there was something amiss. She glanced around and seeing that Pius was unmoved, shrugged and relaxed back into her contemplation. Some of the other sisters, who had hoped for a quiet moment, cleared their throats, but still she did not move. Eventually, Agnes, impatient to be doing something active after her forced inaction in hospital, slid forward on her polished seat.

'Sister,' she whispered, 'that's your bell.'

There was no response.

'Sister—?' She raised her hand as if to tap on her shoulder but Pius turned and Agnes was shocked to see the expression on her face. There was no sign now of the haughty stranger who came into Kildoran those months ago. The lines on her face were faded and she looked frightened. There was something of the look she had about her when they sat in here and faced the crucifix together. 'Can I help?'

Pius shook her head. 'I have to do this for myself.' Then she caught Agnes' hand. 'And I am unbearably afraid.'

Though not entirely sure what sort of momentum things had taken, Agnes knew enough to be certain that whatever Pius was to face now, it had to do with the whole of the rest of her life. Mother Mary was in a frenzy of activity for the past couple of days and Pius had been walking about in a dream. There were endless phone calls and now Pius' summons bell was continuous and by the sound of shuffles and coughs in the

349

chapel, the natives were growing restless. She took a deep breath and tried to remember what her father used to tell her when she was afraid. 'Em – I think the saying is – there is no way forward but a way through. Does that make sense?'

Pius almost smiled. 'It does.' She got to her feet slowly. 'And it is time for me to move forward. I've been standing still for far too long.' She gathered up her prayer books and swept noiselessly up the chapel. At the top of the aisle she stood a moment in front of the large crucifix with her head bowed and Agnes wondered if her courage had deserted her again but it had not. She nodded briefly and then went on her way.

Though the corridors from the convent chapel to the front parlour usually took a few minutes to negotiate, Pius could not remember the journey. One minute she was in the relative safety of the chapel, the next in the hallway with the sound of voices coming from beyond the heavy oak door. She must have knocked. Before she had a chance to change her mind Mother Mary opened the door with a flourish.

'Ah, there you are my dear! Come in, Come in.' Pius stood on the threshold but Mother Mary caught her elbow and ushered her into the room. 'I will leave you to your visitor.'

'You're not staying?'

'No.'

Struggling to control herself Pius pleaded with her. 'Stay. I can't do this alone.'

Mother Mary detached herself from the hand clutching at her sleeve. 'You will not be alone. Have faith.' Then she turned on her heel and left the room.

The sound of the door shutting behind her seemed to echo forever but eventually it was replaced by the crackling of the fire. Though she was on the other side of the room, Pius could feel the heat of it. It seemed to have crossed the space between her and the flame and was burning into the fabric on the back of her veil. She knew her cheeks were burning as well and that she should do something. She was still facing the door and the soft sound of someone breathing in the room told her she should turn but she couldn't. The heat around her was becoming unbearable and there was a feeling of bodies crushing in on either side, pulling at her and all the time the crackling of the fire growing louder ...

'Elly?'

The voice was soft and cracked with age.

'Elly, turn around.'

She put her hands to her ears to drown out the other noises but her fingers caught on the sides of her veil. For a moment she couldn't think what it was. The folds of material felt heavy and there was sweat making the edges sticky. Confused, she pushed the fabric away and the veil slid off her head onto the floor. She could feel the other person move but she held up her hand to stop him. 'Leave it! I'll get it myself.' As she bent down to pick it up she could feel Nell Byrne's anger that day in the home and the frustration of her outburst as the nurses dragged her away. She stood upright and steeled herself to meet her brother's eye.

He was not by the fire as she had thought but standing right behind her. Time had shortened his back and lengthened hers so that they were now the same height and she was looking into his eyes. Where they had once been dark brown they had paled a little now and a thin line of milky confusion ringing the iris betrayed his age. His hair, once so dark, was pure white. Unlike Noel Fagan, his complexion did not have

351

the blowsy abused look of the heavy drinker. He was smartly dressed and had an air about him of one who was well cared for. He held out his hand as if to shake hers. 'Are you well, Elly? It's been a long time.'

She left his hand there and clutched the veil tightly to her chest. 'It's been forever. It's been all of my life.'

He dropped his hand. 'Has it been so bad for you? Have you not been happy at all?'

Her laugh was scornful. 'Happy? Eleanor Morrissey? Should I have been?'

'I hoped you were.'

'You didn't care.'

'Oh, Elly. Can you really believe that?'

'What else was there to believe?' She spat, crossing the room to sit in one of the chairs on either side of a small mahogany tray table. She waited while Patrick took the other chair and moving it round, sat facing her. 'You left me.'

'I didn't leave you. I was taken away – you know that.'

She shrugged away the unspoken accusation. 'I only knew what I was told – you could have told me every thing.'

'You were a child, Elly. I couldn't have told you anything.'

She leaned her face close to his and her eyes blazed with anger. 'Do you have any idea of the pain you could have spared me if you had only told me you were innocent! Do you realise that I have spent fifty years doing penance for a crime that *you didn't commit!*'

There was a moment's silence while he stared back at her. She was conscious of his face close to hers and the touch of his breath on her cheeks. His lips were moving as he struggled to say the words she needed to hear. He only had to say that it was all a terrible mistake, that he should have told her and that it wasn't really her fault that she got it so wrong. He only had to say the right words and she could start to break free of the years of confusion and torment that had plagued her.

'*Fifty years.*'

And still he said nothing.

Instead he raised his hand into the air as if pointing at something and then rested his index finger in the middle of her forehead. Neither of them breathed while his finger slowly moved down her face, smoothing the lines as if it could smooth away all the years since he had last touched her. She wanted to cry out, to tell him to stop but his finger was already on her lips and it rested there.

'Hush, pet,' he whispered, 'don't be angry. I wasn't innocent.' The sound of a raging pulse roared in her ears and he repeated, louder and more insistent. 'You know I wasn't innocent.'

There were tears pouring down her face and she caught his hand and held on as if her life depended on it. 'But you were, Patrick! You were innocent and I got you blamed!'

'Open your eyes, Eleanor Morrissey and look at me!' He was standing now, as angry as she had been a moment before. 'I was *not* an innocent man. I was guilty of a heinous act and I deserved to be punished. Yes, I spent years in jail but I deserved it – don't you understand that? I'm not resentful; I accepted my punishment and moved on. If you're to move on too, you must accept my guilt. *My* guilt. I was angry and hurt and I took it out on the one person who had never let me down in her entire life!' He knelt in front of her. 'In her entire life, Elly. Do you hear me?'

'But I let them take you away.'

'How could you have done otherwise? They'd never have believed you.'

'They would! I'd have told them! I'd have told them you were with me—' She stopped suddenly and looked at him. He was still kneeling and his eyes were fixed on her face. She waited for him to speak. 'I'd have sworn to it.'

'And you'd have been telling the truth, Elly, wouldn't you? I was with you. I was down at the stream with you.' His eyes never left her face. 'Look at me.'

And see what? That the only person who had ever loved had had betrayed her? She shook her head. 'That was a mistake. I got it wrong.'

He caught her hands and squeezed then tightly.

'You got nothing wrong. I was very drunk but sober enough to know what I was doing. There was a madness in me. I have no excuse and you—.' he touched his finger gently to her lips again '—you must make no excuses for me either.'

'But all those years locked up?'

He stood up slowly and brushed the specks off the knees of his trousers. 'I deserved it. You were all better off without me. I did wrong and I deserved to do my time.'

'And did *I*?' She felt the old anger rise up in her again. 'Did *I* deserve to be abandoned?'

'I didn't abandon you, pet.'

'What! How can you say that! You look at me!' Now she was standing, her arms held out by her side. 'I was a child. A child. Look at me now, would you? I'm an old woman – old and bitter. You did your time and then got on with your life.'

'What did you want me to do?' He sounded so desperate that all the energy drained out of her anger.

'I wanted you to – I wanted you to come and tell me that it was all a mistake. That everyone got it wrong. That you and I could just go home.' She sat wearily. 'But you didn't. You'd paid your price and I had to look after myself.'

'That's not true.' His voice was steady now. 'I didn't just abandon you. I found out from Mother Mary, or Sister Mary, as she was then, that you had gone to the nuns so I wrote to them. The convent would tell me nothing, only that you had been there a while and had moved on. I wrote to the Carmodys but they would have nothing to do with me, said you were better off without me. So I came to Kildoran to find you for myself. The house was gone and it looked as if nobody had been round the place in years. When I made some enquiries about it in Kilkenny I found out that nobody would even go onto Morrisseys' land – because of the ghosts!'

'Ghosts?'

'That's what they said. There was supposed to be a ghost on the land.'

She smiled. 'That's ridiculous! What sort of a ghost?'

'The ghost of a young girl who had been desperately unhappy and had drowned herself.'

For the first time, Pius felt the knot inside of herself start to loosen. 'Oh Patrick, and you thought it was me? You thought I was dead?'

'Yes.'

'What did you do then?'

He smiled. 'Well, I nearly hit the bottle again but I didn't. I went to see the solicitors to find out what was to be done about the farm. I couldn't come back and work it and I didn't want to sell it, not yet. It was the only link I had with you. I knew the convent had ownership of your share and I presumed it was

355

because they had been your guardians at the time of your death.' He gestured towards her habit. 'Crazy, I never imagined that you had entered.'

'What else could I have done?'

'Married.'

She laughed suddenly. 'Me? Married? Who'd have married me?'

'Someone. You were lovely.'

'I was never lovely.'

'You were very lovely. You were kind and gentle and caring and loyal and—' suddenly his voice broke, 'and I betrayed you. Oh Elly, I am so sorry.' Now there were tears rolling down his cheeks and she could see him, as he was that day years ago when he had sunk to his knees in a mess of whiskey and chicken feathers. 'I was a coward, afraid of everything: of our mam being dead, of our da being drunk, of the mess I'd make of everything. You were the only one who had faith in me and I betrayed you worst of all.' He took a deep breath. 'So now I've found you again and I want to ask for your forgiveness. I've made my peace with society but I haven't yet made my peace with you. Eleanor, I am so sorry. Can you ever forgive me?'

Pius said nothing. She wasn't even looking at him.

Over his head on the wall above the desk there was a crucifix, a replica of the one in the chapel. Like on the larger one the figure had his head turned away from her but he was different. Where usually she could feel a rage of resentment throbbing from him, there was none. The air in the room was perfectly still. There was no sound of water rushing about her ears; no pulling of an angry mob closing in on her; no whispered threats from beneath a staircase as piercing eyes watched her every move.

'Elly?'

She reached forward and, kneeling in front him, wrapped her arms around his shoulders. For an age they held on to one another until gradually the thin carpet was not enough to protect their aging knees from the wooden floor beneath. She groaned as she tried to rise.

'I'm completely stiff!'

As she started to move the sound of someone laughing stopped her. She looked at Patrick in amazement – it wasn't coming from him. It was her voice. Laughing. She couldn't remember the last time she laughed and as the tears rolled down her face she gulped to control herself, 'Look at us!'

'I though you'd be used to it, with your job.' He held onto the chair and tried to haul himself up.

'Patrick Morrissey! Have a bit of respect, would you! I'm a woman of the cloth.' They both flopped back into their chairs, still laughing.

'God help us, Elly. It's going to take a bit of getting used to.'

Pius felt her body glow with an emotion she had long forgotten – a happiness she hadn't felt for fifty years. It should be so easy now to wipe the slate clean, forgive and forget but fifty years is a long time and she didn't know that she was going to be able for it. 'So you're staying then.'

He shook his head. 'No, I can't ever come back to Kildoran to stay. The Morrisseys are well out of here.'

'But I've only just found you – you can't leave me again!'

'Stop your fussing; you were always the same. I'm not leaving you.' There was the same warm affection in his voice that she could remember from her childhood. 'I'm going back to London with you and Mother Mary. I have a small house there, not far from your convent. We'll see plenty of each other.'

'We'll need to, Patrick,' she whispered. 'I don't think I will be able to do this on my own. A thought struck her. 'Are you married?'

'No, Elly, and you won't be doing it on your own. You've got me. Patrick and Eleanor together again.'

'Like it always was.'

'That's right, Miss Morrissey,' the name didn't sound so foreign on his lips. 'Like it always was.'

CHAPTER 30

E MER RUSHED TO ANSWER THE PHONE that was shrilling in the hallway. She didn't usually have calls so late but since John's death a few people had taken to checking up on her at night. She knew they were concerned about her but really there was no need. She felt fine, just tired and by teatime unwilling to make small talk in the bar. Cora and her brothers were managing there and glad of the extra money they could earn in run-up to Christmas.

'Hello?'

There was a pause at the other end.

'Can I help you?'

'Mrs Fagan?' The voice was hesitant.

'Yes?'

'It's em – it's Sister Pius. I'm sorry to ring you so late but I – we were wondering if we might have a word with you.'

'About Gareth?' At this time of night? Emer looked at her watch – it was after eight.

'No,' there was the old edge of impatience, 'not Gareth. I – I wondered if we might come and see you for a short visit tomorrow? In the afternoon? I believe you are shut for a couple of hours in the afternoon?'

She sounded so flustered that Emer didn't know how to respond. And to whom did 'we' refer? She was just about to ask when Cora stuck her head round the door and held out some notes, mouthing that she needed change. 'Yes, that's fine,' she said quickly, signalling to Cora. 'We're actually shut all afternoon from two to six so anytime then would be fine.'

'Oh, thank you! Thank you!' the woman was positively gushing. 'It'll be nearer four, I imagine, after the school has cleared.'

'Okay, well – I'll see you then.'

'Yes, you will. Thank you.' And she put the phone down.

Emer stood holding the mouthpiece for a few minutes. What was all that about? Sister Pius making an appointment to visit – how very formal. She shrugged; tomorrow wouldn't be too long in coming. Whatever the mystery, she'd find out about it soon enough.

Fagans shut at two o'clock the following afternoon as usual and by half past, Cora had tidied up and was off for the rest of the day. Emer checked the supply of rashers and sausages for the teatime rush and then headed for the kitchen. Gareth was off to a football match against another National School and wouldn't be home till later so she was relishing the thought of an afternoon to catch up on things. Despite his laziness John had left the business in good order. If anything, he had been quite stingy so there was a healthy bank balance to support plans for the shop she had harboured for years. She would make a pot of tea and sit down with the papers to get it all clear in her head before talking to the solicitors and bank.

She made the tea then sat at the table, the papers spread out in front of her. Where to start? She was just organising them into piles when she heard someone in the shop. The front door was always left unlocked in case of emergencies but she was surprised that Pius and her companion hadn't rung the bell. Formal one minute; familiar the next.

Suddenly, there was the tread of footsteps in the hallway outside and a cold clammy feeling began to spread across her forehead. It wasn't Pius and though it sounded like John, it wasn't him either. She turned to face the door. Noel Fagan was standing there, drunk.

'Well would you look at that? The merry widow counting her fortune!' The smell of stale whiskey and rancid memories clung to his coat as he stood there swaying, filling the doorway.

Emer wanted to bolt but there was nowhere she could go. He was blocking the door and to get to the stairs she would have to pass by him. Instead, she barely glanced in his direction. 'There's nothing for you here. Go away.' She tried to keep her voice as steady and indifferent as she could.

'Go away? Go away?' He released his grip on the doorframe and lurched into the room. 'Who the fuck do you think you are? Ordering me out of my own home?'

Emer stood, pushing the chair back with her knees so that it was wedged between them and, still keeping her voice steady, she turned to face him. 'This is not your home.'

'It fucking is! It—'

Without taking her eyes off his face, she picked a long manila envelope off the table and held it out. 'Here's a copy of your father's will. It leaves this place to John – in full. And here,' she turned her hand over, 'is my wedding ring. I am John's wife and we have a son. You are not the heir, you never were.'

Looking as if he was fighting for control, he pulled the chair round and sat down. 'Emer,' he held out his hands, 'I didn't come here to fight with you.'

'Really? Why then?'

He gestured to the heaps of paper on the table. 'Look at that' he said, 'that's not a task for you. You're a woman grieving and with a child to support. You don't need extra responsibilities.' Seeing her face set hard against him, his tone became more suppliant. 'Look, I was brought up here. This was my home until I—'

'Until you—?'

'Until John came along.' There were tears of self-pity in his eyes now and a whinge in his voice. 'It turned my parents' heads – the change of life baby, the miracle. I was pushed to one side. Pushed out of my own home. Pushed—'

'Is that what happened?' She knew she sounded sympathetic.

'You can't imagine what it was like back then, Emer. It was as if I ceased to exist, can you imagine what that was like? All the love that had been mine all my life was suddenly heaped onto the new baby and I was out in the cold.' When she said nothing, he continued, 'I was sent into exile, that's where I was sent. Nineteen years old and no welcome for me in my own home.' He buried his face in his hands.

'So you didn't leave of your own accord?'

He raised his head slightly and addressed his question to the palms of his hands. 'It's my home. Why would I want to leave Kildoran?' His plaintive tone and passive expression sat uncomfortably on a face scarred with anger and hard living.

'Because you raped my mother.'

He didn't move.

'Did you hear what I said?'

No answer.

Emer took a deep breath. 'I said, because you raped my mother.'

He put his hands on either arm of the chair and raised his body slowly. When he was at eye level with her he pushed his face close into hers. 'I heard you.'

'And?'

'And nothing.' As quickly as it had been turned off, the old bravado was back. 'That's bollocks.'

'It's a fact.'

'Yeah?'

His nonchalance was eating into her reserve and Emer felt that at any moment she was going to explode. He was watching her with the ghost of a smile playing on his face. How did she know – that would be the next question and what would she answer to that? That her mother had told her? That her mother, who was known to have lost her mind forty years ago, had given her all the facts? And what could she say then? She clenched the manila envelope and prayed.

'I asked you a question, bitch. Is that a fact?' His breath was hot on her face and his hands already on her shoulders. Against her back Emer felt the heat of the range's hang rail. Nell might have lost her mind but Emer had seen her scars – they were real enough. Ragged angry scars clawing their way up her thighs and kicked inside of her by the man who was now pressing himself against her daughter. Through the sleeves of his coat she could feel how thin his arms were. He looked as if he might keel over any minute but his expression was hard and confident. She opened her mouth. 'Ye—.'

'It's a fact.'

'Whaat—!' At the sound of the strange voice the two of them turned. Standing in the doorway were two people – a nun and an old man.

'Sister Pius?' Emer was so pleased she could have hugged her.

'Good afternoon, Mrs Fagan, you were expecting us?' Her voice was very calm. 'I hope you don't mind us letting ourselves in but the door was open and it's freezing outside. The wind plays havoc with my brother's chest.'

'Your brother?' Emer looked at the man. Although his eyes were as dark as his sister's were pale and his skin sallow, he looked like a male version of her.

'That's right,' Pius' face was glowing. 'This is my brother, Patrick Morrissey.'

As his unsteady world came crashing around his feet, Noel Fagan suddenly realised what it was that had bothered him about the skinny nun that night in the convent. He knew he'd recognised her from somewhere. Like a series of stills from an old film he had flashes of the skinny kid on the farm, scuttling around trying to please. He saw her discomfort as she tried to avoid his hand on the chair; the flash of her knickers as she raced up the school stairs terrified of the painting on the bend – and the look of horror on her face the day the crowd closed in on her as she ran away, leaving her brother and his belt behind. He started to laugh.

'And his adoring little sister. Well, well, quite the reunion. Won't you sit down, Miss Morrissey – or is it not in your habit?' He wiped his eyes with the sleeve of his coat, spluttering in mirth at his own wit.

Emer was staring at Patrick. 'I though you were—'

He smiled at her. 'Everyone did, Mrs Fagan.' He turned his face to Noel. 'Everyone did.'

There was a minute's silence as the four of them surveyed one another. Emer didn't know what might have happened if they hadn't turned up when they did; she didn't know what might happen next. She saw Pius standing beside her brother looking as if she was unsure whether to laugh or to cry; Noel was staring at them as if trying to work out his next move; and Patrick was looking at Emer and his eyes were full of tears.

'You have the look of your mother about you,' he whispered.

It wasn't what she had expected. 'I have?' In Emer's mind there was an old woman, lined with age and injustice.

'She was very pretty.'

Emer half smiled. Of course! The Nell this man was remembering was not an old lady in a nursing home, spitting vicious confusion at whoever crossed her path. This man was remembering the young girl he loved. Loved and left for dead.

As if he could read her mind, Noel snorted. 'Very pretty!'

All three turned on him. Fists clenched, Patrick sprang forward but his sister stopped him. 'No, Patrick, that's not the way! Don't touch him!'

'That's right, Morrissey. Don't do anything. Hide behind little sister's skirt, why don't you?' He brushed imaginary crumbs off the front of his coat. 'Always the fucking same. Coward.'

This time nobody stopped Patrick. With all the strength his body could muster, he hurled himself across the space that divided them. Knowing that his anger would give him the strength that age might deny him, Noel grabbed Emer and pulled her across. For a second there was confusion. In front of her, Patrick's face was suffused in rage and behind her Noel was muttering to himself.

'Still just in time to be too late, Morrissey. Some things never change, do they?' His laughter spat moist onto her neck.

As Patrick's hand tried to reach behind her, Emer clenched her fists and shoved her elbows back as hard as she could. Noel wasn't expecting it. He tried to twist his body out of the way but alcohol dulled his reaction. He lost his footing and slipped, hitting his head on the edge of the hang rail. The sound of metal on bone stopped Patrick in his tracks and he stood looking over Emer's shoulder as Noel crumbled to a heap. Emer didn't turn around but stood there face to face. There was silence in the kitchen.

Eventually, Pius spoke. 'Is he dead?'

Emer looked at her. 'I don't know.'

'Does he have a pulse?'

'I don't know.'

Moving her gently aside, Patrick knelt down and probed amongst the scarves and folds of Noel's coat. 'He's alive,' he said. 'He needs an ambulance.'

Still, Emer didn't move.

'Please,' he caught her hand. 'We can't do nothing – he needs an ambulance. Please call an ambulance.'

Emer's voice was hard. 'My mother needed an ambulance.'

Patrick stood up and turned her round. 'That's right,' he said. 'Your mother needed an ambulance and I didn't get one for her. I was too scared. I ran away.' He looked down at Noel's unconscious body. 'Is that what *you* want to do now? Is that what you really want to do?'

CHAPTER 31

ON THE NIGHT OF THE KILDORAN NATIONAL SCHOOL Christmas Concert, the village hall was packed. As usual, the front rows were left vacant for the guests of honour but from the third row back there was great shuffling and negotiations. Mothers of children with speaking parts jostled for position with mothers responsible for costumes and everywhere, small children climbed onto or under seats. Eventually, Sister Bernard came onto the stage. Seeing her there, the audience fell quiet and the last few stragglers were ushered into the hall just ahead of the parish priest and the sisters due to occupy the front rows.

They trooped up the centre aisle, nodding in recognition to the various familiar faces. Behind them came an assortment of residents from St Thomas' Home who could be trusted not to fall asleep in the first few minutes, or spend the entire performance fiddling with a whirring hearing aid.

Last to enter the hall was Sister Pius and with her, a man who had been staying at the convent. He was well wrapped up and those who happened to glance his way wondered if he might be a retired priest from another parish or a relative of one of the nuns. Whichever, he was neither familiar nor particularly interesting and eyes soon turned back to the stage where the infant class, dressed in a variety of angel costumes was taking its place. Glad of the distraction, Pius decided not to attract any more attention and sat on one of the empty chairs at the back wall. She beckoned Patrick in beside her and they settled themselves as comfortably as a draughty village hall in winter would allow. The piano tinkled the opening bars of *Silent Night* and the children began to sing.

'Excuse me, is this taken?' There was a young woman standing by the empty chair next to Patrick.

'We're not using it.' Pius leaned across and pushed the chair towards her.

'Thanks! We're always the last – takes us ages to unload!' As her coat fell open, they could see the uniform of one of St Thomas' nurses underneath. She put her scarf on the chair. 'Would you keep this space for me, please?' Pius tried not to tut in impatience. The starting time was printed clearly on the tickets and if people couldn't get there on time they really should wait for an interval. And she'd left the door ajar. The draught would be blowing right in on Patrick's chest and she didn't want him catching a chill. All being well, they were due to fly home tomorrow, her time in Kildoran done and a whole life ahead of them. She smiled to herself in the darkness. Maybe Mother Mary had been right to bring her back here. Maybe if she had found Patrick in London it wouldn't have been the same. Kildoran might have hung like a cloud – an unmentionable shadow over both their futures. Now there was no cloud. She turned to Patrick. He must have been thinking the same thing because even in the dim light she could see he was smiling. She reached her hand out and felt the warmth of his.

Around them there were stifled chuckles as the children on stage struggled with the end of the carol's impossibly high notes and then the audience burst into applause. Patrick and Pius clapped too, so caught up in the general air of celebration that neither of them noticed as Bridget struggled back into the hall pushing a wheelchair. She eventually managed to get the back wheels over the step and turned to close the door. She pulled the chair from beside Patrick out of the way and pushed the wheelchair in instead. She had a warm coat on her and plenty of youthful flesh – she could do wind stop for the evening. Fixing the brake on the wheelchair, she leaned over and smoothed the blanket on the old woman's knees.

'There you are,' Pius and Patrick heard her whisper just before the next carol started. 'That should keep you nice and warm, Nell.' She smiled her apologies for the disturbance at the couple watching her. 'Now you just sit back and enjoy the evening.'

At the front of the hall Emer, turning the pages for the pianist, watched the arrivals in horror. When she visited her mother earlier, Nell declared herself unwilling to come out into the cold for the evening. Obviously, she had changed her mind. No doubt the thought of a quiet night in with few nurses around to fuss over her didn't appeal. She was sitting bolt upright in her wheelchair, eyes scanning the stage for a glimpse of Gareth. As each carol started, Emer could see her lean forward then, when Gareth didn't appear, slump back, eyes shut, to wait for the next time. Even the length of the hall wasn't enough to disguise her total lack of interest in anyone but her own grandson. She had come to see him and him alone – thank God, Emer thought. She could not begin to imagine what might happen if Nell turned to the couple sitting rigid to the right of her: Pius had her eyes shut and looked as if she was praying; Patrick was staring ahead in shock.

As Emer watched him, she realised that despite all that he had done, or failed to do in the past, she did not feel any hostility towards Patrick Morrissey. He had loved her mother –

she had no doubt about that – and he paid the price for his cowardice. The Patrick Morrissey who was sitting in Kildoran village hall tonight was not the same Patrick Morrissey who had fled in terror that night fifty years ago. And it was a different man who had cleared a space on her kitchen floor two weeks ago while Sister Pius calmly rang for an ambulance. When Noel Fagan gave that gasp and stopped breathing, it was Patrick who had bent down and given him the kiss of life. The ambulance men praised him when they arrived. While they put Noel on the stretcher, Pius fussed around telling them how she and her brother had wondered at the shop door being left open on a half day and come in to find a drunken man attacking defenceless Mrs Fagan; Emer stood there watching him as he knelt on the floor, his eyes all the time fixed on his sister.

As they carried Noel out, saying there'd be someone round later to get the details, Patrick never took his eyes off Pius' face. 'Was that me?' his voice was barely more than a whisper. 'Was I like him?'

Pius smiled at Emer. 'Listen to him,' she said. She put her hand out to help him up. As the two women pulled him to his feet, she was still smiling. 'I'm sure I've told you this before. You're kind and nice and you take care of me. He's drunk and cruel and he hurts people.' Then she picked up the kettle as if it was the most natural thing in the world to make herself at home in Emer's kitchen and the three of them sat and talked. Gareth came in from his match and if he was surprised to see Sister Pius and a man there, he didn't say. He held his hand out and introduced himself solemnly. 'Hello, I'm Gareth'

'Gareth James by any chance?' Patrick stood and shook the proffered hand.

'How did you know?' Gareth's eyes opened wide.

Patrick held the small hand. 'You're the spit of your granddad.' Emer could see that he was struggling to contain the emotion but he quickly composed himself. 'He was a handsome beast.'

Gareth grinned. 'Was he?'

Patrick threw his hands up in the air. 'Handsomer than I ever was – I'm afraid. None of the rest of us stood a chance.' Over Gareth's head he caught Emer's eye. 'Nor did we deserve it. Your granny married a good man.' Then he patted Gareth's head. 'You have a lot to live up to.'

Gareth sighed. 'I know,' he said, 'Mammy's always telling me.'

The three adults laughed as he headed upstairs to change. Word had already gone around that there had been an incident in the shop and people were beginning to come to offer support in return for the details. Pius and Patrick left, saying they'd be at the convent if she needed them. By the time the Gardai arrived they'd already spoken to the Morrisseys and only needed to confirm that the man had come in uninvited and that Emer was unharmed. They told her he had been seen earlier in Kilkenny and had been thrown out of every pub there for being abusive. He was in hospital now, intensive care. They'd let her know if there was any news but in the meantime, lock the doors when she was alone. Emer had fallen into bed that night, exhausted.

'No more, God, please,' she prayed. 'Let that be the end of it – I can't take any more.'

Now she was standing the top end of Kildoran Village Hall with her mother, albeit asleep, and Patrick Morrissey sitting side by side at the back. Facing her, Matty and Agnes smiled at the children as if they had personally reared every one of them. Further back Bridie Hennessey, who nearly had, was shifting uncomfortably. Helen Burke, resplendent as an angel on the wide windowsill, was instructing the shepherds to get their act together as she had it on authority that they wouldn't be able to spend the entire night lolling about the mountain. From outside there was nervous giggling as the star players prepared to make their entrance.

There was a drum roll and everybody in the hall turned to watch. From their viewpoint on the aisle seats, Agnes and Matty noticed Emer's face and, following her gaze, realised why she looked so pale. Before either of them could think what to do, the doors were flung open to reveal Eilish Hennessey perched on a blanket-covered bicycle with a donkey's head stuck to the front of it. She was giving a very convincing impression of the Blessed Virgin in the throes of labour and beside her, his face suffused in embarrassment as he tried to propel the donkey forward, was Gareth. As they passed the back row, he spotted his granny. If she didn't wake up now, she'd miss it. With a quick apology to his writhing wife, he let go of the donkey and leaned over to Nell.

'Pssst! Granny – it's me – I'm Joseph – look!' There was a moment's panic as Eilish wobbled and nearly lost possession of the pillow she'd stuck under her robe at the last minute. Bridget leapt forward to hold the bicycle.

'It's okay!' she shouted. 'There's a nurse in the house!' A great burst of applause erupted from the audience. Nell woke up.

Gareth was standing in front of her and he was Joseph. Imagine! The starring role! She beamed at him. 'Look at you!' she said. 'Didn't I know you'd get the best part?' Everyone in the hall was turned to watch and she hoped they all knew who he was. He looked so fine in his robes. Bridget had moved from her seat and she couldn't reach her so she turned instead to the man sitting to the right of her. He was all wrapped up in a heavy coat with the collar up and she couldn't see his face so she caught his sleeve and pulled him to her.

'Look!' she urged him. 'That's my grandson! Turn that collar down and look at who it is. Look!'

For a minute nobody in the hall knew where the screams were coming from. One minute the Holy Family had made a precarious entrance and the next minute, chairs were being pushed back and Sister Agnes had dived into the audience, her sleeves already rolled up. Somebody was calling for them all to make a space and Sister Bernard was urging everyone to be calm. From her perch on the windowsill, Helen Burke had an angel's-eye view of the activity.

'Hey, Eilish!' she called over the heads of the crowd. 'You can stop now – I think your mammy is having the baby!' From all corners of the hall, various Hennesseys appeared and Eilish, having discarded her bump unceremoniously, tried to get through. Seeing her frustration, Pius got up to go to her. She put out her hand. 'Eilish! Come here. Your mother will be fine. You stay with me.'

'What's happening? Why are you leaving?' Nell caught her as she tried to squeeze past the wheelchair. 'Tell me! Why is everybody standing up? I can't see – what is it?'

Bridget sat down and put her arm around Nell. 'It's okay, Nell. It seems that Bridie has gone into labour. Don't worry. Dr Rourke is here – he'll take care of her.'

'The doctor? There's not supposed to be a doctor. There were only the two of them in the manger. Why are they changing things? I don't like it. I don't like when they change things.'

Bridget opened her mouth to explain that it wasn't the Blessed Virgin but her mother who was having an unscheduled birth but Pius caught her eye and smiled at her. 'I think perhaps the show is over,' she whispered.

Bridget smiled back. 'I think you're right.' She took a deep breath and started to button her coat. 'You know, Nell,' she said, 'after Gareth there's no point in watching the rest of it. Did you see how well he looked? He was wonderful.' She straightened the blanket and stood up. 'I think we might as well go home now, will we?'

Nell looked round in confusion. People certainly seemed to be leaving. The man beside her had sunk even further under his collar and there was a nun around somewhere fussing over a child in a dress that was much too long. Gareth was trying to manoeuvre a bicycle through the crowd to lean it against the wall and somebody had taken his blanket with the donkey's head saying that it was needed up the hall. She shook her head crossly. 'What's gotten into these people at all—' she muttered. 'Don't they know how to behave at a concert?'

At the top of the Hall it had become immediately obvious to Agnes and Dr Rourke that getting Bridie to a more private location wasn't going to be possible. A quick check revealed that a new Hennessey was well on the way and the best they could hope for was a bit more space and a smaller audience.

'I'm afraid we'll have to leave it at that for this year, ladies and gentlemen.'

'Thank you very much for coming. Now if you could just make your way to the back of the hall, that'd be a great help.'

'On with you now – and thank you.'

Together, Sisters Bernard and Kathleen herded the crowd, helped by the few willing shepherds who remembered that they'd been promised sweets afterwards if they behaved well and were good children. A few parents and some of the sisters positioned themselves at the doors to supervise the exodus and reunite parents and performers. Bridget sat on the edge of her chair waiting for the mêlée to settle before she attempted to manoeuvre Nell over the step. Eventually, the crowd began to thin and Emer appeared, her face flushed with anxiety.

'Mam! Gareth! Are you okay?'

Gareth waved. 'Did you see me, Mammy?'

'I did, pet. You looked brilliant.' Emer's eyes sought out Patrick's then Nell's.

With her beloved grandson dancing in front of her, Nell was smiling broadly – her nightmares forgotten, her secrets told. Patrick raised a questioning eyebrow at Emer who shook her head. The past was done.

'He was wonderful.' Nell pulled on her gloves, 'but then they took his donkey away and changed everything. Nobody wanted to stay and watch it after that, did they?' She turned and addressed her question towards Patrick.

He stood up quickly and taking hold of the handles on the back of her wheelchair, swung it around so that she had her back to him. 'You're perfectly right,' he said. 'Best to leave things as they are.' He released the brake and pushed the chair towards the door. Once they reached the car, he placed a hand gently on Nell's shoulder. 'There you are, safe now.' Then he stood back and motioned to Bridget to take over. 'Goodnight.'

'Goodnight!' Nell called as she pulled herself into the car. 'What a pleasant man. A gentleman. There aren't too many of them around today, I can tell you.'

Bridget winked at Emer and got into the car beside Nell. 'You're right there, Nell,' she said. 'You must tell me how you do it.'

'Oh now,' Pius and Emer heard her say as the car door closed. 'I wasn't short of admirers in my day ... '

Pius took the wheelchair and wheeled it back beside the hall door for the Home's caretaker to collect. She handed Eilish over to Emer and indicated to where Patrick was waiting for her by the convent gate. 'We're leaving tomorrow,' she said, holding out her hand. 'It was good to meet you, Emer.'

Emer took her hand and smiled at her. 'And you. Good luck – both of you.'

Pius' eyes glistened with tears. 'Thank you. Thank you for everything.' Then before anyone knew what was happening she bent down and folded her arms around Gareth and Eilish. 'Be good, you two.' she said in a muffled voice. Then she raised her head and looked into their astonished faces. 'But even more importantly, be happy. It is essential,' and her old bossy voice was back, 'that children know how to be happy.' With that, she winked at them, turned on her heel and walked away.

Emer and the two children stood there watching her as she reached the convent gate. The man was waiting for her and when she got to his side he put out his arm and they walked together up the steps into the warmth of the convent. The onlookers might have said something but at that moment there was a strange cry from the village hall – a strangled sound that started off like pain but grew into a great sound like triumph.

And then all the people who were reluctant to go home just yet, not wanting to leave till the performance was truly over, smiled at each other as another noise pierced the night air.

The shrill pure cry of a new born infant.

Even Bill Brady and his mother joined in the applause.

Also by Adrienne Dines

Toppling Miss April

'*Monica Moran was not the woman she used to be. Or rather she was not just the woman she used to be. She was at least one other woman as well and their combined weight sat heavily on her overburdened bones. Where her breasts had been generous twenty years ago, they were now magnanimous, munificent... If that cleavage was any closer to the ground you could stand a bicycle in it.*'

'A laugh aloud screwball comedy. This is humour sized 44F ... uncontainably funny.' *Meg Gardiner*

'A melange of hilarious misunderstandings and risqué innuendo, which makes it a pleasure to read.' *Mabel Fitzpatrick, Ireland on Sunday*

'Full of clever crossed wires and accompanied by a strong whiff of the menopause, *Toppling Miss April* is an outrageous tale of sex among the over-50s. It's a ridiculous riot! *Emma Walsh, Irish Independent*

The Jigsaw Maker

'*One click of the shutters and all the memories stir and rise and glide slowly towards the light outside...and when the shutters close and they are packed safely, he'd stuff them in his satchel...oblivious to how much his passion for capturing memories was going to cost. And who'd have to pay the price.*'

'The pieces fit together very well.' Fay Weldon

'A brilliant follow-up to Adrienne Dines' debut *Toppling Miss April*, well plotted and very enjoyable.' Lovereading.co.uk

'This seemingly light novel has a dark underbelly – a complex tale of secrets and lies.' *Irish Examiner*